I0817892

GODS AND HEROES

FALL OF PANDEIA

GODS AND HEROES: FALL OF PANDEIA

ISBN: 978-1-7641264-1-0

Brendan is not currently represented by any publishers or literary agents. He can be contacted at:
enquiries@brendanwrightauthor.com

Connect with Brendan:
Instagram: @brendanwrightauthor
Facebook: /brendanwrightauthor
Website: brendanwrightauthor.com

Cover art by Brendan Wright

This book is dedicated to Kenneth Lucarelli, an honorary Hero of Pandeia.

Acknowledgements

I would like to acknowledge each and every one of my Kickstarter backers; Aaron, Allie, Lynn, Christine, Nicole, Don, Thomas, Darryl, Ajda, Carlos, Cecilie, Wendy, Knujon, Onyx, Adams, Andy, Alexandra, Annabelle, Kearin, Afreen, Jake, Ewan, Alexandra, Kenneth, and Damien. Each of you is an absolute legend, and this book would not have happened without your support!

Thank you so, so much.

Mattias

1795

A gentle breeze whispered over the Tarsi countryside. It would have been refreshing, if only Mattias could remove his helmet. His cheek itched where a bead of sweat had settled.

In the distance to the west, a vast darkness loomed. He couldn't be sure, but it seemed to grow each day. It was certainly larger now than it had been when they first arrived in Tarsium. At least the sky above them was clear and blue.

From somewhere nearby, a whistle pierced the silence. A green and blue bird danced through the sky towards a copse of trees. He'd never seen a bird like it. Its tail feathers flowed behind it, longer than its body and sprouting outwards in beautiful patterns.

The men around him, his team, held their weapons tense and ready. The seemingly peaceful country didn't fool these soldiers. Each of them knew that somewhere close by, the enemy waited. Attacks from the Tarsi came without warning, and from nowhere. For almost a year already, the Ermoori had been entrenched in the homeland of their enemy. Mattias never thought he'd be sick of seeing such a beautiful place.

Still, after the oppressive danger surrounding them in the forests of Shanaken, it felt nice to at least be out in the open. Even if they had to stay on guard.

His men were restless; it came off them like a bad smell. Though they fidgeted, they remained vigilant. One of them, Gerard, adjusted his weapon's power setting for the tenth time in an hour, and turned to look at Mattias.

"Any news from the districts, sir?" he asked.

"Nothing since last week," Mattias said, "our forces are still bogged down in the streets. The Tarsi can appear and disappear in those cities just as well as they can out here."

Bryon, another of the younger soldiers merged with Mattias' unit, shifted on his feet.

"We've not even taken any territory, have we?" he said, "I mean, whenever we leave an area, they can just sneak back in behind us."

"That's why we're moving so slowly, Bryon," Geffrey said, "do try to keep up."

"I just meant," Bryon said, "that we're fighting the same way we did in Shanaken. Trying to take land inch by inch. Shouldn't we be hunting the Tarsi, instead?"

Bratton, the older veteran soldier, shook his head.

"How do you suggest we do that," he said, "when those slimy little frogs disappear before we can get our sights on them?"

A rustle came from somewhere as branches shifted; Mattias' entire team snapped their weapons up towards the noise. The low buzz of Ermoori technology powering up surrounded Mattias in a comforting haze.

The faceplate of his helmet, solid black from the outside, showed him every detail of the landscape before him. It was almost like a focusing lens, like the eyeglasses some of the older Overseers wore. The original helmets contained a slim gap at eye level which gave surprisingly good vision, but Prime Overseer Hayne had upgraded them during the last year. Now they could see much more, and in far more detail. Still, looking out towards the noise, Mattias saw nothing but trees. His men shuffled into a combat formation, covering each other as they'd been trained.

They did not fire their weapons; his men would wait until the order, or until they were engaged.

How far they've come, he thought, *from those scared boys who joined my team a year ago*. Though they moved as one now, Mattias' team had been cobbled together from the surviving soldiers of other battalions before they came to Tarsium. Since then, they'd survived dozens of vicious attacks from the Tarsi.

But as Bryon said, they had still barely gained any ground. Any time they ventured further into the countryside, an attack came. No matter how many times they marched through an area, the enemy somehow reappeared. The entire war effort seemed to have ground to a halt.

Perhaps Bryon is right, he thought, *and we should be hunting them instead of trying to claim the land*. But orders were orders; they had been told to do what they were doing, and the Overseers weren't known for taking suggestions.

Another rustle came from the same direction, and Mattias shook himself out of his thoughts.

"Where is it?" one of his soldiers said, "there's nothing there!"

"Hold your nerve, boys," Mattias called, "the Tarsi are nothing but cowards and deceivers."

A half-hearted laugh was his only response. Mattias swivelled to check their flanks; atop the low hill where they'd made their temporary base, there was nothing but the tents, his team and the tank which followed them. He scanned the rolling countryside for more signs. The Tarsi only attacked in groups.

Trees swayed gently, and the deep green grass rippled as breezes changed direction.

They could be anywhere.

Mattias remembered the first attack; mid-march, with no enemy in sight, several soldiers had simply collapsed, screaming and bleeding. Their death had been as swift as it was horrifying, and no enemy had been spotted.

Now, Mattias' team conducted marches from small town to small town. Their orders were to claim Tarsium as part of the new Ermoori empire. Their successes were few and far between. But they always returned, and they were getting better at fighting their unseen enemy.

"Here!" one of his men called, "one of ours!"

Mattias watched an Ermoori soldier stumble from the trees. His weapon was missing, but the solid black armour he wore seemed to be intact. How a soldier had survived wandering alone, Mattias couldn't imagine. His hunting groups returned alive and well—albeit unsuccessful—so this man must have belonged to one of the other battalions stationed outside the districts.

"Soldier," Mattias called to the man, "report. Where have you been?"

The man said nothing, limping to the safety of their base with a hand to his side as though he was grievously wounded. He was lucky to be alive, but the limp looked serious.

Mattias signalled for the unit's doctor, Petor. He was easy to spot; bright red shoulder plates marked his role as healer. Mattias' own shoulder plates were the bright green of a captain, but all his other soldiers' armour was entirely black. Petor's red shoulder plates always brought comfort.

"Check him over," Mattias told the man when he jogged over, "take him to the command tent if you need to remove his armour."

"Yes sir."

"And report to me when you're done."

Mattias cast his eyes over the countryside once more.

"Keep your eyes sharp, men," he said, "this is just the kind of distraction the enemy can use."

He held his weapon ready to fire. The hills and valleys of verdant grass revealed no secrets to him. How were the Tarsi able to appear from nowhere? There had to be an explanation. It couldn't be magic... could it?

Mattias' senses prickled with the intensity of his focus. His men stayed in the formation he'd taught them, a double-layered circle facing outward that surrounded the tank and the command tent. The soldiers in the outer circle kneeled, and those behind stood. When it came time to fight, the kneeling soldiers would fire first, and the standing soldiers would watch for new targets or any complications. If all else failed, there was the tank.

It was a good system. So far, Mattias' team had avoided more casualties than most of the other battalions. Of course, some of that might have been luck... or the placement of their team outside the districts.

Most of the Ermoori army was pushing through the cities, suffering losses but steadily rooting out Tarsi fighters. They hadn't gained much ground in the last month or so, but victory would come. Mattias had to believe that; there was no other way to get through such warfare.

The weapon hummed in his hands, its stock buzzing against his shoulder. The power that Prime Overseer Hayne had created was truly incredible. As difficult as it was to find the enemy, once they were spotted, they didn't stand a chance.

Mattias sighed, quietly enough that no one else would have heard. Another false alarm; there were no enemies. There was nothing but the grass and the breeze.

"Sir," one of his men said, "it's been about an hour since the last change."

Mattias nodded, still watching the trees.

"Change up, men," he called.

The soldiers marched around to the opposite side of the circle. They would scan the terrain now with fresh eyes, as their view had changed. The primary and secondary groups would swap, too; those who were assigned to kneeling would trade places with the soldiers who stood behind them in combat.

A strange feeling crept over Mattias' neck and down his spine. As his men set up in their new positions, a scream rang out; it came from the command tent. The soldiers shouted, searching around them. Mattias went straight for the tent.

The doctor and the returned soldier were fighting, grappling on the ground. Beneath them, the grass had become a slick mess of red. He couldn't tell who was wounded.

"Enough," Mattias shouted, "stop this!"

The doctor, Petor, rolled on top of the soldier and rammed a fist into the man's head. Both men were fully armoured; they couldn't risk a doctor being killed. The blow hit so hard it vibrated through the ground. The men grappled further, shoving at each other, each trying to gain the advantage. As Mattias watched, the blood spread over the grass below them.

Why are they fighting? He couldn't tell what, if anything, had set them against each other. They had ignored his order. Mattias wasn't sure who the wounded soldier was, but it was unlike his own men to ignore a command.

Mattias stepped in close and kicked the unknown soldier off of the doctor. The man moved as if to attack once more, but stopped when he saw Mattias' weapon aimed at his face.

“Who are you?” Mattias demanded. When the soldier said nothing, Mattias tipped his weapon up and back. “Take off your helmet.”

“He’s one of them, sir,” Petor said.

“Are you certain?”

“Why else would he attack me?”

Mattias frowned. An imposter in Ermoori armour meant the enemy had managed to kill a soldier and steal his belongings. So far, every time an Ermoori had fallen, his fellow soldiers retrieved the body and put his armour and weaponry away.

If a Tarsi has obtained armour to disguise themselves once, he thought, *it can happen again*. It was a disconcerting thought.

The soldier, realising he was out of options, slowly reached up and pulled the helmet off. Mattias found himself holding his breath as the sleek black faceplate lifted away. But underneath was an Ermoori face.

“Why didn’t you just say you weren’t Tarsi?” Mattias said.

“Why did you attack me?” Petor asked at the same time.

The soldier said nothing. Mattias watched his closely; his eyes were hollow, haunted, and there was a careful blankness about his expression.

I don’t like this, he thought, *there is something off here*.

There were many men who had been so battered by war that they simply shut down. They didn’t talk, or eat, or sleep. Mattias was lucky not to count himself among them. But this man was different;

of all those struck numb by war, none had suddenly attacked a fellow soldier. He couldn't have been a defector. Why would a defector approach an unfamiliar unit the way he had? Besides, no one turned on Ermoor. So what was it?

The man hasn't reacted to a word we've said, Mattias thought, *I wonder...*

"Petor," he said, "if this man does nothing in ten seconds, I am going to shoot him in the leg."

The doctor exhaled a short laugh from his nostrils.

"Yes, sir," he said.

Mattias waited.

The soldier's expression remained blank.

Mattias squeezed the trigger, and a vivid yellow flash arced from the barrel to the man's thigh. He screamed as the powerful bolt lanced straight through the otherwise impenetrable Ermoori armour.

Petor leapt onto the man and pinned him down, ignoring the open wound and the soldier's screams.

Two more of Mattias' men slipped into the tent, weapons up.

"What's happening, sir?"

Mattias gestured to the messy scene.

"We have a problem," he said.

Danel

1795

Danel rushed down the massive tunnel ahead of his ambush group. Five warriors, against fully armoured Ermoori soldiers. The group was Danel, Kala—a Tarsi agent—and three more Shenza whom Danel didn't know well; Atana, Tanek, and Lenala, who at the least appeared to be skilled and disciplined warriors. Danel was lucky to have them in his group. Though Kala guided them through the tunnels and gathered information from the other Tarsi to help them, the group was technically under Danel's lead.

He had proved himself many times, though he was still terrified of the Ermoori.

Their footsteps didn't echo down here, but the presence of the Tarsi and Shenza around him was still a comfort even without the sound of their movement. The Ermoori were everywhere now. Even with their sneak attacks every day, the Tarsi were barely making a difference.

The tunnels beneath Tarsium had become a home to Danel. Fighting the invaders from the safety of the cool, open darkness was infinitely better than being hunted through the forests of Shanaken. For one thing, the Ermoori had no idea the tunnels existed. And, as much as Danel missed the forests, there was a deep sense of calm within the tunnels. Being underground had suffocated him at first. But almost a year living in darkness had somehow changed him.

Many of the tunnels were set lower down, so that there were inclines to reach the sections of tunnel that connected to the surface. Even so, water constantly flowed through the slim channel set into the centre of each tunnel's floor. It never overflowed, and seemed to always gently babble instead of rushing. The tunnels' ceiling faded into shadow, as tall as the tunnels were wide; at least ten metres. Sometimes, Danel forgot that they were enclosed.

They ran up a long, sloping incline, the rough stone beneath their feet providing excellent grip despite the mud coating every surface. Ahead of them, the incline ended, barely visible in the darkness.

It was almost time for another attack.

He trained every day, with other Shenza and with the Tarsi. Hidden underneath their invaders, the war wasn't as terrifying. Danel didn't have high hopes of winning, but at least he didn't fear for his life every day.

Whenever they could, small groups snuck out of the countless hidden entrances scattered around Tarsium and attacked the Ermoori. Danel's group stuck mostly to Azar. Ermoori soldiers were everywhere despite the constant efforts of the Tarsi to demoralise and repel them. There seemed to be no end to their numbers and resources. Even worse, there was no end to their dedication.

The Tarsi way of fighting seemed to be the only counter to Ermoor's superiority; but it was too slow. They needed a better way. At this rate, the entire population of Tarsium would be wiped out before even half the Ermoori forces were killed.

"Here," said Kala, the Tarsi agent who guided them, "this entrance. There is an Ermoori encampment just south of here."

Danel glanced at the entrance; no matter how many times Kala selected one of the countless secret entrances to the surface above, it baffled him. Every entrance looked identical. Rough stone stairs running against the wall to keep the tunnel open, with a landing at the top large enough to fit seven or eight people comfortably. Though it was dim down here, they could always see. Danel still hadn't figured out how there was any light. The Shenza were now accustomed to the low light, having lived down here for Amalus knew how long, but even when they first arrived they could see.

His small group gathered on the landing. Danel always took a breath before their attacks; though they still held the element of surprise, the Ermoori possessed no weaknesses. Every time he ventured above ground, it could be his last day.

"Any information you can share about this encampment?" Danel asked.

"Only that there are perhaps half a dozen soldiers," Kala said, "and one of their war vehicles."

"Smaller group than usual," Danel said, "that's good news, at least."

She nodded.

"As good as we can hope for, at any rate."

The group shared glances, and readied themselves.

When Kala nodded, they opened the disguised hatch and slipped out into the world above.

Gentle sunlight fell through a copse of trees nestled against the low ground between several hills. Danel breathed fresh air, savouring the smell of grass and tree bark. He waited for everyone to emerge from the hidden entrance, and they headed south.

Most of the time, their attacks didn't result in any real damage being done; they killed Ermoori when they could, but their mission was to reduce morale enough so that the Ermoori couldn't justify the cost of invading Tarsium. So far, Danel didn't feel very successful.

The Ermoori barely reacted to their attacks. Their armour protected them from virtually every form of damage, and they were fanatically loyal to their cause.

Danel crested a hill and watched for signs of the invaders. It took almost no time; they perched atop a smaller hill not far from Danel's group. The soldiers hadn't reacted to them yet. He crouched behind a tree trunk, the others following his lead.

The Ermoori had spread through Tarsium at an alarming rate. With the Tarsi refusing to wage war, the invaders had set up encampments throughout the countryside and even within the three major cities. They never stayed in one place long. They seemed to be attempting to discover how the Tarsi travelled without being seen. Danel wondered if they would ever figure it out; as far as he was concerned, it was pure luck that they hadn't already. All it would take would be one sneak attack to go wrong.

It was afternoon. Though the Ermoori changed watch at dawn and dusk, Danel had yet to see any of them remove their armour or go to sleep. They did have tents set up, where some soldiers retired temporarily; perhaps they slept in those?

Five soldiers stood watch on the low hill, standing in a circle around one of their large war vehicles and a tent. Danel eyed their weapons; *if only there was a way to steal a few*, he thought, *we could turn the tide of the war*. Those weapons were more powerful than anything Danel had ever seen.

Attacking the Ermoori was becoming harder, not just because of their firepower, but because they learned from each encounter. When they first invaded a year ago, they moved through Tarsium in a line, creating a makeshift border along the eastern side. Their groups explored the countryside, expecting Tarsi and Shenza warriors to respond with an army. In those first months, Danel and the others had been able to attack from behind, while the Ermoori were focused on claiming ground.

Then their focus shifted; instead of claiming land, they started hunting for signs of Tarsi and Shenza, abandoning linear progression in favour of protecting from surprise attacks. Now, they stayed in outward-facing circles, keeping watch every hour of the day.

Kala knelt beside him. The others were nearby, behind the trees and watching the invaders carefully. Waiting for the Ermoori to be vulnerable was impractical, but they could watch a group for a while to see if there were any bad habits among their soldiers.

"The two on the northeast side talk to each other a lot," Danel said after a short while, "they'll be the easiest to sneak up on."

"And the vehicle is facing west," Kala said.

"Do we go now? Or closer to dusk?"

Kala sighed, her huge eyes squinting at the Ermoori soldiers.

"We cannot afford to keep waiting," she said, "Ermoor claims more of Tarsium every day."

"Let's go, then," Danel said.

They descended the hill opposite the Ermoori encampment, and circled around towards the north east side. Danel's throat tightened as they drew closer to the invaders. These attacks always left him shaking, wondering desperately if he would live to see tomorrow.

"I'll approach first, from the northwest," Kala whispered, "and try to distract them. You four rush in as soon as you can."

It was the best plan they had; the Ermoori had disregarded every previous tactic by adapting with chilling efficiency. They seemed almost inhuman.

"Remember," Kala added, "focus everything on one soldier. Attack the joints, the neck. Strike fast and retreat even faster."

She'd given them the same reminder the last half dozen attacks. Still, it helped Danel focus. Kala slipped away, and the Shenza drew their swords. The Ermoori watched the landscape around them, blissfully oblivious to Danel and his group.

An idea formed itself suddenly in Danel's mind.

"And grab his weapon, if you can," Danel whispered.

The others looked at him.

"We need a way to kill them," he said, "and those weapons are powerful."

Danel took a deep breath, body tense as he waited out the silence. His blade was heavy, as though it held the weight of all the blood spilled in Ermoor's vicious invasion.

Moments stretched out in a sickening crawl. Danel hefted his blade and wiped the sweat off his forehead. *Any time now*, he thought, *Kala will distract them*. The other Shenza looked as nervous as Danel felt; attacking the Ermoori never got any easier, nor less scary. But they were ready.

A murmur arose from the western side of the hill; Danel heard the voices of the Ermoori.

"Let's go," Danel said.

They crept through the trees towards the invaders. Danel was grateful for the dense forest in the area; they would be able to get quite close before being spotted. He kept his eyes on the two Ermoori closest to them, the two who spoke to each other too much. Waiting for them to turn away towards Kala.

After a brief moment, Danel's group were close enough to hear the low voices of the two soldiers. Finally, one of them looked west. The other was still speaking, but it wouldn't be long now.

"As soon as the one on the left turns away," Danel whispered, "we charge in. Stay silent, stay low."

The others nodded.

Danel breathed carefully, watching. They were so close. He summoned the image in his mind's eye of the attack; rush in to the closest soldier, lunge at the neck with his blade. Keep out of line of the weapon. Disarm the soldier if possible. Then, escape. One attack, one target.

The soldier glanced towards his fellow, and in a flash the four Shenza leapt into motion as one. Danel got there first. The Ermoori turned back to face him just as he raised his blade for the attack.

He stabbed at the man's neck, but his blade bounced off the solid black helmet, the impact jarring Danel's arms right up to the shoulder. Lenala swept her blade down at the soldier's wrist on his weapon arm. He didn't drop the weapon, but smashed the butt of its hilt into her face. Danel heard a crunch as she fell back. Tanek knelt and slipped his blade deftly between the armour plates covering the Ermoori's thigh and calf; he sliced through the clothing underneath and through flesh.

With a strangled scream, the Ermoori soldier crashed to the ground. Danel, breathing heavy now, tried for the neck again; but the enemy had already learnt to tuck his head down, and Danel couldn't pierce the much smaller gap.

Yelling broke the silence, but it was coming from the other side of the encampment. *That will cover the sound of our attack*, Danel thought, *good.* He dropped knee-first onto the downed soldier. A satisfying grunt of pain rising from the Ermoori. Atana grabbed the weapon and wrestled to get it out of his grip.

A flash of yellow light and a heart-stopping crack sounded, and Atana collapsed, half of her head missing as blood and pieces of her brain splattered onto the grass.

"No!" Danel screamed.

Tanek grabbed the enemy's weapon and brought his foot down on his face; it wouldn't have done any damage, but Danel had the opening he needed. He lunged with all his weight, aiming for the centre of the neck. His blade crunched through bone, thudding as it hit the inside of the helmet on the other side.

With a growl, Danel twisted the sword and wrenched it out. A flash of yellow shrieked by him, so close it burned, and at the same time a cracking sound rang out from the western side of the camp.

"Time to go," Danel shouted.

"Kala!" a shout came from below; Lenala stood waiting, blood flowing from her smashed nose. Her eyes were wide, shooting in the direction of the Ermoori's shouts.

"She can get herself out of this," Danel said, "we can't help her."

Lenala looked about to reply, but an enemy soldier spotted them, and a moment later a volley of yellow lightning tore up the ground around them. She made an anguished cry, but she joined Danel when he sprinted towards safety.

Mattias

1795

"He doesn't speak Ermoori?" Commander Darrow asked.

"Not that we can tell," Mattias said, "I said to his face I would shoot him, and he did nothing. Not even a blink."

Commander Darrow barely moved, his impeccable posture unaffected by the armour he wore. His shoulder plates were a pale, shining blue, and a thick stripe of the same blue flowed over the top section of his helmet. His voice was clipped, serious, and rang with the now familiar metallic echo that all armoured Ermoori voices took on.

"Fascinating," the Commander said.

The imposter sat with his head hanging low, his arms tied behind his back around a heavy bench.

"What do we do, sir?"

"You and I," Darrow said slowly, "will bring him to the Prime Overseer. No doubt he will learn much more from this man than you or I ever could."

Mattias nodded. Prime Overseer Hayne's intelligence was unmatched. If anyone could make sense of this, it was him.

"And my unit?" Mattias asked.

"They are to remain here, and hold the area."

"Without me-"

"They will be fine. You have trained them well."

"But sir, they need-"

"Enough, Captain," Commander Darrow said, "you have your orders. You are welcome to take it up with Prime Overseer Hayne, if you believe you know better than your superior officer."

Mattias caught himself before talking back again. He hated the idea of leaving his men on their own, but Darrow was right; they were a disciplined team. Besides, as far as wars went, Tarsium was quiet. Nothing compared to the brutality of the Shanaken forests, teeming with wild life just as desperate to kill them as the Shenza had been. Even the plants had been lethal.

"Yes, sir," he said.

Mattias retied the imposter's hands behind his back and dragged him to his feet. He followed the Commander to his own tank, pushing the imposter in front of him, and ordered two soldiers to drag the man onto the tank's roof and down into the main hatch. When the imposter was secured, Mattias joined the crew inside. Darrow gave the order to deploy, and the tank rumbled as it left Mattias' team behind.

He was glad not to have his face visible; he could hide his unease. His men were well trained and would fight well, but the existence of the imposter soldier presented uncomfortable implications. Had the Tarsi somehow destroyed his mind? Did they have a way of manipulating a person's thoughts so badly that he didn't even recognise his own language?

He had heard the stories about the old mental asylum in Darkpoint; when it first opened, patients had been terrorised by the founder, a ruthless man nicknamed Doctor Fear. Though it was an absurd name, the man himself was terrifying. Rumours of experimentation surrounded him. He had created some kind of chemical that destroyed people's minds. Did the Tarsi somehow replicate that chemical?

Whatever the Tarsi did to this Ermoori man, it was bad. And they might be able to do the same to Mattias' own men. How could anyone fight against an attack on the mind?

Commander Darrow seemed unbothered. Mattias didn't know much about the man, but he possessed the kind of stark confidence that Mattias could only wish for. Even after so long in the Ermoori military, Mattias still felt like a pretender. He wondered if he would ever feel deserving of the respect and devotion his unit held for him.

The imposter still sat in total silence, his face a statue etched in stone. Mattias had never been as unnerved by another person. What was happening behind that expressionless face?

Underneath the tank, the countryside rolled gently from hill to hill. There were no windows other than a small one for the driver. Mattias would have liked to see their journey to the coast and Prime Overseer Hayne's warship, but he contented himself with checking his weapon over. The crew was quiet, though morale was considerably higher than in the teams on the battlefield; Commander's teams were small enough to fit entirely within their tank. They travelled from place to place overseeing the war effort, and saw much less combat, protected as they were. Mattias envied them. He would never admit it out loud, but it was the truth.

Most of an hour passed as the tank rumbled on. Mattias watched the imposter through the entire trip, until the driver reported their arrival.

"Excellent," Commander Darrow said, "send a teleradio transmission to the Prime Overseer."

"Yes, sir."

Mattias climbed out of the tank with a careful eye on the strange soldier. Darrow's men handled the prisoner well; there was a weapon pointed at him the entire time. They gathered outside the tank, then followed Commander Darrow to the pier that had been made to access Overseer Hayne's warship.

A small party stood at the pier to welcome them. Mattias didn't recognise any of them; they were unarmoured, wearing the clothing of government officials instead of soldiers. Commander Darrow greeted them and the entire group proceeded down the pier.

"Prime Overseer Hayne is quite busy," one of the welcoming party said, "as I'm sure you can appreciate. This meeting will have to be brief."

Darrow nodded.

"It will not take long," he said, "but I believe the Prime Overseer will be quite interested in what we have to show him."

The man who had first spoken glanced at Darrow with raised eyebrows, his pinched face sour as his cold gaze took in Mattias. His voice was as cold as his expression.

"We will see," he said.

Hayne's warship was massive; much larger than the ones commanded by the other ranking officers. Rumour had it the Overseer had built a fully-equipped laboratory somewhere inside. It had to be true; even within the last year, there had been several upgrades to armour and weaponry handed out to the higher performing units.

Within the vast ship, Mattias followed the welcoming party through narrow corridors, up flights of stairs and through heavy steel doors. Finally, they stopped before a larger closed door in a wide antechamber. Judging by the direction they'd come, Mattias guessed they had to be somewhere abaft the great cabin.

"Hold here," the pinched-face man said, "the Prime Overseer will call when he is ready."

With a smug look, he slipped through the large door and left them to the gently shifting silence of the antechamber. They didn't wait long. After barely a moment, the door opened and they were waved in.

Prime Overseer Hayne stood with his hands behind his back, looking down at a complex technological interface. Buttons, dials, and glowing lights filled the angled benchtop, surrounding a strange screen of glass with what looked like a map of Pandeia covered in tiny, bright dots.

He didn't react to them at first, taking his time instead to finish whatever it was he was busy with. There were no labels on the bench, but Prime Overseer Hayne occasionally pushed buttons and turned dials with deft, practiced hands. After a short time, he gave a slight nod and cast his icy blue eyes over Mattias and the others.

"This soldier," he said quietly, "does not speak Ermoori, does he?"

Mattias couldn't stop his eyebrows shooting up in surprise. "How did you know that, my lord?"

"He is carefully controlling his expression, but he is unfamiliar with everything around him."

Hayne spoke with a gentle, pondering voice, as though he was speaking with himself. He watched the imposter, hands behind his back once more. Though the Prime Overseer's eyes were as bright and cold as ever, silver hair was beginning to spread from his temples. Mattias had no idea how old the man was, but he looked tired. Running a war couldn't have been easy; Mattias didn't envy him.

"Tell me everything you know," Hayne said to Mattias, "about this man."

"There isn't much to tell, sir. He came from the trees, limping, and unarmed. He didn't respond to anything we said, but after he was alone in the command tent with the doctor a little while, he attacked."

"Without provocation?"

"Not that our doctor said."

A slight nod was his only answer. Then the Prime Overseer looked over the imposter again. He stepped in close and grabbed the man's hair, ignoring the grunt of pain as he pulled his head back. Hayne's eyes showed nothing but sharp intelligence as he leaned in.

"I wonder," the Prime Overseer whispered, "do you feel pain the same way as normal men do?"

What does that *mean*? Mattias thought, *he's speaking as though that soldier is an animal*.

The imposter began struggling, his grunts turning to screams; Mattias realised Hayne was pulling even harder on his hair.

"My lord," Mattias said, "with all due respect, what are you doing?"

Hayne responded in a language Mattias didn't understand. But the imposter stopped screaming and stared, wide-eyed, at the Prime Overseer.

Hayne stepped back suddenly, composed and with his hands behind his back once again.

"You have done well, captain," Hayne said to Mattias, "you may not have realised, but you captured one of the enemy."

"The... the enemy, sir? I don't understand."

"No, I expect you don't. There is still much to learn about the Tarsi, even for me. I would have thought they understood Ermoori… they clearly make terrible spies without speaking their enemy's language. Perhaps this one is inexperienced. It would certainly explain the ease of his capture."

Mattias shook his head. The man before them was Ermoori. No one could disguise themselves that well; especially considering the Tarsi were four foot tall and looked like... well, more or less like frogs. Mattias didn't agree with the derogatory term most soldiers used, but it *was* accurate.

"It appears," Prime Overseer Hayne continued, still to himself, "that the Tarsi physiology is able to shift on a cellular level. Unless it's just another form of..."

He seemed to remember there were other people in the room, and straightened up. Mattias frowned at the words he'd used. He knew the Prime Overseer was intelligent, but he could have sworn several of those words were gibberish. What was a '*cellular level*'?

"This will require more looking into," Overseer Hayne said, "and there will be a reward for you, Captain Sterling. But for the moment, orders have changed."

"Sir?" Commander Darrow asked.

"Any lone Ermoori soldiers approaching our encampments are to be shot on sight."

Danel

1795

The neck is still the biggest vulnerability," Danel said, "but if they know we're aiming for it, it's easy for them to protect it."

After the chaos of battle, the tunnels were beautifully quiet. Danel and the others sat on the stony ground, waiting for Kala to return. Lenala's bleeding had subsided somewhat. They had left Atana's body behind; attempting to retrieve it would have only killed the rest of them.

"The leg joints make a good target," Tanek said, "but what we really need is to disarm more of them."

Lenala nodded.

"Those weapons are far too powerful," she said, nodding at the one in Tanek's hands, "if we could get our hands on even a few more of them..."

"It won't make a difference," Danel said, "we don't know how to use them."

"We can figure it out," Tanek said as he turned the weapon in his hands, "just give me some time."

"It's hard enough killing one," Danel said, "how are we going to steal enough of their weapons to arm our teams?"

"Exactly," Lenala said, "and besides, we don't even know if their weapons can punch through that armour in the first place. If they can't, we're no better off for taking some."

They fell into an uncomfortable silence. Danel rubbed his face, his eyes squeezed shut as he hoped for Kala to return. She was the better leader, even if Danel held the title.

"We could put a larger group together," Lenala said, "enough to overwhelm one of their smaller encampments?"

"Overwhelm?" Tanek scoffed, "are we fighting in different wars? How do you think we'll overwhelm the Ermoori?"

"The distractions work well," Lenala said, "if we have enough Tarsi and Shenza, we can target a larger group of Ermoori after they're distracted. With that weapon firing at them, they'll have no choice but to focus on it. Even if it can't kill them, they'll panic about someone else having their weapons. A few of us will pick off one of theirs, and then we'll take his weapon and run. Just like we did earlier."

Danel thought about it. As far as plans went, it wasn't exactly brilliant; the Tarsi and Shenza were spread across the entire country, launching strategic attacks independent of each other. The Tarsi themselves were somehow able to communicate when they needed to, but organising a large attack like that was likely out of reach.

He wondered if Kala would like the idea. *Where is she*? he thought, *it's been too long*.

"Well," Lenala said, "someone say something. Can we do it?"

"Can we?" Danel said, "possibly." He scratched his cheek and sighed. "Should we? I don't think so. We already barely survived that attack. Getting close to them is far too dangerous."

Tanek said nothing. He looked hollow, like his spirit had already climbed the Eternal Mountain. Lenala shook her head, eyes dropping to the dark tunnel floor. The war was beating them down. Even their victories felt like defeat.

We claim so little, Danel thought, *for the price we pay*.

"If," Tanek said slowly, "and I mean, by the *slightest* chance, if this thing can get through their armour… it will change everything. We can run our surprise attacks from a distance, pick off a few of them, and take their weapons and armour."

Danel nodded. It sounded good. Too good to be true.

"Let's figure out how to make it work, then."

Silence fell over them again. Though they were safe in the tunnels, it wasn't much of a life. The Ermoori were taking everything from them.

They were beginning to go hungry, too; Danel's last proper meal had been two days ago. The tunnels were an excellent way to travel unseen, but Ermoor had taken hold of so much of Tarsium that they'd managed to halt the transport of food and resources. How could they fight an enemy so powerful?

Even if Tarsium had an army, they would have been overrun before long. It only would have meant more bloodshed. The Ermoori were simply too well-organised, too protected, and too many. For the first time, Danel really thought about what Pandeia would look like after the war. The only logical outcome was that the Ermoori controlled the world. Would it be wiser to simply surrender? Or would the invaders refuse to accept a peaceful end to the fighting? They were certainly bloodthirsty, but surely they would end the slaughter if their opponents stopped fighting back...

But he couldn't voice the thought. What would the others think of him? So many Shenza had died; what was the purpose of their deaths if the survivors abandoned the fight?

Danel didn't know how many had died so far, but it must have been in the thousands. Tens of thousands, even. The only positive was that the Ermoori weren't killing innocents in the districts. They seemed only to want fighters dead. It made him think perhaps that surrender *could* work.

Shanaken was taken. If something didn't change soon, Tarsium would be next. The Ermoori showed no signs of slowing; their resources were endless, and they progressed with the brutality and determination of a people who believed in a cause greater than themselves. Danel felt like a cornered forest mouse surrounded by Zuzuk, the giant predators of the Shanaken forests.

A scraping sound crept through the tunnels from a distance like a whisper. The three Shenza leapt to their feet, swords drawn. A sound like that had never come through the tunnels before.

"Who's there?" Danel called.

A low shape dragged itself out of the gloom. Danel took up a defensive stance, ready despite his exhaustion. The shape gradually formed, and Danel gasped as he finally saw what it was.

Kala was barely alive. Her clothing was shredded and bloody, and when she drew closer, Danel realised her left leg ended at the knee in a mangled mess of flesh and bone. Her breath was laboured, rattling desperately through her throat as though she was drowning.

"Kala!" Lenala shouted, as they rushed to her side.

"You're alive," Danel said, "thank Amalus you made it."

"We need to get her to a healer," Tanek said, "right now."

Mattias

1795

Weeks had passed since Prime Overseer Hayne had given the order to shoot Ermoori soldiers returning from enemy territory on sight. So far, they hadn't needed to follow that order; but Mattias knew somewhere deep down that it wouldn't be long before they did. When he returned to his unit, they argued against the order when Mattias relayed it; but by now they had accepted it in grim silence. Every day they hoped, desperately, that they wouldn't see one of their own approaching.

His unit had moved northwest He watched the edges of the forest near their new encampment, hoping—as always—not to see anyone emerge.

Attacks from the Shenza and Tarsi were coming more often now; almost every day. *Either they are becoming desperate*, he thought, *or they are approaching victory*. He didn't know which; battalions were only apprised of the information they needed, which was determined by the Commanders and Prime Overseer Hayne. Their teleradios were used to give orders to the soldiers, not relay information to them.

His men were uneasy, and barely any words were shared between them. Even their meals, such as they were, were eaten in silence. Watch changes too, went by without a word.

Every few days, a command tank appeared to drop off supplies to each of that Commander's units. There was one due today, most likely; Mattias could never be certain when they would show up. If they were too consistent, the enemy would be able to track them. The tank units moved easy, immune to the weight of the war somehow. They must have had to engage in combat; why weren't they suffering as much as Mattias' unit? A part of him briefly wondered if the Tarsi could take over a tank unit; if they could look like Ermoori, who could really be trusted? All it would take was one tank unit to let down their guard.

Mattias shifted on his feet, ignoring the rifle in his hands. If he thought about it too much, his fear would take over, and the need to use it would overwhelm him. With all the glory that had surrounded the Ermoori army, and the war itself, nobody ever talked about the sheer, crushing dread of being a soldier in enemy territory. Only the tank units seemed to live without that dread.

They had been attacked many times in the last few weeks, always by small groups of Shenza, occasionally accompanied by a single Tarsi, if at all. Each time, a swell of gratitude rose up within him that it wasn't Ermoori soldiers emerging from the trees.

"Sir," Geffrey, one of Mattias' most skilled marksmen, said, "is the resupply unit bringing more ammunition this time? They didn't bother last time, and we're running low."

"We can only hope," Mattias said, "if the attacks continue at the pace they're going, we'll run out more quickly than they can keep us stocked."

"What happens then?" Robert, the youngest in the unit, asked.

"We fight hand-to-hand," Mattias said with a shrug.

The handful of soldiers within earshot shuffled uncomfortably at that. He had meant it to sound light-hearted, as though it wasn't a problem; but his men clearly took it to heart.

"Spare your fear, lads," Mattias said, "leave it for the enemy to fear us, not the other way around. Their weapons do nothing against our armour."

But his comment fell flat, and silence crept over the team once more. It wasn't long ago that he could rally them with a few words; the war had sapped their humour as surely as it had taken everything else. Not for the first time, Mattias wondered what the purpose of the war actually was. Even if the fighting stopped today, it seemed to him there would be no victory. The best he could hope for was to survive, and try to live with himself afterwards. If he had to kill a fellow Ermoori, that would be almost impossible.

His body was heavy, the armour weighing him down despite being lightweight. Weeks of little sleep, if any, dragged his mind down at the same time. How long could he keep going like this? And how long could his men remain disciplined and effective if they struggled even to fight the silence and mind-numbing boredom?

A low rumbling sounded from somewhere east: supplies, at last. Mattias crossed the encampment quickly, a grim smile on his face unseen behind his helmet.

The tank came into view around a tall hill, its sleek black armour shining in the sun. Mattias waved and waited for the team to emerge. There were four of them, including Commander Darrow, who greeted Mattias and stood next to him as the soldiers swapped full crates for empty ones.

"New orders, sir?" Mattias asked.

"There is a small town northwest of here," Commander Darrow said, "your team is to take it before sundown. It will be a base of operations for you, and a resupply station for other units."

"Is there an enemy presence?"

"The enemy is everywhere, Mattias," Darrow said, "but in this case, no. No soldiers, no Tarsi spies. The civilians will be easy to deal with."

"Sir," Mattias said, "could you clarify?"

Commander Darrow sighed and looked down his nose at Mattias.

"Clarify what?"

"When you say *deal with...*"

"I'm saying they don't pose a threat. They will not attack."

Mattias let out a relieved breath. He could never tell with Darrow.

"But if they do," the Commander said, "the price of rebellion is death."

A thought, as sudden as it was uncomfortable, bloomed cold in Mattias' head. Darrow was his only source of news and information; the teleradio in Mattias' tank almost never received transmissions, and when it did, they were simple orders. He had to take the opportunity.

"Do you know," Mattias asked, "if any other units have had to... to kill one of their own?"

Darrow gave him an odd look. It seemed to say *why should that matter*?

"Oh yes," he said, his voice cold and vicious, "many. Your unit is particularly fortunate."

"We are," Mattias said, "we've not even lost a man to the enemy."

"Don't make the mistake of thinking yourself invulnerable, Captain Sterling," the Commander said, "many other units have thought the same, before being decimated by a well-timed ambush."

"How many have we lost, sir?"

"In total? Thousands. Likely more."

Mattias let it sink in. He'd never asked before; he knew there had been deaths, of course; but their armour and weapons were supposed to be the ultimate power in Pandeia. Compared to Ermoor, soldiers in the rest of the world were supposed to be as helpless as rats. They wielded swords, wore leather or cloth, and lived in forests. How were they killing so many Ermoori?

"I see," Mattias said, eyes scanning the countryside as the soldiers finished their resupply.

"We will win the war," Commander Darrow said, "before too long. These people are weak. They rely on trickery and surprise, and even then they mostly fail. They have only managed to stall us so long because the Shenza are fighting on their behalf."

It was true; Mattias had barely even seen any Tarsi. It seemed as though there weren't many to begin with. From what he'd heard, the cities were mostly populated by Shenza, Omati, and even Ermoori. The latter made him uncomfortable; why were people leaving the great city of Ermoor to live in a place filled with such uncivilized beings?

Though, he realised, once the war was done, Ermoori cities would be built in every country, and the people would all be living side-by-side after all. He couldn't imagine what that life would look like. How long before the foreign people accepted Ermoor as their rulers? How many times would rebellion need to be stamped out?

How many more would have to die before there was finally peace? Mattias knew the answer to that one, at least; Too many. No matter the number, it was too many.

Commander Darrow left, and Mattias watched the tank pull away and disappear behind the same hill from whence it came.

Mattias called Geffrey to him.

"Fold in," he said, "we leave for our next encampment as soon as we're ready."

"Yes sir," Geffrey said.

The team moved efficiently; they'd packed and moved countless times over the last year. Even in Shanaken they were constantly on the move. They had even developed their own phrases; *fold in* was pack everything up. Simple, but effective.

As his men packed everything into the tank, Mattias realised a way around the Tarsi problem. They could look like anyone, but they couldn't know what the Ermoori were thinking. And they apparently couldn't understand Ermoori...

"Willen!" he called. The young man ran to him.

"Do we have paper? Charcoal?"

"I think so, sir," Willen said.

"Bring it to me."

Not long after, Mattias finished writing a series of notes, holding the paper against the side of their tank. He straightened up and noticed his men had finished their packing and were standing ready.

"Okay, lads," he said, "take a paper each. We use these from now on to make sure the Tarsi aren't among us."

"How does this help?" Robert asked, "it's just random words next to days of the week."

"The Tarsi cannot speak our language," Mattias said, "those are paired code words. I wrote instructions on the back, familiarise yourselves with the pattern and destroy the paper as soon as you can. From now on, we use those codes to address each other if any of us become separated."

He looked at the men around him as they read their papers.

"You know what our orders are, boys," he said, "if we see other Ermoori soldiers without warning. I don't want that to happen to any of you. Stick to the code words, but otherwise try to stay together."

"So, we're still shooting our own," Geffrey asked, "if they don't belong to our unit?"

"I don't like it any more than you, Geffrey," Mattias said, "but yes. And even those within this unit, if they can't recite the correct code."

"Sir," Robert said, "we can't do that. I can't shoot anyone here. They're my brothers."

"Not if they don't know the code," Mattias said, forcing a hard edge into his voice, "we're fighting a different kind of war here, boys.

The enemy can look like one of us. No one is safe, and no one can be trusted if they don't know our code. I'm sorry, I really am. But this is the only way."

Teleradio static buzzed within the tank. Mattias sat alone in the dark, waiting as patiently as he could. He heard nothing from outside the tank; though with the thick metal and static, he only could have heard gunshots.

"Captain Sterling?" a voice finally said, "come in, Captain Sterling?"

"Here."

"I have Prime Overseer Hayne waiting. Go ahead."

A click sounded, and then the static quieted.

"Sir," Mattias said, "I have something to report."

The Prime Overseer's voice came through softly, but so cold that Mattias flinched.

"Tell me, captain. I am a busy man."

"When the orders came through to shoot our own men," Mattias said, "I had an idea. I set codewords dependent on the day of the week, and ordered my men to memorise them and destroy the papers. The Tarsi can't speak Ermoori, or read it, and so I thought each unit could come up with their own codes, so at least if our own team is separated, we could know for sure who's who."

A long silence followed, with only the dim static filling the tank's interior.

"A surprisingly efficient solution," the Prime Overseer said, "and you have implemented this within your team already?"

"Yes, sir."

"You have been… useful, captain. I will remember this."

The line clicked again, and Mattias was plunged into pure, cold silence. He rubbed his chin, strangely unsatisfied with the Prime Overseer's words.

I will remember this.

What did it mean?

"He could have said thank you," he muttered.

Securing his helmet back in place, he opened the tank's main hatch and returned to his men. They were alert, but their misery was as palpable as their tension.

Danel

1795

It took them hours to carry Kala to the nearest Tarsi hub. She was pale, her usually mottled grey skin turned a stark white. Danel had torn a strip from his tunic and tied it tightly around her leg above the wound; she was so weak she hadn't even screamed.

The hub was a small collection of tents and benches set up along the tunnel walls. Some were better equipped than others, permanent homes where the Tarsi conducted military planning and medical care, but most were simply places for them to rest or regroup in relative comfort. There were hundreds, if not thousands, of the hubs nestled in the tunnels throughout all of Tarsium.

They passed several hubs which contained no medical supplies or healers, and were forced to move on.

"The healer's tent is that one," said a Tarsi man keeping watch on the northern side of the tunnel. He looked at Kala's wounds and grimaced. "There may not be much we can do for her," he added.

Danel rushed her into the tent. The healer, another Tarsi, barely glanced up from her work mixing vials of liquid together.

"I can stop the bleeding," she said, "but that's all. We have exhausted our medicines."

"What's all this for, then?" Danel demanded, gesturing at the vials.

"These do not work on their own," the healer said, "I'm trying to make something useful out of what we have left, but there's only so much I can do."

Kala whimpered, a quiet, breathless sound. Outside the tent, Danel had seen dozens of Shenza and a few Tarsi sitting or lying on the stony ground, all sporting wounds of varying seriousness.

We are done for, Danel thought, *we will lose this war by starvation and injuries if we don't get killed by the Ermoori*. It was a sobering thought; even if they somehow managed to survive the invaders, they would die anyway. He let a tense breath out as he watched Kala sink lower into unconsciousness. Her eyes flared open occasionally, but they didn't see Danel or the tunnel; he was certain of it.

Then she whispered something, and her voice was suddenly lucid, almost strong. He heard every word.

"Asheilos," she said, "I finally see you. Take me home. I'm so tired."

The moment she stopped speaking, she faded. Danel heard one final breath escape from her. Her eyes became as still and lifeless as glass. Danel was alone with the healer. She stopped briefly enough to look at Kala.

"It was quick," she said, "that's the best we can hope for here. And now I can give what we have to others who might survive."

Danel almost threw up, his stomach and throat working as his eyes stung from sudden, unbidden tears. In that moment he would have surrendered Tarsium, all of Pandeia, for the war to just end. For no more deaths. *Let the Ermoori have it all*, he thought, *as long as everyone else survives*.

He left the tent, left Kala's body where it lay, and his mind slipped into a cold, numb fugue as he rejoined Tanek and Lenala.

"How goes Kala?" Lenala asked, her broken nose still untreated.

"She..." Danel's voice was hoarse, as though he'd been screaming. He cleared his throat as best he could, and then burst into tears.

"Oh, no," Lenala said. She sprinted for the tent.

A moment later, Danel heard her cry out. Tanek put a hand on his shoulder.

"I'm sorry," he said.

"No," Danel said through ragged breaths, "it's *them* who should be sorry."

Tanek nodded, but said no more. What was there to say?

Lenala emerged from the tent, tears streaming down her face. She looked as lost as Danel felt. They stood in the middle of the tunnel, simply watching the other survivors as they went about their business. Atana's death hit him then too, from the depths of his mind, a fresh horror that his thoughts had hid from him until now. He'd seen it; he'd been right there. And there was nothing he could have done.

Same with Kala. She had been alone when she distracted the Ermoori. He couldn't even imagine the strength it had taken to drag herself back to them. How many others had suffered a similar fate at the hands of the Ermoori? Dying alone, grievously wounded, barely able to speak as foreigners invaded their home.

The tunnel was too big; there were so few people, and those there were sat slumped and hollow. He knew the Shenza had hoped to join forces with the Tarsi and make a stand here, but they were too few and far between to combat the Ermoori. And the survivors of the last year were so beaten down, they possessed no fighting spirit. What could they do? Simply lay down and die? It felt like their only options—surrender, fight, or run—would all end up the same way; they were running out of medicine, tactics, people, and time.

Tanek gestured to a small group of tents further down the tunnel. They were clustered together, a collection of barrels and crates beside them.

"Should we see if they have any food?" he asked.

Danel nodded and they wandered over. A few people stood at the opening of the tents, gaunt and hollow-eyed. There was no smoke coming from the tents, no smells of food. Now that he was closer, he saw the barrels and crates were empty.

Inside the closest tent was a pair of Shenza checking over old pieces of fruit; all of which looked rotten.

There was no grain or rice, no salted fish. Nothing that could last a while, that could fill an empty stomach. Danel watched the two as they examined the fruit; they seemed to be placing all but the most rancid into a crate like the ones outside the tent's entrance, and only throwing away those they absolutely had to.

It was disconcerting. The two Shenza finally called to the hungry loiterers and offered the ruined fruit. They ate ravenously, ignoring small spots of mould and even live fruit flies as they chewed. Fruits that, not long ago, would have offended any self-respecting Shenza. Fruits that would have been thrown from the canopy cities to the forest floor in disgust, were now being eaten without question.

And the Ermoori still looked strong, unflappable in their powerful armour as they spread through the countryside like a sickness. Would they ever have to deal with the consequences of their actions? Danel hoped one day to see a more powerful army rise up and wreak the same destruction on them.

He sighed, turning away from the rotten fruit and shaking his head. His thoughts were not right; the Shenza didn't seek vengeance. They moved with the flow of life.

Peace without weakness.

Strength without aggression.

Growth without forgetting.

The tenets of the Shenza, held sacred by every warrior in Shanaken. Except they were already broken. They had been too weak to stop the Ermoori. In their desperation to strike back, they were all demonstrating aggression. They launched ambushes, exploited weaknesses, retaliated for every attack; these things went against the tenets. And growth without forgetting? The Shenza hadn't grown at all. In the centuries that had passed since the Ermoori first began their attempted invasions, nothing about the Shenza was different.

And now, they were the ones launching attacks on the enemy. Hunting them using tricks and deceit.

We have lost our way. No wonder we lost Shanaken.

And they would lose the war.

Danel entered a new tent. It was empty of both people and food. Only a small bench and a few upturned crates were placed in there; if not for them, Danel would have assumed it had never been used at all.

The next one contained a lone Tarsi woman, whose eyes seemed twice the size they should have; the rest of her was so emaciated that Danel was amazed she was alive. She looked carefully at him, her face slack and her eyes alternating from focused to vacant. Against the tent wall, a pile of large fabric bundles reached up almost to the roof, sloping down like a ramp to stop them from toppling. There was no food, nothing that might help a survivor of the war, wounded or not.

"What are you doing in here?" Danel asked.

When the Tarsi woman spoke, her voice was barely even a whisper, pained and weak.

"I'm going to die, I think." She pointed at the pile of bundles, her slim finger shaking. "Like them."

Mattias

1795

Twyford was nestled in a small forest, invisible from outside the tree line. A small river, barely more than a brook, snaked its way lazily past the tiny town. A few dozen homes, a mill, and a storehouse were all it contained. The storehouse was the target; if they controlled such a building, they could begin stockpiling the resources of the Tarsi, keeping them from falling into enemy hands and effectively laying siege to the entire region.

The tank rolled over the thin dirt road, Mattias walking beside it on the grass. A few Tarsi walked along the dirt roads that connected their homes, but other than that the roads were deserted. The storehouse was quiet, the only real motion coming from the river and the mill drawing from it.

Mattias wondered what resources were already in the storehouse, if any. Surely whatever they had would have already been seized by the Tarsi and Shenza rebels to aid in the war effort... But a part of him hoped they would stumble upon food or perhaps something even better.

Did the Tarsi even use money? Did the Shenza? His attitudes towards the Shenza had changed drastically after fighting against them; they were honourable, and skilled warriors, and braver than most Ermoori. But they still seemed... uncivilized. Almost animalistic. The Tarsi, though, were nothing less than traitorous in their use of sneak attacks and disguises. Though he'd seen them, like the ones in Twyford, he'd never heard them speak other than to scream in pain, and they possessed no honour or bravery that he could see.

Mattias didn't enjoy killing. He hated it, in fact. But he hadn't felt bad for leaving the disguised Tarsi with Prime Overseer Hayne, even though he knew Hayne would kill him when he was done with whatever experiments he needed to conduct. He didn't feel bad for taking Tarsium. He wished it could have been done peacefully, but he could see now that it was impossible. Even if the Tarsi had surrendered, they would have fought back from the shadows, with poison and secret plots. Not like soldiers, like cowards.

Like me.

The thought slashed at him from somewhere deep and dark. The part of him that had survived the Tyran uprising all those years ago by running away. The part of him that had survived stealing the relic from Shanaken by running away. The part of him that he could never confront, that made him hate himself.

No, he thought, *I am a leader and a soldier. I fight, and I kill, and I can do things now that would have broken me years ago. I am no coward. Cowards are not given command of a unit of soldiers and deployed behind enemy lines.*

The commanders and captains weren't scared. The Prime Overseer wasn't scared. And neither was Mattias. He wouldn't allow himself to be.

As they entered the town, Mattias heard gasps and scuffling, then the slam of several wooden doors.

See? he told himself, *those are cowards. I am the fear they hide from*. Tarsi could not be trusted. Their orders had been to shoot any apparent Ermoori soldiers returning from enemy territory; but if they had the chance to kill Tarsi before they could disguise themselves as Ermoori, shouldn't they take it? It was better than shooting at his own people.

Besides, with the Tarsi refusing to fight like soldiers, there was nothing to distinguish combatants from civilians. Which made them all combatants. It didn't take a soldier to poison, or to plunge a blade into someone's neck as they slept.

I am sick of suspecting everyone, he thought, *these cowards shouldn't have such an effect on us*.

There was a Tarsi on the road still, wrapped in a cloak and facing them. A deep hood shrouded their face in shadow.

Mattias looked over the homes, searching for spies or any sign of another sneak attack. It would be just like the Tarsi to put one of their own in the middle of the street as bait so they could launch an attack from the flanks.

"Hey," he called to the lone figure, "off the road, or I will shoot."

"Sir," Geffrey said quietly, "you know they don't speak Ermoori. He can't follow instructions he doesn't understand."

It's a trick, he thought, *whatever this Tarsi is doing, it's some kind of trap*. He cast his eyes over the buildings nearby, watched for enemy soldiers ducking behind cover. He knew there was something wrong, deep within his bones. It didn't matter if they could speak Ermoori. An enemy was an enemy, and Mattias felt far better shooting one of these creatures on sight than he did doubting his own men.

"So be it," he said.

Geffrey called out as Mattias raised the barrel of his rifle and fired. The Tarsi crumpled as a bolt of yellow lightning cracked through his skull.

The Tarsi in the homes around them began wailing, their voices tremulous and discordant. Mattias glanced at all of them, certain an attack would come soon. Their cries were loud, almost painfully so.

"Ready for an attack, boys," he called, his rifle stock against his shoulder.

"Sir," Robert said, "these are civilians. Innocents. There is no attack coming."

"*Innocents*?" he asked, "no, there are no innocent Tarsi. They can all look like one of us, so they are all dangerous."

A door opened suddenly, and a Tarsi ran from the house towards them, screaming horribly. *A war cry*, he thought, *something to disturb their enemies*?

There was something in the creature's hand; a weapon? He couldn't tell, but the Tarsi was running towards them from the other side of the corpse Mattias had shot down. He would want vengeance, if it were someone he knew.

He tried to discern what was in the Tarsi's hand; he really did try. But he couldn't tell, and every moment the creature drew closer was a risk he couldn't take.

His rifle thumped lightly into his shoulder as another bolt of yellow lightning arced through its target. Two bodies littered the road, and the wails grew louder. His men were looking at each other. Their faces were hidden behind their helmets, but they moved with uncertainty. *They don't see*, he thought, *how much danger we're in at any given moment.*

The barrel of the tank rattled as it spun on its tracks; the gunner trying to keep potential targets in sight. Mattias had to fight to control his breathing; everyone was an enemy here, and his men were beginning to lose their composure.

"Sunlight!" he called, hoping the code words might bring them out of their fear.

"Daybreak," his men said back.

They weren't in sync as they usually were, and one or two didn't even answer. He looked at them pointedly.

"Daybreak," they said, begrudgingly.

"Sir, over there!" Geffrey called.

Mattias looked past the Tarsi corpses; an Ermoori in armour approached Twyford from the opposite side of the town. He carried his rifle, unlike the last soldier who'd shown up unannounced. And he didn't look wounded.

"Sunlight!" Mattias bellowed at the unknown soldier.

The man's helmet snapped in the direction of Mattias, but he said nothing. Mattias raised his rifle, barrel at the soldier and finger on the trigger. In response, the soldier did the same.

"Sunlight, damn you!" Mattias shouted again, "last chance!"

"Sir," Geffrey said, "he doesn't know our-"

His words were cut off by the crack of Mattias' rifle; the soldier attempted to duck and run, but the bolt caught him in the neck. His head whipped back from the impact, and he tumbled backwards into the dirt.

“One true God have mercy on us,” Geffrey said, “sir, only *our* unit knows our code words. He’s Ermoori, just not our unit.”

“How can you know that?” Mattias snapped, “he didn’t say a thing, just like the other one. Besides, you’ve been given your orders. Any unknown Ermoori soldiers approaching are shot on sight.”

Just as the last word was spoken, a yellow bolt shrieked past his head and slammed into the tank. His men swept around into combat stances, rifles ready. A lone Tarsi stood in the road, holding the fallen soldier’s rifle. A bare second passed before the street erupted into screaming bolts of lightning.

The Tarsi lived perhaps a heartbeat beyond first pulling the trigger. By the time its body hit the ground, it was mangled beyond recognition; the searing heat and thunderous impact of Ermoori rifle fire tearing it to shreds of jagged flesh and bone.

Mattias sprinted to the ruined body and retrieved the Ermoori rifle. He threw it up to the tank crew, one of whom had opened the top hatch and was looking over the street.

“Robert, Willen,” Mattias said, “bring the armour back here.”

They followed their orders without complaint; but their unease was thick in the air nevertheless. When they returned to the tank, they hoisted the corpse up onto the tank’s hull. The tank crew dragged it inside and Mattias heard clamouring inside as they shoved it into the limited storage space. They never left Ermoori technology behind.

“Now that the locals understand our strength,” Mattias said, it’s time to take the town for ourselves.”

His men looked at each other, then at the Tarsi watching from their windows. They looked like they were about to refuse. Mattias almost lost his temper, but settled for a hard edge in his voice.

"That's an order, boys. Round up the Tarsi, lock them up somewhere out of the way. Any who rebel will be killed."

Kerberos

1796

The war didn't bother Kerberos; he was Thearan, and war was their religion. What bothered him was his scout's reports of the technology being utilised by the Ermoori. That kind of power was far too dangerous in the wrong hands. And Riffolk's hands were the worst of the possible wrong hands.

He had only ever wanted to fix the problems he'd seen in governments, to rule with fairness and create a world that worked for everyone. His family, and every other noble family in Omatus, had been fat, lazy and corrupt. He'd grown up tormented and ridiculed for his love of books. No one around him had understood the power of knowledge, and so Omatus had descended into chaos as noble families squabbled over who sat on the throne without any thought given to what they should do once there.

Kerberos was determined to be different. He had left his name behind, and spent his life building an army. He provided magic to all those who followed him, and gave a fair chance to any who thought they could challenge him. Everything he had now, he had fought for. Earned by hard work. Omatus was his, and he had turned it into a flourishing city without crime, hunger or poverty.

All that was asked of his people was to worship Sithares. Even after the god had turned its back on him, he still made sure Omatus worshipped it. Keeping his people strong by combat was just one way he could make his city great. The price for strength and prosperity had to be paid; if corruption came from greed and laziness, then the opposite would come from discipline and strength. And Sithares was the surest path to those.

It had worked well for the entire course of his rule. His people, at first, were deeply uncomfortable with the idea of dedicating themselves to a god they'd never worshipped before. But as Omatus changed, they came to understand.

A deep, unshakable pride filled Kerberos as he looked over his city. Mid-afternoon sun streamed over the Omati stone that formed most of the buildings and roads. The city shone like a beacon to the rest of the world. A beacon that offered strength and security to any who could pay the price.

The Ermoori had swarmed Shanaken, and were doing the same in Tarsium. By all accounts, they were unstoppable. If left unchecked, they would take Omatus soon. Kerberos' army was strong, perhaps one of the strongest in Pandeia; but they wouldn't be able to stand against the superior armour and weaponry of the Ermoori.

I cannot fight them head on, he thought, *and I cannot allow them to continue taking Pandeia*. The thought of surrendering the city was absurd, but... it was possible that this was his only option. *At least until I can take control for myself.*

Below him, the city was quiet. After all he'd done to wrest it from the claws of failure, the knowledge of Ermoor's impending invasion hit him like a Thearan lion's giant claws.

And then there was Aella. Theara's self-appointed queen. Theara was far more defensible than Omatus; perhaps there was a way the two could work together? He could abandon Omatus altogether, and return with both armies, forcing the Ermoori into the defensive... He could call Aella to come to his defence, with the promise that he would help her against the Ermoori when the time came...

He shook his head, scolding himself for indulging in fantasy. Aella hated him. She hated everything he stood for. A truce would have been too much to hope for, let alone an alliance. Perhaps if the vicious warrior in her gave way to a reasonable leader; but that was too much to hope for, too.

She was so powerful, he thought, *such a pity her intelligence was so lacking.*

If she possessed the same vision and dedication as Kerberos, she might have fully revived Theara. As it was, she had essentially turned it into yet another campsite for the Thearans under her rule. They would not be a threat to him; but they could have been useful. There were very few nomadic tribes left, of late. Most had either joined Kerberos or Aella. Which meant recruiting more Thearans was hardly feasible.

What bothered him just as much as the technological power Ermoor possessed was the scientific mind behind it. Riffolk Hayne was as ruthless as he was brilliant. Before him, the Ermoori had attempted attacks on Shanaken countless times over generations. Their conviction was nothing short of extraordinary; but Riffolk had finally given them the power to match.

Kerberos didn't fear death. What he did fear was the effect it would have on him after he came back; though the Thearans he'd made immortal became more powerful each time they resurrected, their mind was fractured by the experience. Only a little, but it would certainly become worse if repeated over time.

I cannot let them kill me, he thought, *the city needs my mind undamaged.*

The city itself could be rebuilt; it had taken him a long time to change Omatus for the better, but he could do it again. He was immortal, after all. He felt the same as he had decades before. No slower, no weaker. No older.

Perhaps that is how I regain control, he thought, *not by fighting, but by waiting*. Time would mean nothing to him, but it would grind his enemies into dust. It meant watching his city fall, living under Ermoori rule for a lifetime or two; but eventually, he would become its leader once more.

He couldn't tell if it was genius or madness. But based on the reports he'd received, there would be no fighting the Ermoori. If Kerberos' mind was the key to Omatus becoming the best city it could be, then he had to protect it at all costs. Everything else would come later. If it took a few years or a few hundred years, he would make certain Omatus became as great as he knew it could be.

Rushed footsteps pulled him from his reverie. Nomiki, his second in command, appeared on the balcony.

"Our scouts have returned from the east," she said, "thousands of people from Tarsium have fled. They are seeking shelter, protection."

Nomiki never bothered with pleasantries, not even those accorded to royalty or military leaders. Kerberos held a great deal of respect for her; she cared nothing for his title, only for his strength and intelligence. She followed him because of who he was, not because he was a king or a warlord.

"So," he said, "Tarsium has fallen."

“Not yet. Many people have abandoned their homes, because they see how powerful the Ermoori are. But for the moment, the fleeing are merely civilians. The war still rages.”

Kerberos nodded. All the Tarsi were doing was stalling the inevitable. It wouldn’t be long now before the Ermoori appeared in Omatus.

A week later, the Tarsi refugees milled outside the main gates of Omatus. They were downtrodden, and as scared as children watching their first battle. Even those closest to the gates shot furtive glances back the way they’d come, as though the Ermoori had been hounding them since they left.

Mostly they were Omati, Shenza and Ermoori citizens who had been living in Tarsium, but a few Tarsi clustered together here and there. There were wounded among them, but not too many.

Kerberos open the gates, but kept his warriors in a semicircular guard around the entrance. The people before him stared aghast at the warriors; they had perhaps expected a gracious welcome into safety.

One of them, a native Tarsi, stepped forward to address Kerberos.

“Your majesty, King Atillus Argyris,” she said, “we seek your aid in this most desperate of times. We have left our homes and possessions to the ravages of war, and call upon you to provide whatever shelter you can until the fighting is at an end."

Kerberos looked over the people, huddled and frightened, nothing in their eyes but pleading. Weakness. Would they want to enter the city, if they knew Kerberos was planning to give it to the Ermoori anyway? Doubtful. But there was nowhere these people could escape to that Ermoor wouldn't take eventually.

"Omatus is open to all," he called, watching the faces light with relief.

An excited murmur spread through the crowd, and Kerberos watched them begin to celebrate. He held his hands up.

"*If*," he boomed, "you accept Sithares as your one and only god."

The precarious hope that had begun to spread shattered all at once. Some of the desperate even responded with anger, shouting obscenities at Kerberos and the warriors barring the way in. They would have fought, if they weren't so beaten down already.

Kerberos didn't bother drawing his weapon. Shoulders slumped, heads lowered, and defeat was accepted. The message spread through thousands of people within moments. Barely two hundred of them stepped forward, agreeing to worship Sithares. The rest, sparing forlorn glances at Omatus, shambled west. They took hours to disappear over the horizon.

When they were gone, Kerberos had the guard escort those who'd stayed to the fire temple. They were to learn the prayer, and devote themselves to Sithares. The thousands who left were going to die; but these ones had chosen life. Or, at least, had chosen power and strength over fleeing. They had a chance.

He strolled ahead of the group, entering the fire temple before them. Their eyes bulged at the vast room. In its centre burned the great bonfire, taller than two people and equally as wide. Around the walls, spaced evenly, were the smaller coal beds for individual prayer. There were several more of these chambers, a bonfire perpetually raging in each. Thearans knelt at several of the coal beds.

Kerberos gestured for the refugees to kneel facing the bonfire, and stood among them as they did. He watched the flames, the magic within them scorching in its brilliance.

Such a small number, he thought, *but any souls added to the pool of magic is useful*. The number of followers each of the gods had increased that god's power, a fraction of which was divided between the followers themselves. Even adding two hundred people to Sithares' worshippers would increase his power.

He called their attention and recited Sithares' prayer three times. When he was certain they understood, he guided them through reciting the prayer for themselves. The bonfire roared into a whirlwind.

The people screamed as fire erupted over their skin. Kerberos waited for them to realise they weren't in danger. Their screams died down, and finally they settled into numb disbelief. Smiling, Kerberos left the guards to give them a tour of Omatus. If only it were so easy to convert Ermoori to Sithares. The war would be over within a year.

Then again, war itself added to Sithares' power. Perhaps the conflict would provide enough magic to Sithares that Kerberos could fight against Ermoor after all.

Before he realised it, Kerberos was back in the royal quarters, looking over the city. He sighed, the sound whipped away by the breeze. Before Ermoor's invasion, Kerberos had decided to use his power to take all of Pandeia; he had met Riffolk Hayne and had seen the man's ruthless ambition. One of them would end up ruling over Pandeia, it was just a matter of who would end up on the throne.

Riffolk would get there first, of that Kerberos had no doubt. But he wasn't immortal. And though the Ermoori scientist was gathering magic just as Kerberos was, he didn't have the training Kerberos had.

It was only a matter of time. Somehow, at some point, Kerberos would take everything from Riffolk Hayne. He would take the world itself. Riffolk's role in his mission was to pave the way for him; if the Ermoori performed the hard work of taking over, Kerberos could step in later and assume control over the new world. He only had to wait for Riffolk to die of old age.

Kerberos cast his gaze east, past the smoke churning from the fire temple, towards where he knew the Ermoori were currently invading Tarsium. From here, he could see nothing of the war. The horizon was peaceful, still, as it always was.

In the other direction lay the massive black cloud of smoke over Sitharkos. It was growing every day. Soon, even the days would be as dark as night.

He wondered how different the horizon would look when Omatus belonged to Ermoor. Would he be able to live with himself when his city was ground to a pulp in the name of greed? Could he really lay low for however long it took to seize the opportunity to take Omatus back?

He sighed again. Only time would tell. It was a bittersweet feeling to know that he had all the time in the world.

Riffolk

1796

The war had slowed to a crawl. Riffolk watched his instruments carefully every day, every hour, but barely anything changed.

His army won almost every battle they engaged in. He possessed superior resources, weaponry, and numbers. But the Tarsi fought from the shadows, appearing and disappearing like a strong gust of wind on the ocean.

His Detector, able to track and measure magical activity, didn't help to determine where or when the Tarsi would appear. He had no way of knowing even how many Tarsi soldiers there were. The only course of action was to continue pushing, continue laying siege to Tarsium until the Tarsi were forced to either surrender or die.

Riffolk busied himself trying to improve upon the weapons and equipment he'd developed for his soldiers. Worthwhile upgrades were few and far between, but over the last year he'd created several he was proud of.

The helmets were particularly brilliant; he'd managed to merge magic and technology perfectly into the faceplates. His soldiers were able to see further—and in more detail—than any normal man, even in the dark. He'd also driven up the power output of his rifles, so that they could even penetrate the almost unbreakable Ermoori armour. It was a risk, but the added power meant his rifles could shatter the black-bladed swords of the Shenza, and the magical shields they cast.

His ship-bound laboratory contained everything he needed. It was almost better equipped than his hidden one back in Ermoor. He had, after all, transferred all of his most useful tools and resources to his warship before deploying.

All of the work he'd done, the time and resources he'd given to the cause; how was he still being slowed by a rag-tag group of mediocre fighters? They weren't even particularly powerful. His Detector proved that. So why, then, was his army stalled? It was not an issue of numbers. As far as he could tell, it was a lack of usable information. The Tarsi were far too talented with secrets.

I should have done far more research on these creatures, he thought. *How they think. How they behave.*

His research and designs had leapt forward by decades after he had experimented on the Shenza he'd been able to capture. He learned all about their magic, tested their physical limits, and discovered their biological differences from the Ermoori. Thanks to the creatures' sacrifice, Riffolk had finally bridged the gap between magic and technology. It was these breakthroughs that allowed him to build the original Detector, as well as every other design that utilised magic.

Fortunately, Riffolk had obtained one of the Tarsi. The creature had been caught attempting to infiltrate one of his units. It hadn't said a word, and by all accounts seemed incapable of understanding Ermoori. But Riffolk had learned much of their language from an old text his men found back in Shanaken. Apparently, despite the Tarsi's reputation for secret keeping, the Shenza knew a surprising amount about the mysterious beings.

With their language available to him, Riffolk had been gathering books from the three districts as his soldiers took them street by street. There were few secrets in them; Riffolk would have been disappointed if their sensitive data could be obtained so easily. But he learned a lot regardless.

Riffolk now knew that the Tarsi were able to reconfigure their bodies not by magic, but as a natural form of camouflage. As well as that, he knew that most of the Tarsi *could*, in fact, speak Ermoori. They were spies, and had been for decades if not longer.

The creature's lack of response to Ermoori was most likely a careful ruse. Years ago, Riffolk had taken a Shenza captive. He'd studied it carefully; the way it had reacted to him and his words was vastly different to the Tarsi he now held. In his years traveling to new worlds, he had interacted with many people for whom Ermoori was an alien language. None of them behaved the way this creature did when spoken to.

He wondered if its innate ability to physically transform could be manipulated; or better yet, if it could be taken and merged with technology the way he had done with magic. Or if he could apply it to his own body...

Imagine the things he could accomplish, if he could become anybody! Or if he could send perfectly disguised spies of his own into Tarsi territory. He already commanded several elite units dedicated to infiltration and information gathering. They would be perfect candidates.

Even better, he thought, *I could create a device to detect whether a being is using this camouflage regardless of what form it has taken.*

Ideas rushed through his head, some fully-formed and others mere concepts. This would require a lot of careful research.

The captured Tarsi, stripped of the armour it had stolen, hung suspended within a restraint device almost identical to the one he'd used to hold the Shenza years before. The main difference was the set of four metal rods passing through the Tarsi's body. If it tried to change, it would be torn apart. Riffolk had explained this to the creature. Its head had dropped, horror and fear clashing in its eyes. Strange, almost Ermoori eyes.

Riffolk had since taken samples of the Tarsi's skin, blood, and hair. The results were fascinating; the hair simply disintegrated, and the skin slowly became a mottled grey. Unfortunately, Riffolk was limited in the conclusions he could draw from such information. His speciality was in weaponry and technology, not in medicine. All he could do was take notes and hope that the doctors in his employ would be able to make sense of it.

The only conclusion he did come to was that the Tarsi's transformation took active effort; or at least some kind of conscious trigger that ended as soon as he had removed parts of the body. The flesh changed back to its original form the instant its owner lost connection with it.

What other differences are there, he thought, *between their physiology, and my own*? They needed to eat, just like any other living thing. Their natural form seemed amphibious to him, though the captured Tarsi had yet to reveal its real body. He would see it before long; when he killed it. If the skin changed back after being cut off, surely the whole body would change when the creature died? Answers he looked forward to, particularly in the absence of progress in the war effort.

Riffolk watched the creature carefully. Even with its eyes glazed over and its eyelids wavering, it maintained a carefully blank expression.

"You are tenacious," Riffolk said quietly, "I will grant you that. But you fight for naught. The war, your homeland, all of it... it is only a matter of time before you lose it all to me."

He took no pleasure in taunting the creature, but its reactions could teach him a great deal. The mindset of his enemies was even more important than their physiology. How they thought, what they valued, how they adapted to challenges... knowledge like that could win the war in short order.

Still watching, Riffolk drew a knife from its sheath on his belt. He held it up, searching for any sign of fear, anger, or defiance. There was nothing. The creature's eyes roamed listlessly over the shining blade without so much as a blink.

Afterwards, though, was an almost imperceptible, brief flash of determination. *There*, Riffolk thought, *the rebellious nature of the Tarsi is revealed.*

The Tarsi had no traditional army. But it was clear they did possess the mettle to fight. It was their abilities, natural or otherwise, that allowed them to stall his forces so effectively. That, and the unflinching defiance demonstrated by the Tarsi in front of him. They defended their land with a determination that outmatched even the Shenza.

And they had joined forces with the Shenza on top of that. Desperately banding together made sense; he had anticipated as much. But he hadn't expected how quickly they adapted to their new situation.

His own men were taking far longer to adapt. As much as Riffolk was proud of the powerful army he'd created, he couldn't help but wish the soldiers were as effective as his inventions. If only there were a way to create technological soldiers from scratch... but he was a long way from that kind of innovation. Replacement limbs were easy compared to creating an automaton with enough awareness to succeed in combat. The hand he'd created for Arthor Symond was proof; even before he built it, he knew it would work. But building a soldier? It was far more difficult than equipping brainwashed men with armour and weaponry.

He had built protective sentinels for his lab, but their programming was simple. They detected any sign of life, mostly by motion, and attacked anything that wasn't Riffolk.

I must gather data, he thought, *it is information which will win this war.*

The Tarsi closed its eyes, its breathing laboured. How long had it been since restraining the creature? Weeks, it had to be. He hadn't given the Tarsi any food or water. No Ermoori could have lasted this long.

Despite not being soldiers, the Tarsi were far more resilient than they seemed. This one had been shot in the leg, starved, sliced open, and subjected to experimentation. Yet still, it refused to scream or beg. And it refused to die. The war had raged in Tarsium for over a year now; the Ermoori had gained a lot of ground, but he needed a way to control the Tarsi's resources. It all hinged on how long it would take this one to die of starvation. That, and whether or not he could use its natural abilities to build new technology.

Riffolk laid a hand on the creature's shoulder.

"You may take solace in the fact that your death will assist me in creating an empire."

For the first time, Riffolk saw something in the creature's eyes. It looked at him, really looked at him, a vicious edge shining from its eyes.

"You will lose," it said in perfect Ermoori, "whether now or after the war... someday, all that you value will be taken from you."

Paca

1796

The cold Ermoori sky filled Paca's vision. A steely grey that promised plenty of what the Ermoori called rain. Fresh, clean water simply fell from the air up here.

Life on the surface was strange. Even after such a long time living up here, even after the realisation that the Wheels of Life were nothing but exploitation, Paca still dreamed about the dark serenity of the tunnels. She... *missed* those tunnels. The feeling of a stone ceiling close over her head at all times was something she hadn't realised she found so comforting until it was gone.

The darkness was also something she took comfort in without knowing. In Ermoor, wake time was heralded by a burning light in the sky that blazed with a power she couldn't have imagined.

Despite how strange Ermoor was, and the tension that had plagued their introduction to each other, the Ermoori and Tyrans had grown familiar. Life was slow with all the Ermoori soldiers gone. Paca didn't know how to feel about that; her life had been spent working, filling every moment with purpose, only stopping to rest enough to keep working again. Now, there was very little to occupy her time.

They spent time talking amongst themselves. The Tyrans explored Ermoor, tentatively at first, but gradually growing bolder. Paca still hated the feeling of endless sky above her head. How did the Ermoori live with the knowledge that they stood at the bottom of an infinite void?

One of the Ermoori, a woman named Patricia Welling, spent much of her time with the Tyrans. She looked younger than Paca, but that wasn't saying much; it was Paca's experience that Tyrans looked far older than Ermoori even when they weren't.

The door of the building behind Paca clicked closed; Patricia stepped beside her, following her gaze up at the grey sky.

"It must feel strange," the Ermoori woman said, "to finally make it above ground, only to see constant clouds."

"I like the clouds," Paca said, "at least they cover up the… nothingness. But I don't know that I'll ever like being up here." She glanced at Patricia. "Even with the clouds, it feels... like I'm too small.

Like the sky just never stops, and next to that, we're like specks of dirt."

Patricia smiled a sad, gentle smile.

"Yes," she said, "that's exactly what it feels like."

"How do you live with it?" Paca asked, "knowing there's nothing between you and the sky?"

"It seems easier to me than living in darkness. I don't know how you lived with that."

"Well," Paca frowned, "until recently, everything we did was for the Creator. We knew—no, *believed*—that our lives had been designed by God, so there was no room for doubt."

Patricia gave her a strange look. In the bright grey light of Ermoor's daytime, every tiny detail in her face stood out. Her skin was smooth but taught, her blue eyes made grey by the clouds they reflected. Her hair, pulled back in a tight bun, was dark, clean and smooth. She had muscle and stood with a straight back. In that moment, her face seemed to betray a fight raging behind her eyes. She cleared her throat.

"We hold the same faith," she said quietly, "God is the architect of our lives, the giver of purpose. We work day and night for the Overseers. There is little time to worry about the sky above our heads."

"What exactly is the work you do?" Paca asked, still watching the ominously roiling clouds, "I thought the Tyrans provided all the power your people need?"

“Factories,” Patricia said, and then when she saw Paca’s face, “they are like buildings where things are built. They use machinery, probably a lot like the Wheels of Life, to create a lot of things very quickly.”

Paca ran her hands through her hair. It was something she’d never done before; in Tyra, her hands were always dirty. Her hair had been dirty too. Another thing she’d never realised until reaching the surface; hair wasn’t supposed to be knotted and tangled and matted with filth.

“I would like to see these factories,” Paca said, “and the things they create.”

For her whole life, working the Wheels had provided no visible results. Of course, they had been doing it for the glory of the Creator, but still... she imagined seeing something she’d built at the end of a long shift might have made the work easier.

“Perhaps you will,” Patricia said, “resources are dwindling with the war effort, but we work all the time even so. I know your people have given more than enough, but if we shared the work, it might be easier for everyone.”

Paca realised with a start that the idea sounded good to her. Though she hated the Overseers, a life of constant work had forged a deep discomfort in the idea of empty days. Since coming to the surface, there was nothing to occupy her mind, nothing to distract her from the insanity of an endless void looming above.

She knew other Tyrans who felt the same way. Life in Ermoor was... aimless. They were mostly only busy looking for places for everyone to sleep, but Tyrans were far easier to please in that regard than the Ermoori were. For the moment they were crammed into the homes of the Ermoori workers, who had several rooms not used for sleeping and therefore plenty of floor space. It was a fine plan, in the short term. But there were thousands of Tyrans, and only so much floor space in the Ermoori workers' small homes.

Paca—and everyone else, for that matter—worried about the end of the war. The entire Ermoori army would return, and find the Tyrans living with their people on the surface. What would their reaction be?

Most of the time, Tyrans kept to themselves, as did the Ermoori. They spoke, and it was lucky they both spoke the same language; but getting them to trust each other was hard work. The few who attempted this work—Paca, Patricia, and a couple more—had to organise meetings and get everyone talking.

But to what end? When the soldiers returned, they would force the Tyrans back underground again... wouldn't they? So why put so much effort into building a new life up here?

Patricia was staring at her. Paca blinked, and heat tingled over her cheeks.

"Oh," she said, "yes. I think the Tyrans will be happy to have something to do. I don't believe my people know what to do with themselves without work."

"But you fought to escape the work," Patricia said, "didn't you? I really thought you'd argue against helping us."

"Working for faceless demons who lied to us about our God is one thing. Working to help ease the burden of those who took us in... that's very different."

Patricia smiled again. It was as sad and far-away as the first smile, but there was still comfort to be found there.

If only she could find such comfort in the future... but if working together helped keep the Tyrans busy, she was all for it. She just hoped the others would be as happy to help as she'd said.

Karak

1796

Karak's heart squeezed tight in his chest, as though Asheilos themself was crushing it in its fist. Omas' desert roads were all but lifeless. With the war in full swing, very few people had any business travelling. Karak wished he was otherwise occupied.

The small team with him, Zela, Laral, and Koro, rode their horses in silence. All four of them were disguised as Omati. Karak usually felt safe while shifted; but as they neared Omatus, a deep, piercing dread threatened to overcome him. Nothing could lift the burden he carried, knowing that he had to face Kerberos again. The others seemed confident, but Karak knew it had to be a lie; no sane person would feel no fear against a monster such as the king of Omatus.

"They will likely be on guard," Laral said, "with the invasion approaching."

Karak nodded; he was expecting a city on edge. Even Tarsi would struggle to infiltrate at a time like this. Where once they could slip undetected into any city, now they would face far more scrutiny.

"But they will be looking for the Ermoori," Zela said, "not Omati."

"Anyone approaching will be searched," Karak said, "Kerberos does not take chances."

"We have talked this through already," Koro snapped, "all we can do is appear as desperate refugees hoping to enter the city before the war reaches Omas. We are unarmed, and will give them no reason to doubt us."

"After that," Karak added, "we must accept whatever happens."

It was so simple to say, but Karak could barely breathe. He wasn't ready to die, but if he was discovered by Kerberos, there would be no surviving. If it came to that, Karak had no idea what he would do.

"You sound like you've already accepted failure," Koro said, his voice cold, "though that's hardly surprising."

"Koro," Laral warned, "it is not your place to judge."

"I'm stating a simple fact. Karak has failed time and again. He was exiled, for Asheilos' sake."

"Enough," Laral said.

Karak barely noticed them squabble; Kerberos' golden, burning eyes lurked in his thoughts.

Omatus rose before them, close enough now that Karak saw the warriors guarding each entrance. Two stood outside every gate, with hundreds of silhouettes lining the battlements above them. It was exactly as they'd predicted; a city on edge, ready for war.

Even a city like Omatus would fall to the Ermoori; Zeera had said as much after news of the invasion grew worse. Kerberos was powerful—frighteningly so—but even he couldn't destroy the Ermoori.

He might be killed, Karak thought, a sudden desperate hope flashing within his chest, *and good riddance*.

Silence descended once again over the small group. It was almost time for them to become Omati in action as well as form. Karak cleared his throat and assumed a tired, hopeless expression. It was not difficult.

"We're getting close, now," he said, in Oman, "hopefully the guards won't hold us up long so we can find somewhere to rest soon."

The others took his cue, their postures and expressions changing to match the grizzled Omasi faces. Laral nodded, glancing back at Karak.

"And eat," he said, "I can't remember the last proper meal I had."

His voice had become deeper, etched with a scratchiness that sounded like the desert. Laral had always been particularly good at voices. The others said nothing as they approached the nearest gate. Better to let their appearance and expressions do most of the work, at least until the warriors prompted them to talk.

The warriors, one of whom was pure-blooded Thearan, watched them draw close with an easy confidence. Karak wondered if they might enter without issue after all.

But the casual air was a lie; just as they drew within a few metres of the gate, both warriors side-stepped into the passageway, their spears levelled at Karak's group. Laral cleared his throat and manoeuvred his horse to the front of the group.

"We are farmers, we only want-"

"Submit your belongings to be searched," one of the warriors said, "and take off those cloaks. Slowly."

Each of them complied; they carried no weapons, just as Koro had said. Even so, the guards tore through their things with utter disregard. When Karak and the others took off their travel cloaks, one of the warriors patted them down thoroughly while the other kept his spear ready.

"What's this?" the warrior patting Karak down said, "that's an odd weapon for a few farmers to be carrying."

Koro's head snapped around to stare at him. Karak squeezed his eyes shut in a frown, pinching the bridge of his nose with two fingers. *What was I thinking?* he scolded himself, *of course they were going to find it*. He knew, even when he hid the dagger under his belt, that it might cause trouble later on. But what was he to do? Stroll up to Kerberos and let the monster tear him to pieces? If he was attacked again, he wanted to at least fight back. Give the king a scar for his trouble.

"It..." Karak stumbled for some kind of explanation. "It's an old family heirloom," he said, "generations old. I don't want to use it, I just wanted to keep it. Or... or sell it, if I have to."

He could practically feel Koro's eyes on him. The others as well. The Omati guards glanced between them and the dagger, exchanging looks of their own. Karak had to force his breathing to remain even, ignoring his thundering heart as the sun's reflection lanced from the guard's spearheads.

Everything was dry and hot; his mouth, his eyes, his skin, even his clothing leeched moisture from his body. The sun, its heat a weapon wielded by Sithares itself, beat mercilessly down onto Karak.

"Please," Laral said, "we are no warriors. We wish to make no trouble. Keep the dagger for yourselves, if you must. We only want refuge before the war reaches this land."

The warrior who'd patted Karak down hefted the dagger in his hand. It was a Tarsi design, but most wouldn't have recognised it. A moment passed in torturous silence before the Thearan warrior looked at Karak.

"Heirloom, you said?"

"Yes," Karak said, the misery in his voice only partially an act.

"Well," the guard said, "I could let you in to the city. But our orders are to report and detain any who bear weapons."

Karak's throat had squeezed shut. The other three would be furious, even if they were let into Omatus without issue. Beyond that, assuming they survived their mission, Karak would be exiled again, or worse. Why did he bring a dagger? He'd known the plan, and agreed to it.

The warrior watched sunlight slide over the delicate designs as he turned the dagger in his hands.

"Lucky for you," he finally said, "this is an heirloom, not a weapon."

"Thank you," Laral said, "I assure you, it will be used for nothing untoward."

Karak breathed again, pulling in barely a trickle of air as he reached for the dagger. The warrior snatched it out of the way.

"There is a toll, you know," he said, "when I sell this, that should just about cover it for the four of you."

Slowly, he stepped aside, watching with satisfaction as the small group trudged into Omatus. Koro pushed past Karak, leaning in as he did.

"Another failure," he whispered, "why am I not surprised?"

Riffolk

1796

Finally, after weeks of starvation, the captured Tarsi died. Riffolk made certain; he'd planned on cutting into its body to investigate further anyway. Even if transforming back into its Tarsi body didn't convince him, removing its head and organs put all doubts to rest.

There was a small team of doctors and scientists on his warship. Once he had dissected the Tarsi and investigated a little on his own, he sent them in to apply their specialised knowledge.

Even without any conclusions they might draw, Riffolk had plenty to work with. Their ability to change wasn't technically magic, but it was close enough that he knew where to start his experiments. He had built many devices over his career that could closely examine any kind of material.

Over the last few weeks, Riffolk had taken extensive notes on the skin and flesh of the Tarsi. He compared them to the research notes he'd made about the Shenza; the differences were stark.

Normal flesh—to the extent that the Shenza could be considered normal—was a collection of uniform cells that reproduced over and over, but were otherwise inert. Tarsi skin was a mess of overactive cells that all looked different to each other. Even more perplexing, they constantly changed their make-up. At any given point, they could exactly resemble the Shenza cells, or Riffolk's own, or cells that didn't even look like skin.

It will be difficult to replicate this, he thought, *no synthetic material can work this way.*

At the very least, he may be able to create a detector device that could sense the strange cellular activity Tarsi skin was constantly undergoing. It did emanate a low kind of energy…

He sketched a few preliminary blueprints, alterations to the Magic Detector that might just work for Tarsi cells. Until the doctors were done with their examination and research of the Tarsi corpse, Riffolk couldn't begin building anything. He set the blueprints aside. For now, he had to focus on war strategies again. He needed a way forward; a way to break through the stalemate the Tarsi had forced upon him.

With the creature's starvation monitored, Riffolk was certain that a siege would work. It took a while for Tarsi to starve to death, but most of the forces his army fought against were Shenza. Besides, Riffolk commanded more resources than the Tarsi did; even if they were being consumed at a concerning rate. All he had to do was root out their supply lines, caches and systems, and take them for himself. After that, the stall his forces found themselves in would serve him instead of the enemy.

He'd already discovered several stock-houses; most of those were now under his control. He was certain the Tarsi were beginning to run low on food and other resources, but he couldn't stop until they were utterly defeated.

Riffolk stood over one of his work benches in the great cabin, leaving the doctors in his lab. A hollow glass sphere sat within a metal bracket on the wall, humming with bright yellow lightning. By its light he read through reports and maps he'd received from his exploratory battalions.

The maps were rudimentary, the reports brief and vague. He couldn't tell how the Tarsi were moving from place to place without being detected. If they were moving on their own, the explanation would have been obvious; they could change their bodies into potentially limitless shapes and forms. But most of their attacks were performed with a majority of Shenza warriors.

They weren't using vehicles. While quite a number of the horseless carts Riffolk had invented decades before were used in Tarsium, they only worked on paved roads.

It was almost impossible to believe that they were moving around on foot; his soldiers were outfitted with new helmets that allowed them to see clearly at a distance. None of his Commanders had reported seeing Tarsi or Shenza warriors travelling over the countryside.

Looking over the maps and reports spread out in front of him, it at last became clear. The only remaining viable option; an underground tunnel system. They couldn't possibly have built it in response to the Ermoori presence. It seemed to span the entire country, so it had to have been built over a long time.

Assuming it was as old as he suspected, it would also be well-hidden. He read over the maps and reports; even if the battalions didn't know it, there had to be a pattern to the attacks. A way to discern where the tunnel entrances were. Repeated attacks in certain areas, or a pattern in the conflicts that formed a recognisable network....

Now that he knew what to look for, a renewed sense of purpose filled him with buzzing energy. He had been stuck before, though he was loath to admit it. But finally, with this new revelation, he could complete this phase of the war. He looked forward to putting Tarsium behind him.

So far, he had deployed two thirds of his total army, with the remaining third serving as reserves as they underwent further training aboard their warships. That left a sizeable number for Omas and Theara. Most of his forces were alive and well; casualties had been low, well within the acceptable range he'd planned for. Even better, he had smashed both the Shenza and the Tarsi, and he doubted the Omasi or Thearan armies would prove a match to his own.

But he was getting ahead of himself. What mattered now was the network of hidden tunnels that he was almost certain existed beneath the Tarsi countryside. He wouldn't know unless he found it, but there was no other explanation.

Magic could do a lot, but it couldn't make a squad of warriors appear from nowhere. The only magic Riffolk had seen—in this world, at any rate—was based on simple elements; fire, water, air, lightning, and the mysterious solid shadows of the Shenza. There might have been technology capable of such a feat, but it was centuries away from being made.

He had seen something that did almost the same thing... but it couldn't be harnessed or controlled, and there was only one in all of Pandeia. No, he decided the Tarsi couldn't have access to another portal. He would have seen signs of it well before now.

They were simply moving through their country by direct methods without being seen; no magic, no technology. Riffolk had found that usually the simplest answer was the correct one.

Working quickly as his mind continued wandering, Riffolk marked out the locations and times of each attack on one large map of Tarsium. He factored in the three districts, as well as their respective centres of government and power. Around the site of each attack, he drew a small circle; the probable area for a hidden entrance based on how quickly the enemy appeared and disappeared. They could only travel so fast on foot.

There were too many overlaps. Only a few of the reports mentioned the exact direction from which the enemy advanced. He read through them again, marking the directions down where he found them.

That should narrow it down, he thought, *along with sending instructions to each unit to search for anything that could be a hidden door. Large or flat rocks, patches of land that look different…*

He scanned the map intently, marking out possible entrances. There weren't many. The frequency with which they attacked, and the various locations, should have pointed to dozens of entrances. Possibly hundreds. But they had done a good job of masking their origin points.

Still, there were a few places he could begin his search. He had at least narrowed down to a few general areas. In the meantime, his goal was to starve out the resistance until they were weak enough to destroy.

Victory was close. He could feel it.

Mara

1796

Her quarters were dark, cool and quiet. The ancient stone loomed ominously when she first arrived. Now, it held her protectively, like a vast shield keeping their enemies far away. She lay in a half-awake trance, thoughts chasing each other through her unfocused mind.

Months had passed since Mara's accident; causing the cliff to collapse when she'd been threatened by travellers on the road. Fleeing Aethos was a mistake, but Aerene had saved her. Still, since then, Mara felt more fragile than ever.

She couldn't sleep, yet again, and the events of that day whirred through her mind in an unstoppable, repeating cycle. Her panic attack, running from Aethos, the men who threatened her, and then her fall off the cliff. Now that she was safe again, everything that happened was almost like a dream; like just another one of her nightmares. But at the same time, it was all too real.

She knew she possessed a huge amount of magic, but it still took another chosen Hero to save her from a dangerous situation. Despite all her power—despite having been touched by a God—she'd been helpless.

Its power coursed through her constantly. She remembered the first time Power Magic came to her; walking through the streets of Ermoor, a sense of limitless strength filling her entire body. At the time, though it felt strange, she'd been utterly protected. It was as though nothing could have stood in her way, and nothing could have hurt her.

Now, the magic seethed inside her, writhing against her fear and restraint like a caged wild animal. It screamed danger, crackling in her mind in a way that made her heart race. Though Aerene had made her feel safe, her experience with the Ermoori man from the carriage made Riffolk's presence in her mind even more vivid. His face was never far from her mind's eye.

Eliza and Aerene were supportive, and Mara had agreed to train with them. While the idea of using magic again scared her; the fact that it had put her in mortal danger only deepened her terror.

A little while after, Eliza started training her. Her daughter refused to take no as an answer any longer. Her heart swelled, and almost equally terrified, of the woman she'd become. Their training started with failure, but eventually, Mara gained a little more control. Using magic still terrified her; but whenever Eliza was in the room, talking in her gentle and soothing voice, Mara could bring herself to use it.

Even so, memories and visions plagued her constantly. Sitting in her room alone, the scene once again swam into focus, her quiet, dark room fading away.

The desert's heat seared her skin. The sun, blinding in its intensity, burned against her eyes.

And there was the carriage.

It was Riffolk who walked out from behind it this time. But instead of being disintegrated by Mara's lightning, he unleashed his own lightning; it arced out to meet hers, clashing in a monstrous explosion that left them both unscathed. This time, somehow, the cliff didn't crack and break off. Riffolk stood facing her when the dust had settled, an evil grin on his face. He took a step towards her.

"You know," he said, "you can't kill me. And I will find you sooner or later."

Instead of answering, Mara tried to run; just like her other dreams, however, she couldn't move at all. Riffolk laughed, stepping closer to her again.

"You can't escape," he said, "there is nowhere you can hide where I won't find you."

"Leave me alone," Mara said, unable to stop the shaking in her voice, "please. What do you want from me? Why can't you just leave me alone?"

"You're in my head, Mara. The beast I captured tried to get in as well, but I fought it out. I don't know why, but I can't get *you* out, so my only option… is to kill you."

Mara wept; the warmth of her tears vividly real. She knew she was dreaming, but in that moment, it felt as though she really stood in front of Riffolk on the path out of Aethos. Her nightmares were almost always tainted with an unreal edge, despite the terror they brought to her. This one was different; *this is actually Riffolk, talking to me now,* she thought, *I think we're both dreaming the same thing.*

"Where are you?" Riffolk said suddenly, "it feels strange. I'll find you eventually, of course. But this will be far easier for both of us if you just tell me now."

Mara tried shaking her head, but it didn't work. Riffolk's smile twitched as he stared at her; he'd seen her attempt, or could read her thoughts.

"You may think you're being brave," he said, "but I assure you, this is merely stubborn stupidity. The more you deny me, the more I will make you suffer when I find you."

She wanted to tell him to disappear, to die, to go back to Ermoor and forget her. Nothing came out of her mouth but a small, pathetic whine. The sheer weakness she exuded in that moment revolted even herself; a part of her raged at herself, hated herself for letting Riffolk have so much power over her. *I'm supposed to be a Hero,* she thought, *but instead, I'm as small and weak as a wounded pigeon.*

Riffolk laughed again. He took another step, coming within two feet of her. *Close enough to touch,* she thought, *I wonder what happens if he touches me*. Fear struck her heart like a lightning bolt, and her lungs seized. No air flowed in or out, and Mara's heart began slamming against her chest so hard she almost vomited.

"Just tell me," Riffolk said, "just one word."

He reached out, his fingers brushing against her cheek with almost loving tenderness. A memory flashed in front of Mara's eyes; the day she met him, when he was the greatest prize she could have imagined. He'd been charming, elegant, and perfect. *If only I'd seen him for what he really is,* she thought, *I could have begged father not to marry me off to him.*

Mara couldn't move, couldn't speak, even if she'd wanted to. She stared at the horizon beyond Riffolk, willing the nightmare to end. If she could have killed him then, even if it was just in the dream, she would have given anything.

"Where are you?" he asked, still stroking her face, "it's so easy… just tell me. I'll make sure you don't suffer."

His hand slipped gently down her face, and before she knew it, he was gripping her throat with enough force to cut off her breath completely. He squeezed, forcing a tiny, choked squeal from her as pain flashed through her neck.

"I'm getting tired of this game, Mara," Riffolk said, "I don't like you in my head. I need to be very clear with you. You are going to die. Soon. It's just a matter of time."

He squeezed tighter. Mara couldn't even bring her hands up to fight against his grip. *Can he kill me in a dream?* She thought, *am I going to die now?* It was certainly real enough to her. She couldn't breathe, and he kept gripping her throat tighter.

His eyes drew close to hers. Bright blue, brighter than the sky above them and the ocean to her left. She looked deep into his eyes then, and she saw nothing. They were simply voids; two gaping portals that swallowed everything they touched. He would have her; she knew it now. Looking into his empty, cold gaze, the certainty settled into her panicked body that there was truly no escape from him.

Finally, whatever had been holding her still… snapped. She screamed, punching him everywhere she could reach. His gripped loosened, and she shoved against him. They came apart, both sprawling backwards into the dirt.

Mara screamed again, and unleashed her magic in a wave directed at Riffolk. It hit him, exploding in a glorious cascade of sparks. Distantly, under the crackling and hissing of Power Magic, Mara heard Riffolk scream. She couldn't tell if it was rage, or pain, or both; but her fear and rage boiled too hot within her to care.

"Mara!" a voice crashed through the dream, "Mara, wake up!"

Riffolk, and the desert around him, collapsed in a rush as Mara's shoulders were shaken by someone's hands. The dark stone walls of her quarters reappeared, and Aerene and Eliza's faces swam into her vision.

"What happened?" Mara said.

"It's okay," Aerene said, "it's alright, you're safe now. It was just a dream."

Mara shook her head to clear her muddled thoughts. *How do they know I was having a nightmare?* she thought, *unless...* She looked properly at the walls; deep, jagged cracks covered most of the stone, and smoke drifted through the air. The bed below her was mangled and smoking, and the door had been blown into shards of wood strewn over the floor.

A deep crack sounded from somewhere in the walls, reminding Mara painfully of the cliff she'd fallen from. Fear spiked within her again, and her entire body began shaking uncontrollably.

"It's okay," Aerene said again, "we're here. You're okay."

My magic did this, she thought, *it put me in danger on the cliff, and now I've put them in danger. I put Eliza in danger*. She'd almost forgotten how powerful her magic could be. She couldn't simply stop using magic; that didn't change accidents like tonight, or the cliff.

Although she hated to admit it, the path she had to take was clear to her now.

"I'm sorry," she said, "I didn't mean to... I... I don't have control."

She glanced at Eliza, and then at Aerene. *If can't stop myself from using magic in situations like this*, she thought, *I'm a danger to everyone around me. I can't risk hurting Eliza. I have to get it back under my control.*

"I think it's best if I… if I started training properly," she said, "I need to be able to control the magic in me."

Eliza's eyes shone with pride, and hope, and love. Aerene nodded, a similar expression on her face.

"We can both help with that," Aerene said.

Mara smiled back at them, an uneasy smile that masked the terror coursing through her body. But under that terror lay something else, something more powerful. Even in the dream, she'd eventually beaten him. Alone. Her fear controlled her, for now; but if she could get past that…

If Riffolk does find me, she thought, *he'll face all of us, together. And I'll be ready. I have to be.*

Paca

1796

The city of Ermoor was a winding mess of endless roads and buildings. Paca learned that it was separated into districts, like the sectors in Tyra. Most of them served a specific purpose, and Patricia brought Paca and a group of Tyrans to Ivorstorm; the factory district.

Paca watched the reactions of the people they passed; most Ermoori still didn't know about the Tyrans. They stared at Paca openly, a strange expression on their faces.

Tyrans were pale, their clothing simple leather dried and stretched from the skin of diggers; the creatures that nested in and around Tyra. Paca and her people wore no jewellery. They hadn't even known what it was until they saw the Ermoori wearing metal and colourful stones on their fingers, around their necks and through tiny holes in their ears.

Even though the Tyrans had washed themselves in large tubs with hot water, the difference in their skin tone was noticeable. Their hair and eyes were far paler than Ermoori, and there was no way to hide that. Before they'd left for Ivorstorm, Patricia and a few other Ermoori had lent their clothes to Paca's small group. That, at least, had made Paca feel a little less conspicuous.

"You'll need to be careful," Patricia said as they walked, "the soldiers are gone, but a lot of the Overseers are still here. Especially the ones who control the factories."

"What will happen if they see us?"

Patricia hesitated.

"With our clothes on, they'll most likely not realise anything's amiss. They mostly only care about theft and laziness."

Paca nodded; in Tyra, the penalty of laziness was often death. But that wasn't what she feared.

"But what if they *do* realise we're Tyrans?" she asked.

"Try to keep out of sight," Patricia said, "and whatever you do, look busy."

Ivorstorm was massive, with winding streets and looming buildings. Ermoori homes were large, each with several rooms, but in comparison the factories made them look as small as the low stone beds in Tyra. They were tall, but what made Paca's breath catch in her throat was the sheer breadth of them; they took up entire streets, stretching away in either direction so that they looked like an endless wall.

Each factory possessed a door on each side of the building. One of them was always larger and more ornate; this was the main entrance. The factory Patricia led them to had a main entrance with an arched blue door, the handles silver bars that swivelled in place. She led them past the large main doors, and around the corner of the next street to a much smaller grey door. It was metal, and looked imposing to Paca.

The group of Tyrans with them watched, breath held, as Patricia opened the door with a low grunt, and the room beyond filled Paca's vision. A complex system of machinery that Paca couldn't even begin to understand hummed and squealed all around her. Hundreds of Ermoori stood in rows facing waist-high platforms that moved, inspecting the strange things being dragged along by them. Everything moved quickly, and the Ermoori—despite their numbers—could barely keep up with the speed of the moving platforms.

Above them, a series of metal walkways formed a grid overlooking the ground floor. The machinery reached these walkways in many places, and Ermoori workers were stationed up there, though

Paca couldn't see what they were doing. Above even that was a single platform, connected to the walkways below by a staircase and a single walkway. The platform was placed so that the entire factory was visible to the person standing there. The man stood straight-backed, barely moving except to turn every now and then. Paca found herself hoping desperately that their group would avoid the man's gaze.

Still more Ermoori worked along the walls of the factory, packing boxes and moving them to yet another section where more workers carried them through a door to somewhere Paca couldn't see. It was hot, and loud, and Paca found her breathing growing thin. The Wheels were hard work, but at least they were simple. There was one job to do, and the only noise was the steady grinding sound. This factory was chaos by comparison.

"What are they making?" Paca asked.

"Food for the soldiers," Patricia said, "we ship supplies to them every month."

"That's… food?"

The items dragged along the platforms were metal tins, and as Paca looked closer, she saw a grey substance filling each of them.

"Yes, it's processed so it will last as long as they need."

Tyrans lived off of mushrooms and lightleaf, mostly, and she had no idea what the grey paste-looking substance tasted like, but Paca couldn't help feeling ill. *Food should be grown*, she thought, *not built using machinery.*

"Hey!" a deep voice shouted from above, "what are you doing, there?"

Paca froze. Patricia grabbed her arm and marched along the wall with them, looking straight ahead as though she hadn't heard the shout.

"He's looking over there," Patricia whispered, "just move with me, and we'll blend in with the workers."

Her heart thundering in her chest, Paca looked frantically for a way out. A hiding place.

"You!" the Overseer shouted again, "stop what you're doing and come here, now!"

Memories crashed into her mind; the explosion that had killed her friend, Zailen suddenly gone, the booming voice of the demons that seemed to come from the air itself. They were the same people, these Overseers, the ones who'd held Tyra in an unbreakable grip. They were the demons. And they were still here. Even now, after they'd escaped Tyra, the Tyrans remained imprisoned.

Patricia had mentioned other countries; masses of land on the other side of vast expanses of salt water. The idea was difficult to comprehend, but Paca found herself wondering if they worked differently to Ermoor. Was there a place, somewhere out there, where she could be free? Was it possible to live without fearing death every waking moment?

Patricia pulled her over to a section of moving platforms where fewer Ermoori worked. The small group of Tyrans followed, leaning close to hear as Patricia spoke.

"Each of these tins must contain the right type of food, and the right amount of food," she explained, "and cannot contain anything else."

She picked up a tin, looked it over, then placed it back down.

"When you've checked it, put it this way, the short side facing you."

Now that Paca was close, she realised there were several different tins. They were all silver, but were slightly different shapes. One of them contained the grey paste, one contained dry, thin, rectangular things that were a pale brown. Another had what looked like stew; the rarest and most delectable of meals in Tyra. There, they were made from mushrooms and the meat of diggers. The stew tins here seemed to contain meat as well, but everything else was unfamiliar to Paca.

A thud sounded from above them. Despite herself, Paca glanced up; a worker had dropped to her knees before the Overseer on the platform, a hand to her face. The Overseer had stopped watching the factory floor.

"It wasn't us," Paca said, "you were right. It wasn't us he was shouting at."

"Good," Patricia said quietly, "if he hasn't noticed you already, he's unlikely to think you're anything other than Ermoori."

"We just need to give Ermoori clothing to every Tyran," Paca said, "can we do that?"

"I think so."

Above them, the Overseer kicked the worker in the stomach. He ordered her to return to work, and when she didn't rise immediately, he kicked her again.

"Eyes down!" Patricia hissed, "staring at them is a great way to attract the Overseer's attention."

Paca looked back down at the tins of food. She picked up a few, looking at them carefully and then placing them back down as Patricia had done.

Just work, she thought, *head down, mind empty, just like in Tyra. Check a tin, put it down. Don't attract attention*. Is this what her life would be from now on? Instead of walking the Wheels, standing still and staring at food to feed the soldiers so they could continue their massacre?

She'd been happy to help when Patricia first asked, but she hadn't known what the factories made. She hadn't realised they would really be helping the Ermoori soldiers.

But did they have a choice? The Overseers were just as brutal here as the demons had been in Tyra; they didn't treat their own any better. Except in Tyra, Paca observed, the demons were safely behind walls, controlling every aspect of the Tyrans' lives using chaos and fear. This Overseer was alone, on a platform surrounded by workers. If they banded together...

In Tyra, they hadn't known what to expect beyond the walls. They didn't know how many demons there were, what weapons they possessed, or where to go if they survived the fight. Here, the entire factory was visible, as was the lone enemy. Even the escape was clear; a door sat in each of the four walls. The odds were in their favour.

She risked a glance up; the worker was still struggling to rise. The Overseer pulled something from his belt and pointed it at the worker's head. A sick feeling swept through Paca's stomach like a sudden chill.

An explosion and a flash of yellow light leapt from the Overseer's weapon, and blood and chunks of bone sprayed down onto the factory floor. The sound was so loud that the chaos of the factory disappeared under a piercing whine and a thick cloud of heavy silence.

Most of the workers didn't react. Even the ones stained with the blood of their fellow worker simply kept working as though nothing had happened.

The Overseer's eyes caught Paca's. Her stomach, still reeling, froze solid. *Oh no*, she thought.

"You!" the Overseer shouted, pointing his weapon at her.

She flinched, her body tingling in cold dread as she waited for another explosion.

"Work!" Patricia hissed again, "eyes down, don't look at him!"

"Get to work," the Overseer shouted at the same time, "or you're next."

Riffolk

1796

Riffolk rubbed his temples, massaging the pain from his head. His dream had been shockingly vivid. He had found Mara, alone and out in the open, and stoked her fear of him to the breaking point. But she had unleashed a wave of lightning so intense that it threatened to burn through his mind. He'd jolted awake, head throbbing, and left his bed behind to distract himself with work.

The mission now was finding those tunnels.

He had to be careful, lest the Tarsi discover what he was doing. If they knew he was so close to finding their secret, it could undo the biggest advantage he had; surprise. As long as he could get into their tunnels, he could storm them, wiping out the pockets of resistance travelling therein. They had only the one advantage, their ability to appear and disappear at will. In every other way, Riffolk's force was superior. But their advantage was a keen one, and far too effective for his taste. If he took it, they would fall.

His soldiers were closing in. It wouldn't be long now... he could practically see it; the tunnel network, small bands of Tarsi and Shenza huddled together, their false sense of safety shattered as his troops swept through.

To make sure the Tarsi didn't suspect anything, he had decided to disguise his orders as simple manoeuvres. Teams closest to the suspected tunnel entrances were told to search for dropped Ermoori technology and enemy supplies. They would be checking over everything, looking at the ground. Only the Overseers and certain trustworthy commanders knew what they were really looking for. No one else could be trusted.

Even if his soldiers found a tunnel entrance accidentally, he knew they would investigate. And he knew they would figure out its use, and root out the enemy within. If they didn't, they would be executed for treason.

Riffolk had sent the misleading orders out to many battalions, making sure to include those who weren't close to potential entrance sites.

Months passed since he first made the realisation that a network of tunnels had to be beneath Tarsium. Months of slow, careful, secret work. He didn't even work on any new upgrades to his existing designs in order to dedicate his full attention to the search.

He maintained almost constant contact with his commanders via teleradio transmissions, marking his map with every piece of information they provided. And even so, he couldn't be certain his men hadn't missed something. He didn't know how well the Tarsi could hide the entrances, what kind of technology or magic they might be using.

Briefly, he had even drawn up his own blueprints for underground tunnels and hidden entrances, just in case it gave him any new ideas. There was the network underneath Ermoor, of course, but that didn't utilise secret entrances hidden within a natural countryside. They might have been as ancient as each other, the two tunnel networks, but they served very different purposes.

Riffolk was planning the next series of orders for his commanders when a knock at the door shoved him out of his thoughts.

"Enter," he called, unable to keep the annoyance out of his voice.

Bennedict, his royal ambassador, slid into the room without opening the door too wide.

"Your majesty," he said, "your teleradio is shut off."

"Yes," Riffolk said, "my head aches. What messages have you received for me?"

“One of your units has discovered an entrance leading down into what seems to be a network of tunnels.”

Riffolk smiled. He almost laughed.

Bennedict handed him a rough-looking note; coordinates were scrawled on it, marking a place on the Tarsium map that Riffolk had isolated as one of the more likely locations.

“Move two more units to that position,” he said, “one to follow the first into the tunnels, and the other to guard the entrance. I will not have enemies follow us and attack from behind.”

“Yes, your majesty.”

“Relay instructions to the underground units,” Riffolk added, “that they are to search for more ways above ground as they proceed. I want every entrance destroyed so that they cannot be closed and hidden any longer.”

“Yes, your majesty.”

Bennedict left as smoothly as he’d entered, and Riffolk allowed himself a sigh of relief. The Tarsi were on the verge of toppling. The war was almost won.

Omas was next. Riffolk had already drawn up a strategy, and several contingencies depending how the tide of battle turned. If there was one valuable thing he’d learned about war, it was that plans only lasted until the combat began.

He would need to leave a sizeable number of soldiers behind in Tarsium to maintain control. The units he’d left in Shanaken were faring well; construction was underway for a new city to rival Ermoor itself. But the Tarsi were far more difficult than the Shenza. Any soldiers remaining in Tarsium would need to be vigilant, even after things had seemingly calmed down.

Now that he'd found the tunnels, he could free up some time to work on more projects. He was mostly finished with a particularly exciting one, but seeking the tunnels had side-tracked him. His new project sat on a mannequin in the great cabin, inside a lockable cabinet. His own personal armour.

It was lighter than the armour he'd given his soldiers, but even stronger. He'd built it to react to the magic within his own body. It drew strength from the Shadow Magic he could wield, and destructive energy from his Power Magic.

He had also built it to seamlessly cover his entire body. Overlapping plates of black steel were inlaid at each joint. The rivets were so fine they could barely be seen. The actual plates of armour could absorb his magic, but more importantly, they could hold it indefinitely. Since building it, Riffolk had been pouring as much magic into it as he could. He could draw it back when he needed to, or leave it in the armour for almost unbreakable protection.

There was so much magic coursing through the brilliant metal that it vibrated, making his feet tingle from where he stood. The only finishing touches he needed to put on were with the helmet. A smaller version of the magic detector he'd designed years ago, set into the visor. Assuming it worked, he would be able to see powerful magic users lit up right in front of his eyes.

Before discovering the tunnels, Riffolk had also designed a new weapon for himself. It looked more or less like a pistol, but instead of shooting magic-infused bullets, it focused the magic from his armour and fired bolts of pure magic. It also could be used as a medium through which to focus his magic, to give him greater control and power with the spells he cast.

He would have built the same for his entire army, but it only worked with someone who could wield magic. Besides, one should never give away *all* of one's secrets. His subjects had to know that none of them could stand against him if they were ever so inclined. He didn't believe any of his own would commit treason to that extent, but he never presumed to know for certain how things would turn out. There was also the fact that after the war, all of Pandeia's people would be his subjects; he had to demonstrate as publicly as possible how invincible he was.

As Prime Overseer and leader of the Ermoori military, he would stamp out the very idea of rebellion under his new empire before it could even begin.

Mara

1796

After the nightmare, a new sense of strength flowed through her body. It was tentative, faint; but it was there. She remembered training with Mathys all those years ago. Before Eliza, back when the worst thing she had to face were memories of Riffolk. Magic had been a gift to her then, and training had brought her confidence.

She wanted to feel that way again. She wanted to stop being afraid. The magic within her was violent, she knew that. It was dangerous. She realised that the few times she'd been truly in control of it were times she had *wanted* to be violent.

That's the key to taking control, she thought, *I have to embrace what it is to be dangerous. To kill.*

The war was coming. Their mission to destroy Sithares was coming. Mara had no control over that. But if she could remember how to control her magic, train enough to be effective, maybe she could really help. Maybe she could even survive Riffolk.

And they're here for me, she thought, *Eliza and Aerene. They will keep me safe.* Even if she wasn't certain about the other members of The Circle, she trusted Eliza and Aerene implicitly.

Each of the Heroes had been given a room in which to train. So far, Mara hadn't used hers. But she stood in it now, trying to feel the magic within her, trying not to let the panic take over. The room was large, the walls lined with devices that used electricity. Their energy hummed in her mind, not quite visible. The electricity called to her. She only needed to reach for it, and it would be hers.

Except, at the moment, she was alone. She still didn't know what exactly had possessed her to come here without Eliza or Aerene. Perhaps simply to prove to herself that she could.

A part of her knew that practicing alone was a bad idea. But if she only felt okay around others, how could she ever really feel safe? She was glad for Eliza and Aerene, of course; but she had to get used to using magic again on her own terms.

In the last few years, Mara had cut herself off from Power Magic. She could still feel Riffolk's presence in the back of her mind, a cold dread that followed her wherever she went. His rage never wavered. It clawed at her thoughts, dragging them down and threatening to overcome her. Such rage; it had been such a long time since she'd seen him, but his hatred still burned as viciously as when she first fled Ermoor.

How could someone hold on to that much anger for so long? Mara could barely even remember the things that had happened in Ermoor. Why did Riffolk still hate her so much?

She took a deep breath, closing her eyes and forcing thoughts of Riffolk away. Instead she focused on the devices laying against the walls; on the magic within them. If she could just control it for a moment on her own…

All around her, Power Magic hummed, waiting for her to take it. The more she reached out with her senses, the more of it rushed to her will. Her heart beat more quickly, her skin prickling as she willed the magic into her body. A tiny amount, just to feel it flow through her. The feeling was chaotic; both familiar and unknown, exhilarating and hideous. It was primal, ancient, vaster than anything she could have imagined. Powerful. More than powerful; it *was* power. Nothing could stand against it.

And she thought she could control it? Bend it to her will, use it as she wanted? No.

It belongs to no one. Not even Riffolk. But you can channel it, allow it to flow through you. You just need to control yourself, not the magic.

The thoughts almost sounded like they were someone else's. But still, they rang true. They swept gently through her mind, quiet but certain, a sweet embrace within her thoughts. And for the first time in a long time, Mara was calm.

She let out a shaky breath, and sat on the floor. The stone beneath her was cold, rough, the coolness of it spreading through her like the moon's light on a winter night.

Along the walls, the machinery obtained by Zeera and the Tarsi went on gently humming. Riffolk's designs, no doubt. She had no idea how they worked. But the power that ran through them spoke to her, whispered its strengths, begging to be unleashed.

Again, vague memories arose in her mind of first touching that power in Ermoor. At the time she didn't know what she was doing, but the magic leapt to do her bidding anyway. She remembered a feeling of protection, so intense that there had been a strange kind of rift between her and the rest of the world.

She'd killed people that day, but it had been as easy as touching them. And when they'd died, she felt nothing but an otherworldly fascination.

With another slow breath, Mara drew more magic into herself. It arced through her in a rush of buzzing energy. Strength swelled her muscles, and an electric clarity washed over her mind, as though she had been sleeping until this moment.

Power Magic was powerful, of course, but as it sizzled through her body, she realised it was simply a natural force that could be used. Like building a mill on the river, turning the great wheel with its powerful flow. Mara was the vessel, the medium through which Power Magic worked. She was simply a link in the chain of power. A part of the natural world.

She had a place, even if she didn't have full control over it. Warmth filled her heart then, and a gentle smile lifted her lips. It felt good to smile again.

There was more; her mind stretched to fill a greater space. She had been so terrified of the war reaching them, of her duty in helping to destroy Sithares. That fear had stopped her from living, from doing anything.

But mere moments after embracing Power Magic, she was no longer stuck. A weight, so long a part of her that she hadn't consciously felt it, lifted away and left her lighter than the air itself. She could reach out to the magic around her, join herself to it, and become one with every crackling bolt. Her place among it was barely distinguishable; in that moment, the machinery around her became a part of her own body.

Channelling the magic was simply providing a pathway for it to move along; guiding it to move naturally where it needed to. But she could move it in other ways, too. Without opening her eyes, she reached out with her senses and located one of the machines. Taking hold of the energy within it, she willed it to rise.

As though it weighed nothing, the machine swept up into the air, Power Magic flowing through it in pulsing waves. Because the machinery was designed to contain the energy, she could move it the same way she could control the magic itself.

And Mara herself was a perfect channel of that magic...

With a thought, she lifted off the ground, Power Magic flowing between her and each machine in a buzzing web of flashing yellow light. How had she gone so long without using this power? It was exhilarating, holding herself in mid-air with barely any effort. Why had she been scared? Power Magic should have been a gift, there was nothing to fear in its brilliant embrace.

Blue eyes flashed into her mind, sudden and cold. The rage, Riffolk's rage, lanced through her focus, into her head like a blade, and she crashed to the floor.

Can he feel it when I use magic, she thought, *is he punishing me*? She hadn't been aware of him using magic, at least not on any conscious level. Was it possible? Even worse, could he sever her connection to it at will? Or was this just more fear that destroyed her concentration?

She reached out again, past the rage crashing against her mind, and tried to draw magic once more. It was there, flowing freely around her, but... she couldn't connect to it. She sensed it there, but that was all she could do.

Sitting on the rough stone floor, sore from the fall, Mara was suddenly weak again. The way she'd felt in Ermoor, after discovering Riffolk's monstrous nature. In the days before Mathys, when she had only wine to drag her through each day. Her stomach pulled tight into itself, constricting with a force that left her gasping, and she vomited on the floor.

Riffolk's face swam before her eyes, as though he stood before her in a fog. She could almost see the room in which he stood; what was happening? This was like her nightmares, but she was certainly awake… wasn't she?

He looked different now. Older. In her nightmares, he always looked the way he had when she'd lived in Ermoor. This felt more real. How was this possible?

If he could stop her from using magic, force her to see him standing there like there was no distance between them, Mara wasn't as safe as she'd hoped. He smiled, and Mara couldn't help feeling a sickening dread overtake her. His smile was the same as it had always been; knowing and deadly, as though he knew her every thought.

"Fascinating," he said gently, "we really are at the centre of a very powerful convergence of magic."

He stood in a laboratory. A flash of memory hit her before she could do anything to stop it; Mara trapped in Riffolk's underground laboratory, the bang and flash of his weapon and the Tyran woman's head exploding. How had she forgotten that? She remembered that he was a monster, but somehow her mind had hidden the memory from her. He'd murdered someone right in front of her, and barely even blinked. Now, he watched her with the same calculating eyes that had watched that poor girl. But now they were trained on Mara.

"I have been doing some research," Riffolk said, "on the magic that we share. There isn't much information out there, but I have the means to acquire all that there is."

She was stuck. Paralysed. Riffolk's voice did something to her, pierced her mind and gripped her spine.

"We are linked, Mara," he continued, "but you knew that. There is more. I would tell you, but it will be more fun to show you."

He smiled, and a terror stronger than any she'd ever known took her into the dark.

Paca

1796

There were no soldiers in Ermoor. But even so, the Overseers held the city in an unbreakable grip. Thanks to their impeccable armour and weaponry, and the placement of their overwatch platforms, the Ermoori workers didn't dare try a revolt.

But the Tyrans had been trained. And they had faced far worse chances in Tyra than this. She wanted to convince the Ermoori to fight with her, but she knew they wouldn't. A few would die, and the

Ermoori weren't brave enough to face death. They seemed not to be desperate enough to want to fight for freedom.

Outside of the factories, the Ermoori were granted almost complete freedom. They lived in their homes, which were clean and large compared to the cramped, filthy quarters in Tyra. They were fed adequately… or had been, before the war. Now they were given barely enough to avoid starving to death.

Working to create this much food, Paca thought, *and they can't spare enough for the people making it*. In some ways, that was worse than the Tyrans working at the Wheels of Life. At least the Tyrans had never known what they were producing. They grew food for themselves, and never had to hand away anything they needed. The Ermoori stared longingly at the food as it was parcelled away. At the end of their shift, they were handed a small portion of food; enough for one day, so they had to keep working to be fed.

During the work, the Ermoori chattered amongst themselves. They cared a great deal about the social lives of the nobility. Paca had no idea what they were talking about for weeks, until she finally asked Patricia.

"The nobility," she explained, "are the wealthy class. They're not all Overseers, but all Overseers are nobility."

"Wealthy?"

"They… it means they have a lot of money."

Paca frowned, trying to puzzle out what the word might mean.

"Money?" Patricia said, "to buy things. It's, well… I'm not sure how to describe it to someone who's never heard of it."

Another Ermoori worker perked up.

"Money is a way to trade for items or things of value," she said, "it's special notes with writing on them that measures value. You give someone the note, and if it's worth as much as the thing you want, they give it to you."

The concept made no sense to Paca. Even less sense the more she thought about it. They had created an entire system to trade things; why not just trade the things themselves?

"But… you don't have money?" Paca asked, "only the wealthy?"

"Not much," the Ermoori woman—Hannah—said, "since the war, we are paid mostly in food and lodging. What little money we receive is barely enough to pay for a few things, like a drink at a tavern. We try not to think about money too much."

"It used to be better," Patricia said, "we used to be able to shop as we wanted. Not in the way that nobles do, but the cheaper stores in Riverford and Emberhelm. Then came the war, and now the stores that cater to the working class are barely open anymore."

"So why are these wealthy people's lives so interesting?"

"They don't have to work," Patricia said, "and they have everything they could ever want. They fill their time with activities you and I couldn't even imagine."

Paca frowned, trying to imagine an entire life without work. She'd thought about it before, of course; but there was only so much to do in Tyra. A life without purpose might have driven her insane in those dark, dank tunnels. But perhaps she only thought that now, knowing that the Wheels of Life had been pointless. Before she knew any better, she probably would have lived in blissful ignorance. Or contented ignorance, at any rate.

The first little while living in Ermoor had shown her what empty days could look like. Admittedly, it was wonderful to give her body enough rest for once; but after perhaps a quarter of a day, she grew restless. She couldn't think or focus without something to do. There had to be a way to live freely, but with some form of work to do that wasn't based on deception and oppression.

"…lie to each other constantly," Hannah was saying, "it's really quite something, how they treat each other."

Paca blinked, trying to remember what Hannah had said. *These wealthy people sound ridiculous,* she thought, *I'm not sure what I would do without having to work, but it certainly wouldn't be anything like them.*

"How do you know all this," Paca asked, "about their private lives, I mean?"

Hannah and Patricia smiled.

"We don't only work the factories," Patricia said, "a lot of the workers are servants to the nobility."

"Servants?"

"We do the things they don't want to. It's from them we receive most of the money we make… the factories don't pay."

Paca frowned again. In front of her, the bench whirred as it moved the tins by. Paca picked them up one at a time, inspecting them and placing them back again. The work had become second nature now; it was so much easier than turning the Wheels of Life. She couldn't imagine running after someone and doing everything they didn't want to.

"What sort of things do you do for them?"

"Cleaning, mostly," Hannah said, "and getting supplies. Some of them cook, but not everyone."

"If none of these wealthy people have to work, why can't they just do those things for themselves?"

"That's what wealth gets you," Patricia said, "the right to do whatever you want."

A hot, intense rage clawed its way up from somewhere deep within Paca. The nobility and the Overseers of Ermoor spent their days manipulating each other, lying and disrespecting one another. Meanwhile, the workers weren't even given any of the money that was apparently required to obtain things in this city. They had to live off the scraps given to them.

"If they have so much money," Paca said, "why do they need to keep it all? Why not share it with those who need it?"

"Greed," Patricia said, "just because they don't need it, doesn't mean they want anyone else to have it."

They were struggling to get enough food. At the end of each shift, each worker was given one small tin of grey paste. It was vaguely sweet, which only confused Paca. Though there was a little flavour, it mostly tasted like nothing, and had no smell.

Their shift ended, and Paca took her small tin from the Overseer's assistant on the way out the main entrance. Once again, she went unrecognised. The Ermoori cared so little for their workers that they never noticed when the faces changed. It only added to Paca's rage.

On their way home, Paca glanced at the buildings around them. Light glowed from every window they passed. A sick feeling spread through her gut as she finally realised what was wrong.

The homes had power, as did the factories. Paca knew now that the power came from Tyra. The Wheels of Life were their own kind of factory. But the Tyrans weren't turning the Wheels anymore.

"Wait," Paca said to Patricia, "how are the factories working?"

"What do you mean?"

"None of the Tyrans are underground anymore," Paca said, "no one is turning the Wheels. Where is the power coming from?"

Patricia's mouth fell open.

"I didn't, er… I suppose I hadn't thought about it."

Paca could barely breathe; first they'd learned that the Wheels had nothing to do with serving the Creator, and now it seemed that the Wheels weren't even required in the first place. What did they do, if not provide power to Ermoor?

Coming above ground was supposed to be a chance at freedom. But all that had happened so far was more work, more restrictions, and the very real possibility of starvation.

I've come too far to give myself to this sort of life, Paca thought, *we need to make some changes.*

Danel

1796

Danel's stomach growled, cramping painfully in the dark shadows of the underground tunnels. More and more lately, Danel found himself thinking about the kitchens back home. He had been a fisher in Shanaken, and an excellent cook.

His old life was a fog now, like the mist that settled over the forest in the early mornings. He'd forgotten the smell of the forest, the feeling of life all around him. Now his life was silence and the cold tunnels stretching away into the distance. And hunger. Their food had almost entirely run out; the Ermoori had destroyed most of the Tarsi supply lines above ground.

Even worse, they had adjusted their strategies; the Tarsi weren't able to infiltrate the enemy army as they had before. Spies were being rooted out and hunted down with shocking efficiency.

The war was all but lost. Danel wanted to be optimistic, but the Ermoori forces were ruthless. Unstoppable. They couldn't keep going like this for much longer. Those who were still alive were severely weakened by weeks of desperate hunger.

In Shanaken, Danel had been able to acquire food whenever he needed it. The kitchens were well-stocked with herbs and spices in pots, and vegetables in large barrels. There were also the *kenad*, the plump little flightless birds bred for their meat. Those didn't need to be hunted, but Danel had greatly enjoyed cooking them.

He would have eaten anything now. All he could think about was food; even the war was secondary. He didn't think he'd be able to fight anyway. The Ermoori never grew tired. They never ran out of ammunition, or food. They were like a vicious storm that never ran itself down.

Tanek groaned as he stood, holding a hand to his stomach. The man barely complained; the groan was more than he'd said in the last hour or so. In his other hand was the Ermoori weapon. They hadn't learned much about it, though they managed to fire it several times. After that it simply stopped firing. Tanek still took it everywhere with him, hoping he could somehow fix it.

Danel stood, groaning too.

"We can find food," Tanek said, "right? Surely something grows down here."

"I doubt it," Danel said, "but we could maybe find a hidden entrance and try to find something above ground?"

They were in one of the small camps with a few dozen others. It sat in the intersection between three tunnels. The food had run out, and the medicine too. No one spoke to each other, and the tents were empty.

"It's worth trying," Lenala said.

With that, they ventured down one of the tunnels. No one noticed them leaving. The walk was difficult; Danel swayed on his feet, dizzy with hunger. His legs and hands shook.

After a quarter hour or so, they reached one of the entrances up to the surface. They sat on the stairs that led up to the door a while, each needing to catch their breath. It was unlikely they'd find food, but they were desperate. Danel would have killed for real food, though he'd never say that out loud.

"We can't stay up there long," Tanek said, "if we run into the Ermoori, we don't stand a chance."

Danel nodded.

"I'm not even sure what's up there," Lenala said, "I've only seen trees and grass so far, and the trees aren't growing any…"

A sound echoed through the tunnel in the direction they'd come from. It was too muddled to make it out.

"What's—"

"Shh!" Danel cut off Lenala before she could ask the question.

It might have been some kind of fight… the people were at their wit's end, after all. But something about it felt off to Danel. There was a frightening kind of intensity to the noise.

They stared down the tunnel, though it disappeared into darkness. The sound grew, and then Danel's heart froze in his chest as a scream pierced the din, and a flash of yellow light arced into the tunnel wall. Sparks splashed from the cold stone, lighting up the space around them as pieces of stone crashed to the ground.

"Ermoori!" Danel said, "we need to leave, right now!"

"No," Lenala said, "we need to help them."

"Help them? We can barely stand. None of us are *Kaizeluun*. We can't help them."

Tanek nodded.

"Danel is right," he said, "the best we can do is survive. This war won't be won by the likes of us, especially in our state."

"So we're just giving up?"

"I don't see another option," Danel said, "they've found the tunnels. It was our only advantage, and now it's gone. Besides, Tanek hasn't gotten that thing working again."

"You're talking about losing the war," Lenala said, "is this really it?"

"We've been losing," Tanek said, "this whole time. We lost in Shanaken, and we're barely surviving in Tarsium."

Yellow flashes lit up the distant camp. The bulky silhouettes of Ermoori soldiers loomed in the brief flares of their weapons firing. Their shouts were deep and distorted, making their harsh language even uglier.

"Come on," Danel said, "we need to go. Now."

Just as he said it, another bolt of lightning streaked past them, so close its buzzing energy seared his cheek.

"They know we're here!" Tanek hissed, "get out, get out!"

Danel shoved the door open and waved Lenala and Tanek through. A sizzling bolt of lightning slammed into the stairs beside him as he scrambled up and out.

It was dark outside; Danel had no idea what time of day it was when in the tunnels. They ran in the opposite direction from the camp as quickly and as silently as they could. Danel could barely breathe. It was all he could do to stay on his feet as he ran.

They reached a small forest after an hour of running. Danel dropped to the soft ground, the stars above him blurring. He didn't know if they would be safe here, but he just couldn't run anymore. There was nothing left for him to give.

Again, his stomach growled. The other two lowered themselves to the ground as well. A blissful silence enveloped them, and Danel found himself thinking once more about his home. He missed his friends; Delaik, Zel, and Lashana. They had fished together almost every day. Times had been so simple then. Danel hadn't needed to worry about anything, only catching fish and the leisurely training performed by non-*Daishen.*

The Ermoori had only invaded every few years, but to Danel they had been as important as the ambient noise in the forests. If he'd known how bad things would get, he might have… what? Run away in advance? Given the Shenza warning? He sighed. No, there would have been no difference. Nothing he could have done.

"We're really in trouble," Danel said, "Aren't we?"

"We need to find food first," Lenala said, "then we can worry about the war."

Danel forced himself to his feet, shaking worse than ever. In Shanaken, he could find food almost anywhere in the forest. Tarsium was an entirely different thing.

"Let's build a bird trap first," Tanek said, "then we can wait for something while we forage."

"Do they even have *kenads* here?" Lenala asked, "there aren't many other birds that can be trapped so easily."

"We can alter the trap. It will work."

Danel cast his gaze over the forest. There were almost no animals, and those that were there were small. They didn't have bows or arrows. Danel had a dagger, as did Lenala and Tanek. But that was the only weaponry they had; it wouldn't do much for hunting. Perhaps if he was *Kaizuun.*

They built a few traps together, then wandered further into the small forest. Every now and then, a rabbit dashed behind the trees. There were no fruits or vegetables naturally growing anywhere.

After half an hour of sneaking through the forest, they stumbled across a stream. Even from where they stood, Danel could see fish swaying lazily in the water.

"Fish!" Danel said, "finally!"

They ran, though Danel almost stumbled with the weakness in his legs. He drew his dagger and slowed as he approached the stream. Though he didn't have the tools he usually used, fishing was his favourite thing. Even with just a dagger, he should be able to get a couple of fish.

He settled over the water, dagger in hand. The fish twitched whenever he moved; but its reactions were slow, sluggish, as though there were no predators these fish had to worry about.

Good, he thought, *I'd struggle if these fish were anything like in Shanaken.*

Danel hefted the dagger. The fish twitched again, but settled almost instantly. He watched it closely, attuning himself to its gentle swaying.

He rammed the dagger down into the fish's head. A wave of elation bloomed in his chest at the prospect of real food. At the same time, an explosion sounded from nearby, and the booming shouts of Ermoori shattered the quiet ambience of the countryside.

Mattias

1796

The tunnels underneath Tarsium were huge. Mattias' entire unit could almost fit shoulder-to-shoulder across its breadth. It made storming them all too easy. In addition, the Tarsi were all barely standing from weeks of starvation.

For the first time, Mattias felt no fear in combat. He marched alongside his men, confident that victory was theirs. He would not die here, of that he was certain.

Their visors allowed them to see through shadows, and across far distances. Picking off Tarsi here was just target practice. The

Shenza were no better. Seeing them unable to fight gave him a bright flash of satisfaction; he'd seen what they could do when at full strength, and now was his chance to exact revenge.

Most of the tunnels were empty. Mattias kept his unit together, deciding which tunnel to take whenever they branched. Their orders were simple; find and destroy the enemy. Every now and then, a small abandoned camp was nestled against the tunnel walls, or in the intersection between several tunnels. They searched each one they found, though none of the camps contained any food or weapons.

Mattias couldn't believe how close the enemy had been to defeat. Their stalemate had lasted months, during which Tarsi and Shenza attacked regularly. Though the Ermoori had cut off resources wherever they could be found, it seemed to Mattias that they would never die.

But it had all been an act. The enemy was barely alive; unable to muster the strength to regain any land, let alone win the war. It was almost a wonder to Mattias how they'd lasted as long as they did, even with the hidden tunnel network.

The first camp they found contained ten starving Shenza and one Tarsi. Mattias' rifle thudded against his shoulder as he fired round after round into the scattering wretches before him. If he hadn't spent the last two years stuck in the middle of Tarsium waiting for surprise attacks, he might have felt bad for them. But they were cowards, and they fought with no honour. He was beyond pity, beyond empathy for these animals.

An hour later they found a second camp. It looked abandoned, though it would have housed several dozen if it weren't. It lay in the intersection between three tunnels.

He stood in the centre of the camp, directing his men as they searched the tents. They found almost nothing. Satisfied that his men were in control, Mattias looked around himself. The tents were in disrepair. Barrels lay around on the rough stone ground, empty and partially eaten by mould.

Mattias entered a large tent. A half-dead Shenza huddled in a corner, gripping his sword with what little strength he had left. He looked up at Mattias with a hopeless kind of rage. There was no humanity in that face. He had been scared of the Shenza his entire life, but in that moment, all he felt was disgust. Not even pity; its expression was the same as he'd seen on the vermin that infested Ermoor.

The Shenza shifted its balance, moving the blade of its sword to point at Mattias. His armour was as strong as Shenza steel; he didn't need to fear it unless it was able to ram its blade into one of the tiny gaps at his joints.

It said something in its odd language, its voice scratchy and weak. Mattias pushed the lever to shift ammunition type from shadow rounds to electric and cocked the rifle.

"You should have surrendered when you had the chance," he said, raising his rifle to point at the creature's head.

Just as he pulled the trigger, the Shenza slapped aside Mattias' rifle with its blade. The lightning-infused bullet lanced through the tent's wall and slammed into the stone ground beyond. An impact thudded at his neck, and another at his left armpit, and searing heat spread from both.

It stabbed me, he thought, *it got me*. Before it could do any more damage, Mattias fired at its head. The tent flashed with yellow light, and the Shenza's head exploded, spattering the tent with blood.

"Doctor," Mattias shouted, "to me!"

A moment later, Petor rushed into the tent.

"What's happened?" he asked.

The tent swayed in front of Mattias' face, and cold grey blurred the edges of his vision.

"Stabbed," he managed to say, "neck and… and… armpit."

He collapsed, though he didn't feel his body hit the ground. The doctor worked quickly while Mattias wavered in and out of consciousness. There was barely any pain, which surprised him. In fact, he felt nothing.

Some time later, Mattias awoke to the pain he'd expected while Petor had been working to heal him. He still lay on the stone ground of the tent; though now he could feel it beneath him.

His left arm was heavy and cold, but a brilliant pain lanced into his body from the armpit, pushing ruthlessly against his mind. His neck was tight, and the same sharp pain emanated from where he'd been stabbed. The fact that he was alive amazed him; he didn't know of anyone else who'd survived being stabbed in the neck.

"Captain," Petor said, "how are you feeling?"

"Sore," Mattias said, "unsurprisingly. Why didn't I die?"

"I took blood from one of the men," Petor said, "and I got to you quickly. It's good you called out."

"Are the boys okay?" Mattias asked.

Petor nodded, a kind smile on his face.

"There were no other Shenza here," he said, "they're all waiting outside, and keeping guard."

Mattias breathed a sigh of relief, wincing at the pain in his neck. His helmet lay on the ground nearby; he felt strange without it on, even though it meant he could breathe easier.

"How long will it take me to heal?" Mattias asked, "we can't stay here."

The doctor shrugged.

"It will take as long as it takes. Rest, please. The war in Tarsium is all but won."

Danel

1796

Hiding from the Ermoori was becoming almost impossible. They had barely managed to avoid a large group emerging from a tunnel entrance near them just as he caught a fish. They'd had to sprint from the area before they could even eat.

After they discovered the hidden tunnels, the Ermoori had stormed through the entire network, killing any survivors they found. Two more Shenza and a Tarsi agent had joined Danel's group as they fled from a camp while it was being attacked. The Shenza were Zalen and Kenek. Both were *Daishen.* Danel wasn't ashamed to admit he felt a little safer with them around.

Naka, the Tarsi agent, was away, seeking information about the war effort from the other Tarsi. Danel didn't expect good news. In the meantime, the five Shenza kept themselves hidden in a thick copse of trees in the middle of a group of hills. There were no hidden entrances to the tunnel system here, and no other strategic advantages that might attract the Ermoori. Still, they remained on the lookout.

Before she left, Naka had taught them how to find some food in the Tarsi countryside. There wasn't much, but it was just enough to survive. At least until they could get somewhere better.

It turned out there *were* fruits and vegetables in Tarsium; one just needed to know where to look. The trees grew their fruits only in the top layers of branches. And the vegetables—all of them—grew entirely underground. They were part of the root system of several different bushes and flowers. Gathering them took work, and they were hard and bitter, unlike the fruits and vegetables in Shanaken; but it was vastly better than starving.

A small stream burbled through the forest where they hid. From it they took water and fish, although the fish here were small and few.

They ate their food raw; Shenza did not cook with fire. Besides, smoke would immediately draw attention to them, and with the Ermoori hot on their trail, they had to take every precaution. With his stomach cramping and roiling, even the bitter toughness of the root vegetables sang in his mouth.

Another thing the Tarsi seemed not to have was spices and herbs; the root vegetables weren't bad, but he might have killed for some spices. And they would certainly have been improved with cooking.

Every now and then, an explosion rumbled in the distance. They saw no more survivors. Nor, thankfully, did they see any more Ermoori soldiers.

Danel had never felt so powerless. He was cowering in the middle of nowhere while his people died. But what was he to do? Rush at the enemy, and die just to be brave? No. He would survive, however cowardly it might be, and would live to fight another day. Perhaps they could join the forces of Omas and Theara, and fight as one merged army…

The Shenza and Tarsi had already become one group. Would the Omasi—and, more terrifying, the Thearans—actually join them? And even if so, would they be able to beat the Ermoori?

Danel doubted it. He hated admitting that, but with all the Ermoori had done, he simply couldn't bring himself to believe that the war could be won. All he wanted to do was survive. More and more, he found himself wondering if it would be better to surrender. He wasn't sure what the Ermoori would do to the surviving warriors; but by all accounts, they weren't killing civilians.

"Naka has been away a while," Kenek said, "how long do we wait?"

"Before what?" Tanek said, "what do you think we'll be doing if she doesn't come back?"

Kenek frowned at Tanek, his expression saying it should have been obvious.

"Getting out of here."

"And going where?"

"Anywhere," Kenek said, "where the Ermoori *aren't*."

Danel scoffed; he couldn't stop himself. Kenek rounded on him.

"What," he said, "you want to just stay here? Wait for the Ermoori to find us?"

"I want to wait for Naka," Danel said, "she will return."

"Even if she does, what good will it do? She can't help us fight, the Tarsi aren't warriors."

"She will bring information," Lenala said, "to help us. There must be something, some weakness or blind spot we can use against them."

"We've been searching for weaknesses for three years," Kenek said, "since they first breached the tree line in Shanaken. They have none. And they're only growing stronger."

Danel sighed; he couldn't argue with Kenek's point. He had been thinking the same thing just before the conversation. Even so, he found himself unable to admit it out loud. If Naka did return with information, what good would it do now? The Tarsi and Shenza were scattered, and those who remained were starving, wounded, or both. Knowing an enemy's weakness didn't matter if you were too weak to exploit it.

"Their weapons are continuously being improved, that's true," Naka said as she emerged from behind a tree, "as is their armour. Fighting them head-on will very likely result in death."

Lenala let out a surprised laugh and embraced Naka. Danel did the same, but the others simply gave grim smiles; mustering enthusiasm was difficult in the face of certain annihilation.

"Our saviour returns," Kenek said, "and in one piece."

"What have you discovered?" Lenala asked, "is there anything we can use?"

Naka sat on the ground. She looked exhausted, even more than the rest of them.

"I managed to reach a representative of the Circle of Shadows," she said, "and they shared their plan. Part of it, anyway. They never share everything they know."

For a moment, Naka simply stared at the ground in front of her. There was a deep, profound sadness emanating from her eyes. Danel's stomach sank into a freezing pool; he knew with sudden, chilling certainty that there was only bad news.

"Good to know they have a plan," Kenek said.

"It never felt like there was a plan," Tanek said, "like the tunnels. The Circle really messed up there."

"What do you mean?" Naka said, "the tunnels were one of our most effective tools against the Ermoori."

"Sure," Tanek said, "except why didn't they flood them as soon as the Ermoori went down there? They could have done it, right?"

Naka frowned.

"All of our fighters were down there," she said, "starving and weak. By the time we evacuated, the Ermoori were already on their way out too. Besides, several of the tunnels *were* flooded. But the Ermoori got to us too quickly."

Tanek leaned in.

"How many Ermoori did we kill?"

"I don't know."

"Not enough," Kenek said, "and we're getting off track. What are we doing? What plan did the Circle share with you?"

Naka looked up at them all. Her giant eyes, silver speckled with blue, gave away a fragility that broke Danel's heart. She looked like a traumatised child. Danel had once retrieved a frightened *Kuulshen* from the forest, after she had attempted to hunt on her own. At only twelve years old, the girl had been attacked by a *zuzuk*, and barely survived. When she recovered from the attack, Danel visited her. She had looked at him the way Naka looked at the group now.

"Well," Naka said, "we are to… leave Tarsium."

"Leave?" Kenek demanded, "and what, just let the Ermoori take all of it?"

"That is the plan."

Kenek's mouth opened and closed in outrage. Naka held her hand up.

"There is a more complex plan in place," she said, "one that we do not need to know right now. I can promise you, we will return to Tarsium, and Shanaken. But first, we must trust the Circle."

Over the course of the war, the Tarsi had explained a little about the Circle of Shadows. Only a few details, mostly from Kala before she died. They were a secret organisation that influenced the trajectory of power in the world. They couldn't have been too powerful, though; if they possessed the influence Kala had implied, they would have been able to stop the Ermoori.

"We don't *need to know*?" Kenek said, "How are we to trust the Circle if they refuse to tell us anything?"

Naka stared at Kenek, her eyes steely as the corners of her mouth turned down.

"Who are you to demand the Circle's secrets?"

"I'm one of the people who is going to die," Kenek said, "because they don't want to tell us what's really happening."

"Do you believe in Amalus?"

Kenek scoffed.

"Of course I do."

"Even when it doesn't tell you its plan?"

"That's different," Kenek said, "the members of the Circle are just people. The Gods only speak to their Heroes."

"Do you know why that is?"

Kenek frowned, but said nothing.

"They can speak to anyone," Naka said, "at any time. So why not you? Why not everyone?"

"They're gods," Kenek said, "they're busy."

"And you don't think the Circle is busy?"

Kenek growled, his dark red eyes flared at Naka.

"Are you really comparing a secret organisation of Tarsi to the Gods? How arrogant *are* you?"

"I'm merely suggesting that there are many things you don't need to know. That there are secrets you are not entitled to, which will be safer being carried by a few. The Gods know that, as does the Circle."

With a sigh that sounded more like a scoff, Kenek ran his hands through his long black hair. He sat down across from Naka, as far from her as he could without separating from the group. Danel had to stop himself from shaking his head. Kenek made some fair points, but he was only sowing discord among their small group. None of them wanted to leave Tarsium—they hadn't wanted to leave Shanaken, either—but if it meant getting away from the Ermoori, Danel agreed with Naka.

"How many of us are left?" Danel asked, "did the Circle tell you?"

Naka grimaced, and a sharp cold pierced Danel's heart.

"Not many," she said, "more than you might think, but nowhere near enough to combat Ermoor."

"There is no force in Pandeia that can combat Ermoor," Kenek said, "that's why you were supposed to be finding information we could use against them, so we wouldn't have to fight them head-on. Instead, we're just running away."

"We are following a plan," Naka said, "your complaint about being in the dark is noted, Kenek. But it doesn't change anything. We will go to Omas, and we will learn the Circle's plan when and if they choose to reveal it. You can join us… or you can stay behind, and take your chances with the Ermoori."

Riffolk

1796

No matter how many times he took it, victory never lost its brilliance. Tarsium was his. As he predicted, once he found the tunnel network, the enemy's resolve collapsed. His forces had swept through the tunnels with commendable speed.

A handful of his Commanders and Overseers stood before him in the command room of his warship. They looked at him with unwavering dedication, some of them battle-hardened and some fresh-faced as though they had just travelled directly from Ermoor. Riffolk watched each man carefully; even now, after the battle was won, he suspected the Tarsi might have infiltrated his chain of command. It wasn't enough to ruin things, he just had to restrict the information he fed them.

"As before," he told them, "a small force will remain here to maintain control. We have successfully broken the enemy, they are unlikely to rebel until they have regrouped. Even if they do, it will be a small and ineffective attack that the remaining forces will easily be able to handle."

This wasn't strictly true, of course; when a rebellion formed, it would be one based on secrecy and infiltration. It would be slow, patient, and subtle. But if there were Tarsi here, he wanted them to think he hadn't considered that. So far, his forces moved like a blunt instrument, without subtlety, storming the battlefield and overwhelming the enemy through sheer power. Even finding the tunnels had been made to look like an accident.

"Our next destination," Riffolk continued, "is Omas. We will take Omatus first, being the closest city. I will send a small force to Theara, but they will merely be keeping an eye on the Thearans there. I don't believe Queen Aella is still there, but it does have a presence of some kind. Even if they have no loyalty to the rest of Pandeia, their love for war cannot be overstated. They will fight if they see the opportunity, and we need to know if an army leaves the city."

The men before him nodded along to his words. They stood with impeccable posture, hands behind their backs as was required when being addressed by a superior officer. None behaved differently than usual. None watched the others for clues on how to act. It might have convinced him, if he didn't already know how tricky the Tarsi could be.

"After Omatus, I will send out new orders. Until then, focus on taking the city."

The commanders and Overseers saluted and left. Riffolk returned to his lab; he only used the command room for these meetings, and for military planning when his lab wasn't available. His new suit of armour lay on a workbench, the helmet disassembled so he could work on the visor.

His lab was the only place in the warship that he knew was entirely safe from spies. He kept it locked at all times. More than that, he'd built a kind of lock that could only be opened by forming a unique key from Shadow Magic; it was impossible to pick. As a further security measure, Riffolk had developed a code with which he wrote his notes and designs. They would look like gibberish to anyone but him.

The Tarsi represented a difficult obstacle; it wasn't normal warfare when the enemy could appear as anyone. As frustrating as it was, Riffolk relished the intellectual challenge. It forced him to think things through far more carefully, forced him to adapt in ways that were making him deadlier. They didn't know it, but they were helping him become the powerful man he knew he was destined to be. His latest victory against them proved it.

Other than carefully watching for undercover Tarsi, Riffolk was pushing himself with his technological designs. The Detector he'd designed was attuned to the natural energy that magic exuded. He built it to be incredibly sensitive, so that it would pick up magic used anywhere in Pandeia.

The visor of his new helmet had been built the same way, but far less sensitive; it would only pick up magical energy within its line of sight. He'd developed a reactive metal alloy that worked similarly to light bulbs. It was set into the Shadow-Magic-reinforced glass of the visor in a mesh pattern; he could see through it clearly, but it would light up in response to being aligned with magic.

It was almost ready. He only had to reassemble it, give it a final look-over, and then test wear it. He was actively involved in the war in Tarsium, but not to the extent he planned to be for Omas. Omatus was the beginning of the end of the war. The cities along the western coast of Omas were either abandoned or had no real military with which to defend themselves. As far as Riffolk was concerned, they were non-existent.

Theara, on the other hand, was unique; the people there would be much harder to defeat. By all accounts, Theara's reputation as impenetrable was well-earned. But with the low level of magic present within its walls, Riffolk was certain most of the Thearans were elsewhere; Aethos, if he was correct. Where most of the magic in Pandeia was currently focused. The collection of lights on his Detector indicating magic in Aethos was blinding.

His army was regrouping on the coast as he sat in the lab. Within hours, they would be on their way to Omas. The men were mostly in good health, and in acceptable spirits. Months of stalemate had chipped away at their morale, but now that things were moving again, that would improve.

The fleet was ready. His men were ready. They had collected a vast mass of Tarsi resources to put towards the war effort going forward.

A gentle knock broke the silence. Riffolk threw a tarp over his armour and opened the door to find Bennedict.

"Your majesty," Bennedict said, "the commanders are ready to give the order, at your convenience."

"Good. I will be out momentarily."

Bennedict nodded, and backed out of the doorway. He never looked at anything but Riffolk, or the floor. Impeccably professional, as always. Riffolk turned back to his armour; it was time to reveal it to the world. He would wear it without the helmet to address the army, but he was proud of how the armour looked without the helmet anyway. He specifically designed it to be elegant and practical so that it could be worn as military dress.

It took half an hour to put on the suit, but once it was on, Riffolk felt more himself than he had in years; with Mara's constant presence in his head, and the war taking its toll, feeling this way was more and more rare.

The magic he'd channelled into the armour fed into him, creating a perpetual cycle of energy that worked like the energy storage orbs he'd designed. All it took was the initial infusion of magic, and it would remain active until used up. With the armour on, magic flowed into him, and it only took a little concentration to direct some of it back into the armour.

In addition to the magic cycling through the armour and his own body, he had designed a new kind of material which absorbed natural energies. He'd needed to create a new receptive material for each magic type, and spaced them across his armour at various points. If they came into contact with magic, a low percentage of that energy would be taken into the suit as fuel that Riffolk could then absorb himself. He had tweaked the material to be as reactive as possible, but there was only so much magic it could take in before it became overloaded. Still, a little was better than nothing.

The more they attack me, he thought with satisfaction, *the more powerful I become.*

His new weapon sat in a special holster attached to the thigh plate. It was designed to channel his own magic directly via the cable connecting its hilt to his suit. There were no bullets or ammunition; it shot bolts of pure magic. It was, for all intents and purposes, a pure conductor for magic to flow through. Casting spells took focus and practice; but with his new firearm, magic would be as easy to wield for him as a normal pistol.

With the armour on, Riffolk headed for the pier. The ship was empty. His footsteps echoed down the sleek, silent hallways. Images of his blueprints followed along in his mind's eye as he glanced around the ship. He loved nothing more than seeing his designs made real.

Outside, Riffolk strolled onto the ramp, seeing thousands of his soldiers standing at attention in rows. Each battalion formed a square, with its commander at the head. Riffolk smiled at the awed murmuring that met his arrival.

When he reached the shore and approached the army, a cheer exploded over him. The men were as keen as Riffolk himself to finish the war. He was glad to have good news for them today.

In front of the amassed army, a podium had been erected along with a microphone and amplifier.

"Today," Riffolk said, "is the beginning of our final tour of Pandeia."

This was met with another wave of cheers. Silence settled over the men the instant Riffolk lifted his hand.

"The Omasi are not as duplicitous or cowardly as the Tarsi," Riffolk continued, "they will be much more straightforward in combat. We are to take Omatus first. The only defences they possess are a thick stone wall around the city. This will fall to our tanks even easier than the mighty trees of Shanaken."

Laughter arose this time, genuine and hearty. Riffolk nodded, trying to seem encouraging to the soldiers. It was new for him, but morale was important at this crucial stage of the war.

"Your commanders have been given the battle plan for Omatus already," Riffolk said, "you will be briefed by them on the journey. You will find more than enough ammunition on each warship, as well as new rations. Repairs or replacement pieces of armour can be organised through your commanders."

He looked over the soldiers. Most had their helmets on the ground next to their feet, to show their faces to their Prime Overseer. Riffolk wondered how many of them were Tarsi in disguise. He would most likely never know, but as long as he could seize and maintain control of Pandeia, he didn't care how many Tarsi kept themselves hidden among his numbers. He'd never be vulnerable to their schemes if he suspected everyone.

"Most importantly," he called out, "remember *why* we fight. We fight this war to make Pandeia a better place. To bring civilisation to these… *people*. We fight for the good of all."

Without a moment's hesitation, the cry rang out from every soldier gathered before him.

"For the good of all!"

Danel

1797

Tarsius bustled with desperate energy. The Tarsi trading settlement on Omas' east coast, usually busy, had become a crowded hurricane of motion. Tarsi, Shenza, Thearans and Omati prepared to evacuate before the Ermoori arrived.

Danel's group trudged into the settlement. Above them, the smoke-covered sky seethed like a filthy grey ocean. The grey dirt of Omas had darkened to almost black beneath their feet.

"We were lucky to find a boat," Danel said, "now we need to get to Aethos."

"We will find a way," Naka said.

"What about the other surviving fighters?" Lenala said, "if we're all split up, how can we be sure they'll all make it to Aethos?"

Naka sighed, casting her eyes over the street.

"Our channels of communication have broken down," she said, "but the Circle has spread the message to evacuate as far as they can. All we can do is make it to Aethos, and hope the others do the same."

Tanek grumbled, the expression on his face almost as dark as the roiling sky.

"Before this war," he said, "I believed the Tarsi knew everything. And their reputation… able to make rule breakers disappear, and to disappear themselves… Now I can see you're only people, just like the rest of us."

"People who took us in," Danel said, "when we needed it. People who fought with us."

Lenala smiled at Danel, the warmth of it almost enough to wash away the tension in the air.

Tanek turned on Danel.

"What good did that do?" he spat, "all we did was slow them down a little. Thousands of us still died in Tarsium, and now we're scattered and fleeing."

"You've done nothing but complain," Danel said, "since you joined us. Our best chance is in Aethos," Danel said, "it's where everyone is headed. Some may not make it, but that doesn't change the situation."

"Danel is right, Tanek," Lenala said, "none of us like it, but nowhere else in Pandeia is safe."

"What about Aros?" Tanek said, "other than Theara, it's the most defensible city in Pandeia. High in the Omasi mountain ranges, somewhere Ermoor would probably struggle to get to."

"The Thearans of Aros are suspicious of outsiders," Naka said, "anyone but a Tarsi would have a hard time gaining entry."

"The cities on the western coast, then," Tanek said, "on the other side of the mountains. It'll take the Ermoori ages to get there."

"You are welcome to go there," Naka said, "and try your luck. But our plan will not change. The Circle is in Aethos. That is where we need to be."

Tanek didn't leave them, but he brooded in cold silence after that. They followed the crowd as it began pouring towards the western gate; most of the population apparently planned to travel as one group. There were no supplies left to purchase, and no time to rest. So, Danel and the others simply followed.

He assumed this group would head for Aethos, but if they didn't, Danel and his group could still travel with them for as long as they were going in the same direction. And in a crowd as vast as this, they were far more protected.

Danel didn't look forward to travelling in a small group. He only hoped they could reach Aethos before the Ermoori.

Lenala placed her hand gently on his shoulder as they walked, a small gesture, but one that sent a wave of soothing comfort through him.

The journey took a long time; more than two months, by Danel's estimate. Omas' desert was almost unbearable. Intense heat, vicious winds, and terrain that changed between soft, ever-shifting sand and rocky, cracked, hard-packed earth.

Deadly animals lurked everywhere, though at any given moment the desert looked utterly uninhabited. There were almost no trees, except for the occasional dead skeletons reaching towards the dark grey smoke above them, clawing with sharp branches as though desperate to swipe the smoke clear.

They walked for most of each day. In the forests back home, Danel loved getting from place to place. Not so in Omas; in many ways, it was the exact opposite of Shanaken.

"I thought all the smoke would at least make it a little cooler," Danel panted, "how does the sun's heat make it through all that?"

"Sithares is more powerful than it's ever been before," Naka said, "that is no ordinary smoke."

Kenek nodded, a grim smile slashed across his face. "The God of Fire is turning all of Pandeia into an oven. Great. So even if we somehow survive Ermoor's invasion, we'll be cooked to death anyway."

"It's only the desert," Danel said, "in the cities it's not so bad."

"For the moment," Kenek said, "but how long will that last?"

"Hush," Naka waved for them to quiet down, "save your energy for the journey."

The only moments he enjoyed in the entire journey were the nights. They set up tents and lay down, finally resting after countless hours trudging over unforgiving land. After a few weeks, Lenala asked if she could share Danel's tent. Despite the heat and the smoke, nights in Omas were as cold as the southern ocean in the dead of winter. Danel agreed—perhaps a little too enthusiastically—and with that, they grew much closer. Nights became something he looked forward to, not just for the rest, but for the company. They talked about anything that came to mind as they held each other for warmth. Then they lapsed gradually into silence, the vicious desert outside forgotten.

Ermoor can take the rest of Pandeia, he thought one night, *as long as I have Lenala, everything will be alright.*

Though long and difficult, the rest of their march through Omas was uneventful. They never saw any Ermoori. When Aethos finally appeared before them, Danel breathed a heavy sigh of relief. *We made it*, he thought, *somewhere safe*.

Naka had spoken about the Circle of Shadows as though they were capable of destroying Ermoor. As though they knew everything. Danel hoped it was true; if even part of it was, he'd feel better.

The last few hours of walking were the longest and most difficult; watching the city gradually inching towards them served to highlight how far they still had to walk.

But finally, legs aching, lungs burning, they reached the gate. It was almost as impressive as the trees in Shanaken; massive, ornate, and ancient. The noise of the wind behind them shrank under the gate's deep grinding as it opened. A small group stood waiting to welcome them, a Tarsi woman in front.

"Before you enter," she said, her voice raised to address the crowd, "it is important to know who among you is willing and able to fight. Ermoor will reach us before too long. We only stand a chance with as many of you helping as possible."

Thousands of hands rose. Danel and Lenala put their hands up along with the others. With that decided, the Tarsi woman and her consort stood aside, and the massive group from Tarsius ventured into the city.

Aethos was beautiful. Nothing compared to Shanaken, of course; but there were far more plants and trees here than anywhere else he'd been since leaving his home. The people were welcoming, smiling and waving as they passed without fear or suspicion. For the first time since the war began, Danel felt safe.

If only it could last.

Paca

1797

The factories in Ivorstorm worked through the day, and lay like the corpses of gargantuan beasts each night. There were other factories, further south, that were entirely abandoned. Paca didn't understand why they weren't being used. Ermoor's army needed vast amounts of food and other resources to function, and there were still plenty of nobles living in Ermoor who relied on the factories. Why would they shut any of them down?

It wasn't for lack of power; Paca still reeled from the revelation that the Wheels of Life stopping made no difference to

Ermoor's available power. The factories were massive. If nothing else, their abandonment represented a horrible waste. In Tyra, hundreds of people slept in the same room, their stone benches filling most of the floorspace. Paca couldn't imagine wasting such a space.

She stood before one of them now, its high walls disappearing into the fog of the cold night, the strange yellow lights that lined every street reflecting off the thick haze to create an ethereal scene. The concealing mists made Paca far more comfortable than she felt during the day. In fact, almost everything about the nights in Ermoor was better to her than the days.

There was a curfew in place in Ermoor, but with almost no soldiers around, nights were free to explore. The Ermoori didn't dare leave their houses after sundown, but Paca found herself craving the quiet darkness, and the fog above her head that covered the endless void.

A skittering sound came from the alleyway between two buildings; several rats rushed down the street. Though Ermoor looked clean, it was mostly an illusion. They swept their rubbish into alleyways, and only kept clean those things that were in plain view. By comparison, Tyra's dirt and filth covered everything.

But at least it was honest.

Along with yellow lights lining the street were poles topped with strangely-shaped contraptions. They regularly erupted into horribly scratchy, loud voices throughout the day. At night they remained mercifully silent. When they did speak, they announced the evils of the world outside of Ermoor. At the same time they sang the praises of Ermoor itself. They were so worshipful of their own city that it bordered on delusion.

Paca watched the rats disappear into the swirling mists. She wondered if the nobles and Overseers ever spotted rats. The small critters almost never showed themselves during the day. It must have been easy to love their city if they only ever saw polished streets and endless resources.

She checked the factory's doors; they were locked fast. Guarded during the day, and locked at night. There had to be a way to bypass the doors. They weren't like the portals in Tyra that appeared in the walls; there were handles and keyholes. Though Paca wasn't used to these things, she suspected there was a way to unlock them without the key. Or, perhaps, a way to obtain a key from somewhere…

Thinking, Paca wandered back towards the Ermoori houses she shared with the others. Despite being more luxurious than anywhere in Tyra, even Paca had to admit the houses were far too cramped. They had been fine for a short while, but two years had passed since coming to the surface, and both the Ermoori and the Tyrans were eager to have their own space.

Despite Paca's insistence that the Overseers could be overrun, the Ermoori simply weren't willing to risk a fight. Every shift, Paca imagined sneaking up to the Overseer's platform and killing him. They could be free, could create a new world where the people had everything they needed. Without an Overseer controlling things, the food they made here could go to the people who made it. All she wanted was a life lived on her own terms. She could work happily every day, if she knew it had a purpose; but not for Overseers who worked them to death, and paid them with barely enough food to survive.

It would take years, if it ever happened at all. But it wouldn't happen without the Ermoori's help. And that started with the abandoned factories.

Paca slipped into Patricia's house quietly. Her sense of time was still changing, but she always erred on the cautious side when she wasn't sure how late it was. The Ermoori were already sick of sharing their space with the Tyrans; Paca didn't want to cause more trouble by waking them in the middle of the night.

But to her surprise, Patricia was awake. She sat in the small kitchen, a weathered mug in both hands. Her blue eyes were dark in the dim light. A candle flickered softly on the bench, its light barely enough to cover the small surface on which it sat.

"Where do you go?" she asked.

"What do you mean?"

"At nights. Just now, where did you go?"

Paca sighed, glancing back towards the house's front door.

"I just… wander."

"But why?"

"I like the night," she said, "it reminds me of home. I can explore, and I don't have to see the sky above me."

Patricia frowned, placing her mug down on the small kitchen bench. Paca still stood near the entrance; there was only the one chair.

"I didn't think you'd miss a place like that," Patricia said, "after all the things you've said about it. It sounds horrible."

"No worse than Ermoor."

Patricia made a face like Paca had swatted her mug onto the floor.

"How can you say that?" she said, "you were forced to work in darkness and dirt your whole life! Ermoor is the best place in Pandeia."

"The Ermoori are forced to work as well," Paca said, "for scraps of food that aren't even enough to keep you fed. The Overseers murder anyone who doesn't obey. What about it is the best, exactly?"

"Well," Patricia shook her head, "it's… civilised. It's clean, and we have God's love. We are His favoured people."

"If you're favoured," Paca said, "I'd hate to see what this God of yours does to his enemies."

"He condemns them."

Paca sighed.

"After half my life serving our Creator," she said, "we learned that he was never real. All the purpose we thought we had was false. The punishments we suffered were meted out by men. Nothing more. It was your Overseers, your soldiers, doing that to us. Lying to us. There was never a master beyond this realm, watching over us, providing for us."

"Not the Creator," Patricia said, "but *our* God, the one true God, is real, and he is what makes Ermoor great."

"Are you happy?" Paca asked.

"God has blessed me with a productive life."

"That's not an answer."

"We must be content with what God provides."

Paca suppressed a laugh, though there was no humour in it. She shook her head.

"That's also not an answer. Patricia, are you *happy*?"

The Ermoori woman hesitated. She looked at Paca, then stared into her mug. Wisps of steam gently curled from whatever drink she had made. It smelled like tea, but that didn't narrow it down; the Ermoori had at least a hundred different kinds of tea, and Paca couldn't tell any of them apart.

"I suppose," Patricia said slowly, "that is to say… well…"

Her frown deepened. Then, with no warning but the quiver of her lower lip, tears sprang from her eyes. Her breath hitched and she hid her face in her hands.

"Oh, dear," she said between sobs, "I apologise, it's improper to weep in company."

"I… what?"

"It's unladylike," Patricia said, "we aren't supposed to cry unless we're alone."

Paca's jaw dropped.

“That’s insane, Patricia,” she said, “crying is normal. Everyone does it. Who told you that you can only cry when you’re alone?”

“God,” Patricia said, “everyone in Ermoor knows it.”

“So your God actually spoke to you?”

Patricia shook her head, her tears subsiding a little.

“Not like that,” she said, “it’s in the Holy Tome.”

She’d heard Ermoori talking about the Holy Tome several times over the last two years. At first she knew nothing of books, but now she understood what they were. Even so, she struggled to believe that people would let a book dictate their every action.

“You live by the Tome,” Paca said, “but what has it ever given you in return?”

“Purpose,” Patricia said, “something to live for.”

“And an unhappy life. I’m sorry, Patricia, but I don’t see why you should live so devoutly when it brings you such misery.”

For a long moment, Patricia stared into her tea. The tears had stopped, but what replaced it was a heart-breaking emptiness in her eyes. She sniffed every now and then, but no more tears came.

“I suppose,” she said hesitantly, “that that is how you must have felt, when you discovered your God wasn’t real. But I need you to understand, Paca… you cannot sway me from my faith.” She took a long, quiet drink of her tea. “I will always believe,” she finally said, “but what you’re saying about Ermoor… well… I *am* unhappy.”

“It seems to me that most people are unhappy,” Paca said, “and I think we might have the opportunity to do something about it.”

“You’re not talking about rushing the factory Overseer again, are you?” Patricia said.

“No,” Paca said, “but… I *do* think it would work.”

“We’re not doing that, Paca. It’s too dangerous.”

Paca waved her hand dismissively.

“I know,” she said, “that’s not what I’m saying.”

Patricia watched her, eyes still numb, though an edge of curiosity shone from them.

“There are at least three abandoned factories in Ermoor,” Paca said, “probably twice that. They’re locked, but if we could find a way to get into them, we could set them up as housing for the Tyrans.”

Patricia shook her head.

“The locks were designed by the Prime Overseer,” she said, “Riffolk Hayne. He’s a genius. No one will be able to break into them.”

“What about the keys?”

“You want to *steal* from an Overseer?”

Paca cleared her throat.

“Can it be done?”

“It’s too dangerous.”

“That’s not what I asked.”

“It technically *could* be done,” Patricia said, “but the Overseers are dangerous. You know that. They have no mercy. The only person who could get close enough to them is their servants, and I'm not willing to put any of them in that much danger."

"If they can find out where the keys are," Paca said, "and when the house might be empty, I can do it."

"I don't want to put *you* in that much danger either, Paca."

"You're not putting me in danger," Paca said, "it's my choice."

Patricia took a slow breath. She looked at Paca with an intensity she hadn't expected.

"Is this worth your life?" she asked, "just for more sleeping space? If an Overseer sees you, he won't ask questions. He won't give you a chance to escape or give excuses. He'll kill you."

"I know," Paca said, "I know. But, damn it all, Patricia, I'm *sick* of living like this. So are you. All the Ermoori workers, all the Tyrans, we all want a better life. And I think we deserve it. If I must risk my life to get it, I will. Gladly."

Mattias

1797

Mattias passed the time in the warship playing dice games with his unit. Their ships docked on the eastern shore of Tarsium, so they had to circle around to make landfall near Omatus. The trip was to take over a month, even considering the speed with which Hayne's warships travelled; weaving around landmarks and circumventing the country took time.

Tarsium was finally behind them. Omas was a desert, but other than that Mattias looked forward to more straightforward warfare.

He'd be able to stand next to his men, the enemy ahead of them, with no doubt in his mind about who he was fighting.

His men were in high spirits. Now that Omas was so close, they were keen to put the memories of Tarsium away. They had bonded as soldiers now, as a group of brothers, and in their travel time were acting as brothers did. Games, drink, swapping stories, and training together filled every day.

The warship was massive, and even with two thousand soldiers on board, there were plentiful rooms where the soldiers could spend their time. Mattias had recovered from his wounds, and spent as much time in the common rooms as his unit.

He still couldn't believe the Shenza had managed to stab through the resilient fabric in the joints of his armour; not just once, but twice. He could have sworn it was stronger than that. Prime Overseer Hayne had said it would take a powerful lunge from a Shenza blade… but the creature that had attacked him was barely alive. He knew the armour itself was strong; he'd taken countless hits from enemy blades without even a scratch.

Thearans were vicious warriors. But by all accounts, they were brutes with no sense of tactics; Mattias didn't think he'd have to worry about precise strikes to his joints from them. They used no battle formations, had no command structure, and fought entirely as individuals. It was a wonder to Mattias that they still existed at all. But for him, at least, it meant an easier battle.

They were to attack Omatus first. For perhaps the first time, Mattias found himself actually looking forward to the fight. Omatus was not known for its military capabilities. Thearans had a presence within the city, but the Omati were a separate people. They hadn't waged war in thousands of years.

A rush of laughter rose up from the handful of soldiers in the common room. Mattias glanced up to see them huddled around a table; with a smile, he shook thoughts of the war aside and leaned in with them.

"That's thirty for you, Bratton," Geffrey said, "and you deserve them, too."

Bratton was older than most of Mattias' unit. The hair at his temples was grey, and deep lines were set into his face around the eyes. But he'd been a soldier his whole life, and thirty push-ups was easy for him. He finished quickly, and the soldiers booed at the ease of the challenge.

"Your roll, sir," Bratton said when he returned to his feet, "if you're still playing, that is."

He must have skipped a few turns; his unit had become used to his tendency to let his mind wander. While he was thinking, the world slipped away behind his thoughts until he might as well have been blind.

"Yes, yes," Mattias said, "of course."

There were five dice in the game of Overseer's Order. The player rolled one at a time, and had to make either a set of the same number, or a run of sequential numbers. Each dice could be re-rolled once, and the men took bets between each roll to liven things up.

Mattias rolled a two. The men launched into excited chatter, shouting bets over each other before Mattias rolled the next dice. There were bets on each outcome; he would gain a set, or a run, or he would lose. When the shouting died down, Mattias rolled the second dice.

Cheers and boos erupted through the room as the dice settled on a three. Those who had bet on Mattias losing began their push-ups, and the rest started haggling their bets for the next roll.

The next was a five; Mattias re-rolled, but got another five. With a theatrical sigh, he gave the dice to Gerard, performed thirty push-ups, and sat back down. His men gave a supportive cheer, and then settled into betting on Gerard's game.

He stretched his shoulders; though mostly healed, the push-ups pulled at his scars, leaving them tight and sore. Military fatigues didn't help. They were fitted, soft but rugged, and the deep blue that represented Ermoor. And they allowed far more movement than his armour, which made it more likely to overexert himself.

As odd as it was, Mattias felt strange without his armour on. It was in his quarters, along with his weapons; he found himself wanting to retrieve it at least a few times a day. He didn't miss combat, of course; but he hated being dressed in non-armoured clothing. Their military fatigues were comfortable, but so lightweight compared to his armour that it was like wearing nothing. Even in the safety of the warship, Mattias didn't like the feeling.

He still woke up every night, a cold sweat soaking through his nightclothes. The nightmares only grew worse with time; even his first encounter with a Shenza in the tunnels of Tyra still haunted him. He wondered if those memories would ever fade enough to let him sleep. But every battle he survived added to the vast dark cloud in his mind. Several times, he'd slept in his full armour, just to feel protected.

Though they had gotten very little sleep in the forests of Shanaken, they dug trenches and slept without ever removing their armour. And, though many of his nightmares crawled up from those forests, there was a strange comfort in feeling the same way he'd felt back then.

Mattias left his men playing and ventured back to his quarters. Captains and commanders were given private quarters, so he didn't have to be quite as conscious of the available space as his unit, who shared a room between ten men.

His armour lay neatly on a bench, his rifle and other weapons next to it. Despite already completing it today, Mattias stripped the rifle and cleaned it. The process gave him a focused kind of peace. Overseer Hayne's rifles were so impeccably designed and built that each part gave a satisfying click as it snapped back together. There were no screws or rivets to undo, one just needed to understand the catches and buttons to activate, and the order in which to do so.

After stripping, cleaning, and reassembling his rifle, Mattias sharpened his knife. The blade of it was black, like the armour. It was supposed to remain sharp for much longer than standard steel blades, but Mattias liked to be sure.

The next step was polishing his armour. There were no nicks or scuff marks, so this was easy. It had been built to be put on by the wearer without the need for assistance, and it fit together as crisply as the rifle. The secret was multiple layers for each section of the armour; the under layer covered limbs and lesser areas, each plate of which was connected by strips of the tough fabric that Overseer Hayne had promised would stand up to Shenza blades. Atop the under layers were shells that fastened over the top of the major vulnerable areas.

It all connected to form an almost impenetrable set of armour. Mattias never ceased to be amazed at the genius of the design. When it was polished, he placed the pieces back on the bench, organised to make it easy—and fast—to put on.

The last step in Mattias' maintenance ritual was looking over all the pouches and the gear included therein. Every soldier's suit had a belt lined with pouches made from the same tough material that joined the armour plates together, and a backpack. The material was waterproof, and invulnerable to anything that could be found outside. Most of the contents was spare ammunition, ration tins, and basic medical supplies.

With all his checks done, Mattias sat on the bed and looked over his quarters. The design was sparse and cold, with no thought given to decoration. There was the bed, the bench, and two chests for storage. A porthole was set into the hull, though Mattias' quarters were in the lower levels of the ship. The view was minimal, but Mattias appreciated natural light wherever it could be found.

He kept the quarters neat, though that was easy enough with so few belongings. The soldiers didn't need to buy anything during the war, so they only had their armour, weapons, and fatigues. A few of them had brought mementos of their families or other loved ones, but many—like Mattias himself—didn't have families of their own. He'd brought a book, which had been read countless times by now, but that was all.

The book was worn and weathered, the text a little faded. It had been given to him by his father on his fifteenth birthday. *The Adventures of Wilhelm Templeton*, it was called, and it was the one thing his father and he had in common. Wilhelm Templeton was a master marksman and a devoted agent of the Twelve Crowns. There were a handful of books in the series, but this was the first, and in Mattias' opinion, the best. He kept it in his backpack whenever he was on duty.

Not many of the other soldiers had brought books with them. Though it made him feel closer to his father, it was one of the things that separated him from his men. Most preferred card or dice games to pass the time.

They would arrive in Omatus within a day or two. Fear and relief crashed together in his mind; the fear he had come to expect, but relief? That was strange. He didn't want to fight, but the fact that they no longer had to face a hidden enemy made the looming battle far easier to face.

I have my men, he thought, *and my armour. So long as I have those, I can fight*.

Kerberos

1797

Kerberos watched the Ermoori army approach. His own army was ready; news of the war had streamed in constantly over the last two years, and Kerberos made sure his warriors trained extensively to prepare. Although Sithares had abandoned him as Hero, Kerberos never lost the ability to wield Fire Magic. He had taught as many of the Omati people as possible to wield it also, and they had been training alongside his warriors.

The enemy soldiers concerned him. But what concerned him even more were the vehicles with them, vehicles that seemed to carry cannons on top. Omatus was easy to defend against warriors; but those cannons were powerful enough to fell the mighty trees of Shanaken. And Ermoori armour was almost as strong as the unbreakable blades of the Shenza.

When word reached Kerberos that the war showed no sign of stopping, he'd sent scouts to watch the fighting from a distance. He understood the Ermoori well enough now to know exactly how they fought. But it wasn't simply a matter of matching strategy; if his enemy was unstoppable, understanding how they fought wouldn't make any difference.

He needed a back-up plan. Fortunately, he had several. But with the Ermoori on his doorstep, he would have to be careful. They were not to be underestimated.

Kerberos sighed. All the work he'd done over the decades to build Omatus into a city of prosperity and power, and it would be undone in one battle. He had thought about this battle for months, years, about all the possible outcomes, and he kept coming to the same conclusion.

Omatus, at least in the short term, was doomed. He would be able to hold them off, and perhaps even provide them with a real challenge. But when all was said and done, Hayne had built a force to rival even the ancient Thearans.

Ideally, he would give Omatus to Riffolk and simply wait for the man to grow old, or for some other opportunity to present itself. Then he could take it back. But Omatus' strength came from Sithares, from Fire Magic, which required conflict. If he gave in, he would be weakening his city. His people, whose religion was based on war, would never support his rule again.

Doomed if we fight, he thought, *and doomed if we do not*. But the only option was to fight. He couldn't let down the people he had taught to worship Sithares; they *had* to fight.

His scouts had updated him up right up until the Ermoori landed on the shores of Omas. Their movements were consistent, their strategies simple. From what Kerberos had been told, either Riffolk hadn't bothered giving his soldiers specific orders, or he wasn't a particularly strategic commander; the soldiers seemed well-trained, but they fought in simple terms. They relied on the technology Riffolk had designed. It was no wonder they were unsuccessful in their attempts to take Shanaken up until now.

Kerberos knew what he would do, given Hayne's resources. They would concentrate cannon fire into a section of the wall, storm the break, and most likely repeat the process with another section of the city wall. Meanwhile, any spare cannons would fire over the walls into the city proper. This would destabilise his forces, shatter morale, and deal significant damage to a lot of the city's infrastructure. With all of that, Kerberos would struggle to maintain control over his army, let alone organise counter attacks.

Even if Riffolk Hayne didn't utilise that strategy, Kerberos knew it would be something even more devastating.

The only weakness that Kerberos could determine was their unfailing adherence to their army's command structure. They followed orders strictly, to a fault. He knew Hayne was with them, too. If he could reach their leader…

Gentle footsteps entered his quarters.

"Kerberos," Nomiki said, "Will we wait for them to strike?"

He shook his head.

"They have not attacked yet," he said, "I will approach and speak to them."

She spared a glance towards the amassed army.

"They may not give you much of a chance to speak," she said, "they have been letting civilians live, but not leaders or warriors. Do you really want to give them such a great chance to kill you?"

"I don't believe they will," Kerberos said, "their leader is with them. He will want to confront me."

"Because he knows you?"

"Because we have met before, yes. He respects me, as much as he is capable of respecting another being."

Nomiki nodded. There was no real fear in her eyes. She was Thearan down to the bone; she lived and breathed war. It would take more than some well-armoured Ermoori to scare someone like her.

"As you wish," she said, "we will wait for your signal."

"In the meantime, keep an eye on those vehicles," Kerberos said, "it is time to get our people into the lower levels of the arena.

Anyone who can fight needs to wait around the inside of the wall, and watch for a breach."

"I will pass on the orders. If I don't hear from you, we will meet where we agreed."

An hour later, Kerberos stood at the main gate. It was the only entrance into Omatus now; he had ordered all the side gates barred and reinforced. He wore his armour, and the thick chain of his Demon's Tail wrapped around his torso in the simple but secure pattern that would allow him to deploy it at short notice. Its spiked ball hung secure on his belt, and the Thearan spearhead rested in a sheath at his back. Next to that was his Soul Blade. All his warriors were armed and awaiting the attack.

The city was as ready as it would ever be.

With a gesture from Kerberos, the guards opened the gate. He strolled out onto the hard-packed grey dirt. The Ermoori stood confidently, their weapons held ready but not aimed. There was no leader waiting to speak to him. A short time later, one of the vehicles came to a stop in front of Kerberos.

Riffolk Hayne emerged from a hatch atop the vehicle and climbed down to the ground. He was in full armour, a seamless helmet covering his head and face. Kerberos only recognised the man by his bearing, build, and the unique elegance of his armour.

"Kerberos," the man said in Oman, "also known as Atillus Argyris. King of Omatus. We are presented with a unique opportunity for mutual benefit."

A pity he is wearing that helmet, Kerberos thought, *I could have ended the war right here. I wonder if the armour can withstand Fire Magic*. He would have checked, but if it failed he'd be instantly killed. The fact that he would return from the dead didn't stop him from wanting to avoid death. He couldn't afford a fractured mind at such a pivotal moment in Omatus' history.

"State your offer," Kerberos said, "let us be done with this."

Hayne remained perfectly still.

"I'm sure you know what I have to say. Pandeia is mine. One way or another, I will take Omatus. If you surrender without a fight, you will remain its leader, free to rule as you wish, second only to me in matters of interest to all of Pandeia."

"If nothing changes in Omatus under your… *ownership*," Kerberos said, "why do you need to take it at all?"

There was a pause, during which Kerberos could have sworn the Ermoori man smiled.

"If all of Pandeia is united," Hayne said, "we can work towards a better future. Is that not what you want for Omatus?"

"I have already built a better future for my city."

Hayne shook his head.

"Do you not see the potential here?" he asked with a broad sweep of his arm, "this technology can be used for good. I can provide endless resources, safety, scientific education… I can bring about a new age of enlightenment."

Kerberos watched the man speak. He stood tall, feet planted like a civilian instead of a soldier. His stance was open. It was clear he believed what he was saying. Whether he could deliver on the promise was a different matter, but at least for now, he was being genuine. His posture told Kerberos everything.

As difficult as it was to accept, Kerberos was almost tempted by Hayne's offer. To avoid the fight, and gain all the resources and privileges of a more advanced country.

But he knew it wasn't that simple. If he bowed to Hayne now, he would be in servitude. His entire city would be under Ermoor's control. After that, Hayne could do whatever he wanted to Omatus. There would be countless soldiers loyal to him there, which meant resisting his rule would become impossible. Omatus would belong to Riffolk, no matter his promises to the contrary.

Hayne's head cocked slightly, as though he could see Kerberos' thoughts.

"Consider your answer carefully," the Ermoori man said, "I will get what I want either way. We do not have to fight."

He is desperate to avoid conflict, Kerberos thought, *which means he believes he could lose*.

"If you do not want to fight," Kerberos said, "you could simply leave. This war would not have started were it not for you."

"You refuse, then," Hayne said, "for what? Pride?"

"For my people," Kerberos said, "for my city. I have built Omatus from nothing into a beacon of strength and power. We must fight any opponent who threatens us. It is our duty, as followers of Sithares."

Riffolk spared a glance at the city. His movements were loose, easy, as though he was untouchable. As though he had never experienced fear.

Perhaps I can rip that helmet off, he thought, *and roast the man inside his fancy armour*.

"I expected more from you, Kerberos," Hayne said, "I had hoped you could be reasonable."

"How could I reason with you or your army? Did you give the Shenza or the Tarsi a chance to be reasonable?"

"They do not think the way you and I do, Kerberos. After so long fighting us back, the Shenza never would have stopped to hear me out. And the Tarsi, well… they were born for subjugation. They have nothing but camouflage, coward's tools. They already lived in the shadows, I simply gave them a new shadow under which to hide."

"There is no reasoning with a madman," Kerberos said, "for all your technological marvels, that is all you are. There will be no truce. You will have to fight for every piece of Omatus you wish to claim."

"Very well," Hayne said with a careless sigh, "the war continues. So be it."

He turned his back on Kerberos and gestured to his army.

Countless bolts of yellow lightning screamed from their weapons, slamming into the stone walls of Omatus with explosive power. Kerberos growled, twirling the Demon's Tail in a series of tight loops until the chain was unwound. It took barely a moment. He hurled the spiked ball at Hayne. It hit him in the back, throwing him to the ground. Kerberos yanked at the thick chain, hurling the spiked ball back to his waiting left hand. He held the spearhead in his right hand like a sword, ready for Hayne to counter.

As soon as the Ermoori soldiers saw Hayne on the ground, they targeted Kerberos; bolts of lightning arced towards him instead of the wall.

He dropped the spiked ball, readied a fireball and launched it at the closest vehicle, then another at a group of Ermoori soldiers. A bolt from an Ermoori rifle caught him on the thigh; a searing, brilliant pain slashed through his entire body. Another landed in his gut, and he fell to his knees.

A vicious kind of buzzing slashed through his muscles, forcing them to contract until he couldn't move. Hot blood drenched his legs, flowing from the wounds in his gut and thigh.

No, he thought, *this is not where I die*.

He forced Fire Magic through his body, feeding the flames with rage and sheer determination. When he unleashed it, the Fire enveloped him.

Energy and strength rushed through him, and suddenly he was on his feet again. Lightning slammed into him once more, but now it only stung. He drew his sword; the Soul Blade forged by Sithares itself. Soldiers screamed as he swung the blade through their armour like it was nothing. They saw their weapons hit him with no effect, and panic set in. They fled, screaming to their fellow soldiers, and a new volley of bright yellow bolts shrieked at him from further away.

Kerberos launched himself at another group of Ermoori, hacking into their flesh through their armour ruthlessly. He didn't have much time; becoming a Fire Wight made one incredibly powerful, but it drained Fire Magic at a shocking rate. He needed to deal as much damage as he could in the time he had, but he also needed to escape before returning to his weakened state.

The vehicle he'd thrown a fireball at turned to aim its cannon at him; its armour was unscathed. His stomach lurched with a sudden impact, and he looked down to see an Ermoori had rammed a knife into him. He cut the man's head off and pulled the knife free. The metal was warped and twisted, so hot from his Wight form that it was almost molten.

Kerberos snapped back to look at the vehicle just as it fired. It hit him square in the face, blinding him as the force of it threw him backwards through the air.

He hit the ground hard, only feeling a slight impact thanks to his increased strength and durability. If not for his Wight form, he would have been destroyed. Moving with his momentum, he rolled backwards and sprang onto his feet. Thousands of Ermoori fired at him. The vehicle cannons boomed, their projectiles slamming into the ground around him.

They surrounded him. Ignoring the lightning that thudded against him, he cast his eyes over the enemy, looking for anything that might help. A bolt of lightning streaked past his head from behind him, missing him by a hair. It hit an Ermoori in front of Kerberos just as the man looked about to fire at him. The flashing yellow bolt cracked straight through the armour plating of his chest, and he dropped without a sound.

His magic was running out; at least, his Fire Magic. But Power Magic... He summoned a bolt of lightning of his own and hurled it at a soldier. Just as he'd hoped, it tore through the armour and ripped a gash in the man's stomach. He died screaming. Kerberos grabbed the fallen Ermoori weapon, looking over it quickly.

A handle lay at the bottom, with a curved piece at the end that looked like it was designed to sit against his shoulder. Just in front of the handle was a small piece of metal that curved like a sickle. He held it as the Ermoori did and pulled the small piece of metal; the weapon shoved against his shoulder as a loud crack sounded, and a bolt of lightning shot out into the mass of soldiers before him. Kerberos twirled and fired at the vehicle. A dent appeared; a very small dent. Not good enough.

He couldn't use Shadow Magic as a shield against the Ermoori weapons; it was clearly susceptible to the yellow lightning of Power Magic. The other magic types available to him wouldn't help much, either. Kerberos attacked the soldiers between him and the city, pushing to get back.

While Kerberos was dealing with the attack on him, a large group of Ermoori soldiers had amassed at the city gate. The wall of Omatus shook as cannon fire exploded against it, barely missing the their own soldiers. He couldn't see where Hayne had gone. Kerberos sheathed his Soul Blade and sprinted for the city. He hated abandoning a fight, but his magic was almost gone.

As he ran, he launched bolt after bolt of Power Magic into the Ermoori soldiers closest to him. Dozens of them died, and dozens more were struck down by errant bolts shot by their own soldiers targeting Kerberos. He only wished he could have killed more of them.

The gate was closed; he had ordered it so when he left to speak with Hayne. Ermoori swarmed at the great door, shooting with their weapons and giving victorious screams whenever cannon fire hit. *I need a way in*, he thought, *unless they destroy the gate first*.

Kerberos drew his Soul Blade and hacked at the Ermoori between him and the gate. Those at the gate didn't hear over the noise of battle, and Kerberos ignored the attacks from those behind him.

With a final, shuddering boom, the main gate collapsed. Ermoori rushed into the city, met by thousands of Kerberos' own warriors. The clash of both armies was like a wave hitting a rocky cliff, and Kerberos pushed the attack from behind until he broke through to his warriors.

Just in time; as he stepped into the Thearan ranks, his magic burned up, and he dropped to one knee. They fought around him, trying to force a blockade between their king and the enemy.

It didn't last long. Though Kerberos' Soul Blade could slice through their armour, just about nothing else could. They pushed ruthlessly against the Thearans and Omati, their weapons flashing as bolts of lightning arced through the air.

Kerberos forced himself to his feet. Hundreds of Thearans lay dead on the cold grey stone already. Those who had belonged to his original tribe would be resurrected, but for now they would be of no help. There was no stopping the Ermoori; they smashed through Kerberos' army in a matter of moments. Their shining black armour was pristine, even after facing Thearan steel and Fire Magic.

An explosion rocked the ground under his feet, and a massive section of the wall to his right crumbled. An instant later, one of the vehicles ploughed through the newly made gap, followed by masses of Ermoori soldiers.

It is time, he thought, *Omatus will fall. But I will return, and when I do, I will take Pandeia for myself.*

Kerberos fought viciously, his Soul Blade flashing in the light of countless fireballs thrown by his Thearan warriors. As he fought, he made his way towards the palace. If he could get away, he would be able to bide his time until he was ready to strike back.

"Kerberos!"

Nomiki appeared at his side, and he smiled. He was glad to have her here in this moment. She whistled, loud and clear, and within a moment his most trusted warriors ran to join them.

"We need to get Kerberos out of here safely," Nomiki said, "Omatus can survive the Ermoori for a while, but this will all be for nought if we lose the king."

They nodded and formed a circle around Kerberos. He sheathed his Soul Blade once more, and they ran for the palace.

The instant they started moving, the Ermoori shouted, and a barrage of lightning filled the air around them.

"If the king falls," Nomiki shouted above the chaos, "we must hide—"

An explosion of searing pain hit his chest. He saw yellow, and then the sky above him. The blue of it turned to cold, stark white, and he only had time to think *Hayne will pay* before the Fire took him.

Karak

1797

Months after arriving in Omatus, Karak still hadn't made a move. He and his team watched Kerberos. They searched for opportunities, though Karak did everything in his power not to confront the murderous king. He found excuses, didn't report the few opportunities he did see, and went as long as he could without completing his mission.

He thought the others might have known what he was up to, but they never said anything. Of course, there were arguments about how long it was taking; but no suspicion against Karak.

"I swear," Koro said, "we could have taken it today. Kerberos didn't step foot in his quarters almost the entire day."

They were together in a safehouse; the Tarsi owned dozens of such houses throughout Pandeia.

"We need to be careful," Karak said, "you remember what he did in Azar, right? He's only become more powerful since then."

"He's not a God, Karak. He can be defeated."

Koro stood, stepping towards Karak.

"But we're not even talking about fighting him," he said, "we just need to sneak into his quarters. Take the book. You've done it before."

"I almost died. Twice."

"You didn't have us," Laral said quietly.

"I did have a team."

Zela sighed, and gestured for them to quiet.

"What exactly are we waiting for?" she asked, "what situation will make you comfortable with going in there?"

"I... don't know. We just need to be *sure* he won't show up before we've left. We need a distraction. Something big."

"How do we make that much noise without making it obvious it's a distraction?"

"There's not much that can scare Kerberos," Karak said, "nor is there much that can take his attention. He is a man of... intense focus. He is intelligent, powerful, and driven."

"I'm not hearing any suggestions," Koro said, "unless your plan is to kneel and accept him as your king."

"My point," Karak said as patiently as he could, "is that it's not going to be easy to trick someone like Kerberos. The things he holds as important are few. He will not care for an attack by a small team. He will not react to minor disturbances in the city. If we are to take his attention away from the book, it will require something incredible. Something big."

Koro threw his hands up, an irritated smile on his face as he stared at Karak incredulously.

"You've said that already. Like *what*?"

"Like the war?" Laral said, "the Ermoori attacking Omatus. That would do it, right?"

Karak nodded.

"It's only a matter of time before they get here, too," he said, "Tarsium is all but theirs."

Zela strolled to a small chair next to Laral and sat down.

"So, we wait for the war to reach us," she said, "and then we take the book while the fighting rages."

"We'll have a narrow margin of time," Koro said, "the fighting must be in full swing, but not for so long that the Ermoori are too close to the palace."

Karak ran his hand over his bald head.

"And we need to be absolutely certain Kerberos is part of the battle," he said.

“Okay,” Koro said, “we’ll watch for the Ermoori. We’ll wait until the battle actually starts. Then, when we’re sure Kerberos is busy fighting, we’ll take the book.”

Karak’s heart beat harder than it should have. *There is no excuse now*, he thought, *no way to get out of taking the book.* The only positive was that they still had time before the Ermoori reached Omatus.

Time passed, tense and still, as though the city held its breath. Karak had heard about the power and resources wielded by the Ermoori. He couldn’t believe he’d found himself in this situation; waiting for them to arrive in a walled-off city, waiting for them to attack. It was almost like praying for his own death.

Then, all at once, the Ermoori appeared.

They took Omatus with a speed and ferocity that sent cold waves of sickening shock through Karak’s body. They had taken months to seize control of Shanaken, and almost two years for Tarsium. While it was terrifying, Karak couldn’t help but be relieved; It was just as they’d planned. With his city under attack, Kerberos would be far too busy to keep an eye on the book of Sithares.

Their safehouse was in Omatus’ main city region in the southeast, near the great bridge. Omatus consisted of two large circular sections connected by the massive bridge that spanned the

Alpheus River. The lower region was smaller, home to the royal palace, the high nobles' homes, and markets that catered to the wealthy. With the great bridge being Kerberos' only way to get from the palace to the main city gates, Karak and his team witnessed the king making his way towards battle.

Even that tiny glimpse was enough to set Karak's skin alight with tingling fear. Kerberos possessed the presence of a Hero, one of the ancients who could decimate entire armies single-handedly. He moved with the implacable confidence of a God.

Karak just had to make sure they got out of the city before the Ermoori got to the palace.

"How long do we wait now?" Zela asked, "before we go to the palace?"

"Just a few moments more," Karak said, "just so we know Kerberos is engaged in combat."

"Would he have left a guard behind?" Laral asked.

"No way to know until we're there," Koro said, "but royal guards are far easier to sneak by than Kerberos. We should be fine."

Shifting back into Omati forms, the four Tarsi left their safehouse and ran for the palace. They would have looked like civilians fleeing the battle.

There were no warriors between them and the palace; it seemed Kerberos had sent most of them to the northwest region of the city in preparation. Karak was certain that warriors would be present somewhere nearby. It was only a matter of hoping they'd be ignored long enough to take the book.

As they approached the palace, they heard combat begin in earnest behind them. Explosions made the giant stones rumble even from the opposite side of the bridge.

Placed sparingly around the outer wall on the palace side of the city were small entrances for merchants and supplies. Karak saw one, tiny from the distance; it had been barred, and a small group of Thearans stood waiting for an attack. *I knew there would be warriors around here*, he thought, *hopefully they're only keeping watch over the wall, and not inside the palace*.

Paca

1797

Paca," Patricia said, "this is Lorena, Juliet, and Adaline."

The women nodded to her as they were introduced. Heavy rain slashed against the windows outside, and a fire gently crackled in the hearth near them. Bad weather was another thing Paca had slowly become accustomed to; in Tyra, there were no seasons, no rain or wind. There was only the dark.

"So *you're* the one," Juliet said, "who wants to steal from an Overseer. I expected someone... scarier."

Juliet's hair was a pale orange, glowing pale yellow from the flickering fire. She looked somehow timid and brave at the same time.

"How many people have heard about this?" Paca asked.

Juliet and Adaline both smiled.

"Many of us," Adaline said, "word spreads through us faster than scandal through the nobles."

Adaline looked barely older than a child; large blue eyes and pouting lips, with wispy, pale brown hair. By contrast, her voice was knowing and secretive. It was just like Tyra. Children had no time to be children; they had to grow up fast enough to keep up with the demand on their minds and bodies.

"Not everything is gossip," Paca said, "we need secrets if we are to survive."

Juliet laughed.

"You need a lot more than secrets."

"Juliet," Patricia said, "please. We're here to listen to Paca. If she's right—and I believe she is—we could create living space for every Tyran. No more crowded homes. And we could do it without the Overseers ever knowing."

Adaline shifted in her seat, sweeping a hand through her hair, her eyes darting through the room.

"The Overseers know everything," she said quietly.

"If they did," Paca said, "they would be here right now, putting a stop to this conversation."

A sudden silence gripped the three women sitting across from Paca and Patricia, as though they expected the door to be smashed down at any moment.

"Patricia told me one of you works for the Overseer of production," Paca said, "which of you is it?"

Lorena raised her hand.

"I do," she whispered.

"How often are you in his house?"

"Most days," Lorena said, "I have sisters who work in the factories, but I was lucky. Overseer Salwey took a liking to me over the other girls who applied."

Paca nodded, watching the girl closely.

"What does your job require you to do?"

Lorena took a slow, shaky breath. Her eyes, a dark blue deeper than any pit Paca had ever come across in Tyra, remained stuck on the floor.

"Anything and everything the Salweys need," she said, "most often cleaning and cooking, and taking care of the children."

"Are you given access to any keys, or information? Do you know where the secrets are kept?"

"He would never give his keys to anyone," Lorena said, "not even another Overseer. They have their own rules that must be followed. I know where his safe is, where he keeps valuables... but I don't know what's in there, or how to unlock it."

"Does he wear his keys?"

"Every day. There is a pouch on his belt, but it would be difficult to open. I heard him say once that it was designed by Riffolk Hayne to be impossible to pickpocket."

Paca nodded. She never would have attempted stealing from an Overseer if it meant taking directly from his person.

"Does he have spare copies," she asked, "of his keys?"

"I doubt it." A spark lit up Lorena's eyes, and she frowned. "but after one of his factories shut down, I think... I believe his set of keys looked smaller."

That's it, Paca thought, *he keeps his unused keys elsewhere. The safe, most likely*. It made the mission far simpler.

"Is the house ever empty?" she asked.

Lorena frowned again, her lips pulled thin in concentration.

"Every now and then," she said, "but it's hard to tell when. His wife, Peggy, likes to go shopping. But when she does, I usually stay at the house with the children."

"Could you take them somewhere," Paca asked, "for a short while?"

Lorena's face went pale. She looked at the girls next to her, at the fire, at the dark window rattling from the rain. She fidgeted her hands, entwining them over and over, squeezing until her skin turned white. She never once looked at Paca.

"I... I could," she said, "but it would be unusual. The kids would talk, and Elijah—Mister Salwey—would have questions."

"We can't attract any attention," Patricia said, "questions from an Overseer could topple the whole thing."

"I know," Paca said, "let me handle that. I just need the house empty for an hour or so."

"How, exactly," Juliet said, "will you *handle* an Overseer asking questions?"

"And how do you expect to break into a safe," Adaline said, "designed by Overseer Hayne? Did they even *have* locks in Tyra?"

"No," Paca said, "there were no locks. Our entire city was a cage, and we had no possessions to keep from one another. We'll get into the safe the same way we get into the factory."

She had never seen keys or locks before coming to the surface. But they were simple enough to understand, compared to many of the other things she'd learned. Each key was a specific shape, and each lock could only be opened by a certain key.

Paca watched the fire. It never ceased to amaze her; the light and the warmth of it, the gentle crackling. Tyrans would have given anything for such a luxury. They certainly needed it more than the Ermoori; despite the storm outside, it had already been warm in the house before they lit the fire.

"The safe doesn't use a key," Lorena said, "it's a code. Overseer Hayne built safes that unlock with buttons instead of keys."

"So, we need the code."

"You make it sound so simple," Adaline said, "but the code is not a key. You can't steal it. And it's not like you can simply ask him what it is."

Paca turned back to Lorena.

"Are there any numbers with particular meaning to him?" she asked, "birthdays? Anniversaries?"

Both were also new concepts to Paca; Tyrans didn't have any days of significance, and certainly didn't celebrate the day of their birth. Even the concept of days and nights was foreign to them before they lived in Ermoor.

"Overseer Salwey pays as much attention to birthdays and anniversaries as any other man," Lorena said, "and he doesn't talk to me about important things."

"I need you to try to find out what the code could be," Paca said, "however you can."

"No," Juliet said, "Overseer Salwey will know what part she played immediately. It's far too dangerous."

"If it comes to that," Paca said, "I will make it look like a random crime, so that Lorena isn't suspected."

Juliet scoffed.

"Random crime? There *is* no crime in Ermoor. There hasn't been for decades. Not since the Spectre."

"But if they don't know who did it," Paca said, "and don't have a reason to suspect Lorena, then how could they possibly find out what happened?"

"They will take anyone," Lorena said, "any workers they think might know even the tiniest detail. And they'll force us to talk."

Keys were made of metal, which was forged and shaped every day in some of the factories in Ermoor. The workers in those factories would know how to shape metal to their needs…

If we know the shape, she thought, *and we can bring it to those workers, then we might be able to make a key.*

"If we could get one of the workers from the metal-based factories to make a copy of the key," Paca said, "and return it while the house is empty... they wouldn't even know anything had happened."

Lorena and Juliet frowned at her, doubt written all over their faces.

"It's… flimsy," Patricia said, "but if we don't attract the attention of the Overseers, it just might work."

Eliza

1797

Eliza dove to the side, barely dodging under a sweeping kick from Aerene. She rolled to her feet and sent a weak bolt at Aerene's leg. The Austris Aran slipped diagonally through the air without even a twitch of her wings; Eliza's bolt hit the wall. She was getting better at controlling the power of her magical attacks. For now, she had to keep the power low, but control would allow her to fight better. Channelling more power into her attacks hadn't ever been much of an issue for her, but more precision would mean her attacks would be far more effective.

Aerene spun in a tight arc, sending a blade-like slash of Air Magic right at Eliza's head. She ducked low and reached out her hand, fingers splayed. She summoned a viciously crackling ball of energy in her palm. At the same time, behind Aerene, a smaller ball of lightning pulsed to life. Eliza snapped her hand into a fist; the magic in her hand exploded in a bright flash while the lightning behind Aerene slammed into her back.

"Nice trick," the Austris Aran said, "creating a separate origin point to confuse your opponent."

Eliza beamed; praise from Aerene was always genuine. She had developed quite a collection of techniques over the last little while. It had become one of her favourite things to come up with new ways to use magic. She wasn't sure how well she'd be able to use them in real battle if it came to that, but practicing them with Aerene was helping her immensely.

"Have you ever been in battle?" she asked Aerene.

"No. Other than fighting wild animals, that is. But that's quite different."

"The benefits of living in a floating city, I suppose," Eliza said, "thousands of kilometres away from any other cities."

Aerene smiled.

"We have always been ready for the war," Aerene said, "you don't need to worry about that."

"The war against Sithares," Eliza said, "but not Ermoor."

"Shaela killed a whole team of them decades ago. They may be more powerful now, but they've never had to face an army of Austris Arans."

"They've also never broken through the tree line of Shanaken before," Eliza said, "until this war. It's different. They might actually win."

"They won't."

Eliza nodded, but she couldn't bring herself to believe it. Neither could she accept defeat before the fight began; all she could do was train hard, and push away thoughts about what might happen if the Ermoori did win.

"We likely won't see real battle, anyway," Eliza said with a slight shake of her head, "we'll be waging magical war on Sithares in the temple by the time the Ermoori arrive. We're still not even ready to cast the spells."

"Eliza, you won't be casting the spells anyway. You know that. You'll just be there to support your mother."

The words stung, even though Eliza knew they were true. Over the last couple years, Aerene had been helping Eliza by telling her much of what the Circle discussed. They shared almost everything with each other, despite the Circle's secrecy. There were still things Aerene couldn't tell her, of course; but Eliza knew all about the ritual to destroy Sithares.

"My point remains," Eliza said, "we won't be seeing real battle unless the Ermoori arrive really soon, or after Sithares is dead."

“I’m not certain that’s true,” Aerene said, “the battle will go on for a while. History shows that is usually the case.”

“Won’t destroying Sithares also take a while? It can’t be easy killing a god.”

Aerene smiled again.

“I suppose we won’t know until it happens,” she said, “but either way, we will face it together.”

With that, she leapt at Eliza, a wide grin on her face. Eliza threw herself sideways, gathering a lightning ball as she rolled into a combat stance. Aerene was already in the air again. They had trained together so many times now, they knew each other’s fighting style as well as they knew their own.

Aerene never stopped moving. Her attacks were measured, precise, and only performed when Aerene was certain she could get away with it. While it meant Eliza had to be watchful while they sparred, it also meant openings for attack were plentiful.

They traded blows for at least half an hour before they collapsed in the centre of the room. Eliza’s training room was shared with her mother, large enough to spar and practice but lined with machines that flowed with electricity. Aerene could use magic no matter where she was, but for Eliza to keep using it for an extended time, she needed to absorb magic from an outside source. Electricity was perhaps the most difficult kind of magic to use, if for no other reason than it almost never occurred in nature.

Air Magic, by contrast, must have been like… well, breathing. It was everywhere. Eliza wondered what it was like, to constantly feel magic around her. She worried about fighting in a war without machines around from which to draw power. What would she do when she ran out of magic? She could fight hand-to-hand thanks to Mathys, but that wouldn't help against heavily armoured soldiers with technological weaponry.

Eliza lay on her back, feeling her breath slowly return to its normal rhythm. Sweat made her clothes cling to her skin. Heat streamed constantly from the roiling black clouds above the city. She looked at Aerene; the blue-skinned woman wasn't sweating at all. She sat on the floor instead of lying down, and as far as Eliza could tell, wasn't even out of breath.

"Is it Air Magic," Eliza said, "that allows you to fight without running out of breath?"

Aerene glanced at her, watching her face, watching her chest rise and fall as it finally slowed down.

"I… didn't realise people could run out of breath," she said, "how strange."

"You've never noticed it after we spar?"

"I suppose I thought it was an affectation," she said, "like when people sigh."

Eliza laughed. She had become used to the sight of Austris Arans despite their blue skin and giant golden wings. Sometimes it was difficult to remember just how different they were.

"You thought I just sighed a lot after every practice battle?"

"It's no stranger than anything else people do out of habit."

With another laugh, Eliza shook her head and then shifted to look up to the ceiling. It was hemispherical, plain and smooth, except for the wide windows that lined its base. They were large enough for Austris Arans to fly in and out of, as with every window in the city.

Whenever she could, Eliza tried to enjoy this time. Her days were spent training, and she'd always loved training. It wouldn't be long before both wars began in Austris Ara; the magical one against Sithares, and the physical one against Ermoor. She was terrified, of course, but she refused to let terror overtake her the way it was doing to her mother.

At least Aerene and Eliza could spend time together, laughing about stupid things and learning magic. She realised in that moment that she had no idea what the future might look like even next year, let alone when she was her mother's age. The entirety of Pandeia might look different, depending who won the war. And if they failed against Sithares? It didn't bear thinking about.

Eliza sat up, rest her elbows on her knees and looking again at Aerene. She seemed as young as Eliza, but she knew that was an illusion. What didn't look like merely illusion was the Austris Aran girl's calm. She was always serene, and humbler by far than any other Austris Aran Eliza had met. Eliza still couldn't believe how long Aerene's people lived for.

"Are you scared of death?" she asked, the thought escaping her mouth before it had fully formed in her head.

Aerene's face took on a far-away quality, a slight frown as her eyes stared at nothing.

"I… suppose," she said slowly, "I haven't really thought about it. It's still, well, a long way off."

She chuckled lightly. Eliza nodded; I *wouldn't be scared of death either, if I was Austris Aran*, she thought.

"Don't worry," Aerene said gently, "it's a long way off for you, too. We'll protect each other, that's what the Circle is for."

Karak

1797

The palace was guarded; each entrance was locked tight, with two Thearans keeping watch. But without Kerberos, and with most of the Thearans caught up in the fighting, sneaking in would be significantly easier.

"Last time I was here," Karak said, "I shifted into an animal and went from the roof to the balcony of the royal quarters. We should be able to do that again. We'll just need to watch for more guards... since the book was stolen once before, Kerberos might have guards posted at all times near it now."

They circled around the building, keeping out of sight of Thearans. The south eastern side of the palace was quiet, and ornate enough to be climbable. There were no patrols, for which Karak was grateful; but the area out of sight of any guards was incredibly small. They could shift into animals, which would make them less conspicuous, but they would most likely be seen at some point.

"Okay," Karak said, "one of us stays here. The other three climb the wall and cross the roof. We drop to the balcony, take out any guards we find, take the book, and bail."

"Sounds simple enough," Koro said, "who stays behind?"

"I will," Zela said. No one argued with her.

They shifted, the group of three into birds and Zela into a dog. They carried the black metal box; the only thing that could allow them to safely carry the book of Sithares. They should be able to grab it now, and get out quickly.

From the palace roof, they could see most of the city. Even the larger section beyond the bridge, though they could see only the buildings and the main street.

Karak held the black box in both claws of his bird form. They flew low over the roof, and when they reached the opposite edge, Karak placed the box down as gently as he could. It was time. The book was almost theirs once again. After all he'd been through, he wasn't even sure why he wanted to help the Circle so badly anymore. They had cast him out after he committed the grievous sin of sharing

Tarsi secrets with an outsider. Since then, nothing he did changed his standing with them.

For a while, he'd contented himself with living in Omatus. He'd even briefly lived as Anamas Argyris. But that all ended when the Circle contacted him asking for more help, asking him to atone for his past once again.

It was his fault Kerberos had come to Azar. It was his fault, at least partially, that Kerberos was so versed in magic; he had taught the man, back when he was a boy, how to use Deias, the ancient language that carried magic within its words. That was well before the boy Atillus became Kerberos. He never could have known how much damage he'd cause all these decades later.

Zeera held it against him, as did all the other Tarsi. He didn't blame them. But he was beginning to wonder why he should have to work tirelessly, not to mention put himself in so much danger, if they were never going to forgive him.

Not for the first time, Karak wondered how many things would be different if he'd never taken the job teaching Atillus Argyris. Would Kerberos be as powerful now? Would some other Tarsi have taken the job instead? There were plenty of Tarsi who knew *Deias*; perhaps someone else would have turned into an outcast. Would Karak have even stayed with the Circle?

The balcony below them was wide, providing a view of the entire city. Karak listened for any movement inside the royal quarters.

There was nothing. The three Tarsi glanced at each other; it was now or never.

"Karak," Koro whispered, "when we drop down, you cast a blinding spell just in case. Laral and I will shift into sand panthers to take anyone out. We get the book, at any cost."

Laral and Karak nodded. Technically, Karak was in charge of the group; but now wasn't the time to fight for control. Karak prepared his spell while the other two shifted. A few moments of concentration was all it took for each of them.

Memories flooded Karak's mind, the familiarity of his task sending a dry, hot burst of sickness through his stomach. He had come here to steal the book, and he had come here attempting to assassinate Kerberos. He could still feel the beating Kerberos had dealt him. He was amazed, even now, that he'd survived. Kerberos was some kind of eternal punishment; he was cursed to confront the brutal king over and over until the Thearan finally killed him.

He wondered if that was what Zeera really wanted. If that was why she kept sending him on such dangerous missions. He had been thinking lately that even if he succeeded in bringing the book back to Zeera, he'd still be considered an outsider. Zeera was certainly still cold towards him, though there was at least a little empathy in her voice the last time they spoke…

Unless I imagined that.

They dropped onto the balcony, Karak fighting to keep his wits. Beyond the open doorway, the room looked empty. The spell in

Karak's hand grew warm, glowing with its power. They snuck into the room, Karak's heart slamming against his chest.

Despite making almost no sound, a reaction came from outside the room, just past the hallway doors. Karak heard the shuffling of armoured warriors, the hissing of weapons being drawn from their scabbards. He had expected as much; he only hoped there would be one or two guards. Then, at least, they stood a chance.

The doors opened, and four Thearan guards rushed in. Again, A horrible sickness arose within his body. He couldn't shake the memories out of his head. They clung to him, clawing like monsters, paralysing him as though they wielded poison. With more focus than he thought he possessed, Karak threw the spell at the Thearan warriors.

The flash of white light was brilliant. Immediately, the other two Tarsi leapt at the Thearans, slashing and biting with their sand panther forms. Karak stepped back to seek the book. He didn't want to leave the others to fight four guards, but their mission was the book, and they couldn't get it if all three of them were dead.

But it wasn't in the room. Karak's heart stopped. *What now*? There were only so many places it could be; but every moment he spent looking was a danger.

A strangled scream cut through the chaos as Koro tore into a Thearan's neck. The woman collapsed. One of the other warriors leapt over her corpse, lunging at Koro with a short spear. The blade caught him on the hind leg. It cut deep, and Koro let out a scream, his real voice strange coming from the sand panther's mouth.

The Thearans pressed their attack; it was now three against three, but Koro's wound looked bad. *And I don't know where to begin looking for the book*, Karak thought, *this is a nightmare*.

It might have been down in the secret room behind Omatus' royal library. But that seemed too obvious, since Kerberos had already used it to imprison Aella. Perhaps in the throne room, though there would be a much larger guard given the size of the room and its accessibility.

I could just run, he thought, *get out of Omatus before the war gets too bad.*

But if the Circle lost the war, and Karak could have prevented it… would he really be able to live with himself? *Probably not*. And if any Circle members—or any of the Tarsi, for that matter—survived, Karak would be hunted down.

The fighting grew more intense as the Thearans pushed Koro and Laral towards the balcony. Karak searched for a safe way down. He didn't know if Koro would be able to shift into a bird and fly down, with his injured leg. But if they didn't escape soon, they'd all be dead.

As he turned back to the fight, a small group of Thearans sprinted from the battle towards the bridge. Yellow bolts of lightning followed them. In the centre of the group, Karak saw him. Kerberos. He went cold and numb from head to toe. The king of Omatus was on his way back to the palace.

He knows, Karak thought, *he knows the book is being stolen, and he's coming to kill me*. Behind him, the Thearans noticed the same thing as they spilled onto the balcony. They stopped attacking, instead holding their weapons pointed at the Tarsi.

"Why is the king coming back?" one of them said, "are we losing the battle?"

"No," another said, "Kerberos never loses."

One of the yellow bolts blasted straight through Kerberos' chest. The giant Thearan fell to the stone ground. His personal guard grabbed him, dragging him off the road and into a small group of houses. Karak lost sight of them.

"He…" the second Thearan said, "did he just get…"

"You three," the third one said, "better not have had anything to do with this attack."

"Why would we be in league with the Ermoori?" Koro snapped, "those monsters are trying to destroy everything."

"Then what are you doing here?"

"We're trying to save the world," Karak said, "from *your* god."

"Karak," Laral hissed in Tarsi, "why would you tell them that?"

"Sometimes the truth is the only option."

"I don't think this is one of those times," Koro said.

"What are you saying?" one of the Thearans asked, "speak Oman!"

"You should be fighting the Ermoori right now," Koro said, "instead of holding three Tarsi hostage in the royal quarters. You're about to lose this city."

"You know nothing," the warrior said, "Kerberos cannot be killed. We will never lose Omatus. And you cannot save Pandeia from the Fire."

"Why would you *want* the world to burn?" Karak asked.

The Thearan watching him sneered.

"Sithares rewards those loyal to it. You wouldn't understand loyalty, you sneaking little frogs."

"Laral," Karak said in Tarsi, "Koro. We need to get off this balcony. Koro, can you shift?"

"It'll be a challenge," Koro whispered, "but if I have to, yes. I think so."

"Birds?"

"Birds."

"On three?"

"What are you saying?" a Thearan shouted again.

"One."

The change began within his body; it could be close to instant, with enough focus. The Thearans edged closer, their weapons shining in the sun.

"Two."

"Sithares burn you, frogs, *what are you saying*?"

"Three."

Karak completed the shift into bird form the instant after he leapt over the balcony's railing. Laral did the same. Koro screamed and plummeted to the ground. His body hit the stone with a thin smack; Tarsi were small, and Koro had only partly shifted into bird form. He weighed enough for the fall to kill him, but only just. Even if it hadn't been, a Thearan spear jutted from his broken body.

"We need to get out of here," Laral said.

"We need the book," Karak said, "it's the only way to end this. At any cost, remember?"

"How do we get it? They know we're here now, there's no sneaking past them."

"Let's reunite with Zela," Karak said, "then we'll make a new plan. We need to move fast, before the Ermoori reach the palace."

Laral looked as though he was going to argue, but glanced up at the balcony and nodded.

They flew around the building, watching for more warriors. There were a handful, but none were alarmed by their presence; the Thearans inside the palace must not have spread the word just yet. Karak prayed to Asheilos for good luck, knowing it would make no difference but hoping nonetheless.

Zela was nowhere to be found. Karak and Laral landed at the place where they'd last split up, but there was no trace of her. *Now what*? Karak thought, *this entire mission is falling apart*.

"Perhaps she was caught," Laral said quietly, "should we search for her?"

"The book is the mission," Karak said, "I tried to tell Zeera how dangerous this was. By Asheilos, we'll never get this damned book."

All he wanted was to be done with this. The Circle, Sithares, Kerberos; all of it. He just wanted to live his own life, free of debt to the Circle. To not have to worry about the Gods or the war. Was it really so much to ask? Karak wasn't even the Hero, but his entire life seemed devoted to the war against Sithares anyway.

Shouts rang out from around the corner; Karak heard the thudding of too many footsteps.

"They know we're here," Laral said, "where do we go?"

"Wait," Karak said, "listen."

The shouts were Oman, and Karak could only just make out what they were saying in the chaos.

"Get it! Don't let it get away!"

"It's Zela!" Karak said, "she must have the book."

Laral frowned, moving restlessly, edging away from where the shouts were coming.

"Can't you hear what they're saying?" Karak asked, "they wouldn't be shouting those things if they were rushing to attack us. They're trying to stop something from being stolen."

"They're almost here," Laral said, "Karak, we need to go."

"Just wait."

Zela rushed around the corner, gripping a bundle wrapped in what looked like Thearan scaled leather. *Clever*, Karak thought, *most animals in Theara and Omas can withstand intense heat and flame*. Why hadn't he thought of that?

They ran together towards the nearest stretch of the city's wall. Carrying the book over might be difficult, but if they could shift into birds again, they could fly straight over the wall and make their way to Aethos. *We just need to avoid the Thearans*, he thought, *and the Ermoori*.

"Zela," Karak said as they ran, "we need to carry the book together over the wall."

She said nothing, but gave him a quick look of determination. Thearan arrows whistled past them. The wall stretched above, almost close enough.

Among their footfalls, and the clattering of arrows against stone around them, Karak heard a wet thud sound. Zela gasped. She stumbled, dropping the book. Karak fought against every impulse in his body and stopped. Zela dropped to one knee, an arrow sticking out of her chest.

"Oh, no," Karak said, "Zela, we need to—"

"Go," she whispered, "take the book, run. This is your last chance."

Arrows slashed through the air.

"Karak!" Laral screamed, "get the book!"

"I'm sorry," he said to Zela.

She smiled weakly, her grey eyes already dazed. Karak forced himself to turn from her. He snatched the book and sprinted back to

Laral. They held the book together, preparing to shift. A fireball slammed into the wall right next to them. The Thearans were almost upon them.

Karak looked at Laral, trying to appear confident. He could tell from the fear in her eyes that he'd failed.

"Birds on three?" he said.

Kerberos

1797

In the decades since he first read Sithares' prayer aloud, he had never been burned. Fire had become nothing to him but energy. A tool to be used. But now, Kerberos felt it all. His skin, his eyes, even the inside of his mouth as he screamed; the fire ate his flesh like a wild animal. But no matter how long he burned, his body was never destroyed. He simply kept burning.

There was no ground beneath him, no sky above. Nothing but fire. The crackling of his skin and the roar of flame filled his ears, but above that was the vicious laughter of Sithares.

He lost all sense of time. After what must have been a lifetime—or several—he forgot who he had been before the Fire. His memories burned away until there was only pain.

A long time after that, the fires around him shifted, rushing around him as though he was falling. He slammed into something unrelenting, and suddenly, finally, the Fire was no more. Solid grey stone lay beneath him. There were half-destroyed buildings all around him, covered in black scorch marks. He heard the sounds of battle. He knew he should have known where he was. Something about the city called to him. But he couldn't remember anything.

He looked at his hands, at the weapon on his belt. Physically, he felt incredible; but his mind was scattered, unable to make sense of anything around him. Despite that, the battle in the city echoed in his soul. Something pulled him towards it. Whoever he was, it was someone who loved to fight.

"Kerberos," a woman's voice came from somewhere behind him. He turned, and found a warrior looking at him with something like fierce devotion.

Is that my name?

"We must leave the city," the woman said, "those were the orders you gave before you died."

The orders I gave, he thought, *so I am a leader of some kind. A leader who died... and came back.* He didn't recognise the woman in front of him, but he knew she was trustworthy; just like the city called to him, and the song of battle echoed in his soul, this warrior was deeply connected to him.

"So be it," he said.

She handed him a large cloak, which he threw over his head and shoulders without a word.

"Many people saw you die," she said, "for now, it suits you to let them believe it."

They left the alleyway, the woman running in front of him so he could follow.

"What is your name?" he asked.

She hesitated, shot a look at him, and then sighed.

"Nomiki," she said, "I am your second in command. In matters of war, at any rate."

"And what am I?"

"The king. Of Omatus."

He gestured behind them.

"And this is Omatus?"

Nomiki nodded.

A short while later, they reached a massive wall. There were guards, dressed in the same kind of armour as Kerberos and Nomiki. Their eyes went wide the instant they saw his face.

"Your highness," one of them said, "we will open the gate for you."

Nomiki stepped in close to the man.

"Tell the warriors they are to get out of the city if the tide of battle turns against us," she said, "the Ermoori are executing every combatant who survives. Civilians will be fine."

"Yes, my lord," the guard said.

Though Nomiki had told him he was king, Kerberos didn't feel comfortable being addressed as *your highness*. Nomiki turned and watched the city behind them as the guards went about clearing their way. Kerberos did the same; from here, they couldn't see much of the fighting, but he could tell most of it was southeast of them. There was a massive building, which Kerberos took to be a royal palace. It seemed to be the focus of the battle.

"Your highness," a guard said, "the gate is open."

He turned to see open, grey desert. Nomiki and Kerberos rushed through the gate, sprinting west away from Omatus. Behind him, explosions rumbled in the city. The sounds of death faded the further he ran. A strange clash of both relief and intense longing roiled in his heart; he was glad to be clear of the fighting, but an almost overpowering urge begged him to turn back.

"Omatus will be ours again," Nomiki said, "we will return to fight for it."

Almost as though she can read my mind, he thought, *she answered a question I did not ask.*

"Tell me about our opponent," he said, "I remember nothing about them."

As they ran, Nomiki taught him about the Ermoori. The more he learned, the more rage boiled up from somewhere deep and primal within him. He couldn't fully explain it, but he wanted them all dead. When Nomiki mentioned the name of their leader, his vision blurred red, and Fire leapt over his skin. *Riffolk Hayne*. The name exploded within his mind, chaotic memories flooding into the cracks that his death had caused.

He remembered fighting the man, one-on-one, in an enclosed space. Speaking with him, a tense kind of respect between them. Nothing more specific than that, but the feeling of rage could not be ignored.

"We can slow down, now," Nomiki said after a few hours, "we're far enough ahead of anyone else who might leave the city."

They slowed to a walk.

"Most people escaping from the war have headed towards Aethos," Nomiki said, "southwest of here. I suggest we do the same. It will be easiest to hide among large crowds, especially refugees."

Kerberos nodded.

"How far is Aethos?"

"A fair way yet," Nomiki said, "far enough that we'll need to camp somewhere."

"No," Kerberos said, "we will keep moving until we get there. As fast as we can."

They ran in silence for the rest of that day. When they were tired, they walked. Somehow, they didn't see a single other person on the road. Kerberos was glad; he was tall, and broad, and easily recognisable. Even in a crowd, he could likely be picked out. But he would deal with that when he came to it. In the meantime, they just had to get to Aethos.

And Kerberos had to try to fix his fractured mind before the war reached him.

Mattias

1797

Thearans fought like desperate, wild animals. They launched themselves at the Ermoori, slashing and hacking with spears and swords. Their arrows were thicker and hit much harder than the Shenza, though they still weren't enough to get through Ermoori armour. The fighting was brutal. Mattias could barely stand for all the Thearans smashing heavy steel blades into his armour plates. When he killed one, another leaped over the corpse to fill the gap. They screamed as they fought, not in pain but anger.

It was almost as though each and every Thearan warrior was fighting to avenge a grievous injustice done to them by the Ermoori. For them, it seemed personal. Mattias held the line with his unit, shouting orders over the chaos as the enemy attempted to swarm them. His men fought valiantly, their morale absolute.

The Thearans wore armour, but each warrior wore different sets. It was simple steel plating that only covered small areas; shoulder pauldrons, chest plates, gauntlets, occasionally thigh plates. For almost every one of them, it left a lot of exposed skin. His men made the most of it. Each soldier had a hunting knife on their belt, and almost every one of his unit held their knives in their left hand, stabbing and slicing the Thearans who came too close. Meanwhile, they held their rifles in their right hand, firing into the screaming throng.

Mattias couldn't have been more proud of them. They fought in the main sector of the city, pushing through whenever they could. The tanks outside the city's walls sent round after round into the city proper, raining explosive destruction down onto the stone buildings.

Beneath his feet, the entire city shook. The wall was broken and shattered behind them. Their enemy fought viciously, contained within the city walls like countless caged beasts. Something happened to Mattias in that moment.

It felt like waking up. Suddenly, he could see the battlefield without any fear. He saw the rhythm of combat, of the two armies attacking one another. He felt alive.

"Group three and four," he shouted, "back to reserve position. Group one and two, concentrate fire on our front!"

Immediately, his men responded. Group five stayed with him, as usual. Half his unit fell back, climbing onto the wrecked wall to gain the high ground. The other half fired entirely into the warriors directly in front of Mattias. Once groups three and four were in position, they fired down into the same area. The response was as fast as it was drastic; a gap bloomed in the enemy lines, and Ermoori soldiers rushed in to fill it. A cheer rose up from the men.

But even such a blow did nothing to enemy morale. They kept fighting with the same vigour, as though nothing had happened. Not even a glance was spared for their own fallen warriors.

Mattias fired into the enemy ranks, shifting his aim between each shot. He aimed for the chest; the easiest shot that would still kill the target. His men did the same. They fired as efficiently as he did. They stood straight-backed in neat groups, aiming with practiced skill. Even when the Thearans reached them, they fought hand-to-hand gracefully.

They lost no ground. With Mattias' strategy in place, they punched through the enemy's defences, until they moved so far into the city that they had to call a stop to the tank attacks. And still, the Thearans fought without restraint.

Arrows streaked into the Ermoori forces. Not only that, but balls of roaring fire slammed into them from somewhere in the ranks of Thearans. One of them hit the stone ground near Mattias, throwing him off his feet. He shook off the blurred vision that took over, and checked the place of impact.

Two of his soldiers were on the ground as well, but their armour had held. There was no blood, no obvious wounds. Mattias forced himself to his feet and snatched his rifle from the ground. *We can do that, too*, he thought.

He took one of the explosive traps from a pouch on his belt, set it to explode on impact, and hurled it over the Thearans closest to him.

"Set your traps to blow," he shouted to his unit, "throw them! Let's show these savages what Ermoor can do!"

His own trap exploded, and the Ermoori cheered. Within a moment, explosions littered the battlefield. The Thearans responded with screams of rage, and their fighting became even more intense. *They only get stronger*, Mattias thought with wonder, *it's almost as if they're fuelled by rage*.

It took hours for them to reach the bridge. When they did, Mattias couldn't believe the size of it; wide enough for a whole group of his unit to walk side-by-side, and long enough that he would have struggled to shoot anything on the other side. Below it was the massive river Alpheus, which fed into the ocean to his left. The warships could be seen on the banks far below, impressive even from this distance.

The Thearans were waiting for them; perhaps a battalion's worth of them had amassed on the other side of the bridge, with smaller groups spaced along the bridge's length. Thearan archers stood along the opposite cliff, waiting for the Ermoori to approach. Even knowing their arrows wouldn't puncture his armour, Mattias couldn't help but feel intimidated.

Fires appeared in bright orange flares in the distance. Mattias could have sworn the Thearans were holding the fire in their hands... *If the Shenza using magic wasn't clear enough*, he thought, *the Thearans have made it obvious that magic is real*. Where else had those fireballs come from earlier? The Thearans didn't possess projectile weapons other than bows; nothing that could produce explosives like the ones his unit had experienced.

Ermoori were supposed to not believe in magic. One of the core tenets of the exploratory forces was to eradicate any traces of magic. Teleradio broadcasts back in Ermoor talked about the problematic beliefs of savages throughout Pandeia; their beliefs in magic went against the One True God. Mattias wasn't sure what he believed anymore, but he knew the Shenza could do things no normal person should have been able to do.

For a long moment, both armies stood facing each other in silence. The Thearans his men were fighting had retreated further along the bridge. They looked ready to fight again, as though the battle so far had been merely a warm-up.

His own men were tired, but ready. The Thearans stayed put. Mattias frowned; he would have expected them to attack first. *They're hoping to draw us onto the bridge*, he thought, *no doubt they think they can deal more damage to us there*. The bridge was ancient, massive, and—though he hated to admit it—impressive. *If this was Ermoor*, he thought, *the Overseers would simply destroy the bridge with the enemy on it*. Surely the Thearans wouldn't do the same…

A deep rumbling rose up from the ground beneath him. Behind him, the fleet of tanks rolled up the main street. Soldiers parted around them, cheering as they ground to a stop at the bridge's entrance. Even if Mattias and his men would have struggled to hit the enemy on the other side of the bridge, the tanks wouldn't. And they could do a lot more damage.

When they'd stormed the tunnels underneath Tarsium, shooting the enemy had been easy. With the tanks lined up in rows of three, Mattias was beginning to feel the same way. The Thearans' plan to wait for them to attack might have been effective if Ermoor didn't possess dozens of indestructible tanks; now it was almost unfair. Omatus was theirs.

A low grinding sound came from the gently idling tanks as their barrels took aim. Mattias stared into the waiting Thearan ranks. They simply stood, waiting, as though they didn't care about the tanks. As though they were happy to die.

Or as though they have no idea what the tanks are capable of, he thought, despite watching them destroy the city wall.

With no further warning, the tanks opened fire. Their rounds were solid Ermoori steel that came to a wicked point, reinforced somehow with thick bolts of yellow lightning. They were almost exactly what the rifles fired, but a hundred times larger. The rounds slammed into the cliff, the buildings, and the waiting Thearans in a catastrophic maelstrom of death and destruction.

The Thearans on the bridge screamed and sprinted at them. As one, Mattias' unit took aim and fired into the rushing horde. They fell by the dozen, some of them bursting into flame as they did. Mattias ran out of lightning rounds, and switched to what they called dark rounds; pitch black bullets that made very little sound but could pierce almost anything. He fired again and again, watching with satisfaction as the dark rounds streaked right through the Thearans' steel armour.

It wasn't until the bridge was empty that Mattias realised most of the Thearans had fled. Across the gorge, the street was abandoned. A cheer spread through his unit, and the other soldiers picked it up.

The tanks wasted no time; they rumbled over the bridge, a unit walking beside each one, their rifles up and ready. Mattias scanned the city ahead of him, but there were no more Thearans.

A strange kind of silence fell over them. During the war, Mattias had experienced many different kinds of silence; there was the tense quiet before a battle began, the relieved stillness of safety. A silence built from shock followed a surprise attack, and there was an uncomfortable silence whenever they found themselves behind enemy lines, just like in Tarsium.

But this one was different. There was a heaviness to it, and he was left with the undeniable sensation that the battle wasn't over. The Thearans had not given up, of that he was certain.

As he reached the other side of the bridge, a brilliant roar filled his ears and Mattias was thrown forward by a wall of searing fire. His ears rang, and its heat flashed into his skin despite his armour protecting him from the worst of the flames.

Mattias picked himself up off the stony ground yet again.

Where did that come from?

Behind the tanks, the bridge itself was undamaged, only a black scorch mark covering the stone. It emanated from the centre, where mere moments before were a slew of Thearan corpses. They must have been thrown off the bridge in the explosion… but what had caused the explosion in the first place? There was no trace of a weapon. But he had seen the Thearans erupt in flame after being shot down; surely an explosion of that scale—or any scale, for that matter—couldn't have come from a person…

The tanks were unharmed, unsurprisingly; but those soldiers closest to the blast lay still where they'd fallen. A few dozen soldiers were killed, but that was all. For such a huge explosion, it was a low death toll, though still more men than they'd lost in a while. Mattias checked his team. When he knew they were okay, they set to work again.

They spent the next few hours scouring Omatus, searching every building and alley for more Thearans. But there was no trace of them. The royal palace lay empty and cold, like a corpse. Mattias searched the building with his unit, alongside other units he didn't know, but still they found nothing.

After they made certain the palace was empty, Commander Darrow sent a transmission to Prime Overseer Hayne, followed by return orders to spread through Omatus and begin keeping the peace. Just as they had in Tarsium and Shanaken before that, they were to let civilians live, and execute any warriors they found.

Before he had finished briefing his unit to move out, Mattias saw the Prime Overseer stroll into Omatus' royal palace. His weapon—a single pistol—was as unique as his gold-streaked armour. From what Mattias could tell, there was no ammunition cartridge. Its barrel was thicker, and there were strange, small orbs built into the main chamber where the rounds would normally go. They glowed with yellow energy. A cable of some kind linked the pistol to the Prime Overseer's armour.

Overseer Hayne wore no helmet. His face was serene, utterly confident, and he looked at the royal palace as though it had been built just for him.

Paca

1797

Do this right," Lorena said, "and for God's sake, don't get caught. You have no idea what I had to do to get this."

She handed Paca a small scrap of paper with symbols written in a scratchy hand. She couldn't read, of course; but she didn't need to know what the symbols said to identify them on the safe.

They were back in the main room of Patricia's house, but now it was just the two of them. Barely a week had passed. Another week of heightened tensions, cramped living spaces, and long shifts in the factories.

"I'll be in and out," Paca said, "all you need to do is take the children out while Overseer Salwey's wife is shopping."

"In two days' time, right?" Lorena said.

"An hour or two after midday," Paca said with a nod, "when there are less people on the streets."

Lorena fidgeted, wringing her hands together in rubbing motions as though washing them. She stared at the scrap of paper she'd handed to Paca.

"You shouldn't do this," she whispered, "you don't know the Overseers. If you're caught, if something goes wrong—*anything* goes wrong—they'll kill dozens of us. Likely more. Please, don't do this."

Paca shook her head.

"What's the alternative?" she asked, "keep living the way we are? Our people can barely stand each other. It's been too long, Lorena. We need to make space. Even if nothing else changes in this Creator-forsaken place, we at least need our own sleeping quarters."

Lorena crossed her arms, eyes pointed straight down. She looked on the verge of tears. But she said nothing.

Two days later, Paca waited in an alley near the Salweys' house. She still wasn't good at telling the time of day, but Patricia had given her an old timepiece, and taught her how to read it.

It was time.

She couldn't stand out on the street; according to Ermoori sensibilities, a woman alone during work hours, doing nothing, would invite attention. She wore trousers and a man's shirt and jacket. A sturdy hat sat on her head, her hair pulled up inside it. But even so, it wouldn't take much more than a second glance from an onlooker to spot Paca as a woman.

It was a cloudy day, but strangely warm. The days had been getting warmer and warmer, though most of what she'd heard from the Ermoori until now was complaints of the year-round cold. Paca glanced both ways down the street and walked as casually as she could manage to the house.

She tried the door, her breath held in her throat as she listened for people on the street; it was unlocked, just as Lorena had promised. Taking one last quick glance around her, she slipped in through the door.

It was the first noble's house Paca had seen from the inside. Even before she'd entered, the difference was evident; it was massive and ornate, and two stories tall. Inside, it was even more unreal. Smooth marbled stone floors lay under a white ceiling covered in intricate patterns. The walls were divided into halves; the top half painted the deep blue that represented Ermoor, and the bottom half a dark brown wood.

Paca wandered further down the main corridor. Silence filled the rich space, a strange mix of relief and dread churning in her stomach.

She crept up the stairs, then followed the upper corridor to the right. At its end, another corridor went left. The west wing, as Lorena called it. At the far end of the west wing was Overseer Salwey's office. The door wasn't locked; Paca turned the knob and pushed gently.

"Hello," Overseer Salwey said, "Paca, is it?"

Confident, cruel eyes shone from a worn face framed by short silver hair. His broad shoulders filled out the imperious Overseer uniform he wore. He held a weapon in one hand; one of the Ermoori guns that could tear through a person with ease. It was pointed at Paca's chest. The Overseer smiled.

"Would you like to know what I love most about the workers like you?" he asked, "you're all so naive. You really thought you were friends."

He gestured behind him; Lorena sat on the wooden chair in front of the desk. Her eyes were cast down, tears streaming down her cheeks. In a sudden rush, rage consumed Paca. Her heart thundered, her mind roaring in a tempest of violence.

"*You're* the naive ones," Paca said, "for believing yourselves to be invincible. Your time will come, you'll see."

Overseer Salwey laughed; a light-hearted sound, his face showing genuine good humour. But the gun never wavered. He looked at her like she was no more important to him than the wall behind her.

"Do you even know what we want?" she asked, "or who we actually are?"

"You wanted to steal from me," Salwey said, "that's all I care about. Your name means nothing."

"All we want is a place to sleep," Paca said, "enough pay to live comfortably." She took a step towards him, her arms spread, hands splayed. "And my name *should* mean something to you, Overseer. It's Paca. I'm not one of your workers; I'm Tyran."

He didn't react at all.

So, she thought, *Lorena told him everything*.

"You had somewhere to live," the Overseer said, "and you abandoned it. You think we owe you anything, because you people left your own homes to flood our streets?"

Paca took another slow step forwards, forcing her rage down.

"All we want is one of the empty factories. One of the ones you own."

"Ridiculous. I won't just *give* you a factory."

"It's not in use. What would you lose by letting us sleep there?"

"It's *my* factory," Salwey said, "You cannot use it."

"What do you suggest we do then," Paca snapped, "if we have nowhere to live?"

Overseer Salwey's smile turned sour. He shrugged, his hands spreading out in a gesture of total apathy.

"Go back to where you came from," he said.

Paca lunged at him, screaming as she grabbed the gun and shoved it away from her. It exploded, a flash of light rushing over her vision. She twisted it out of his hand.

The Overseer growled and threw her to the ground. But she had the gun. He lunged at her; she yanked at the gun's trigger.

Another explosion erupted in her ears. Another brief flash of light obscured her vision. And then the room refocused in front of her, now a horrifying mess. Blood covered the floor, the wall behind the Overseer, and Lorena.

And Lorena...

A chunk of her head was missing. One of her eyes was wide, dull and glistening at the same time. The other had rolled back and filled with blood. Her mouth hung open listlessly.

The Overseer lay on the ground, choking and weakly groaning. His stomach had become a ragged hole.

Paca placed the gun next to her, and ran her hands over her face. Lorena betrayed her. All she had been trying to do was find a place for the Tyrans to live. Lorena's own home was cramped, just like all the others. Why would she take the Overseers' side?

I never would have wanted her dead, she thought, *even after I saw her here*.

But there was nothing she could do about what had happened. All she could do was get the factory key, and hope no one noticed the key was gone. An Overseer's death was bad enough; hopefully it would take attention away from anything else.

She stood, ignoring Overseer Salwey's gurgling coughs.

Where is the safe? she thought, *Lorena told me it was inside something...*

The study was a little larger than the workers' main rooms. Each wall was lined with bookshelves and glass-door cabinets; one of the bookshelves had a pair of wooden doors in its lower half instead of glass.

She stepped quietly over Salwey and knelt by the cabinet. When she opened it, she let out a sigh of relief. The safe sat inside.

Paca fished in her pocket for the scrap of paper, finally bringing it out; it was a little smudged, but still readable.

A strangled snarl came from behind her, and Salwey grabbed her wrist. He yanked her backwards, shoving himself on top of her, closing his hands over her throat.

"You wretched whore," he said through haggard breaths, as blood-laced saliva drooled from his mouth, "I'll kill you!"

He put all his weight onto her throat, squeezing so hard that blinding spots exploded over her eyes. She hit his arms, tried to claw his hands away, but nothing worked. Even through the haze of white spots, Salwey's eyes bore into her own. They were wider than she had ever seen a person's eyes; bloodshot, and brimming with utter madness.

"I'll kill you," he screamed again, "I'll... I..."

The grip on her throat lessened, and Salwey's eyes fluttered. His breathing turned more jagged. Paca glanced at his wound; ripped up organs were half-hanging out of him, thick blood and viscera seeping from it slowly.

He made one last choking sound, and collapsed on top of her. The wound was slick against her body, as his blood soaked through her clothing.

She squirmed out from under him, her heart a panicked rhythm with his full weight crushing her. At last, she shoved against him and came free. Dark red blood had soaked completely through her shirt. Her arms were coated in it too, up to the elbows. She stood, shaking, and returned to the safe.

Next to the safe door was a large square of buttons with Ermoori numbers stamped on them. She tried to recall the written numbers, but they eluded her; she searched her pocket again, but the paper wasn't there.

"No," she said, "it's here. It has to be."

There were no scraps of paper on the ground. She scrambled, breath coming in tight gasps.

She swept her hands through the pooled blood covering much of the floor, but found no paper. Then she looked at Salwey. His corpse, sprawled on the marble, was the only place left to search.

He was on top of me, she thought, *after I took the paper out*.

Paca pulled his body from its resting place, grunting with the effort. She could barely see a sodden rectangle amongst the blood underneath him.

She fought against the dread building in her stomach, and gently picked it up.

It fell apart, the symbols erased by Salwey's thick, dark blood. Paca sat down in the pool of blood, wrapped her arms around her knees, and wept.

Karak

1797

Karak was only a few hours from Omatus when it was taken. He could still see the city in the distance behind him, as swarms of Thearans poured from the southeastern gates.

Explosions still echoed occasionally, low and grating. Then, all of a sudden, a massive blast of fire rose up from the northern side of the city centre; near where Kerberos had been gunned down. It engulfed a huge chunk of the city in a brief but powerful roar of deep red flame.

"What in Asheilos' name was *that*?" asked Laral.

“I’ve no idea,” Karak said, “but I’m sure it has something to do with Kerberos.”

“But he died. We saw it.”

Karak shook his head, remembering what he’d seen in the city.

“We saw him shot,” he said, “I wouldn’t trust anything so mundane to kill a man such as Kerberos.”

“He collapsed, and didn’t get up.”

Karak ran his head over his head.

“We *can’t* assume he’s dead,” Karak said, “even if all the evidence points to it. I won’t trust that he’s really dead until I see the corpse myself.”

Even then, he thought, *I wouldn’t want to get too close, even to his corpse*.

Laral gave him a strange look, but said no more.

“Come,” Karak said, “we need to keep ahead of the people fleeing Omatus.”

The book was in Karak’s pack; he’d had to take almost everything else out to fit it, and even then, the bag was bulging. It felt to him as though he carried the heaviest weight in Pandeia. If the Thearans found him carrying it, they would murder him immediately… whether Kerberos lived or not.

They had already shifted into Omati forms. *Now we just need to get to Aethos unharmed*, he thought, *and this will finally be over*. With the Circle in possession of Sithares’ book, Karak’s debt would be paid, and he wouldn’t have to do any more for them.

He thought he'd escaped his debt once before, when he decided to live in disguise in Omatus. But Zeera found him; she seemed to know where he was at all times. His only real chance at a normal life was to repay the debt, and get the book to Zeera. Even though he'd failed more than once, she wouldn't be able to deny his freedom when the Circle were finally able to destroy Sithares.

I will disappear, he thought, *the moment Sithares is dead. I will go somewhere the Ermoori can't invade, somewhere the Circle won't follow. Aros, perhaps. Or even Tarsheil… if it still exists.* If it was down there somewhere, at the bottom of the ocean, there may even have been Tarsi living there still. The original colony, blissfully unaware of the Ermoori.

In the meantime, he had to survive until they reached Aethos. Laral walked beside him in silence. He glanced at Karak every few moments.

"What is it?" Karak asked, "speak your mind, Laral."

"I'm just wondering what happened," he said, "that made you fall from the Circle's good graces. No one really talks about it, other than rumours. And I don't listen to rumours."

"Most of them are probably true."

"I'd still prefer to hear it from you."

Karak scoffed and shook his head.

"And I'd prefer not to tell it."

Laral might have sighed, but it was difficult to tell over the wind and their heavy breathing.

Before long, they approached the Alpheus. They walked alongside it. Laral had lapsed into silence once again, his breathing gruff and short. Even next to the Alpheus, the air was so dry that Karak's mouth itched. Above them, the black clouds from Sitharkos continued their slow march over Pandeia. They covered most of Omas now.

"Do you think there will be no fire at all," Laral said, "when Sithares is dead?"

"Fire itself will remain," Karak said, "but Fire Magic will die out, I think."

"I wonder if Kerberos will be weaker."

"Let's hope so."

Karak didn't believe it. When it came to Kerberos, he refused to get his hopes up. The Thearan king was an unstoppable, monstrous force, and nothing could convince Karak otherwise. As far as he was concerned, killing Kerberos would be more difficult even than killing Sithares.

"Do you think the Circle will try to assassinate Kerberos after the war?" Laral asked.

"They would," Karak said, "if they thought there was even a remote possibility they could succeed."

"I think you're far too scared of him."

"You wouldn't think that if you'd ever been face-to-face with him," Karak snapped, "anyone who isn't afraid of Kerberos is a fool.

Zeera knows how dangerous he is. You'd mind that, if you had any sense."

Laral smiled, but there was no humour in it. He didn't reply. The Alpheus rushed by them, its deep waters tainted dark grey by the reflection of the smoke above them. Now that they were far enough from Omatus, the mountains between them and the small town of Mara loomed before them.

Karak glanced behind them often; if the Omati moved too quickly, there was a chance they'd catch up. Most of the warriors in Omatus were Thearan now, part of Kerberos' tribe. They came from the deserts, and were used to moving quickly through harsh terrain. They would move faster than Karak and Laral, no doubt... but Karak had left the city hours earlier than them.

We'll just have to keep pace as long as we can, he thought, *and hope we aren't caught out*.

Some time later, Karak looked back again, and froze.

"What is it?" Laral said, following Karak's gaze and gasping when he saw the two figures.

"Oh, no," he said, "is that... Is that *him*?"

"Do you know anyone else that tall?" Karak said, then shot a glance at Laral. "I told you he wasn't killed."

"Now is not the time for that, Karak."

Kerberos sprinted towards them, another Thearan beside him. Were they running at Karak? Did they know he had the book? Karak's heart thundered, his already dry mouth scratching as he struggled to breathe.

"We need to hide!" Laral hissed.

"Cross the river," Karak said, "shift to birds and carry the book across. Hopefully he won't see us."

The Alpheus was wide and deep, but compared to flying over Omatus' great wall, it wasn't so difficult. On the other side, they sprinted up a small hill and into the trees on its peak. Karak shoved the leather-wrapped book behind a large tree. He poked his head out from behind it, watching for signs of Kerberos.

For a heart-stopping moment, Karak couldn't see him. *He's found us*, he thought, *he's crossing the river now*. But then he saw them; still a way back, but coming closer by the second. Karak shifted the colour and texture of his skin to look like grass. Laral noticed, and did the same. They watched in tense silence as the two Thearans ran alongside the Alpheus.

Then they passed. They ran on, Kerberos shooting a glance in Karak's direction but apparently seeing nothing. The man's face was gentler than he remembered. Focused, but without the sheer rage he had exhibited.

"Kerberos heading to Aethos is... not good news," Laral said, "the Circle must be warned."

"What difference will that make?" Karak asked, "he's powerful enough to destroy the Circle if he wants. There's nothing anyone can do about it, warning or no."

"Karak! How can you say that? Don't you care that they could all die?"

Karak tried to find the words to say that it didn't matter if he cared; Kerberos couldn't be stopped. But his hesitation was answer enough for Laral.

"I can't believe this," he said, "you really don't want to help them?"

"What do you expect me to do," Karak said, "go and kill him myself? Try to outrun him and prepare the entire army at Aethos to try to take him down?"

"If you won't, I will."

"*What*?"

"I'll shift into bird form," Laral said, "outpace them, and warn Zeera. You can bring the book."

Without another word, Laral shifted. He sprang into the air as a sleek grey falcon, disappearing within moments. Karak picked up the book and looked back the way they'd come. The crowd of Thearans approached, a dark patch on the grey horizon. Like a coming storm.

Riffolk

1797

Omatus fell in a matter of hours; perhaps half a day. As he had in Tarsium, Riffolk toured the city once it was his. He expected to find Atillus, but the king was gone.

Not a total surprise, he thought, *the palace would have been much harder to take if the king had stayed behind.*

The magic detector built into his helmet picked up no traces of active magic in Omatus. A pity; Atillus had possessed the book of Sithares, and Riffolk would have loved to add it to his collection. He made a note to himself to check the larger detector in his warship; it was months now since he'd last checked it.

His soldiers stared as he passed them. He had taken off his helmet before touring the city, so the men could see his face. When he approached, they stood taller, followed all correct etiquette. His presence turned them into the best of themselves. Over the last few months, Riffolk had begun thinking about the future of Pandeia. The world he would build, and the legacy he would leave behind.

The Ermoori already thought of him as a genius and a great leader. His newer subjects, however, would take a lot more convincing. But once his power was uncontested, they would see that his real priority was science. He only needed their resources, not their suffering. They'd see, eventually, that they could live comfortably under Ermoori rule. That they were only in danger if they chose to rebel against him.

Omatus possessed everything he needed to build a great city. Obviously, it would need to be expanded; but, just as in Tarsium, the foundations were there.

Riffolk watched his soldiers round up the civilians. They would search for weapons, execute any who possessed them, and let the others go. For now, only Shanaken was undergoing construction. The other new cities would come later, when Riffolk had fully consolidated control of Pandeia.

Occasionally, the crack of a rifle echoed through the stone streets. There was no more fighting, but weapons seemed to be a common possession for the Omati.

The battle was far easier than he had anticipated, but there was something that bothered him; the roiling black clouds emanating from the northwest, covering most of the sky above Omatus. He knew there was magic there, and a massive amount of it. The only logical conclusion was that the volcano of Sitharkos was the home of the physical avatar of Sithares.

Every God had an avatar, as well as the physical manifestation of their magical ability; the book. Their avatars held limited power. Riffolk proved that by capturing Taranos all those years ago. But if Sithares was able to create such a drastic atmospheric change, its power must have been far greater than he thought.

Potentially concerning, he thought, *but I will deal with that when the opportunity presents itself.*

The next move was a slight split of his forces. A battalion would go to Tarsius, the trading settlement north of Omatus. After that, the same battalion was to travel up to Theara. But most of his forces were heading for Aethos; it was where he suspected Mara of being, and where the strange gathering of magical people were concentrated.

With Omatus firmly under his control, Riffolk returned to his warship. He had to call the remainder of his forces to Omatus before they began their march to Aethos. A large chunk of his army had still seen no combat. It meant they would be fresh and eager, rested, ready to fight. They had been training on their warships, waiting for the order to deploy.

For the first time in months, Riffolk checked his detector. Aethos was a teeming mass of bright lights. The light to the far south was gone. Had whatever people in that foreign land travelled to Aethos as well? The detector couldn't be broken already, and he hadn't adjusted the sensitivity settings.

He trusted his design. Aethos had been a hotbed of magical activity for most of the war; if there was a group of people gathering there, and magic had disappeared from the unknown regions to the south, it stood to reason they were there now.

Theara contained very little magic. Perhaps the rumours of its abandonment were true; but even if they weren't, a battalion would suffice to take the city.

Along Omas' west coast were four cities, none of which had any magical presence. His research indicated that their populations were smaller than Omatus, and their military forces were minimal at best. They were barely worth thinking about. The battalion assigned to taking Theara could sweep down the western coast and take each city on their own.

After the detector, Riffolk looked over his other devices. He had built multiple, each with its own display screen, and each showing different values. One measured output from the factories in Ermoor against the rate of consumption by his battalions. One of them tracked the movements of his Overseers, commanders and captains via the beacons installed in their armour. There was his teleradio console, which had a basic screen to show which channel it was currently connected to. And then, in its own corner of the lab, his workbench was laid out with blueprints and pieces of his designs. There was a screen on it too, a simple cataloguing system into which he had transposed his blueprints in every detail.

His biggest problem at the moment was resources; he was bleeding Ermoor dry for this war, even after taking everything he could from Shanaken and Tarsium. The factories were slowing down. He had been stockpiling ammunition, tinned food, and batteries for years. But war was a constant drain of each.

They would be able to fight perhaps another few months before they ran out of ammunition. Food was slightly easier, but the ration tins being processed in Ermoor were designed to keep well in travel; any fresh food they seized from their opponents went bad far too quickly. Riffolk had to finish the war, and take over existing supply lines that ran between the cities. It was lucky that such robust trade routes had already been established between Shanaken, Tarsium, and Omas. With time, he could install much more efficient vehicles that would vastly improve the sharing of resources throughout Pandeia. But for now, he had to rely on what already existed.

Riffolk's lab was outfitted to produce copies of his designs; most of them were built using Shadow Magic, which he could provide himself, but he'd also built a machine that synthesized magic. In its bowels was the book of Amalus. Another machine sat next to it with the book of Taranos contained within. They were an endless source of magic; all Riffolk had to do was build a machine that could draw that magic out and form it into solid pieces.

Shadow Magic was already able to form itself into an unbreakable metal. It wasn't as powerful when formed by a machine, but it worked better than anticipated. The only catch was that it took time to build things using the machines. He had been able to produce upgraded armour and weaponry for many units during the last year, but production time was too slow; most of the machine's time was spent producing more ammunition.

The machines whirred even now, a bullet rolling from the chute at the bottom every few moments. From there it landed on a moving belt which carried it through a small gap in the wall, then dropped it into a box waiting in the main storage room. When the box was full, soldiers took it and replaced it with an empty box.

In Ermoor he'd built much larger versions of these machines. He had been able to manufacture hundreds of thousands of rounds of ammunition. But it wasn't enough. If the war went on too much longer, his soldiers would be fighting with their combat knives and their fists. At least their armour would hold up, if it came to that. Though fighting at close quarters would open them up to more precise attacks; a sharp enough blade could pierce the softer fabric between armour plates.

He didn't want to resort to hand-to-hand warfare. The only option was an all-out attack. Overwhelm the enemy as quickly as possible, and cause as much damage as they could. Destroy their morale in one massive hit.

Unlike the armour he'd given to his soldiers, Riffolk's armour recycled his magic through its plating, storing it in smaller versions of the batteries he'd designed years ago. They were built into the armour plates themselves, and connected by wiring. The wire connected to his gauntlets, which in turn created a circuit when he held his weapons. He didn't need to use ammunition. It was a pity he couldn't give a suit like this to every soldier; but it only worked with a magic user.

He double-checked everything again, and then set up the teleradio for a new transmission. He sent a message to Arthor Symond, and then opened the live channel to his overseers and commanders.

"Attention first battalion," he said, "Commander Selway?"

"Selway reporting, sir," the young commander's voice replied almost immediately, low static filling Riffolk's lab.

"Your battalion is to head north," Riffolk said, "you will take Tarsius, then head north to Theara. From there, you will take each city down the western coast of Omas and meet me in Aethos."

"Understood, sir."

Riffolk flipped a few switches, changing channels to speak with all the commanders other than Selway.

"All commanders," he said, "prepare to march for Aethos. The last days of the war are approaching. We must strike without mercy, without hesitation, if we are to show these savages the error of their ways. For the good of all."

Static crackled as a chorus of responses rushed through the speaker.

"For the good of all!"

Eliza

1797

Mathys Corby had been the first truly heroic person Eliza met. He was like a father to her, but so much more than that. He'd been a teacher. He taught her more than anyone else Eliza knew, and he never treated her like she was a stupid child.

He had even taught her about magic; he couldn't use magic himself, but he somehow knew how to control it, how to focus it, better even than some real magicians. In Eliza's life, which had been defined by fear and paranoia, Mathys had been like a sturdy home keeping the storm away.

To Eliza, the four years since his death had felt both like an age and like a moment. Similar to a dream, within which there was no sense of time passing.

What would he do, she thought, *were he with us now*?

Her mother would have been able to stand with confidence, Eliza knew that much. They wouldn't have had to go through months of Mara's grim, grieving silence. The Circle might have been better equipped to fight their enemies with Mathys to guide them.

So many things that might have been.

Eliza had never lost a loved one before. While her mother was grieving, Eliza needed to be strong, to be there to support her when she couldn't take care of herself. But it meant she hadn't been able to grieve herself. She had cried, of course. And she missed him every day. But for four years, she'd not had the time, nor the space, to grieve him properly. Her mother's pain and grief had to come first. Even when Eliza was alone, she hadn't been able to confront the cold dark void that arose when she thought of Mathys' death.

Today, for some reason, his death rose up and took her in a cold, iron-like grip. Aerene asked her to train again in the morning, and Lashek offered to spar a little while after that. She turned them both down.

She didn't even see her mother for the midday meal, as they had done together every day in Aethos. Instead, she lay in her bed, trying to remember what life had been like back in Saford. Before the Circle, before the war.

The days had been simple, if not particularly exciting. Mathys took care of the things Eliza and her mother couldn't. They worked together on everything else. Mathys had looked the same throughout Eliza's whole life; a little grey in his hair, lines in his face, but eyes clear and sure, like the ocean glistening in sunlight.

He seemed to know everything, but when he didn't, he was the first to admit it. Eliza hadn't met many people; being in hiding from the Ermoori meant they needed to spend almost all their time in the house. But out of all those she had met, Mathys was the only one who really listened to her. No matter what she had to say, no matter what else was going on, he always made the time to hear her.

When she was little, her mother didn't want her knowing about the Spectre of Ermoor. Eventually, she learned all about it, and it was Mathys who taught her. He showed her the equipment he'd used as the Spectre, and when he finally began training her, he showed her combat techniques unique to the Spectre.

He trusted her with knowledge that no one else in Pandeia possessed. He trained her to be a better fighter, and magician, than almost anyone else could be. All that for someone who wasn't even his blood.

Eliza had almost nothing of Mathys'. His surviving Spectre gear was back in Saford, hidden under the house. He'd been wearing a suit when he died, but he had spares of everything. If Eliza survived this insane war, she would go back to the house. She'd live there, the way Mathys had lived, and continue taking care of her mother.

If there was somewhere spirits lived after they died, Eliza hoped Mathys would see the legacy he'd left behind. She hoped he was at peace. But most of all, she hoped he was proud of her and her mother. They were fighting to save the world, and Mara was fighting just to function normally.

She still heard his voice occasionally, echoing in the distance of her memories. The lessons he taught her. The advice he'd given, and the stories of his life he'd shared.

He existed almost as a spirit in her mind; just as her father's presence haunted her.

Eliza never set out to think about Riffolk Hayne. But he still appeared, like a beacon pulling her towards him. She never met him, but she knew exactly what he looked like. Even his voice was familiar to her. But more than anything else, his power flashed through her mind, vivid and hungry. She could recognise his presence by that power alone.

If Mathys were still here, he would have protected them from Riffolk. He would have come up with a plan, a strategy that would have played out exactly as he wanted it to. Without him, it was down to Eliza and the Circle Heroes. They were powerful, of course; but they didn't think the way Mathys did, not even Zeera.

Her mother would be unable to fight him. Eliza knew this with absolute certainty. She was beginning to improve her confidence, and had agreed to train with Aerene and Eliza. But it was clear she still had a long way to go.

I just wish Mathys was still here, she thought, *if for no other reason than to see his face again*.

Mara

1797

Mara's training room was finally beginning to feel familiar, a place she could go to centre herself. Using magic still made her uncomfortable, but she was slowly getting used to it again. The secret was feeding her own rage. She took the hatred and fury that emanated from Riffolk, and she made it her own. She imagined killing him. She made herself *want* to kill him, to inflict pain. It wasn't as difficult as she had first expected.

She spent at least a few hours a day in her training room now. Usually by herself, but sometimes with Eliza. She stood in the centre, alone, feeling electricity flow through the machines. There was always magic within her, but drawing it from elsewhere meant she could grow the power in her body exponentially. It buzzed and crackled through her.

They trained every day now. With Ermoor drawing close, there was no choice but to prepare as much as they could. Mara still struggled with nightmares of Riffolk. But as her control over the magic within her grew, so too did the control she had over her emotions.

When he appeared in her dreams now, sneering and powerful, Mara stood her ground. She had to force herself to do so, but it was more than she'd managed before.

Worse than her nightmares was the fact that Riffolk had begun to appear even when Mara was awake. His face lurked in the edges of her vision at all times, icy blue eyes shining with hatred. *He knows where I am*, she thought, *he's closing in, I can feel it*. Even if he didn't know exactly where, Ermoor was taking more and more of Pandeia. It was only a matter of time before they arrived at Aethos. And when they did…

I just hope the Circle is enough to stop him.

She focused on the magic within her. Her eyes were closed, and still Riffolk was there. Gritting her teeth, she fed the beast that was her fury. The helplessness he made her feel, and the weakness, and the fear; she hated him for it. He deserved to pay for making her feel that way.

Though the magic she possessed frightened her, it hadn't always been that way. When she first used it, it protected her. *And it will again*, she thought, *I just need to stop being afraid of it*. She was far more afraid of Riffolk than of Power Magic; just had to train herself to stop fearing her magic altogether.

Her heart beat quickly as the magic coursed through her. It could destroy things easily, but she needed more than simple destruction. She needed control. Zeera had said many times that magic could be used in countless creative ways, and that a magicians' real power came not from the amount of magic they could wield, but from *how* they used their magic.

A ball of crackling yellow lightning formed in her hand. She forced it to keep its shape as it shifted, streaks of yellow arcing from it to hit the room around her. Power Magic didn't naturally form together like water or fire; it sought to take form as bolts, lancing from its origin to the closest point.

A little while ago, Eliza had tried to show Mara how to contain a huge amount of magic within a sphere. It failed, but at least for a moment, Mara had held it by herself.

She was succeeding now, but with far less magic. Still, it was something. Enough to encourage her to keep training. And rage was beginning to feel better than fear. When it crept into her mind, the Power Magic within her swelled to meet it. They worked in conjunction, each amplifying the other.

Riffolk's face was still there. Not quite in focus, but visible enough in the corners of her vision. Her heart hammered, fear rising up, threatening to swallow the rage.

No, she thought, *I am in control.*

The ball of lightning in her hand grew twofold, as though it believed her thoughts. Mara wondered whether her fear had controlled the magic previously; if it responded to her thoughts, why not her emotions? It only gave her more motivation to try to master her fear.

She battled against the fear, trying to block out Riffolk's face. When that failed, she stamped it down, tuning into her hate instead. Her heart filled her ears with its booming and she gritted her teeth against the cacophony in her mind. It was hard enough to focus lately; she couldn't imagine being able to control herself if she came face-to-face with Riffolk.

Paca

1797

"You *killed* her?" Patricia shouted, "why would you do that?"

Paca tried—and failed—to control her breathing. She had changed clothes, bathed in scalding water as she scrubbed viciously at her skin. Her hands and arms were still pink from the blood. After that she had returned to Patricia's home and sat alone, silent in the kitchen until the factory shift was over.

"I don't think it was me," she said, "the gun went off in his hand first, I only shot once, and that was—"

"It's still your fault she's dead," Patricia said, her voice cold, "you could have walked away. You could have done what Overseer Salwey told you to do."

"He didn't tell me to do anything," Paca said, "he was just going to kill me."

Patricia let out a rushed breath. It was only the two of them in the kitchen; Patricia had sent the others to the house next door so they could talk in private.

"So you killed him first?" Patricia asked, "and Lorena? And you didn't even get the key, Paca! What are we supposed to do now?"

"I don't know!" Paca snapped, "I don't know, okay? It all happened so fast. Lorena betrayed us, Patricia. We were never going to get the key."

"She wouldn't have done that, Paca. Why would she? What would she have gained?"

"The Overseers have more control over their servants than the regular workers," Paca said, "it was almost like... she *had* to tell him the truth, even though she didn't want to."

"That makes you killing her even worse."

Paca sighed, shutting her eyes. When she opened them again, Patricia was staring at her, arms crossed, mouth pressed into a tight downward curve.

The sun had set, but an uncomfortable warmth still lay in the air. Regardless, the Ermoori lit fires in their hearths, as though something compelled them to do so no matter the temperature. Paca was sweating, her chaotic heartbeat and ragged breathing only making it worse.

"I know," she said as evenly as she could, "but it was an accident. And even then, I really think Salwey fired the shot that killed her."

"It doesn't matter, Paca. An Overseer is dead." She paced the kitchen as she spoke, gesturing with a hand that was shaking. "If they'd caught us stealing a key, those responsible would have been killed. But murder of an Overseer? They'll kill dozens. Hundreds, just to make a point."

"Then we need to act first," Paca said.

Word spread faster than any rumour in Ermoor's history. Salwey's wife found him shortly after Paca fled the mansion; they had been home, hiding in the opposite wing until Salwey had dealt with Paca. She had heard the gun go off, but remained where she was, presumably until the house had settled into silence.

Paca tried to assemble a group of fighters, tried to band them together before the Overseers tightened their grip on the city. But it was too late; within a day, the Overseers began punishing workers for no reason, working them even harder, and, worst of all, reduced their meagre pay lower than it had ever been. Most of the workers knew what happened; but they didn't know who to blame.

At least, not at first.

She couldn't be certain that Patricia had told everyone, but it seemed most likely. It felt like a betrayal; but it shouldn't have. Paca was at fault. But as word spread of her involvement, the people lost sight of their goal. They were supposed to find enough space for the Tyrans, so all the people in Ermoor could live in at least some comfort. After that, they needed to fight for more pay and better conditions.

Instead of the people working together against their Overseers, anger and fear infected them against Paca and each other. And with every moment that passed, they paid dearly.

The Overseer in Paca's factory watched them intently, his smile a crooked and vicious slash across his face. He held his weapon free of its holster at all times, finger resting lightly on the trigger. Tension filled the massive room like fog, dragging thickly through her throat.

They worked in a frenzy, terrified to make the slightest mistake. But the fear worked against them; Paca heard a clatter to her left as an unsealed tin fell to the floor.

"Up!" the Overseer barked, "now!"

The girl was far younger than Paca. Head down, she rushed to obey. No one else reacted. Paca focused on her work, but glanced up whenever she could. The Overseer trained his gun on her head, and muttered something Paca couldn't hear.

"My husband," the young girl said in a wavering, sobbing voice, "is a soldier. I have a child at home. Please, don't—"

"You want to make your husband a widower?" the Overseer shouted, "you want your child going hungry tonight, wondering where his mother his? Do it. Now."

I should have stolen the gun, Paca thought, *then I could at least have stood up to this Overseer*.

The girl wept loudly, pulling her dress awkwardly over her head. Paca watched the other workers' eyes remain planted on their stations. She looked back up as the girl dropped her dress on the metal catwalk, revealing a simple cotton shift underneath. But the Overseer didn't look pleased.

"Why are you stopping now?" he asked, raising his voice so everyone could hear, "it wouldn't be much of a punishment if I left you in such a modest shift. Take it off."

His teeth were bared like an animal, his eyes roaming over her body with a hunger that churned Paca's stomach.

The girl hung her head. Her shoulders rocked, but Paca couldn't hear her sobs. The Overseer turned his gun to the side and fired without warning. In the open space of the factory, its boom rocked through her body. The girl jumped, whimpering, her cries wavering.

"Now!" the Overseer screamed.

She pulled the shift off, her slim figure pale and trembling. Rage thrashed within Paca's chest. It burned, clawed at her, stopped her breath in its tracks as it fought to escape her.

The Overseer stared at the young girl's body.

“Good,” he said, “now you’ll stay like that until the shift ends. If no one makes any further mistakes, I might let you put your clothes back on before you go home.”

Paca clenched her teeth, forcing herself to keep working through the rage.

I swear, she thought, *that man—that monster—will pay.*

Riffolk

1797

It was time. Omatus was his, and his soldiers had spent enough time in the city that they had asserted control. Even with a culture like the Thearans, they finally recognised the folly of battling Riffolk's army. Fights broke out every day, but Riffolk came to recognise them as expressions of Theara's cultural expectations rather than genuine revolt.

He foresaw some minor rebellions, but nothing his men couldn't handle. Enough of them had died that any fighting force they could gather would be woefully outnumbered.

They marched for Aethos in almost endless ranks. Riffolk led the army in his own tank, watching the horizon through the small periscope he'd designed. Each journey to a new battlefield so far had been by water; if it were possible, Riffolk would have done the same for Aethos. But land was by far the more efficient option. Besides, a large number of his forces were being deployed for the first time. They would be fresh and ready.

Supplies were dwindling. And despite the intensity of his victories, the enemy in Aethos was growing. The Shenza had fled to Tarsium, and the Tarsi then to Omas. After the battle of Omatus, thousands of Omati and Thearans fled west as well. No doubt they had banded together against the threat of a mutual enemy. It barely mattered; Aethos was small, nothing compared to the places the Ermoori had fought and won so far. A combined army of dregs was still merely dregs.

Within the dark confines of the tank, Riffolk's personal guard sat in silence. They were loyal, highly skilled, and immaculate in their professionalism. He had selected only the absolute best. His favourite quality in this small team, though, was their comfort with silence. They spoke only when necessary, and never bothered Riffolk outside of emergencies.

He was free to watch his army's progress through the periscope, and let his mind wander. Calculating the possible numbers they would face in Aethos was difficult, but not impossible; he enjoyed such exercises, even if they couldn't result in solid fact.

It was safe to presume thousands of Shenza had made it to Tarsium, given how many of them were killed in battle over the last couple years. To be safe, Riffolk assumed thousands more were alive and well in Aethos. The Tarsi were far more difficult. No one knew how many existed, but it wasn't many compared to the other races. But they were worth more than a Shenza warrior anyway, even if there were fewer of them. Thousands more Thearans and Omati fled from Omatus.

Ten thousand combatants, perhaps twenty.

At least in Aethos, he thought, *they will not have the advantage of hidden tunnels. Nor the element of surprise.*

Every time a Tarsi had faced his soldiers on an even battlefield, they had been destroyed with ease. Almost all his armour was accounted for, so they had no way to infiltrate his ranks without him knowing. They would be useless against him in Aethos.

The Thearans were vicious warriors, but they used no strategy, and followed no chain of command. Fighting alongside two allies, they would most likely be a liability to those fighting beside them. Now that he really thought about it, *none* of the rebels seemed to have a chain of command. Riffolk didn't believe the fear-mongering propaganda he transmitted through his teleradio system in Ermoor; but the lack of leadership in his enemy's forces certainly painted an unflattering portrait of their societies.

In some ways, it was shocking the war had lasted this long. He understood why it took so long to breach the forest in Shanaken; but once they did, Riffolk should have been able to take Pandeia faster. Though the Ermoori public believed Shenza and the others to be animals, Riffolk had given them the benefit of the doubt. Why would they not possess rich social and political networks? After all, living in a forest didn't preclude one from being civilised, or from developing some form of leadership.

But Riffolk had apparently been wrong in thinking so highly of them. They displayed the occasional spark of low cunning; organised ambushes, short-term tactics. But nothing like Riffolk would have expected. If anything, it only validated his belief that he could build a better Pandeia.

Their last stand against him had little chance of success. As much as they'd had time to recover and prepare, they simply didn't possess the necessary discipline, organisation, manpower, or resources.

There was one unknown; the people that his detector had discovered in the southern regions, off the map, who were now in Aethos. They were powerful magicians. *Very* powerful. That was the only thing he knew about them. Given the ability of his enemies so far, Riffolk remained confident. But he didn't like unknowns.

He couldn't even begin to theorise about these mysterious southern forces. In the absence of any knowledge, Riffolk refused to make assumptions.

I must prepare for the worst, he thought; *another ten or twenty thousand combatants... powerful ones.*

With the situation unfolding as it was, there wasn't much strategizing to be done. All he could do was strike Aethos ruthlessly, and do as much damage as possible all at once. Their walls would crumble the same as Omatus'. After that, it would be straight warfare. Simple, stupid fighting. Riffolk loved designing weapons, but their use outside of experimentation bored him.

The fighting was a means to an end. If Riffolk believed Pandeia was capable of submitting to his rule without a fight, he would have taken a different path.

He cast his eyes again over the ranks of soldiers marching through the desert. Their steps were synchronised, pounding the dry grey earth beneath their feet in a steady rhythm. They moved like automatons; Riffolk smiled at their uniformity. He could almost believe they weren't humans, but machines instead. An army of machines, descending on his opponents with unfeeling efficiency.

Imagine how easy it would be to root out Tarsi spies if my forces were machine, he thought, *there would be no armour for them to steal. Just the machines' casing.*

The Tarsi were watching, no doubt reporting his movements to Aethos somehow. They didn't possess the transmitting technology of Riffolk's teleradios, but they had to be able to send messages quickly by other means; as lacking as their strategic ability was, they had passed information to each other with shocking efficiency in Tarsium.

On top of that, they were able to change their physical bodies to exactly match the features, skin tone, height, and voices of the Ermoori. Ever since learning of this, Riffolk had trusted no one within his own army. He only told his plans to those who absolutely had to know. Even then, he kept contingencies in place for every one of the plans he shared with his command. He would not leave his victory to chance.

Zeera

1797

The Omati are on their way," Zeera said, "with the refugees from Tarsius, and many of the warriors from Tarsium, our united army is almost complete."

Aella shifted in her chair, her face restless and troubled.

"Those Omati are loyal to Kerberos," she said, "are you certain they can be trusted?"

"Their choices are to fight with us against the Ermoori," Zeera said, "or face the Ermoori alone. And without a city to shelter them."

"Kerberos will be with them," Lashek said, "the threat he poses is too great. Even if the Omati join us, he will never be a true ally to the Circle."

"Exactly," Aella said, "no matter what happens, we cannot trust Kerberos or those who follow him."

"News has it Kerberos is dead," Zeera said.

"You can't believe that," Aella said, "not after I told you about the deal he made with Sithares. Dying is temporary for us."

"He's not with the Omati," Zeera said, "my scouts have checked. Why else would he be missing?"

"He will have a plan," Aella said, "he always does. If you think he is not here, then he is. If you believe you are safe from him, you are wrong."

"Aren't queens supposed to inspire their people?" Lashek said, "not that I don't agree with you, but I can't imagine your warriors fighting a war for you if that's how you give a pep talk."

For once, Zeera agreed with Lashek. She would have loved for Aella to be on her side once in a while. Zeera feared Kerberos; they all did. Especially after the attack on Azar. But that didn't mean they should let his existence control their actions. Zeera sighed and turned to Aella again.

"Even if Kerberos comes for us, why would he fight us before the Ermoori arrive? He will only weaken his own army. It makes far more sense to form a truce."

"And then?" the Thearan queen said, "once Ermoor is defeated, there will be nothing to stop him destroying us,"

"We have the Austris Arans," Zeera said, "and the Heroes. You can beat Kerberos in a fair fight, you've said as much yourself."

"He won't make it a fair fight," Aella said. She closed her eyes, and her face became tired all at once. She ran her hand through her stark white hair, and fixed her golden eyes on Zeera once again. "I am worried, Zeera, that you don't understand how grave a threat Kerberos represents. I know we have higher priorities right now, but we cannot ignore him. He must be stopped, and I will do everything in my power to make sure that happens… with or without your support."

"Now *that* sounded queenly," Lashek said.

"I agree that Kerberos must be eliminated as a threat," Zeera said, "but if it comes down to a choice, destroying Sithares is far more important. We will move against Kerberos when the time is right, Aella. I promise. But you must be open to the possibility that he has no wish to come here, and we may not need to face him at all."

"He wants power," Aella said, "he wants to rule. It's why he went to Omatus. If Ermoor is taking Pandeia, that presents an opportunity for Kerberos to take it from them in turn. Why wouldn't he come to Aethos, if that's where the final battle will take place?"

"The same reason he won't fight you in a fair battle," Zeera replied, "He is only interested in a fight he knows he can win."

To her credit, Aella nodded. She let out a small sigh, her shoulders dropping.

"Perhaps you are right," she said, "but I will not let down my guard. We must remain vigilant."

"We will," Zeera said with a nod.

Tension still sat heavy in the room. Zeera couldn't remember the last time she relaxed. Even her sleep was fraught, her dreams chaotic and dreadful.

Every day that passed brought Ermoor closer. And with the spell to destroy Sithares still incomplete, and the sky growing darker and hotter, they were running out of time. *Sithares, Ermoor, and Kerberos*, she thought, *three unbeatable foes converging on us all at the same time.*

And what could Zeera do? Train? Pray? They hosted a combined army of tens of thousands now, but even so… could they really hope to win?

At least Mara's mood was improving. She was even training. What had helped Zeera through the last few years was her study of magic; she hoped the same could happen for Mara. Perhaps teaching Mara would provide Zeera with enough distraction to get her mind off of the looming danger.

"Mara," she said, feeling a pang of sorrow for the pale woman when she jumped at Zeera's voice, "come with me. I would like to speak with you."

Mara

1797

"That's it," Zeera said quietly, "well done."

A flickering symbol gently lit Mara's palm. Within a moment, it buzzed painfully, reminding Mara of the crackling of Power Magic, before it evaporated, leaving nothing behind.

They had been at it for hours now. Mara had requested Zeera teach her one symbol at a time; when she first began teaching her, she traced several symbols separately, and Mara had been overwhelmed.

Zeera was kind and patient, and she broke the symbol down into simple lines and curves, which Mara practiced piece by piece. Finally, after countless repetitions, Mara had recreated a whole symbol on her palm. Alone, a symbol did nothing. It was magic focused temporarily into a rune, barely controlled until it was chained into an actual spell. But once combined into a full word, the magic within the language of Deias was honed. Mara imagined it the way forging weapons had been described to her by Aella. Raw metal on its own was nothing; but once it was forged into a tool, it held its shape forever.

It was a strange feeling. Power Magic worked on intuition; it could be improved with practice, but actually using it was hard to describe except as a feeling. But Deias was almost exactly the opposite. It worked entirely by knowledge and precision, and could be taught to anyone.

"Draw it again," Zeera said, "repetition builds familiarity, and that leads to accuracy. Reliability."

Mara traced the symbol again, remembering each line and curve one at a time. Her palm tingled as the magic glowed. She had been so terrified to learn Deias, but now that she was doing it, there was almost no fear. Deias wasn't a vicious power within her that demanded to be unleashed. She couldn't destroy the room, or collapse a cliff; she only had to draw the right shapes.

Why was I so scared? she thought, *I should have started this ages ago*.

Women weren't taught much in Ermoor. Mara still remembered growing up there, believing that she couldn't learn the things men did. Thinking she deserved the tiny life imposed on girls like her. When she found out she was to marry Riffolk, the most overwhelming elation rushed through her body. At the time, it was the highest she could hope to climb.

How naïve I was, she thought, *believing everything they told me. Believing Riffolk was who everyone wanted him to be.*

If she could only reach back through time, back to when she had been there. If she knew then what she knew now, she would have killed Riffolk before he gained Power Magic. Before he had become Prime Overseer. Before the war.

But if he'd never been given Power Magic, neither would Mara. Without that, she doubted she would have possessed the strength or the ability to kill him.

"Mara?" Zeera asked.

"Oh," she shook her head, "sorry, I was… thinking."

"Anything I need to be aware of?"

Zeera's voice was gentle, but Mara could hear the eagerness behind that, the pressure on her to know everything.

"No," Mara said, "it was… no, nothing. Just thinking about the past."

Zeera nodded. There was a look in her eyes that said she often did the same.

"It's a special kind of darkness," the Tarsi woman said, "the past. Our memories. They can taste sweet, even as they tear at our hearts. Tread carefully, Mara."

I was stupid for wishing to change the past, Mara thought, *I should be focusing on changing the future*. But even with Power Magic, and the Circle, could she really do what needed to be done? She was getting the hang of Deias, but Zeera was teaching her a very simple spell one symbol at a time; how long would it take her to learn the real spell?

On top of that, the other Heroes began learning Deias far earlier than Mara. She was playing catch-up, but moving too slowly. *Why did I wait*, she thought, *fear? Is that all*? Looking back on it, the fear seemed so small. She had been in real danger a few times; but most of the time, the only thing she'd had to fear was the thought of Riffolk. Only the thought, not the man himself. So why had she been paralysed for so long?

"Let's focus," Zeera said, her voice cutting through Mara's churning thoughts, "draw the symbol again."

She did, but the third line went crooked, and her palm buzzed painfully as the spell burned away.

"It's alright," Zeera said, "try again."

Mara sighed, rubbing her palm where the spell had failed.

"How do you control fear?" she asked Zeera, "I can't get past it. Every time I feel like I've made some progress, it comes back."

Zeera frowned.

"I don't believe you *can* control it," she said, "you just need to get used to the way it feels. If you're accustomed to it, you will be able to think more clearly when it comes."

It made no sense to Mara. The whole problem was that she couldn't get used to it, no matter what she did. It grabbed her heart, her mind, and squeezed. She couldn't breathe when it took her, let alone think clearly.

There has to be a way to control it, she thought, *there must be*. Zeera wouldn't have lied to her, but maybe there was something she didn't know… Mara had to hope, otherwise fear would always be waiting to overtake her. *Riffolk can be beaten*, she thought, *he's not a God. He's a man.* Somewhere deep down, Power Magic pulsed like the distant glow of a far-off storm.

Zeera cleared her throat gently, and gave Mara a look.

"We must keep practicing," she said, "I know you have a lot on your mind, but this is the most important thing."

"More important than the possibility of freezing when it comes time to act?"

With a quick sigh, Zeera gave her a short, sharp smile.

"The surest way to combat fear," she said, "is intense training. If you practice something to the point that you can do it without thinking, then your fear will not stand in the way."

Mara fought against the urge to snap at Zeera. No matter what she said, the Circle's leader never changed her mind.

She knows, a voice that sounded like Riffolk's said, *that you cannot do what needs to be done. She is merely humouring you.*

"No," Mara whispered.

"What?"

"I can do it," she said, louder this time, "he won't convince me. Zeera, tell me I can do this. Please."

"Of course you can."

You have no power that can stop me, Riffolk's voice said, *there is nothing you can do.*

A sick, cold feeling spread through Mara's gut. She couldn't understand what it was, but suddenly she knew something was wrong. Riffolk had been plaguing her since she first escaped him, but this was different somehow.

"Mara," Zeera prodded, "what is it?"

"It's... *him*," Mara said, "in my mind. At least, I think it is. Something is off about it."

"If it's different," Zeera said, "could it be Taranos? You've said Taranos has never spoken to you."

Mara paused.

Was it possible? The others had heard the Gods in their heads... what if Taranos simply sounded similar to Riffolk?

Aerene had told her recently that she only had to think for Aurath to hear her. She wondered if Taranos had spoken to her before, but she'd mistaken it for Riffolk. Or if the only reason the God never spoke to her was that she never reached out.

Are you there, she thought, *can you hear me*?

Silence beat down on her like the heat of the sun.

Kerberos

1797

They had been running for days. Or had they? He wasn't certain of anything anymore. Nomiki called him Kerberos, but the name Atillus kept floating up through his murky thoughts. Broken pieces of memory flashed in his mind without order, like shattered glass reflecting sunlight as it fell through the air.

Who am I?

After a moment's hesitation, he realised he had been waiting for something to answer him. Expectation filled him, almost as though a voice should have been speaking to him from somewhere unknowable.

Wait… There *had* been a voice. Somehow, in his previous life, a voice spoke to his mind directly. He couldn't remember anything more, except that the voice stirred up a buzzing storm within his chest. What was it? Where had it come from? And why was it silent now?

"Nomiki," he said, "tell me about myself. What kind of man was I, before I was killed?"

Though it was daytime, the thick black smoke churning above them turned the desert into a dark grey void. Despite that, a vicious heat filled the air. It rushed into his lungs, scratching and burning. Kerberos found himself strangely unbothered by the heat, other than its effects on his breathing.

"You were commanding," she said, "certain, and you displayed more integrity than I have ever seen in another living person."

Kerberos—or perhaps Atillus—searched for those things within himself. He knew much about the Ermoori and their horrific invasion of Pandeia, thanks to Nomiki… but he didn't know himself.

"You planned everything," Nomiki continued, "I can tell you the plans you shared with me, but I'm sure there were many more you never told anyone."

"Tell me everything you know."

Nomiki told him about his earlier days in the Omasi deserts. He had joined a small tribe at around sixteen years of age, and eventually fought his way to the title of Tribe Leader. He taught Fire Magic to every Thearan who followed him. Over a period of years, Kerberos had overtaken more and more tribes, joining them all to his own.

All of this, which took twenty years, had turned out to be Kerberos' long-term plan to return to the secret city of his birth, Omatus, and claim the crown as king. His real name was Atillus Argyris, middle son of the Argyris family.

He had spent two decades in the brutal deserts of Omas, facing danger and death, all to achieve a singular and seemingly unrelated goal. As they ran, and Nomiki talked, Kerberos' mind went back to Omatus. It was no wonder the city had called to him; it was his city. He had not only been born into it, but had earned the role of king.

Knowing his connection to the city made him furious to be leaving it behind to the Ermoori. Though the details Nomiki told him were unfamiliar to him, the logic behind them made perfect sense. No matter how long it took, Kerberos would take Omatus back.

Nomiki paused for a brief moment, breathing heavily as they ran. Then she went on, her eyes level with the horizon, glistening gold in the dark grey around them.

"When the war started," she said, "you were already planning ways to destroy Riffolk. He'd sent spies to Omatus to steal the book of Sithares. He was gathering each book in an attempt to gain and study the magic within them."

"Did he succeed?"

"Not entirely. You killed the spies, and went to Ermoor yourself to confront him. You read the prayers for Power and Shadow Magic, and gained them for yourself."

Kerberos frowned; he searched within himself, and found several wells of vibrant energy waiting to be tapped.

"Then," Nomiki said, "you went to Azar and learned the prayer of Asheilos. You broke into the headquarters of the Circle of Shadows, and took what you wanted. They were powerless against you. A group of powerful magicians dedicated to destroying Sithares, and you swept them aside like they were nothing."

"Fire Magic feels more powerful than the others," Kerberos said, "but coupled *with* the others, any magician would be able to defeat any opponent."

"There is no space for modesty here, Kerberos," Nomiki replied, "very few magicians could have done what you did."

She glanced at him, her eyes narrowed.

"There was something else," she said, "something you told no one but me."

"Speak."

"It was called Deias. A form of magic accessible by anyone, unlike the elemental magic of the Gods. There are some spells which will be useful in Aethos."

They slowed to a walk and she showed him how it worked. It was a written language, the runes of which possessed innate magical power. The runes were drawn one over the other until a word was made. Once the spell was complete, it manifested as a physical piece of magic. Nomiki taught him a spell to disguise his face. It only worked on the face; he could do nothing about his height or bulk.

"The effect is temporary," Nomiki said, "and it takes energy to cast it, so be careful about when and where you use Deias."

Kerberos nodded. He practiced as they walked, going over the runes until he knew them properly. It didn't take long; patterns came to him easily, it seemed.

They ran again, eventually drawing close to the Alpheus just before it snaked into a massive mountain range.

"Through the mountains," Kerberos said, "or around them?"

"These aren't as difficult to get through as those in the desert proper," Nomiki said, "it will be faster to go straight through."

A strange feeling sparked within him then, and a dim shadow fell over them both. Kerberos glanced up to see a large bird, barely visible in the grey sky.

"I've never seen anything like that before," Nomiki said, "it's certainly not native to Omas."

Without hesitation, Kerberos brought a ball of Fire to his palm and launched it at the bird. Though his body instinctively knew how to wield magic, his broken mind was at a loss; the fireball screamed past its target, and the bird dived.

"Get it!" Kerberos said.

They launched into a sprint, Nomiki hurling fireballs as Kerberos focused on controlling the magic within him.

Ahead of them, the bird swooped into the trees. They almost lost it, but something bloomed in the corner of his mind; a pull, dragging him in the direction he'd last seen the creature. He sensed something similar as they ran parallel to the Alpheus, but had ignored it.

Can I sense magic? he thought, *or is it something else*?

Nomiki's Fire streaked through the air, but she had lost sight of the bird and Kerberos shouted through the roaring chaos.

"There, between those trees. It is hiding behind a trunk."

Nomiki didn't question him. She didn't hesitate even a moment, immediately sending two fireballs arcing into the tree Kerberos indicated.

I do hope I deserve the loyalty of a warrior like that, Kerberos thought, *she is incredible*.

The tree cracked, fire sweeping up its surface and consuming its leaves within moments. Kerberos sprinted for the creature as it readied itself to flee again. Nomiki was half a step behind him, heading for the other side of the tree.

Just as they caught sight of the bird, it streaked from the branch and disappeared over the trees.

"It is heading for Aethos," Kerberos said, "and it does not move much faster than we do. If we push, we can catch up to it."

The next few hours were a blur of chaos; Kerberos and Nomiki crashing through the forest as quickly as they could. They used Fire Magic to help them, burning their way through the trees and fuelling their strength with its raging energy.

Ahead of them, the bird twirled in the air, narrowly avoiding their attacks. It looked different now, smaller and a similar colour to the trees. Kerberos could still feel its presence in his mind somehow. He was getting used to using Fire Magic again, figuring out how to control each fireball's path through the air. He could make them follow the bird; each successive attack was getting closer to hitting the creature.

Finally, just as the mountain range fell away around them and the desert opened up once more, Kerberos hit the bird's wing with a glancing blow. The ball exploded. An instant later, Nomiki's latest attack struck the creature too. It dropped from the sky and slammed into the grey dirt.

They ran up to it, and Kerberos frowned when he saw it up close; it was a short humanoid creature with mottled grey skin, giant eyes and no hair. Nomiki knelt and inspected the body.

"Tarsi," she said, "no doubt on its way to report the fate of Omatus to the Circle of Shadows."

Kerberos nodded, facing west towards Aethos. He would have sent scouts out for information at a time like this as well.

"It's lucky we caught it," Nomiki said, "before it could tell Aethos you survived the battle."

"You told me about the Circle," Kerberos said, "and about my bargain with Sithares. If they are as well-resourced as you say, they will already know of our immortality. We must assume they know I am alive, even without this scout."

Nomiki stood, glancing in the same direction as Kerberos before looking at the man himself.

"I hadn't considered that," she said, "but it makes sense. We will need to be even more careful than I anticipated when we arrive."

"I was hoping for more travelling refugees," Kerberos said, "so that we could blend in with a group."

"Perhaps we should have waited for the Omati fleeing your city," Nomiki said.

"No. We needed to get ahead of them and the Ermoori. I need some time before the war reaches Aethos."

They left the body where it had fallen, and ran west.

By the time they reached Aethos, the horizon bled deep crimson. To the south, the city stretched out over the cliff in a massive overhang, with no visible support structure.

"That's new," Nomiki said, "we had heard rumours, but to see it…"

"What is it?"

"It could only be Austris Ara," Nomiki said, "the mythical city that worships the God of Air. They must have joined the Circle. I thought it wasn't real."

"Austris Ara," Kerberos mused, "an entire city of Air Magicians ready to fight Ermoor…"

Air Magicians…

"I need to get into that city," Kerberos said, "whatever it takes."

Nomiki nodded. Again, there was no questioning or hesitation from her. *I would be lost without her*, he thought, *with my mind as broken as it is*.

"The only way is through Aethos," Nomiki said, "so our immediate plan remains the same. We will seek entry posing as mercenaries, and lay low until the opportunity presents itself to infiltrate Austris Ara."

"Then, we disguise ourselves as Omati," Kerberos said, "or Austris Arans, and seek out the book of Aurath."

He possessed four types of magic now. With Air Magic added, he would be the first person in history to wield all five at once. No one knew what that much power would do to the one who possessed it, but there were theories. Nomiki had discussed them with him at length.

"Do you really believe it could turn me into a God?" Kerberos asked.

"Four decades ago, I wouldn't have believed any of what is happening now. I wouldn't have believed any of the things you achieved out in the deserts." She smiled, a wistful look as her golden eyes twinkled. "Back then, none of us believed in Sithares. We were living the old ways, but with no understanding of what our culture really meant. You changed all that. If anyone could become a God, Kerberos… it is you."

Paca

1797

Weeks passed, weeks of pain and grim work amidst the constant threat of death or worse. When the workers first discovered Paca's part in Salwey's death, they treated her with open contempt. Many of them ignored her completely. But she was also shoved, yelled at, and cast out from the common living spaces.

After the first week of the Overseer's new horrific regime, their hatred finally found a new target. The Overseers pushed them harder every day. Paca waited as long as she could, enduring the work, the threat. Twice she stood naked on the catwalk, trying to ignore the gun's barrel trained on her and the Overseer's ravenous eyes roaming over her body.

It was the second time standing like this that she got the idea.

The Ermoori women were so driven by shame and modesty that being naked left them paralysed. Paca hated the man's eyes on her body, but she had grown up in near total darkness, and cramped living quarters. Her people had no time for shame. The gun was her biggest concern; but during her second punishment, she watched it more closely.

One Overseer must watch all the workers, she thought, *and he cannot focus on everything at once...*

She thought about it a while after that second time standing naked in front of the Overseer. He relaxed a little as soon as her clothes hit the catwalk, as though stripping someone of their modesty gave him more power, more confidence. As though it reduced the likelihood of an uprising.

After the shift ended, and her second punishment, Paca walked home with the others. There had been a moment on that catwalk, where the Overseer noticed the workers moving slower than normal. He shouted at them to speed up. In that brief moment, the gun dipped as he leaned to the side. It was barely an instant. She hadn't reacted in time. But if Paca watched, waited; if she was ready for the next time...

Each factory was controlled by one Overseer. His gun was the only reason Paca's people hadn't already taken him down. That, and his position up on the catwalks; there was no way to sneak up to him without being seen and shot.

For the first time since Salwey's death, Patricia approached her that night. Paca sat outside on the short wooden stairwell that joined Patricia's tiny house to the street. She had taken to sitting out there every night during their supper, staring into the fog and thinking about Ermoor. This far south, the cobblestone streets began breaking down into dirt roads that led gradually into swampland. Insects chirped constantly here, the sound by turns harsh and soothing.

"There is still some food inside," Patricia said, "if you'd like some. I know the others haven't been too generous lately."

"Thank you," Paca said, "but no. I'm not hungry."

Why am I lying about that, she thought, *what do I gain from going without a meal*?

"I'm sorry about today," Patricia said.

"It's not the first time."

"Still... what the Overseer is doing... it needs to be stopped. I've heard from the other factories that they're being treated the same."

Paca stared into the soft, shifting grey fog that covered everything.

What will it take to just live a comfortable life? She thought.

"I'm not surprised," she said instead, "the Overseers have no reason not to be terrible to us."

"*What*?"

She shook her head, gesturing dismissively with a hand.

"I just mean their world is so different from ours. They're *rewarded* for being ruthless. It makes sense for them to use us the way they do, take what they want." She sighed, picking at the old wood underneath her. "Our religion was phony. We learned that the hard way. But theirs is even more phony... I've been on the surface what, a couple years now? And even then, it's obvious to me."

"What do you mean?" Patricia asked, "what's obvious?"

"They talk about their God being loving, about how being faithful to Him is the most honourable thing anyone can do. But look at the way they treat even their own people. Does anything they do actually fit with their teachings?"

Patricia looked as though she was about to respond, but frowned instead. After a moment, she sighed.

"I suppose you're right," she said, "again. You already altered my faith, you know. Everything, really. I used to believe Ermoor was perfect. Looking back on it now, I can't believe we put up with life under the Overseers all this time."

"We don't have to," Paca said, "I have an idea."

Three days later, they stood at their stations, working harder than ever. But now they had a plan.

Some of the workers disagreed with Paca; it meant a couple of the factories wouldn't be joining in their mission, but there were still enough of them to make a difference.

At least, I really hope so.

She checked the large clock near the factory ceiling; she was fluent now at reading the time. Their plan depended on it, so that everything happened at the same time across each factory. Taking a deep breath, Paca dropped the unsealed tin in her hands. Though the factory was filled with buzzing, rumbling, and humming, the clatter of the tin sounded like an explosion.

"You!" the Overseer shouted, "up here, now!"

There were already two other workers on the catwalk. Paca took a long breath and trudged up the metal stairs, trying to stop her heart from racing.

She stepped in front of the other two workers. The Overseer levelled his gun at her; *so far, according to plan*, she thought, *now comes the difficult part*. He gestured with the gun, eyebrows raised expectantly, and she complied.

Only a little longer.

All she had to do was wait, now; let the Overseer believe he still held all the power.

They had already agreed on the timing; one hour after Paca was put on the catwalk, the Overseer would die. She kept her eyes on the clock, forcing herself to appear meek.

When the time came, Paca was ready.

The sudden clatter of another tin hitting the floor struck the same instant as the hour. Paca snapped her eyes back to the Overseer.

Have to time it perfectly.

He leaned to the side, searching quickly for the culprit. As he found her, his face contorted into a scowl, and he jabbed a finger towards her. As he did, the barrel of his gun dropped.

Paca leapt at him, one hand snatching the gun and the other—formed as a fist—ramming into his temple with all the force she could muster. She twisted the gun down. It fired, its deafening roar shaking her to the core. Her body lit up as though on fire, every part of her screaming with the intensity of the moment.

She wrestled the gun from him as he hit her anywhere he could reach. The other girls on the catwalk rushed him, pinning him down as Paca half-fell, half-crawled away with the gun.

It was then she saw the jagged wound in her leg. An instant later, the pain hit; a rush of vicious, sharp pulses shooting through her thigh so brilliant that her vision disappeared under a flash of sickening white.

"Release me!" the Overseer shouted, "all of you are dead, you hear me? Dead!"

"Shut up," one of the naked workers pinning him down said, her voice trembling and fragile, "we're in control now."

Paca's vision swam in and out as her breathing faltered. Pain still streaked through her body, but her focus was fading.

After a while, gentle hands took hold of her.

“Paca,” Patricia’s voice said from somewhere, “oh, God. Give me the gun. Someone, tear that shift! We need to stop the bleeding. Quickly, she won’t last much longer!”

As she fell into a cold fog, Paca heard one last booming roar; the gun had been fired again.

It was the last thing Paca heard.

Karak

1797

In a life of mistakes and failures, Karak couldn't remember his last genuine victory. As he emerged from the mountain range, breathing heavily, the open desert assaulted him with its vicious dry winds. Aethos stood on the horizon.

He trudged through the sand, every muscle burning in the dark grey heat. *So close*, he thought, *only a little longer*. Perhaps less than a day, if he didn't stop moving.

The book seemed to grow heavier the longer he carried it. Sand coated his lungs and throat, making him rattle with every breath. He hadn't been wounded in their escape from Omatus, but he may as well have taken arrows to the chest and limbs.

I am going to die out here, he thought, *with Aethos in sight. The book will never reach Zeera. I cannot make it.*

He had given so much to repay his transgressions. None of it was enough; even in death, he knew Zeera would never forgive him. Not unless he got the book back to her in time.

One step, and another. He stopped looking ahead, stopped hoping that Aethos would draw closer. There was only the next step, and the scratching heat of the desert. His feet were raw; he dared not look back at his tracks in case he saw blood.

Everything was pain. Pain, and blurred shades of grey. It was as if the world itself sought to keep him from his mission.

Perhaps I have died already, he thought, *and this is the punishment that awaits cowards and traitors*. Maybe he would walk for the rest of eternity, Aethos always on the horizon, desert winds forever battering him with searing grey sand. How would he know? He already had no idea how long he'd been walking.

He barely felt the book in his hands; he had to keep glancing down to make sure he still held it. His feet and legs burned one moment, and then went sickeningly cold and numb the next.

The desert stretched before him. He trudged on, now, out of pure spite. *I will make it*, he thought, *even if it kills me. It will be worth it to see Zeera's shocked face*. He had failed too many times before. Never again. If this was to be his fate, so be it; he would walk forever.

Later, whether a day or a week, he would never know, Aethos loomed before him. He looked down again at the book; it was nestled in his chapped arms. His eyes were so dry that blinking only hurt more.

"Hey!" someone called from above, "are you Karak?"

They spoke Tarsi.

"Is this real?" Karak tried to yell back, his voice the same hissing rasp as his footfalls on the sand dunes.

The gate in front of him creaked open, and two Tarsi rushed forward to help him walk. They tried to take the book, but Karak pulled his arms tight around it.

"For Zeera," he croaked, "only… for her."

Their hands pulled away from the book, slipping instead under Karak's own arms. They took some of his weight, and Karak might have wept if the desert hadn't already sucked all the moisture from his body. The flat stone ground of Aethos slapped against his raw feet, pain lancing through him even with the two Tarsi assisting him.

They took him straight to Zeera through blessedly cool hallways. When their eyes met, her mouth dropped open. But instead of disbelief, her eyes shone with concern.

"Karak," she said, "you look like a corpse. Asheilos bless you, it's a wonder you're alive."

Karak tried to tell her that he finally had her damned book, but all that came out of his mouth was a dry rattle.

"Get him water," Zeera snapped, "as much as you can, right now."

The Tarsi who had helped him set him gently down on a chair and rushed away. Zeera took hold of the book, and Karak had to force himself to let go; his fingers had held it so hard for so long that relaxing them was almost impossible.

"Well done, Karak," she said, "your debt is paid. Rest."

She had barely finished speaking when the cool, tidy room slipped away.

Riffolk

1797

The journey was long and slow. He had designed the tanks to be impenetrable and powerful, but they moved slowly over shifting desert sands.

First the thick forests slowing us down, he thought, *then the hills of Tarsium. And now the desert.*

He had to wonder when he would finally see his tanks go at full speed. The horseless carts he invented could move much faster than the general public realised. Given enough time, and the resources he'd gain after the war was done, he'd be able to create vehicles far beyond anything he'd done so far.

There were hundreds of blueprints waiting on the war's end. Things he designed as a purely theoretical exercise, things that simply weren't possible until now. But with all of Pandeia belonging to him, all of its resources his, there was no end to what he could build. Each country was flush with unmined minerals, unique living materials, and other untapped resources. The petrified trees in Theara's Dead Forest were technically wood, but with the strength of steel. The natural minerals in Tarsium contained endless useful properties. And the brilliantly deadly animals of the Shanaken forests possessed venoms and other useable defence mechanisms.

Before the war, Riffolk had conducted missions to obtain many of the resources he knew existed throughout Pandeia. There was still much he didn't know, but he knew enough to draw up hundreds of designs. The people of Pandeia thought his invasion was the first time he had taken from them, but he had seized much more than just their land, and for a long time before the war.

Before even that, he had travelled to places the people of Pandeia couldn't even imagine. He had seen magic, had seen technologies, that were impossible in this world. Since those travels, all Riffolk wanted was to outdo what he had seen others achieve. And now he could.

His blueprints were locked away in the command room of his warship. With the long, slow journey in his tank, he longed for a workspace where he could create new ideas.

Not long now, he thought, *once Aethos is taken, I can focus all my time on producing new technologies.*

The soldiers with him—his elite personal team—sat with perfect posture. They kept their helmets on, their rifles resting in the slots next to each of their seats. At first, they had held their rifles ready; but eventually their captain asked Riffolk's permission to store them instead. If they were attacked, they wouldn't need the rifles anyway. The tank would handle most attackers without the need for his soldiers to get involved.

Even after putting their rifles away, they remained silent and professional. The army stopped each night for rest, erecting tents and scavenging for food. Riffolk stayed within his tank most of the time, but every few nights he met with the commanders in their tent, measuring their progress on the map and discussing military plans for Aethos.

Natural sources of food were hard to come by. Even so far south, where the desert gave way to more trees and other signs of life, there was little to eat. The soldiers hunted birds, but those were barely worth cooking. There were large lizards, which no one was willing to eat, and massive spiders the men shot but avoided going near. How did the Thearans survive out in the desert proper? At least here the Alpheus provided fresh water from the mountains. What did they do to survive where there were no rivers or flora? Riffolk was a genius, but there were many things he didn't know. Living off of nature was one of them, he wasn't ashamed to admit.

No one should live like that, he thought, scrounging around a desert for the barest hint of food. When I finally have my way, there will be no savagery of this kind ever again.

Civilization would come to all.

A few days from Aethos, Riffolk's teleradio crackled to life in the dim confines of his tank.

"My lord?" a voice said through the rough static, "can you hear me?"

"Speak," Riffolk said.

The voice broke constantly, static hissing through the garbled words. Riffolk only made out a few words.

"... the workers... organised... Tyrans... several Overseers..."

"Stop," Riffolk said, "stop the tank. Open the hatches, extend the receiving line."

The soldiers obeyed instantly. His tank ground to a halt. When the hatches opened, he was hit by a dry, oppressive heat so strong that it pulled sweat from his skin even through his armour. He pulled the teleradio out to the tank's roof, and plugged in the bulky earphones he had designed for privacy. Sitting on the tank, he settled into a somewhat comfortable position.

He clicked the transmit button on his portable teleradio.

"Repeat," he said, "the line is bad."

"My lord," the Overseer said, "the workers have started a revolt. They've somehow organised themselves, with escaped Tyrans. Yesterday they took over most of the factories, and several Overseers were killed."

Riffolk sighed, shaking his head gently.

"I *knew* I should have had them all killed when I had the chance," he said to himself.

And perhaps I should have left a unit behind after all, he thought, *not that Arthor was right.*

He hit the transmit button again.

"Where is the Lord Commander?" he asked, "he should be organising a response. And it should have been him notifying me."

Riffolk was met with silence.

So, he thought, *Arthor finally let his conscience overtake his loyalty. But was it desertion, or suicide*?

"Answer me, Overseer," he said, "I will not ask again."

"My... my lord," he said, "I thought you knew. I was told you had already been informed... no one knows where Lord Commander Symond is. He's been missing almost two years now."

Desertion, then. I'm surprised it took him that long. He must know there is nowhere he can hide that I won't find him.

"I will deal with Arthor later," Riffolk said, "and I will punish Overseer Hanlon for his negligence."

Hanlon was always a spineless creature, Riffolk thought, *his only saving grace was his talent for organisation. But the Overseer for Governance should have known he had to inform me of drastic changes. What he did is almost as bad as desertion.*

"What is your name, Overseer?" he asked.

"Bernadi, my lord," he said, "Elliott Bernadi."

"You have done well, Bernadi. I will not forget your loyalty."

"Thank you, my lord."

Riffolk cast his eyes over the desert to the north. Tyrans and Ermoori workers joining forces; it was as ridiculous as it was dangerous. Not for the first time, a swell of relief rushed over him, that he had rendered Tyra's energy production redundant.

The factories are another matter. We need them.

"Is the factory production still halted?"

"Yes, my lord."

"And they want more pay, do they? Or is it more… *respect*?"

"Well, both, my lord," Bernadi said, "and they want a place for the Tyrans to live."

Riffolk sighed again. Control had been so much simpler when the people had been kept in the shadows. When he had ruled from the shadows. He didn't regret becoming a public figure; but the Tyrans first discovering the nature of their confinement was a pity. Now the rest of his people would know there were secrets being kept from them. And he would have to share more resources among the people just to feed more hungry mouths, instead of into his research.

Still, Riffolk's goal was to create a cohesive global society, one in which all his technology could be utilised. To achieve it—like it or not—he had to keep his people happy. Otherwise, all his time would be spent stamping out rebellions.

He closed his eyes.

"Fine."

"My lord?"

"Give it to them, Overseer," he said, "whatever they want. Our resources are running low. It's far more important that we keep the factories working. We'll deal with the rebels responsible after the war. Keep a note of the likeliest suspects."

"Yes, my lord."

Mara

1797

Aerene sat across from Mara in the Ermoori training room, poised and graceful. The blue of her skin glowed even without direct sunlight. There was a slight smile on her face as she looked back at Mara.

"How are you feeling, Mara?" she asked.

"I… well, I don't really know."

Aerene nodded slowly. She did everything slowly, except sparring. Mara had to remind herself of how old Aerene was.

"So much has happened in your life," the Austris Aran woman said, "I'm sure all of it has been overwhelming individually, let alone altogether."

"It's not so much what *has* happened," Mara said, "but what's going to happen."

"Yes, the war is weighing on us all."

"Not just the war," Mara said, "the ritual to destroy Sithares… Aerene, have you ever been certain of something happening in the future? I mean, a specific thing, that you had no way of knowing?"

"No," Aerene said, "not in the way that you mean. Time is a fabric unseen to all but the Gods. We can only see the finished patterns they weave when our time comes."

Mara cleared her throat, trying to breathe through the hammering of her heart.

"For a while now," she said, "I have known… *known*, with total certainty, that I will die at the end of all this. How can I explain this feeling?"

"Just so. A feeling."

"No." Mara shook her head, her arms crossed. "That's just it. It's more than just a feeling. I know it just as well as I know the sun will rise each day."

"If that is true," Aerene said, "and you have glimpsed the fabric before it is woven… peace can only be found in acceptance. If you know what will happen, it only means you have seen your part in the coming events. It changes nothing. All we can do is play our parts as best we can."

"So, I simply accept my fate? Lie down and let myself die?"

"Of course not," Aerene said, "we all must die eventually, Mara. Even the Austris Arans. But we still control our actions until that time comes. You can still fight. You can still help us."

Mara took a shaky breath.

"It's the fear," she said, "it stops me from doing anything. How can I help if I'm paralysed?"

"You must remember our mission," Aerene said, "the reason we are fighting. Fear is momentary, it... it only appears to stand in our way. But our purpose, what we will gain from winning, *that* is forever. You need only stand against fear for a moment to win."

Lashek

1797

The Austris Arans were immensely powerful. Lashek still had trouble trusting them, but even with their sheer power, they still trained and sparred diligently. He respected that about them, albeit begrudgingly.

He had taken to watching Aerene and Eliza spar together. If there was one thing that could convince him to trust the Austris Arans, it was the friendship those two shared.

They moved in perfect, complementary patterns. *How many times have they trained together*? Lashek wondered, *to move so well*?

He didn't envy whoever came face-to-face against the two of them in a real battle.

Eliza's stance was impeccable, her balance never wavering. Her skin buzzed with yellow lightning. She stayed low, hands spread apart, each crackling with ready attack spells. Aerene floated a foot above the ground, wings spread, a look of serenity melding with intense focus on her blue face.

They traded blows, magic arcing around the room. Lashek held his *Kaizuun*, watching them with Shadow Magic revealing much more than his eyes alone could. Aerene was powerful, there was no denying that; but Eliza was something else. The aura around her was so powerful he didn't even need the *Kaizuun* to feel it. No matter how many times he held his *Kaizuun* near her, Lashek never failed to be shocked by her sheer power.

He was almost just as shocked at how close Eliza and Aerene were. There had been no period of suspicion or doubt for the two young women. From the first day they met, they had been friends. Lashek discovered a day or so after Mara escaped from Aethos that Aerene had been the one to find and save her.

Was that enough for him to trust them? Shaela had refused Zeera's plea to the Austris Arans to search of Sithares' book. She even refused to fight against the Ermoori, if they arrived after the book was destroyed.

Aerene swept sideways across the room, narrowly avoiding a bolt of lightning. A blistering barrage of Air and Power sliced through the room from both women, too fast for Lashek to follow it all. Though Aerene's power couldn't match Eliza's, she possessed a mastery of technique that Lashek had never seen before.

The Austris Arans were more or less immortal, and had never lost touch with their God; they learned magic the way Shenza children learned to use swords.

All that knowledge, he thought, *and all that power… and they would still stand back and watch us be destroyed by the Ermoori.* Lashek's entire nation had been built by Amalus to defend Shanaken. Protecting the forest, and maintaining the balance of life within it, were all that his people knew. He couldn't imagine how empty life must be without such a purpose.

He had been struggling with anger against the Austris Arans, but in that moment—without warning—something different rippled through his body. It was cold and quiet, stilling the rage.

Pity. I pity these immortal beings.

They lived thousands of years, wielding power unseen by the rest of Pandeia for generations. But they had no purpose. Their exiled city drifted through the southern skies while they prayed and hunted, simply… waiting.

Waiting to be called on by the Circle, he thought, *no wonder they resent us.*

The newfound pity within him was accompanied by something even more miraculous; calm. For the first time in a long time, Lashek was at peace.

You are almost ready.

Amalus' voice was gentle, but filled his mind with a power that left him breathless. It had been months, likely even years, since he'd heard that voice.

You must live by the tenets. When you can do so, the path forward will be revealed.

He frowned; *why wasn't I told before now?* The Shenza were supposed to live without anger. He knew that, of course; but his feelings towards the Austris Arans were justified. And he hadn't acted upon them, at least not with physical violence.

But you were *told. Countless times, from when you were old enough to talk, you were taught to adhere to the tenets.*

"I didn't know it applied to this," Lashek whispered, "you could have told me earlier."

The tenets apply to all situations. You do not pick and choose when to live by them.

There was a slight pause, and Lashek could have sworn he *felt* Amalus smile.

And if I had told you to let go of your anger earlier, would you have been able to do so?

"I, well…" he sighed. "I suppose I wouldn't have found it so easy."

I could not have done it for you. We can only interact with the physical world in certain ways. You must find the path forward for yourself.

Lashek closed his eyes, shutting out the flashes of light and sound in the room. *The tenets*. No Shenza could forget them.

Peace without weakness.

Strength without aggression.

Growth without forgetting.

The Shenza were peaceful, strong, and looked to the future. They always remembered their past. They never sought out violence, but they would defend their land against any foe. He couldn't remember the last time he stopped to really think about the tenets.

I have been angry too long, he thought, *and what have I reaped from it?*

He took a deep breath. His hand still lay on the hilt of his *kaizuun*, its energy flowing into him. It sat in its sheath, a viciously sharp blade, providing him with the ability to see magic. Power flowed through his body even without the blade being drawn.

Peace without weakness.

He looked at Aerene. Even in the midst of intense training, her face was still, a slight smile lighting her gentle features. Her brow was furrowed in concentration, but there was no anger there.

Strength without aggression.

Lashek had come so far. But in the shadow of the looming war, and in his anger at the Austris Arans and the Ermoori, he had forgotten where he'd come from. His purpose. *We lost Shanaken*, he thought, *but we cannot lose the war*. They were all more powerful than they had been before; every member of the Circle. Lashek had been grievously wounded when Kerberos broke into their headquarters in Azar, but he had trained intensely before then. And again ever since he'd recovered enough to train once more. But his fear and anger had overtaken him; he knew that now. *I am a protector,* he thought, *if not of Shanaken, then all of Pandeia.*

Growth without forgetting.

Eliza and Aerene moved off to the side, sitting on a stone bench against the wall. Eliza was panting, beads of sweat on her forehead. Aerene looked as calm and composed as ever. She didn't sweat.

Lashek ran his hand over his face. It was time to live by the third tenet. It was time to grow.

"Aerene," he said, "are you up for a sparring match with me?"

Paca

1797

Pain was the first thing she felt. Then her eyes opened, and a small, fire-lit room faded into focus. She lay on a small couch, just large enough for her to lie down.

She groaned as she adjusted her position and her thigh flared viciously. The room was empty of people, but decorated in the same style as Patricia's house. She wore a simple white ankle-length shift, more comfortable than the standard clothing worn by most Ermoori workers. Its fabric was shockingly smooth, like oil made solid.

Paca let out a breath, closing her eyes as her mind refused to clear. She pulled the shift up to see the wound; it was wrapped in clean white fabric. Pain still pulsed from the wound, but it helped not being able to see it.

"Ah, you're awake," a woman's voice said from behind Paca, "good. How do you feel?"

Paca tried to say something, but her throat was so dry that she choked instead.

"Oh, dear," the woman said, "hold on a moment."

She came back a moment later with a mug of water, finally coming into Paca's view as she handed the mug to her.

"My name's Sarah. We've not met yet, but I know Patricia quite well. I work as a nurse, but Patricia told me to be ready today in case I was needed."

Paca drank the water, closing her eyes as her parched throat softened. She cleared her throat.

"Thank you," she said, "but what about everyone else? The factories? What's happened?"

Sarah frowned slightly. She was a little older than Paca, her face gentle and kind, creased with lines. Her greying hair was tied back neatly.

"I wasn't told much about what you were doing," she said, "I'm sorry, but I don't know."

"Where is Patricia? Anyone else from the factories?"

"You need rest, Paca," Sarah said, "I'm sorry, but I have no answers for you right now. Frankly, you're lucky to be alive at all. Please, drink more water, and get some sleep."

She awoke to the room looking exactly as it had before. There was no way to tell what time it was. A mug of water sat on a small table next to her; she downed it all. Next to the table was an odd metal pole, with a transparent bag of liquid hanging from a hook at the top. A cable ran from the bag's bottom to the crook of Paca's elbow, which was wrapped with fresh white fabric.

Paca groaned again, her mind still foggy. She had never experienced this before. No matter how much she shook her head, her head never cleared.

Low voices arose from nearby. They grew louder, and then Paca heard footsteps enter the room.

"—sure I heard her wake up," Patricia's voice said, "yes, see?"

"Patricia," Paca said, "finally. Tell me everything."

Patricia sat in a chair opposite Paca, eyes as wide as her smile. Sarah sat next to her, though she looked far more concerned.

"We lost a few people," Patricia said quietly as her expression mellowed, "but it was a success. We took the factories, sent workers to tell Overseers in Millbourne, and made our demands."

"So now we wait for their response?" Paca asked, "are the factories still under our control? What about the Overseers we captured?"

Her mind raced, still fuzzy and stumbling over so many thoughts.

"They are ready to meet with us, Paca. We've been waiting on you. Sarah has been looking after you as much as she can, so as soon as you're feeling better—"

"I am!" she said, "if they want to meet with us, we should go!"

"You're in no state," Sarah said, "the medications you're on, the wound... You still need to heal."

Paca shook her head, "I'm fine. I just need some food, and to clear my head. This is too important to wait any longer."

Almost two hours later, they were taken to an imposing building in Millbourne. Paca could finally think again, though she was still a little woozy and her leg burned with every step.

Four government officials stood at the back of the room, each aiming a pistol at her. She sat next to Patricia. Across from them at the large heavy wooden desk sat the Overseer of Production, a silver-haired man named Harrison Archer. He moved slowly, head turning from Paca to Patricia and back again.

“You have killed several Overseers,” he said in a chillingly calm voice, “and disrupted the flow of sorely needed resources to Prime Overseer Hayne’s forces. And now you sit here, demanding to be rewarded for the damage you have wrought.”

“We don’t want a reward,” Paca said, “we want our basic needs met without toiling away for our entire lives.”

“You are workers,” Archer said, “that is your purpose. The fact that you have caused this much damage should mean a death sentence for you.” His lips curled up into a distasteful snarl as he snatched a sheet of paper from the desk. “However… I have been advised that our priority is the war.”

Patricia glanced at her, wearing the same frown as Paca.

“What does that mean?” Paca asked.

“It means,” Archer said in a cold, clipped voice, “that in the short term, we will do whatever it takes to resume production in the factories.”

“Good,” Patricia said, “we need more pay, we need living spaces for the Tyrans, and we need to be treated better by the Overseers. I think it’s also important that we—”

Overseer Archer held up a finger.

“Enough,” he snapped, “don’t look so pleased with yourselves just yet. Let me make it clear to you that there will still be consequences.”

He stood, and the officials behind him shifted to keep both women in their sights.

"You will be granted your demands," Archer continued, "and the workers will begin their work again as soon as possible. But you two—" he jabbed a finger towards them, "—and all the other rebels who participated in your treasonous little plot, well… after the war is done, you will all be executed. Publicly."

Kerberos

1797

Aethos was tense, thousands upon thousands of warriors frantically training for the coming battle. They mingled, clearly attempting to combine their respective strategies and skills into a cohesive army. Among the chaos, Kerberos and Nomiki were ushered in disguised as Omati.

Shenza, Omati, Thearans, Tarsi, and Austris Arans all lived together. They trained and ate together. Despite being in the midst of a brutal war, they shared compassion for each other. Despite each following a different leader, they had formed an alliance without conflict between them. Kerberos couldn't remember his previous plans—only what Nomiki had told him—but he knew he wanted Omatus to be a thriving, peaceful city. Even without his memories, the urge to do right by his city was powerful.

Seeing the people of Pandeia banding together so effectively gave him hope for the future of Omatus; peace was on the horizon, even if a dangerous enemy stood in the path. He needed only to survive until the war was done. Eventually, Omatus would be his again. If he could gain Air Magic, his goal would only be that much easier. He could be a God himself… destroy Ermoor with a mere thought, and take power over all of Pandeia.

Nomiki walked beside him in silence. They pushed through the tide of the crowd, tall white spires that peaked over Aethos' rooftops marking their way towards Austris Ara. Curious eyes followed him; with his face disguised, there was less chance of discovery, but he towered above the people they passed.

Aethos twisted and turned before them, its ancient streets lined with equally ancient-looking trees. The architecture was similar to that of Omatus, but with taller roofs and large open windows. Most of the buildings were made from the same grey stone. A few, however, were built from the white stone Kerberos could see in Austris Ara. They had the look of temples, large and ornate.

As they approached the border between Austris Ara and Aethos, the streets grew quieter. Austris Arans were tall, almost as tall as Kerberos. But they ignored any people who weren't their own kind. Kerberos and Nomiki simply walked into the city.

"That largest building," Nomiki whispered, "must be their temple. The book will be there."

Kerberos nodded. He had been thinking the same thing. The Austris Arans were arrogant and prideful; they would not hide their God's book the way others had.

People of Omasi descent filled the streets of Austris Ara; they were ignored just as Kerberos and Nomiki were. Called Aethans, they dressed simply, their eyes downcast. *Servants*, he thought, *or slaves*. Before Kerberos ruled Omatus, slavery had been rampant throughout the city and its surrounding farmlands. Kerberos had put an end to it.

But as downtrodden as the Aethans looked, there was a sense of purpose in their eyes, and their stance. It was as though they *wanted* to be in service to the Austris Arans.

Kerberos affected the same stance as those around him. It barely mattered; he could have dropped his disguise entirely, for all the Austris Arans seemed to care. They walked towards the temple. No one looked at them, not even the Aethans; but Kerberos couldn't help feeling uneasy as they approached the massive stone building.

Could it be a trap, he thought, *does the Circle know I am here*?

He cast his eyes over the neat stone streets.

"Watch for the Circle," he whispered, "this is part of their city now too."

“They are busy,” Nomiki whispered back, “preparing to fight the Ermoori.” She glanced around her. “Still, let’s get to the book quickly.”

Lashek

1797

His *Kaizuun* gave a slight hiss as he swung it down. He breathed evenly, the motions of the *Zuunshai* flowing through his body, deeper than thought. Around him, in the shadows of his training room, were ancient trees and young plants. They had been transplanted from all around Aethos.

He breathed in the dark, damp smell of earth, leaves and bark. The *Kaizuun* was perfectly balanced in his hand. Its blade moved as precisely as if it were one of his limbs. The trees around him left a sense in the air, a feeling that told him where they were. He could move easily through the room with his eyes closed, even while performing the *Zuunshai.*

The final move was a downward stroke. Lashek sheathed his blade, eyes closed in the dim room. Despite keeping his breaths even, his heart refused to slow. The war was almost upon them.

He moved to the room's centre, untied his *Kaizuun* from his waist sash, and sat on the soft dark earth. The blade lay across his lap, his hand on its hilt. He focused on nothing but the air flowing in and out of his lungs.

Two years ago, Lashek had found peace in what Amalus called Shadow Meditation. It had taught him how to perform it long ago, back in Shanaken.

I need to get back to that, he thought, *my soul is too troubled to think clearly.*

Before he tried, he calmed his mind. It took a long time. He let go of his frustrations, his doubts, his fears. There had to be nothing in his head, a clean slate, so that he could be receptive to Shadow Meditation.

He had already found some measure of forgiveness for the Austris Arans; a sudden and surprising revelation while watching Aerene and Eliza spar. If he could do that, he could let go of everything else. *Only for a little while*, he thought, *until I can find what I need in the Shadows.*

In the years since arriving in Aethos, the trees and plants in Lashek's training room had grown. Some of them were almost tall enough to reach the high ceiling. Their life energies filled the room like a mist, cool against his skin and tingling in his lungs.

When he attempted Shadow Meditation two years ago, he had managed to connect to the life throughout Aethos; not only that in his training room. It was overwhelming, but it was only through such diversity that he'd managed to find the peace he needed. Over the two years since, that peace had dwindled. If he was going to survive the coming war, he needed it back.

Gently, slowly, Lashek reached out to the magic around him. Shadow Meditation could lead to vast knowledge, or it could result in madness. The key to surviving it with the mind intact was to give in to the sheer volume of information and energy. It was like the ocean; a person couldn't fight against a wave, or the tide. They could only learn to work with the water's natural forces. Lashek immersed himself in the swirling life that flowed around him, like lowering himself into a deep, dark lake.

At first, he was lost. Ancient memories stored within the plants of Aethos swept over him all at once. There was nothing but chaos, like a crowd of voices screaming over each other.

He tried to let it flow, tried to catch something he could understand. All of a sudden, the chaos thrashed his mind, a flare of vicious noise that clawed at his head. He was lost in it now. The room was gone, his body left behind. All that existed was his mind, weak as it was, and centuries—no, *millennia*—of memory stored in the old trees of Aethos, overlapping simultaneously.

Pain seared his mind. A dark, open void approached. It was happening; he was being pulled towards an abyss. Madness. Lashek fought against the tide, holding himself together as he dragged his way back to the training room.

He gasped as the Shadows subsided and he came back to his body. His head ached as though it had been frozen solid. The room was dark, cool, and… strange. For a moment, it was unfamiliar to him. He blinked in the darkness, casting his gaze around the trees. How long had he been lost in Shadow?

His body was tense and sore. He stood groggily, grunting as he stretched. Pulsing echoes of the memories he'd experienced clashed, his mind reeling from the sheer weight of it.

"Too much," he said quietly, "*way* too much."

It was a wonder he could still think at all.

How had the meditation helped him so much last time?

You are so close. Trust yourself, and Shadow Magic.

His *Kaizuun* gave him strength. But it didn't stop his rushing thoughts, or his racing heart. *Trust myself,* he wondered, *sure. Why not. That's how wars are won, isn't it? Just believe in myself.*

There was no answer from Amalus, but he could have sworn the God of Shadows rolled its eyes.

Do Gods even have *eyes*?

There was no answer to that one from Amalus.

Lashek walked gingerly to the closest tree. Its bark was smooth under his hand, its leaves large and grey in the dim light.

He remembered finding the knowledge that life would continue no matter what carnage was wrought by the war. It still amazed him that trees and plants possessed memories. Even so, how were they so certain that everything would be okay? *Life will continue*, their memories had said, *regardless of war, no matter how many die; the Shenza will live on*.

But how could he believe that? Ermoor was destroying everything in their path. They had massacred his people, levelled many of the great trees in Shanaken. They were stripping cultures to the bone, and laying the foundations for their own oppressive country to spread to all of Pandeia.

How would the Shenza live on if every part of their lives was decimated?

The year's end was drawing near. For some reason, that left him with a sense of urgency. Perhaps the thought of a new year was simply a reminder of the war marching inexorably towards them.

Amalus said nothing more, but a kind of reassurance swelled from it to him. It came from the tree too, and from all the life in Aethos. He grabbed it, seized it with as much will as he could muster.

Things will happen as they must, he thought, *there is little I can do to control the flow of events*. The words weren't entirely his; there was a peace and wisdom to them that certainly didn't belong to

Lashek. Nevertheless, it rang true. He only had to hold onto the thoughts long enough to meditate.

Again, he sat on the cool black earth. He settled his *Kaizuun* on his lap, resting his hand on its hilt. His heart still beat too fast; he breathed as slowly as he could.

Here we go again, he thought, *settle your mind, Lashek... if you can.*

The trees around him, the earth below him, and the air above him all swirled with energy. It was old and slow, like a vast ocean. There were countless layers of it, weaving together and veering apart, flowing through the room in graceful waves.

All he had to do was let it take him. With a gentle exhale, Lashek settled into the magic.

Immediately, he was swept into the chaos again. But he relaxed and let his mind move with it. Memories, like echoing thoughts, crashed over him, all at once. He wasn't looking for anything specific; last time he had gained reassurance and perspective… *that would be nice*, he thought, *but maybe the trees have changed their mind recently*.

There were countless plants in Aethos. In this state, Lashek heard all of them at the same time. They didn't *think*, exactly; but they did possess experiences that lived within Shadow Magic itself. It battered his mind like a storm made of memories.

How far back do they go? he wondered.

As if in response, the tide of memory rushed around him, until a drastically different Aethos appeared in his mind's eye. It was colourful; vibrant paints coated each stone surface, and the trees were young and flowering along every street.

Lashek was still caught in the tide. It took him into Austris Ara, which was entirely unchanged, and into the massive temple. Four Heroes stood at the stone dais; the original Circle's Heroes.

On the dais in front of them lay a large steel chest. It was closed and locked, and the Heroes surrounding it looked exhausted.

They've just trapped Sithares, he thought, *this is it. The end of the first war of the Gods*. Lashek peered at the dais; two scrolls lay close to the Austris Aran Hero. They were whole, Deias runes written neatly across both.

The spell... the *complete* spell.

I wish I could have seen how they managed to write the runes down without them disappearing, he thought, *Zeera and Aerene don't even know how that was done*.

Shadow Magic pulled at him, the tide trying to move him through memories. It took everything Lashek had to stay in place. He took a step towards the scrolls, fighting for every inch his foot moved. The room was cold; empty, despite the Heroes in front of him. They hadn't seen him, but he wasn't sure if that meant they couldn't, or if they were simply focused on other things.

"We will split responsibility for the scrolls," the Austris Aran Hero said, facing the Tarsi Hero, "I will take half into the southern reaches. You will keep the other, and bury it as deeply as you can."

Lashek pushed further, barely moving, grunting with the effort. An unimaginable weight pulled him down, as though he was the Eternal Mountain itself attempting to walk across Pandeia.

He was moving so slowly. How long had he been trying to cross the room?

The Heroes were still speaking, but he could no longer hear them. Their voices had become blurry and slow, fading into the background. Time and memories dragged at him with so much force he could barely think.

He stared at the scroll which contained the missing runes. It was all that mattered. If he could read them, memorise them...

But even as he thought it, his mind buckled under the pressure of moving against the tide. *Shadow Meditation can lead to vast knowledge*, Amalus had said, *or it can lead to madness*.

Lashek pushed harder, speeding up as much as he could. The Heroes took their scrolls and walked towards the door into the temple, the Tarsi thankfully last. With a scream, Lashek forced himself forward; he had to move with focus, pure force of will. His body was sitting in his training room. It felt like a physical effort, but he had to remind himself it wasn't. *Focus*, he told himself. *You can move by thinking*.

They were almost out the door. He pushed through the strangely thick air, moving with his mind instead of his body. *I need to go faster*, he thought, *I'm so slow*.

Everything was slow; but Lashek was even slower. Why? He had appeared in the past, such a long time ago, but now he was here, he could barely move. *I made it here. I can make it to the scroll. Focus, Lashek.*

He had only begun meditating to find peace; but in trying to follow the tenets, Shadow Magic was presenting him with the chance to complete the spell they needed. *I just need to reach it*, he thought, *come on. Just a little closer*. But no matter how hard he pushed, he couldn't close the distance.

A quiet voice, so quiet it seemed to reach him from a vast distance, floated into his mind.

When you fight the flow, it fights back. Open your mind, let it happen.

Lashek forced himself to relax; it felt strange, almost like he was giving up. But the Heroes didn't get any further away from him. Instead, everything stopped.

He took a breath. Trying to control the flow of Shadow Meditation was how he'd failed earlier. If he wasn't careful, it could also lead to insanity. What good would reading the scroll do if he lost his mind in the endeavour?

Peace. Without weakness.

Amalus had known; this was his fate. But he had to stick to the tenets. Just as he did when he began the meditation, he let go. He opened his mind. He stopped trying to grasp the thing he needed, stopped trying to force his way through the room.

He kept his mind loose, but held the scroll at the centre of his thoughts. *Trust Amalus*, he thought, *and Shadow Magic*.

At first, nothing happened. But as he relaxed further into the Shadows, time began to move again. The Heroes moved again, walking slowly through the door. Lashek moved too; but it was more like the room slipped past him.

The scroll drew close. He lifted his hand, but he couldn't touch it. *Too eager*, he thought, *let it happen*. He could only get the scroll if he stopped trying to get it.

As ridiculous as that sounded.

Around him, the room swirled like smoke. Suddenly a different room materialised; it was small and empty but for the scroll resting on a stone pedestal. There was no sign of the Heroes. Nothing between Lashek and the scroll.

Before he did anything else, even reach for it, he took another deep breath. He had to be sure this was the real opportunity.

Finally, he touched the corner of the paper. It was real; its rough texture whispered against his skin, its dry dusty smell clung to his nostrils.

Before he could pick it up or read it, he was pulled backwards. The room distorted around him, lengthening as he moved, the scroll staying where it was for a moment. Desperate now, Lashek snatched at the scroll. He took hold of the corner, and then everything happened all at once.

A rushing sound roared in his ears, and the room flew away from him so fast he couldn't breathe.

"No!" he screamed.

Around him a hurricane of darkness swept him into its chaos. He felt nothing, saw nothing, only the rushing sound so loud he thought it would destroy him.

He woke up slowly, not feeling much of anything. It was as though his mind was dripping slowly from the endless void of Shadow Magic back into his body. When he was fully awake, fully himself again, he sat up. His back was damp from the cool earth, but his hand held onto something dry.

Blinking, he opened his hand. A scrap of paper, crumpled and torn, fluttered down to the dirt.

Kerberos

1797

The Air Temple was massive. Kerberos and Nomiki strolled through its hallways, searching as subtly as they could. Every now and then, they had to duck into a room to avoid Aethans. The Austris Arans ignored them, but not all of the Aethans did.

Austris Ara was quieter than Aethos. There were people everywhere, but they moved slower. There was no pervasive sense of dread here, like there was in Aethos. It was almost as though the Austris Arans didn't care about the war at all. Kerberos might have believed they had no intention to fight in the first place. They certainly weren't training as hard as the other armies.

They headed up every flight of stairs they found; it stood to reason that Air Magicians would place their temples and holy artifacts up high, where there was nothing else but air.

His memory was still failing him. Not only that, his thoughts were scattered, many of them coming from nowhere and clashing with the others. He couldn't even be certain he was thinking the same way he would have before resurrecting… was he the same person? Would he reach the same conclusions now, or make the same decisions?

The process of dying and coming back might have even allowed Sithares the opportunity to corrupt him further.

All I want is justice, he thought, *civilisation. Peace*.

But at the same time, there was an urge within him, powerful and deep; to fight. To kill. How could he do what was best for Omatus with that hunger burning inside him? And was it really him, or Sithares? The God of Fire infected people's minds, twisting their thoughts and emotions until they were merely a puppet. A tool, to be used and discarded.

Kerberos had been discarded; before he died, Sithares abandoned him because he only wanted to rule peacefully over Omatus. When Nomiki told him, a strange kind of awe crept into her voice, as though she couldn't quite believe he would make such a choice.

Nomiki inhaled sharply, a quiet hiss of surprise.

“Do you hear that?” she asked.

Kerberos nodded.

“A group,” he said, “most likely Aethans.”

They slipped silently through a wide double door into a large room full of shelves. Each shelf contained dozens of scrolls and books, almost all of which looked ancient. Several of them were covered in familiar runes. A brief flare of hope sparked in Kerberos’ chest, but he quelled it; the Book of Aurath was unlikely to be in this room. He couldn’t feel any magic.

Footsteps grew louder outside the door. *At least four*, he thought, *but maybe five or six*. The Aethans often moved in groups. But they were meek, and always unarmed. If Kerberos and Nomiki had to fight, it would be an easy win.

Kerberos motioned for Nomiki to wait against the wall next to the door. He did the same on the opposite side.

“Wait,” a deep voice in the hallway said, “there’s someone here.”

A moment of silence crept through the door. Kerberos and Nomiki carried only a dagger each; Aethans weren’t allowed weapons, and a dagger was all they could conceal.

Both doors opened. Five Aethans entered the room, followed by an Austris Aran. He was taller than Kerberos, and floated a handspan above the floor. He was the only one with a weapon. Kerberos couldn’t see Nomiki. They hadn’t made a plan of attack. But there were seconds—at most—until they’d be seen.

Kerberos and Nomiki stepped out from behind their doors at almost the same moment. They both launched a fire ball at the Austris Aran.

He blocked one, but the other slammed into his back, exploding, flame clinging to him as he screamed.

The Aethans panicked. They were frozen in place, too terrified to run and too weak to fight. Nomiki threw another fireball at the Austris Aran, who barely managed to deflect it with Air Magic. Kerberos drew his dagger, rammed it into the throat of the nearest Aethan, and shoved the dying man into one of his fellows hard enough to throw them both to the ground. He leapt over them and buried his blade in the Austris Aran's side.

With a roar, the blue-skinned man twirled, Air Magic exploding out from him in an unstoppable wave. Kerberos was flung backwards into the wall.

"You dare sneak into Austris Ara?" the man said, "you will pay for your insolence."

Kerberos said nothing, as did Nomiki. They glanced at each other, and Kerberos nodded. Instantly, Nomiki launched herself at the Austris Aran. Barely a moment later, Kerberos rushed at the man as well.

"Fight, you useless vermin!" the Austris Aran shouted, "or I'll throw you off the city myself."

The four surviving Aethans attacked; but their movements were furtive, weak. They attempted to drag Kerberos from their master, but even the three closest to him couldn't do it. The last Aethan was on Nomiki's side, trying in vain to distract her from the Austris Aran.

Kerberos slammed his fist into the face of one of the Aethans. There was a wet smacking sound and the man dropped heavily, his head cracking against the hard floor.

The Austris Aran swept Kerberos up in another powerful Air Magic throw. Kerberos twisted in the air, preparing to brace himself against the opposite wall as he launched a blade made of Shadow at his attacker. He barely even thought about it; it just made sense to him, without practice or planning. The blade moved so quickly even he didn't see it; he only saw the spray of purple blood on the opposite wall.

With a grunt, the Austris Aran dropped to his knees. Kerberos landed balanced and ready. There were still Aethans to kill; survivors couldn't be allowed.

One of them seemed to have had the same idea; he scrambled for the door. If he could raise an alarm, get the attention of other Austris Arans, Kerberos and Nomiki would be overwhelmed. Even as things were, the noise of combat likely meant they had mere moments before discovery.

Kerberos sent another blade at the Aethan, but it thudded into the door next to the man's head. He shrieked and ducked, clawing at the door handle. Nomiki threw herself at him, ramming her blade into his head through the temple.

The Austris Aran was still alive; barely. Kerberos' Shadow Blade had sliced straight through the chest, right where the heart would be on a man. Did Austris Arans possess the same anatomy as Thearans, other than the wings? Judging by the man's laboured breathing and rapidly slackening gaze, at least their hearts were in the same place.

Kerberos stepped in close, swatting the Austris Aran's hands away from their attempt at disarming him. He slashed the blue man's face, again and again, ignoring his screams. When there was almost nothing left of the man's face, Kerberos took a handful of golden hair and slammed his head into the floor hard enough to feel the impact all the way up to his shoulder.

"Oh no," one of the Aethans said, "by Aurath, what have you *done*?"

Another of the Aethans vomited, dropping to his knees as the colour drained from his face.

Nomiki killed all but one of the remaining Aethans, the last trying to flee and not even reaching the door as Kerberos cut him down. They waited in silence, listening for more guards or servants. For the moment, there were none.

"We will not have long," Nomiki said, "but we are close to the top floor of the temple."

"Wait," Kerberos said.

A series of scrolls on one of the shelves was covered in familiar runes. Deias. He snatched them, tucked them into his belt, and nodded to Nomiki. Anything he could learn about Deias was valuable.

If only there was time to look through the rest of the material here, he thought.

They rushed through the hallways, daggers in hand. He had hoped to get through the temple without raising any suspicion, but the further in they ventured, the more conspicuous they looked. They had to get to the book, and back out again, without drawing the attention of the entire Austris Aran army.

All I need is time enough to read the prayer, he thought, *after that, I will possess all the magic in Pandeia.*

A deep, cold energy leeched into him from somewhere nearby. It had to be the book. The Austris Arans themselves emanated magic in powerful waves, but this was different.

A pair of Aethans almost ran into them as they turned a corner; without pausing to think, Kerberos buried his blade to the hilt in the closest man's eye socket. The second drew in a breath to scream, but Nomiki slashed his throat before he could shout. He held his spurting throat, mouth gaping as he tried to breathe.

They left the corpses where they fell; they had no time to clean the blood, so moving the bodies was wasted effort.

One more flight of stairs, wider and more ornate than any of the previous flights, led up to a large golden double door. They looked at each other; this was the place. Now was the time. He only wished he was fully himself, so he could experience the importance of this moment without the fog of death filling his mind.

They opened the door together. Beyond it was a rooftop, open to the wind rushing in from the south. He looked to the southern horizon; with his memory broken, there was no way to be sure, but it felt to him that he'd never seen the ocean this way before.

He vaguely remembered being on a ship, but what little crept up from the fog was the cramped cabin in the ship's belly. Had he been hiding? Smuggling himself someplace?

White stone columns lined the rooftop, but there was no ceiling connecting them. There were several stone daises. One directly in front of them on the opposite side to the door, and one on each far side of the roof. On the centre dais stood a pedestal; the other two were empty.

They approached, Kerberos peering over the roof for a sign of the book, straining to hear through the wind in case the door behind them opened.

The pedestal faced away from them. He couldn't tell what was on it, if anything. If the book was here, the Austris Arans were arrogant. There were no vaults, no locked doors, nothing to stop a thief from taking their most prized possession.

The humming of its magic pressed insistently into his body. It was on the pedestal. He *knew* it was.

"I will only need a moment," he said, "to memorise the words. After that, we need to find a fast way out."

“If we both read the prayer,” Nomiki said, “we could use Air Magic to escape… a risk, but a calculated one. We are both talented with magic.”

“Are you suggesting we fly out of here?”

“It would be faster than walking.”

“If we succeed.”

They rounded the pedestal; the book wasn’t there. But still, somehow, Kerberos sensed its presence.

What is that, he wondered as something shifted against the pedestal’s top.

It resembled a trick of the light, like the sun reflecting off of something completely transparent. He placed his hand on the pedestal; but it stopped before he could touch the stone.

“Of course,” Nomiki said quietly, “the book of Sithares is bound in Fire. This one is bound in Air.”

Kerberos slid his hand to the edge and pulled up gently; as he opened the book, pages materialised before him. He smiled as he read the prayer aloud. Nomiki’s voice joined his own.

When they finished, a hurricane erupted around them. The wind was so vicious Kerberos was certain he would be thrown off the temple roof. But he didn’t move. It was as though the Air moved through him, like he weighed nothing at all.

It was then, in that moment of exaltation, that Kerberos realised they were both floating. Kerberos focused, and in response to his thoughts, he rose further into the air. It was almost too easy; all it took was a little concentration.

By the time the wind died down, both Kerberos and Nomiki were standing on the roof again.

Kerberos had never experienced such power.

Finally, he thought, *all five magics are mine*. Even with his memory broken, he knew how long he had waited to possess each of the elemental magic types. It was said that any who could do it would become a God; but despite feeling more powerful than ever, he felt nothing like a God.

Now was no time to wonder about it; echoing footsteps sounded from behind them, muffled by the wind and the closed golden door. Nomiki's eyes snapped to look at him. They both looked at the edge of the roof.

"Now or never," Nomiki said, "do we fly, or fight?"

Kerberos glanced back at the door.

Without another thought, he leapt off the roof.

Zeera

1797

She had been reading non-stop for hours. Her eyes were dry, her back aching. The Austris Arans and the Tarsi both kept records of history, but she had found no reference to the missing part of the spell. She couldn't remember the last time she'd slept.

So when Lashek offered her a scrap of paper, she sighed in frustration.

It was late in the afternoon. A tiny nub of wax was all that remained of her latest candle. The papers and books she had read lay in a huge pile to her left, to her right a much shorter pile. She rubbed her eyes, breathing in a slow pattern, when he barged into the room.

"Zeera," he panted as he rushed through the door, "you need to see this."

The last thing I need is some note, she thought, *I've read everything twice over already.*

But something about the paper sent a slight chill through her chest. It wasn't until she saw the runes on it that she realised what it was. Her heart stopped. The entire *world* stopped. After all her searching, all her stressing… and Lashek simply handed it to her.

"W–where?" she whispered, "how?"

"It's a long story," Lashek said, "and honestly, you wouldn't believe me if I told you."

"Lashek. This is important."

"I... well, Shadow Magic allows for a sort of meditation. I communed with the life in Aethos."

"You mean to say that the trees and plants in the city told you where to find this?"

"Not exactly."

"Out with it, Lashek," Zeera snapped.

"Yes, yes. Well, I wasn't told where the scroll was... I was taken there."

"To the scroll? But we have the scroll."

"I went back to when it was whole."

Zeera took a deep breath, rubbing her eyes. It really had been too long since she'd slept.

"You travelled," she said, "through time itself?"

"Not on purpose. It was more like I was... dragged through time, while thoroughly confused. Not as exciting as it sounds. Honestly, I wouldn't recommend it."

He was there, then, she thought, *back with the original Heroes*.

"Did you meet them?"

Lashek shook his head, scratching his chin. He was frowning, his eyes looking at nothing.

"No," he said, "it felt more like a dream than anything. I don't remember, but I don't think I even saw their faces."

Zeera read the runes. She tried to commit them to memory; it would take a little while. Especially fitting it into the sequence of runes they'd already memorised.

"We need to assemble the Heroes," Zeera said, "and double our efforts to learn the spell."

Aella

1798

The first day of the new year arrived without ceremony. Above her, the smoke seemed closer, pushing down on them with boiling malice. Aella could only hope the Circle succeeded in its mission so that the next year began in better spirits. The smoky, burning sky was only the beginning of their troubles.

Thousands of Omati had marched through the desert, gradually changing from a blur on the horizon to a sea of faces outside Aethos' gates. Aella stood on the wall above the gates, intently scanning the people's faces.

There was no sign of Kerberos so far.

"Do you think he's there, among his people?" Shaela asked. They had stood in place since the approaching army drew close enough to make out individuals' features.

"He is not dead," Aella said, "of that I am certain. But whether he is hiding in the crowd, or elsewhere, lying in wait… it's impossible to tell without inspecting each person before they enter. And even that isn't possible."

"He could be in the city already," Shaela said, "Aella, I… there was an attack within Austris Ara a few days ago. Two Aethans, one very tall. They killed an Austris Aran and made it up to the Air Temple's roof. No Aethan would do this. Even if they tried, they wouldn't be able to kill one of my people."

Aella's throat constricted.

He wields Air Magic now.

"Why didn't you tell me? Or Zeera?"

"The Austris Arans are a proud people, Aella. They did not want this kind of weakness known to anyone, not even the Circle."

Aella could have screamed. Her heart thundered as her cheeks flushed.

"It's not an admission of weakness to notify us that *Kerberos* is inside the city! Have you not been listening to me, Shaela? He is the most dangerous being in Pandeia. Even more so now that he has Air Magic."

Shaela's face remained still. It was difficult to read Austris Aran's eyes, but Shaela's shone with grim acceptance.

"We can have some agents search the city," Shaela said, "but Zeera is unconvinced his threat is as great as you claim."

"He possesses all five magics, Shaela. And he is the most ruthless warrior in history. He will stop at nothing to achieve his goals. But regardless of his intentions, no one should wield that much power. No one."

"I understand," Shaela said, "I will order a small team to sweep the city. But with the description being Aethan, it means his ability to disguise himself is… problematic."

"Looking is better than doing nothing," Aella said, "even if we don't find him." She gestured to the crowd before them. "Same as with the Omati."

Shaela nodded.

"Zeera will let them in either way. The best we can do is keep watch over the crowd as they pass through the gates."

At least there is someone else in the Circle who's finally taking the threat of Kerberos seriously. Even if she kept his attack from me at first.

The beginning of the year was usually cold; the vicious heat jarred her. The smoke pouring from Sitharkos had become so bad that they could barely tell the time of day. She knew it was before noon, but they had taken to keeping torches lit at all hours to combat the dark.

Underneath them, a deep groan echoed through the stone of Aethos' great wall as the gates opened and closed again. Zeera approached the waiting Omati, and snatches of the talk between her and the leaders of the crowd drifted up to Aella. She couldn't hear enough to follow the conversation, but there was no need; nothing important was being discussed. Zeera's goal was to make sure the large group of warriors was looking to join them, and to watch for Kerberos. If they were aggressive, the gates would be closed and the crowd turned away. If Kerberos was with them...

Zeera may not want it, she thought, *but I will find a way to kill him. There is no other option.*

She could do it. Even with his extra magic, somehow, she would make certain he couldn't pose a threat. Shaela listened to her when she spoke of Kerberos; as much as the Austris Aran woman didn't want to, Aella was sure she would fight against Kerberos if the need arose.

"He should be easy to spot," Aella said, "even from a distance. Men of his size are rare."

"There are only three people tall enough in this crowd to be noticeable," Shaela said, "none of them match the description you gave me."

Aella peered at the vast crowd before them. She frowned at Shaela.

"How can you possibly know that?"

"Austris Arans have good vision."

"The crowd is huge," Aella said, "and it's so dark."

"... *Quite* good vision."

"Fine," Aella said, "if you could see all that, why didn't you tell me earlier?"

Shaela's full-white eyes passed over the thousands milling ahead of them. Often, Aella forgot it wasn't Shaela who had been chosen by Aurath; she possessed the gravitas of royalty, and the confidence to match.

"It took a little time to check."

Aella forced a laugh back down before it escaped. Of all the people she'd met since joining the Circle, Shaela was quickly becoming her favourite. Her humour was subtle, her intelligence vast, and her power... very few people in Pandeia possessed as much as the Austris Arans, and Shaela was one of the most powerful of their kind.

She could give Kerberos a real challenge. Her and I together... Now that would be a force to be reckoned with.

It was the first time Aella had considered the two fighting together, despite them both being members of the Circle. The Austris Arans tended to keep to themselves. They seemed to consider the problems of Pandeia beneath them; Zeera was concerned of late that the ancient beings wouldn't bother helping in the war. But Aella knew better.

She knew the feeling of carrying limitless power. Of wondering when there would ever be a chance to unleash it. The doubt, almost a certainty, eating away at her soul, that no one could stand up to her.

Perhaps it was Sithares. Or Fire Magic, eating away at her. But she thought it was just power. She was a queen, and one of the most powerful magicians in Pandeia; she knew very well the effect that power had on a person. Magic was a dangerous thing, not just to the wielder's opponents, but to the wielder. It pulsed with an energy that demanded action, like a storm forcing people to shelter. It pulled at her, almost whispering in its desperation.

"You are certain," she said to Shaela, "that he is not among them?"

"Yes," Shaela said.

"And I am certain he's not dead."

"He could be waiting," Shaela said, "hiding somewhere until the war is done."

"Or he could already be here. In the city."

"Impossible. Anyone would recognise Kerberos. Aethos is full of Circle agents."

Aella shook her head.

"Those agents are vastly outnumbered by warriors clamouring to train and prepare for the Ermoori. So few of the warriors here actually know anything about the Circle. They may have heard of Kerberos, but they wouldn't know him."

"The Omati would "

"And they're the most likely to be hiding his existence from us," Aella said, "we will receive no help from them to identify him."

"But their actions could give away their secret," Shaela said, "with so many trying to come into Aethos, it will be difficult for them to maintain a lie."

"We don't have the time to question each warrior. How would we discover a lie amongst thousands of people?"

Shaela narrowed her eyes, mouth firm in a tiny frown of concentration. She watched the army below them, eyes in constant motion.

"We don't need to talk to them to discover a secret," she said, "we only need to watch."

"We? I can see nothing helpful, Shaela."

"I will call some more Austris Arans to watch for suspicious activity, then."

Aella nodded, staring over the dimly lit crowd as Shaela flew away. Along with the oppressive smoke dominating the sky above her, Kerberos' disappearance settled over her in a foreboding haze. He would be waiting for the perfect opportunity to strike.

Even though Sithares had chosen her—and abandoned Kerberos—his power was unbelievable. If anything, he had only become more powerful since.

It seems, she thought, *that Sithares is not quite the ally one would have expected it to be.*

A short while later, Shaela returned with three more Austris Aran warriors. Two of them flew out over the army, swooping through the sky above, their faces turning constantly. Shaela and the other warrior remained next to Aella.

Aella peered into the crowd, an uneasy tension rising in her gut as the massive army below them rallied to be let in.

Perhaps an hour later, their searching was cut short when Zeera finally opened the gates proper. Omati warriors streamed in. Above her, the two Austris Arans flew faster as they searched the slowly dwindling crowd.

Kerberos is nearby, she thought, *I know it*.

Eliza

1798

Aethos suddenly felt small. There were already enough people training and living in the ancient city, but now that the Omati had arrived, there was almost nowhere she could go to be alone.

Her training room, which she shared with her mother, and her quarters, were the only rooms she knew wouldn't be occupied. Even then; interruptions were common. Circle agents scurried between the Heroes, constantly bringing messages or summoning them to another meeting.

I wanted so badly to be involved, she thought with a sigh, *I really shouldn't be complaining.*

The vast majority of Aethos had no idea about the Circle's mission to destroy Sithares. They cared only for the Ermoori army making its way towards them; and Eliza didn't blame them. But it was amazing to see how many people barely paid the roiling smoke above them any mind.

Days were short and dark now. She woke up in darkness, trained in darkness, and went to bed in darkness. And always, the heat shoved down on them, like a vast hand pushing her to the ground.

A long time ago, Mathys had told her briefly what it was like to be the Spectre.

I barely saw sunlight, he'd said, *especially in the first year or two. It took time to build the Spectre into the kind of symbol that scared away the criminals that plagued Ermoor at the time. I was so passionate, back then. I really believed I could change the country. But whatever difference I made, if any at all, came at a steep cost.*

In a strange way, she almost felt closer to him now. She trained every day, and spent all her time in darkness.

She tried to imagine his life back then. Her mother tried to stop Mathys from telling her too much about the Spectre; but every now and then, in moments of training when her mother wasn't nearby, he confided in her. He had been so alone. The entire city had seemed intent to destroy him; even the military he served hated the Spectre.

Eliza wasn't hated. But the Ermoori marched towards them, and the world itself was on the brink of destruction. On top of that, the leader of Ermoor haunted her dreams still.

She had grown up on the run; Mathys and Mara fled Ermoor before Eliza was born, and they'd remained in hiding ever since. It had to be similar to what Mathys experienced all those decades ago. *I do know how he felt*, she told herself, *what it must have been like to be the Spectre*.

Not for the first time, Eliza wondered about the afterlife. Gods were real, she knew that; but there was no doctrine she had heard that mentioned what the Gods did with the souls of their followers. Was Mathys out there somewhere now, watching over her?

Just as she couldn't feel Taranos' presence, there was no sense of Mathys.

But he must be somewhere, she thought, *he can't just be... gone. Can he*?

He was far too important, far too brilliant, to no longer exist.

Kerberos. Eliza hadn't seen him herself; Zeera herded her and her mother into a safe room while the Circle had defended its headquarters in Azar. But she had seen the destruction he left in his wake. Mathys' burned corpse, unrecognisable except for the armour he'd worn. The ceiling caved in, fire and smoke filling the hallway. Kerberos had murdered or grievously wounded dozens, and then simply disappeared.

Eliza knew she wasn't the only one who wanted the king of Omatus dead. But if she had a say, she'd be the one to kill him. Whatever it took.

She just had to survive the war, and the Circle's attempt to destroy Sithares. Then she could focus on hunting Kerberos down. He would pay for what he'd done to Mathys.

Riffolk Hayne had to pay, too. He'd ruined her mother's life before Eliza had even been born. Eliza had never met him, but she felt as though she knew him. His face had haunted her mind since before she could remember. His rage thrashed against her consciousness almost every day.

She realised his presence hadn't changed during the war, despite Riffolk drawing closer to them by the day. *I thought he would get... louder, or something*, she thought, *but it's the same as when he was in Ermoor*.

Did he know where they were? She certainly couldn't tell his location from the presence in her head. *No*, she decided, *no, he can't*. It was a coincidence that he marched his army to Aethos; it was the furthest city from Ermoor, after all. It stood to reason he would reach them last.

And when he finally faces the Circle, she thought, *he won't know what he's walking into*.

Aella

1798

Flashes of deep orange lit up the black smoke above them; the sky itself was a storm made of fire. Pure, blistering heat crashed down on Aella. Sithares was growing far too powerful.

Yes. Power. Can you feel it, child? The end of the world is coming.

She had been ignoring that voice for so long that she gasped at its sudden strength.

"What happens after that," she said, "after you've burned the world down? Do you know what happens to fire when it runs out of fuel? It dies."

Yes. That is its nature.

"If you will die either way," Aella said, "why does it matter to you if you burn Pandeia down or not?"

You are not listening to me, child. It is my nature. I cannot change it any more than you can change the desert winds.

"A god with no free will? Ridiculous."

There is much you do not know about my kind.

A gentle voice broke through Aella's thoughts.

"Who are you talking to?"

Zeera stepped out onto the wall from the staircase. She wore a thick cloak which she had soaked in water; the Tarsi were struggling more than anyone else in the heat.

"No one," Aella said.

Zeera stared out over the desert. There was no sign on her face that she'd even heard Aella speak. Only a strange, sad kind of patience.

Aella sighed.

"Sithares," she said.

Zeera nodded.

"It has grown more powerful than it was when the Circle first trapped it. It was gloating, I suppose?"

"More or less."

"Well," a sardonic voice said from behind them.

Lashek joined them, hand resting on his Shadow Blade's hilt.

"It didn't happen to accidentally let slip a weakness of some kind, did it?" he asked, "it's just... I'm getting sore, carrying the fate of the world by myself."

Zeera barely rolled her eyes; the slightest movement that Aella would have missed had she not already been looking at the short Tarsi woman.

"What in the Gods' name are you talking about?" she said, her voice betraying a hint of humour.

"I found the missing piece, remember? We'd all be lost without me. Still, if Sithares told you anything useful..."

Aella smiled.

"It told me we must sacrifice a dear friend, and then it will disappear."

Lashek ran his hand through his long black hair.

"Lucky for me," he said, "none of you are my friends."

How long had it been since she had been able to joke with friends? Her life before Kerberos was a blur at the best of times, but she almost remembered a time of carefree hunting, laughing and training, with...

Athanasius.

What had happened to him? When his name appeared in her mind, something wrenched within her heart. But was it betrayal, or something worse?

"Aella," Lashek said, "I was only joking."

"Yes," she said, "I know. I know."

Lashek gave her a strange look, and then raised his eyebrows at Zeera.

"Aella, are you okay?" Zeera asked.

Most of the time, she felt every bit the queen she was. But her mind was fractured, and sometimes she couldn't help but get lost in the scattered thoughts, the broken pieces of memories from a different life. She could have sworn she remembered Athanasius. So why could she recall nothing of him now?

Kerberos took him from you. Killed him right in front of you, while you were unarmed and powerless.

A flash of memory seared her mind's eye; in the distance, a dead body plummeting to the ground as Kerberos stood above, shining blade in his hand.

But was it real? Or was Sithares manipulating her?

He did not even need to do it. He only killed Athanasius to hurt you. To show you that he could.

"Stop it!" she screamed.

Zeera stepped back from her.

"I'll take that as a no," Lashek said.

"Lashek," Zeera snapped, "stop talking. Aella... What is happening?"

"Nothing," Aella said, "I need some rest."

She had no idea what time of day it was. When had she last slept? All she could remember with any clarity was the set of spells they had been practicing. Everything else had fallen away. It was a wonder—and a blessing—that the scar on her mind from death didn't seem to affect new memories.

"Get some rest, then," Zeera said gently, "our health and strength are paramount if we are to have any hope of defeating Sithares."

Aella looked at the dark grey sands of Omas. She couldn't see any movement, but she knew the winds were vicious. Even her broken memories would never let go of the brutality of those deserts. She still remembered the sting of sand rushing past her on searing wind. Shifting dunes, every step more difficult than the one before. The endless grey.

Rest. The concept was strange to Aella; she had grown up a nomad, constantly marching, training, or hunting. The only rest for a Thearan was sleep, and even then, only when necessary.

Taking the city of Theara as its queen was a blur. But even glimpsing what she could of her broken memories, she knew she had sat on a throne for long periods. *That must count as rest*, she thought, *of a sort*.

But would rest even help? She wasn't really tired, not in the way Zeera had understood. Sleep couldn't heal a fractured mind. Still, she gave a gentle nod and turned to Zeera.

"I will," she said, "but you must promise to stay vigilant. Kerberos is a threat, and none of us know where he is."

Zeera smiled, placing a hand on Aella's forearm.

"You are safe, Aella," she said, "I promise."

Aella trudged down the stairs into the city's courtyard entrance. Despite the cloying heat and disheartening darkness, Aethos was still beautiful. She couldn't remember if she'd thought of it that way when she first arrived, but it was true. Perhaps now, knowing it would soon be taken, she saw it with new eyes. A fragile, unguarded bird's nest waiting for a hungry Deathclaw.

Even in the courtyard, hundreds of people trained. To their credit, the Omati were mingling well since their arrival. Surviving a battle against Ermoor had clearly given them focus.

I cannot let down my guard yet, she thought, *Kerberos could still be here. And the Omati benefit from merging with us for now... but the moment Ermoor is defeated, they will be perfectly placed to attack us*. For all she knew, they had already been given orders to that effect.

Yes, Kerberos will be planning your downfall to occur very soon. His warriors are loyal to him, no matter what the war brings. Your army may outnumber them, but he does not want to destroy the Circle's army. Only you.

Aella pushed away Sithares' voice as she watched the training around her. Ignoring it was becoming more difficult by the day; before long, it would be consuming her every thought.

It will drive me mad, she thought, *and there is nothing I can do to stop it*.

Had it done the same to Kerberos? Surely... Sithares' effect on one's mind was as destructive as its effect on everything else. She felt it even now, burning away at her mind.

You cannot escape it. Just as your pitiful little group cannot defeat me.

She sighed heavily, squeezing her eyes shut. The sounds of magic and swords clashing rang through the streets. She didn't even fear the war's outcome any longer; she only wanted it all to be done. Just to return to Theara, to her life. Or to welcome death, if that was her fate; with Sithares destroyed, there was no guarantee her immortality would remain.

Her quarters, as with the other Circle members' quarters, were still in Aethos proper. But the temple where they would be fighting Sithares had been changed to the main Air Temple in Austris Ara. It meant the building her quarters were attached to had become quieter; no one but the Heroes were permitted near their quarters, and there was no need to guard a building that served no purpose beyond sleep. Not with an entire army living in the city.

When she reached the building, she sighed again as she stepped into its quiet hallways. The noise behind her dimmed to a cloudy echo. It wasn't until she undressed and lay on her bed that she realised she was, in fact, utterly exhausted.

Even the thought of Kerberos possibly being in Aethos didn't stop her from falling into a cold, dreamless sleep.

Eliza

1798

Sweat poured from Eliza, pleasantly cool against her skin. Zeera motioned with a hand; the water she'd been using for their sparring match flowed back into her two waterskins. Eliza was suddenly struck by how far they'd all come.

Even Zeera wasn't so casual with magic when we first met, she thought, *it has become so much easier for all of us*.

She wondered if Riffolk had trained as much as the Circle members. His presence in her mind was powerful; but power and training were different things. Mara was terrified of him, but with all the practice they were getting, Eliza wasn't so sure he was as unbeatable as her mother feared.

His army was perhaps another issue, though; they had decimated every opponent they'd faced.

But if I can get to him, she thought, *one-on-one…*

"Your control is excellent," Zeera said, "you have taken great strides."

"I was just thinking the same about you," Eliza said.

Zeera nodded. It was how she expressed gratitude, particularly when she was in a humble mood. Eliza wished the Circle's leader was a little more confident; she had barely held the Heroes together after the attack from Kerberos. A little confidence might have made all the difference. Not that she blamed Zeera. Eliza would have struggled with it too.

The training room—the one Eliza and Mara shared—was cool and quiet, though it had warmed significantly with their training. Energy still buzzed within the machines lining the walls. Eliza let the magic she'd been holding go, feeling it crackle as it dissipated. She had grown accustomed to holding magic in her body most of the time, but it felt good to let go of it every now and then. It made her body feel… quiet. Peaceful.

"Do you think it's enough?" she asked.

"What do you mean?"

"All this," she gestured around the room, then between the two of them, "this training. Do you think we can win this war?"

Zeera's eyes were huge, their pale silver shining in the dim room.

"We have a better chance now than ever," she said quietly.

"How long do you think we have left?"

"Not long. But we should be ready to cast the spell any day now. My only hope is that we can fully cast it before the Ermoori get here."

Eliza nodded. They had spent hours every day practicing and learning since Lashek mysteriously produced the spell's missing runes. She didn't know how the others felt, but it seemed to her that they were ready. Eliza watched them practice now, and even she had memorised most of the runes.

"It's my mother," she said, "isn't it? She's the only reason the Heroes weren't ready before now."

A short, sharp sigh was Zeera's only response at first. She frowned, eyes pulling down to the ground.

"We cannot place blame here, Eliza," she said, "we are supposed to be a unified team."

"I didn't mean… I only meant that she took a little while to start, not that I blame her. I would never blame her, not with what she's been through."

Zeera gave another one of her sad, distant smiles and looked up at Eliza.

"What matters now is that we are almost ready," she said, "and with that in mind… Eliza, I need you to support your mother through the coming days. I know you have already been a source of strength to her, but the form that takes may need to change."

Eliza frowned, watching Zeera's giant eyes as they searched her own, wide with concern.

"What do you mean?"

"I need you to tell her that things will be okay," Zeera said quietly, "that everything will turn out alright. I need you to soothe her fears."

"You… you want me to lie to her," Eliza said flatly, "that's what you're really saying."

Zeera drew in a breath, and something flashed in her eyes; a change, a decision.

"Eliza," she said, "I—"

Rushed footsteps echoed from the hallway, and both women spun to see a Circle agent run into the room.

"Zeera," she said, "they're here. The Ermoori are here."

Aerene

1798

Aerene floated high above Aethos, her vision picking up every little detail of the distant soldiers.

There were thousands of them, black armour shining even in the darkness. They carried no torches, no shields. They sang no war chants. Without fanfare, they simply marched through the dark grey desert towards Aethos. They wore helmets that covered their faces entirely.

Shaela floated next to her.

"So," she said to Aerene, "there it is. The war."

“We still have time,” Aerene said, “to defeat Sithares. They’re a couple of days march from here.”

Shaela looked at her, a grim smile on her face.

“It will take that long for you and the other Heroes to prepare, even if you begin now. And then what? We fight their war for them? After fighting off a God?”

“We fight their war *with* them. You are not really suggesting we disappear the moment Sithares is gone, are you?”

“We owe these people only what was agreed upon in our contract.”

Aerene clenched her jaw, rage rushing up to fill her with its sickening intensity.

“So the people of Aethos are dead. All of Pandeia, crushed under the boots of the Ermoori.”

Shaela frowned, turning to look at her with a look of bewildered annoyance.

“You say that as though you think I *want* them dead.”

“Don’t you?”

With a scoff, Shaela shook her head.

“Of course I don’t,” she said, “I am merely considering the wellbeing of my people. As should you. A head-on battle does not give us a high enough likelihood of victory, let alone survival.”

“You were just saying how powerful we are.”

"Yes," Shaela said, "but these beings wield technology beyond our means to fight. I killed a small group of them two decades ago. Do you remember that?"

Aerene nodded, her eyes back on the army marching towards them.

"Well, they were easy to kill then. Their armour was weaker, their weapons less powerful, and they did not know what they were walking into."

Shaela glanced briefly at Aerene, and then continued as she stared at the soldiers too.

"Now it is different. Their armour alone is… impenetrable, by all accounts. There is an entire army of them, and their weapons are beyond what should be possible."

"Magic," Aerene said with a nod, "I can feel it too."

"We cannot fight that, Aerene," Shaela said, "not directly."

"We may have to."

"Not if we can defeat Sithares in time," Shaela said.

Without another word, she plummeted towards the city. Aerene followed.

They landed lightly on the warm stone ground. Scouts had clearly spread the word already; all around them, the people moved with a frenzied new energy, the non-combatants gathering whatever food they could and the warriors training even harder.

Aerene's spearline hung from her belt, all but untouched since Austris Ara landed in Aethos. She had hunted all her life; those skills didn't need as much practice as Air Magic and Deias.

"We should seek out Zeera," Aerene said, "with the Ermoori so close, she will want to meet with the Heroes."

Aerene was right; Zeera had sent a Circle agent out to summon each of the Heroes, as well as Shaela and Eliza. They met at the Air Temple in Austris Ara.

"We are at the threshold," Zeera said, "there are perhaps two days until the Ermoori reach the gates. I think we are ready… we *must* be ready."

"How long will it take to cast the spell?" Eliza asked.

"It is hard to say," Zeera said, "but Sithares will put up a fight, and we will have to focus entirely on the spell until it is done."

Lashek cleared his throat.

"So… hours?" he asked, "days? Years? Do we at least get to take some breaks?"

"I don't have the answers," Zeera said, "Sithares is more powerful than it's ever been. All we can do is put as much magic into the spell as we can."

"And hope the Ermoori don't break in here in the meantime," Lashek said with a dark chuckle.

"Yes," Zeera said, "and that brings me to my next point. Shaela. You are powerful, skilled, and not one of the Heroes. You must stay outside the temple, and kill anyone who approaches before we are finished."

"No," Shaela said.

"Shaela," Aerene snapped, "you cannot refuse. This is our mission. We are a team."

"I am the Hero's guard," Shaela said, "I must be with the Hero of Austris Ara at all times."

"You will be protecting *all* the Heroes," Zeera said, "by standing guard outside the temple. We need someone we can trust, who is powerful enough to deal with anyone who comes for us."

"Flattery will not change my mind."

"It was not intended as flattery."

Aerene stepped close to Shaela, placing a hand on her shoulder.

"Please," she whispered, "for me."

A gentle breeze swept through the temple's wind tunnel.

For a long, searing moment, Shaela said nothing. The Heroes watched her, and she stared out into the grey distance to the south.

Finally, she turned back to Aerene.

"Fine," she said, "but the moment Sithares is dead—the very *instant*—I will return to your side. That is my condition."

Karak

1798

The quarters he'd been given were cramped, but so sparse that it made the limited space seem like a cavern. The only furniture was a narrow bench against the farthest wall. There were a couple of waterskins on the floor next to it. There were no windows.

How long have I been here for?

Groggily, stiffly, he pushed himself to sitting. He was naked, the room blessedly cool. His wounds had mostly—but not completely—healed, though his throat was as viciously dry as the desert he'd walked through. He ran his hands over his head, rubbed his eyes, and twisted to lay his feet on the floor. His clothes lay at the foot of the bed.

I wonder how soon I'm expected to be up and active again, he thought, *or if I've paid my debts well enough to deserve a rest.*

His new quarters sent a message; he may have made up for his failings, but he was starting from the bottom of the Circle's hierarchy again. It wasn't surprising. Selling Tarsi secrets to an outsider was about as serious a crime as a Tarsi could commit. Even worse, the outsider in question had turned out to be Kerberos.

He took one of the waterskins, drank his fill, and poured some over his bare skin. He longed for a flooded room, or at the least a tub of water to lie in. His body was frail, dried out.

Tarsi aren't meant to live in deserts, he thought, *it'll be a blessing if I never see a grain of sand again.*

He slipped into his clothes with a grunt of effort; his body wasn't entirely done healing just yet. The clothing had been cleaned, and was still a little damp. For that, at least, he was grateful.

Light footsteps sounded from the hallway; Karak looked up just in time to see Zeera.

"Back on your feet," she said, "just in time."

Karak's heart sank.

More missions to go on. I won't survive any more.

"What's happening?" he asked.

"The hour is upon us," Zeera' said, "the Circle must fulfil its purpose."

Karak hesitated, frowning.

Zeera would never ask me to be directly involved in their plan, he thought, *I haven't earned nearly that much trust.*

"Then what part am I to play?" he asked instead.

"Ermoor is at the gate," Zeera said, "so most of Aethos will be fighting. I need a few loyal people to stand watch outside the temple. To... intervene, if the enemy reaches us before our job is done."

Karak scoffed; he couldn't help it. He gestured to himself.

"I've not even healed, Zeera," he said, "I can barely stand, let alone *intervene*."

"We are out of options," Zeera said, "and you will not be alone. I am placing agents and guards at various places between the temple and the city's entrance. You will not necessarily have to fight. You can simply watch, and report any developments to Shaela."

Suddenly, something bloomed within him that he hadn't felt in a long, long time; hope. Optimism. He could survive the war, he could get out of it unscathed.

Zeera was giving him a chance.

"I'd be a scout? A lookout?"

"Yes," Zeera said, "but you will report directly to the temple guard. And you will only do so if the worst comes to pass."

He nodded, fighting the urge to smile. After the trials Zeera had put him through over the years, this was almost too good to be true.

I will watch the fighting from a safe distance, he thought, *and I will be shifted the whole time. I won't even be near the battle.*

Even before the war came upon them, Karak had been certain he would die in the service of the Circle. He'd been forced to face Kerberos more than once, stealing from him the most important item in Pandeia. The one time Karak came face-to-face with Kerberos, the man almost killed him as easily as if he'd been a newborn kitten.

"Karak," Zeera said, "are you ready for this last assignment?"

"Another healing potion or two," he said, "and I should be. I don't suppose you have any spare?"

Zeera gave a solemn nod.

"I will have the healers bring some to you."

Aerene

1798

The air had changed. It was still, and yet it buzzed with threat. They were on the Air Temple's roof, where the stone dais stood waiting. In the distance, the dark mass of the Ermoori army loomed a few hours beyond Aethos' gates.

Any moment now, the final battle would begin. Zeera was rushing to prepare them for the spells, guiding Circle agents as they placed everything the Heroes would need around the dais. The book of Sithares sat on the pedestal in the centre of the dais. The Circle was gathered, and they were almost ready. It was now or never; Ermoor was almost close enough to attack.

Shaela had gathered several of the royal guards, and was briefing them on their mission. Aerene approached quietly, trying not to draw attention to herself until Shaela finished speaking.

"...has her own spies who will report to me," Shaela was saying, "but I want you above the temple, watching from a better vantage point. We must be vigilant, and never assume to know everything the battlefield holds."

The royal guards saw her and bowed. Shaela nodded grimly; she was still in a bad mood from being told to guard the temple.

"Go," Shaela said to the guards before turning to fully face Aerene. "Aerene. Are you ready?"

"As ready as I will ever be," Aerene said.

Shaela nodded, her white eyes somehow cold and gentle at the same time. Others seemed to only see the cold. Aerene had once, too. But now she knew Shaela better.

"You know the spells," Shaela said, "you have the magic. Just focus on your mission, and the rest will follow."

She is wise. It is good advice.

Aerene stifled a gasp... mostly. Hearing Aurath's voice could be disconcerting, when she wasn't expecting it.

"Aurath?" Shaela asked with a raised eyebrow.

Aerene glanced around; she couldn't explain why, but in that moment, it felt wrong to talk openly about the Gods' whispered voices.

"Yes," she said, "it told me to follow your advice. It said you are wise."

"Of course it did. I know what I'm talking about."

"Wise people tend not to be so self-assured, Shaela," Aerene said, playfully shoving Shaela's arm, "perhaps you aren't quite as wise as Aurath said."

Shaela's smile was slow and dim, like the sun hidden behind those black-grey clouds of smoke choking Pandeia.

"That may be true," she said, "sometimes I think the Gods have more faith in us than we do in them."

Aerene couldn't stop her mouth from opening; how was she supposed to respond to that? It was utterly unlike Shaela. Aerene watched her turn south, her back to the Ermoori, her white eyes glistening as they searched the distance.

"Sometimes," she said again, "I wonder why the Austris Arans ever joined the Circle."

Where is this coming from? Aerene wondered, *Shaela is never this... morose.*

She is facing the largest war this world has ever seen. As are you. It is natural to examine one's life, one's values and choices, near the end.

Aerene fought to keep her face blank. *Near the end?* she thought, *are you saying that Shaela is going to die? Or that I am?* With a sinking feeling, Aerene looked up at the roiling black smoke above them. Flames of deep orange flashed almost constantly from within the smoke.

Or is this the end for all of us?

But Aurath didn't respond.

"Shaela."

The Hero's Guard took a moment to respond. Her eyes still lingered on the southern horizon. Would Austris Ara ever float above those oceans again? After this war, would there even be an Austris Ara at all?

"Don't worry about me," Shaela said, "focus on what you must do."

"Listen," Aerene said quietly, "I just wanted to... well, if something happens, and you... or I..."

Shaela nodded, the cold melting from her eyes. She placed a hand on Aerene's shoulder.

Aurath help me, she thought, *I'm not prepared for this.*

She took a deep breath.

"I just wanted to say... thank you. For-"

"I am not dead," Shaela said, "yet. Save your thanks for after this is all over."

Her voice was gentle. Her eyes were gentle, kinder than they had ever been. The air rushed quietly from Aerene's lungs, leaving an empty, weak feeling behind. *I shouldn't be surprised*, she thought, *Shaela has never been particularly open with her feelings*.

So quietly that Aerene almost didn't hear it, Shaela sighed.

"I am sorry, Aerene. You were only trying to express your gratitude."

Without warning, Shaela pulled her into a tight embrace.

"You are a brilliant Hero," Shaela whispered, "and I am proud to have served you. Whatever happens, remember that."

Aerene's eyes stung as tears welled and toppled down her cheeks. She wanted to tell Shaela that she couldn't have done any of the things she'd done since being chosen if it hadn't been for Shaela. She wanted to tell Shaela that she had been a better friend to her than anyone Aerene had ever known.

But her breath caught in her throat, and the tears wouldn't stop. *I just wanted to thank her*.

They held each other for a long moment, until Aerene began to fear letting go. When they let each other go, it would be saying goodbye. Aerene had to join the other Heroes at the dais, and Shaela had to guard the temple. What if this was the last they ever saw of each other?

Shaela pulled away, and her chest tightened painfully.

"Be careful, Shaela," she said, "please. This can't be goodbye."

Zeera

1798

Asheilos hadn't spoken to Zeera in a long time. It was a strange feeling, her realisation that in those years she hadn't *needed* her God. But the war was mere moments from starting.

She needed Asheilos now.

But she couldn't hear its voice. For the last few hours, Zeera had been silently praying as she rushed to prepare the Circle for their last mission. The last battle. She had been imagining it for so long, it was hard to believe it was really about to happen.

Circle agents moved the necessary equipment into place around the dais, under Zeera's direction. Two Ermoori machines, large engines that created and held Power Magic. A vented stone basin filled with wooden logs ready to be set alight. A tub full of water. And a tree, taller than any of them, in a massive clay pot. The latter had to be carried up to the Air Temple by a team of Austris Arans; they only helped begrudgingly.

Mara and Eliza stood by the machines, both glowing yellow as they absorbed Power Magic. Aella was praying, and Lashek was performing the blade dance of the Shenza.

Aerene was speaking to her people, convincing them to join the fight against the Ermoori. Shaela had previously promised they would defend Aethos while they lived here; but only until Sithares was destroyed. It was likely all they could expect of the guardians. Besides, even with the Austris Arans' help, it was almost impossible for them to win against the Ermoori.

I have to focus on the Heroes.

The Circle agents finished placing their equipment and left the Heroes to their mission. A few moments later, Aerene glided down to the temple roof, her face set.

No luck there, Zeera thought, *I am not surprised*.

The Heroes' energy grew with each passing moment. Zeera sensed each of them, their power, their resolve. Their fear.

Are we ready?

She honestly couldn't say. They knew the spells, and they had talked endlessly about what to expect... But the truth was, no one knew for certain. Even the oldest Austris Arans alive today were too young to have seen it in person. They did possess more accurate historical records than any other people of Pandeia, but these were disputed even among their own historians.

Some believed the Heroes were unable to kill Sithares, and trapping it had been the only option. Others thought that trapping the God of Fire had been a kind of punishment, something worse than merely being destroyed. And still more thought that the original Circle decided to restrain Sithares for their own, possibly nefarious purposes.

Zeera didn't believe that. The Circle had existed to save Pandeia from Sithares. There had to be a reason why the Circle made the choice they did. Some reason Sithares wasn't destroyed.

"Asheilos," she whispered, "please, give me guidance. Give me reassurance. Something. Anything."

You are on the right path. Focus your energy on destroying Sithares. The war will happen as it happens.

Her chest tightened, squeezing her heart to a shuddering stop. *That sounds ominous*, she thought, *as though we can do nothing to change the outcome of the war*. For a while, there had been a part of her that knew this. Deep down, in a way that she couldn't have articulated; a wordless, creeping kind of dread. But hearing Asheilos' voice tell her to let it happen brought it up to her conscious mind, turning it into a real fear.

They were going to lose the war.

From the Air Temple, through the columns that lined the roof's edges, she could just make out the dark stain on the desert that was the Ermoori army. Thousands of warriors, all but invulnerable.

In a way, it was almost a relief. Zeera had been fearing the war, and wondering about its outcome, for years. Now she only had to wonder about her own survival. By all accounts, the Ermoori had been sparing those who surrendered. Or those who had not fought, at any rate. It would be easy for the Tarsi to appear innocent; the other members of the Circle may not be so lucky. But then again, the Heroes of the Circle weren't actually fighting against the Ermoori. Would they be spared?

Doubtful. As far as Zeera knew—and she knew quite a lot—Riffolk Hayne was ruthless as he was intelligent. He wouldn't stand the existence of magicians as powerful as the Heroes, even if they hadn't fought against his soldiers. They were a threat to him, regardless of their intentions.

You must remain hidden. After the war. Keep the Circle unbroken.

Zeera frowned as Asheilos' voice faded. *After the war*. It was the first time in months she'd thought about what life might be like when all this was over. With Ermoor in control of all of Pandeia, what kind of life would they live?

Keep the Circle unbroken. She had struggled enough keeping the Heroes together over the last few years; how would she do so with Pandeia held tightly in Ermoor's fist?

She didn't know enough about Ermoor's culture, but she knew it wasn't a good place to live. And after the war, every country would be forced to live in a similar way. They worshipped a false god; would all of Pandeia have to do the same? Turn their back on Asheilos, Aurath, and Amalus? The only positive she imagined in that scenario was that Sithares would be forgotten. If there was a chance the God of Fire could return—and given what Lashek had told her about Amalus, there was—forcing the people of Pandeia to never worship Sithares would make it all but impossible.

The Circle would fade into the shadows; if they could live in secrecy, they could maintain their religion in secrecy too. They only had to stay out of trouble.

In the new world, Mara and Eliza would be fine. Lashek and Aella, too; there were plenty of Thearans and Shenza left alive, enough that they could blend in. But the Austris Arans… to the Ermoori, they were an unknown, and would make up a huge number of the forces fighting in this final battle. Zeera worried for them. She could disappear into a crowd, look like anyone. But the Austris Arans stuck out in every way.

On the other hand… the Austris Arans were experts with Deias, more so than even the Tarsi. Perhaps they could hide after all. Zeera had never seen them use Deias to cast disguise spells, but that didn't mean they couldn't.

"Aerene," Zeera called, "come here."

The Austris Aran girl approached immediately.

"Do your people know how to change their appearance," Zeera asked, "using Deias?"

"They would never need to," Aerene said, "no Austris Aran feels the need to alter our bodies."

"I am not talking in generalities, Aerene. I mean after this is all done. When the Ermoori are in control."

Aerene gave a small gasp.

"How can you say that, Zeera?"

"Look at them." She pointed north, where the Ermoori waited in the distance. "They have beaten every existing military in Pandeia. And they still look as though they're fresh to the battlefield. We cannot win this fight."

"Why are you telling me this?"

Zeera tried—and failed—to hide a sigh.

"I am worried Ermoor will forever see Austris Arans as enemies," she said quietly, "and our only survival tactic after the war will be secrecy. Hiding."

"It will not matter," Aerene said, "I spoke with my people, as you suggested. When Sithares is destroyed, my people will most likely return to the southern skies. There will be no need to hide. Our lives will return to normal."

Zeera didn't bother hiding her sigh this time.

"I should have known," she said, "the Austris Arans never had any interest in defending against the Ermoori."

"I do not feel good about it either, Zeera. Were it up to me, I would have Austris Ara stay and fight until the end, but even I cannot sway them on this. They will defend Aethos while we are here, but the moment Sithares is destroyed, they will leave."

I should not be surprised. Austris Arans are all as stubborn as Shaela, and she was difficult enough to convince. Even then, she never promised her people would remain in Aethos after Sithares is destroyed. She seemed hesitant enough to confirm they would help fight the Ermoori at all.

For Zeera's entire life, she had been loyal to the Circle of Shadows. Legends of the great Austris Arans, the guardians of Pandeia, had filled her heart with vibrant light. They were supposed to protect Pandeia.

The contract they had made revolved around Sithares, of course. When the original Circle captured it instead of destroying it, they swore to fight together again if Sithares ever escaped.

They never agreed to fight a war against technologically advanced invaders. But even so, they were the guardians.

Zeera cast her eyes over the Heroes once again. They had built up more magic than she would have thought possible. It took time, but they were finally almost ready. As well as the tub of water prepared by the Circle agents, Zeera had soaked her tunic and trousers in water, and opened the two full waterskins on her belt.

The energy shared by the team crackled with furious purpose. Now that the moment was imminent, there was nothing but focus in each of their eyes.

Between them, the book of Sithares sat on the stone pedestal, magic coming off it in aggressive waves. The runes in her mind's eye as they appeared, one after the other. She knew them now. They all did, at least in theory; they had spent a long time learning them. But now they would have to actually cast the spells. And there was no room for error.

A deep rumble rose up from the temple roof, followed closely by a crunching boom. Smoke and dust billowed from the direction of the main gates.

The final battle had begun.

"Okay, Heroes," she said, "we are out of time. The spells must be cast. Now."

Riffolk

1798

It stood defiant before him; Aethos, the last city free from his rule. An army cobbled together from the dregs of those already defeated. Yet still, they faced him. Still, they refused to yield.

His own army was immaculate. A third of his forces were fresh, unscathed, unmarred. Their armour buffed and spotless. He had kept them in reserve until now, placing them at the head of the throng for the march to the final battle. Eager soldiers, still swept up in the promise of glory.

He peered at the rag-tag warriors standing on the city wall a little closer; their torn clothing had been cleaned, but not repaired. Many of them were wounded. Riffolk couldn't see their eyes clearly, but their stance made it clear; they were defeated already. Riffolk smiled behind his visor. All the years he'd spent planning, all the designs... it all led to this. And it couldn't have played out more perfectly.

Even now, a fraction of his forces were building foundations for a new city in Shanaken. He had dozens of bureaucrats designing improved infrastructure for the existing cities in Tarsium and Omas. A new age of technology and information was coming. He only had to sweep away the remnants of the old world.

And the last of those remnants have collected themselves, he thought, *how convenient for me*.

Aethos was large, and made larger by the circular land mass now attached to the cliff's edge on the city's southern border. At first he had been baffled by it; no such mass existed on any known maps. But it didn't take him long to come to a conclusion.

Twenty years ago, Riffolk had detected powerful magic somewhere in the southern oceans, beyond any charted territories. Through his research he'd known of several types of magic, and now he understood that the core of those magics was elemental in nature. He knew that the Tarsi were stewards of Water Magic. So it stood to reason that those people who lived beyond his reach wielded Air

Magic. How else could a city go from the southern reaches of Pandeia to a cliff's edge in Omas?

His conclusion was proven correct; tall, winged beings flew above the city, sweeping out into the air above his army.

"Prime Overseer," one of the commanders said, "sir, the men are beginning to show doubt. Those... things, up there. They almost look like..."

He drifted into uncomfortable silence. The propaganda pushed on Ermoor's people had created a culture of such fear and repression that they would rather say nothing than question what they could see with their own eyes. It hadn't been Riffolk's idea; the old leaders, the Twelve Crowns, came up with that one centuries ago. Riffolk had merely perfected the method of dissemination.

"You may speak freely, commander," Riffolk prompted.

He would not be the one to put a name to these fears; it had to come from the soldiers themselves.

The commander's faceplate turned to watch the men of his battalion, then glanced up at the flying beings. His body language was tight, tense. Even with proven armour and the deadliest weapon Pandeia had ever seen in his hands, the man was terrified.

"They look like people," the commander finally said, "people with *wings*. Forgive me, Prime Overseer, but... that sounds like magic to me."

Riffolk regarded the man as lightly as he could.

They have been told that magic does not exist, he thought, *but at the same time, they have been taught to hate it. To want it rooted out and destroyed. Now they have the chance.*

"And if it were true," he said, "what difference would it make?"

"Magic doesn't exist."

Riffolk watched the flying beings for a moment, allowing their undeniable majesty to fill him with a sense of awe. It was rare he was impressed, but the blue-skinned creatures were stunning. And an entire city flying through the air was something even he couldn't hope to replicate.

But flying vehicles… yes, there was potential there. Ideas began to flow, blueprints forming in the back of his mind.

Finally, he turned back to the commander.

"When I was young," he said, "the highest technology we had was the street lamps, and older versions of the factories. Simple things. When I first built the horseless cart, my mother thought it was magic. No matter no many times I explained the mechanics of its function, she could not understand."

"Forgive me, Prime Overseer," the commander repeated, "I don't understand why you're telling me this."

Riffolk watched his eyes drag back to the beings above them. He held his rifle tight, as though if he let go, he might fall to the ground. *Such simple minds*, he thought, *they fear so much.*

"Commander," he said, "have you seen lightning? Heard the thunder that follows?"

The man nodded.

"And could you explain exactly how it happens?"

This was met with a frown, and a fumble for answers so intense Riffolk could almost hear the desperation in his mind.

"How about the energy used to power the technology in Ermoor? Could you explain that?"

Again, the man remained silent as he searched for something to say. Riffolk cast his eyes over the army amassed behind him.

"Magic is not something to be feared, commander," he said, "it is no different than any other natural force. Many could be convinced that the technology I have developed is magic."

"Are you saying that magic *is* real?" the commander asked, eyes wide and brows furrowed.

"I am saying it does not matter. The opponents we face today are just people. We will kill them, just as we did the Shenza and Tarsi before them."

"Is magic not against God?"

Riffolk had to force himself not to scoff. After all, the man was only repeating what he had grown up being told.

"Oh, yes," he said instead, "that is part of the reason we fight this war. To teach the savages of Pandeia a better way. To show them our technology and civilised society will always win out against heresy."

It seemed to be enough. The commander nodded grimly and checked over his rifle. Riffolk looked over his army, then once again at the walls of Aethos.

The tension was building. His army was ready, more than ready, and Riffolk had never felt more alive.

"Prime Overseer, sir?" the commander shuffled uncomfortably on his feet, "with all due respect, sir… what are we waiting for?"

"Fear," Riffolk said quietly, "is a powerful tool. It can motivate, or it can paralyse. Our soldiers will be motivated by this moment of apprehension. They have moved from victory to victory. The enemy, however, is beaten down. Desperate." He drew his weapon and checked it over. "They are aware of the threat they face. Waiting for us to strike will demoralise them."

The commander looked at Riffolk as though he'd grown a third eye on his face.

"You're waiting on purpose," the man said, "to make them more scared of us?"

"You forget your place, commander," Riffolk said, "you do not have the right to judge my tactics."

This is what the Lord Commander should be dealing with, he thought, *soothing the doubts of commanders, making sure the army is working optimally*. Riffolk had not missed Arthor much over the last few years, but now he did. *Arthor loves his soldiers*.

"Sorry, sir, of course not, sir," the commander stammered, "I only… well, it's just that… have they not been through enough?"

"*I* say what's enough!" Riffolk snapped. He pointed at the gates. "That is our enemy. They will kill you without hesitation, given the opportunity. They live in open disregard for Ermoor's way of life. I remind you, commander, that sympathising with the enemy is akin to treason."

The commander grew still, his face suddenly pale. He stepped back into rank.

It was almost time. Impatience fluttered through his waiting army like a breeze shuffling fallen leaves. They wanted to fight, wanted to win, and by the time he gave the order, they would leap at the chance to finish his war.

Aethos perched on a cliff, high walls cutting it off from the rest of Omas. The walls would not stand up to his tanks, but until he blew them down, the only way into the city was the main gates. It meant the enemy was cornered. Thousands of Ermoori soldiers, most of whom were fresh and unharmed, waited to fight the thousands of survivors before him.

It still confused him how stubborn the people of Pandeia were being; even at their worst, his soldiers were killing enemy combatants at a staggering ratio. Now his men had every advantage. Even banded together, the enemy could not possibly hope to win.

Riffolk had allowed those who surrendered to live; so why would these doomed warriors continue fighting? After the war, Riffolk was going to turn Pandeia into a paradise for all of its people. They had seen his technology. Even in Tarsium and Omas, his horseless carts—and other conveniences he'd designed—were used. Why did they not realise that Ermoor's rule was in their best interests? It was like a doctor having to fight their patient just to administer the medication that would save their life.

Sometimes, he thought, *we must force the people to live the lives that best suit them. Even if they can't see. Especially then.*

Of course, Riffolk wasn't fighting solely for the good of all. But a stable, flourishing world in which technology was treasured meant he could spend his time pursuing further technological developments. Most would benefit the world, but that was a side effect rather than the goal. The technology itself was the goal.

With an entire world bowing down to him, there would be almost no limit to what Riffolk could accomplish.

He smiled.

"Commanders," he called, "give the order. It is time to end this war."

Lashek

1798

Shadow Magic flowed through his body, pouring strength into his muscles, and certainty into his heart. Zeera called for Aerene, and the two had a quiet conversation. Lashek pushed the voices away, pushed everything away until there was only Shadow Magic. His *Kaizuun* slicing through the hot wind. His eyes were closed; an experienced *Kaizeluun* could perform the *Zuunshai* without looking.

He had performed the *Zuunshai* many times in a row now. Each time, his strength grew. His connection to Shadow Magic deepened with every slash of the blade. It was stronger now than it had been in a long time; since he'd lived in the forests of Shanaken.

I might even be ready, he thought, *to cast these spells.*

A low sound rolled over him, breaking his concentration enough to make him stumble.

"Okay, Heroes," Zeera said, "we are out of time. The spells must be cast. Now."

With the *Zuunshai* flooding his body with magic, he saw the temple roof anew. To his left was the pedestal, the southern point that saw the most wind. In the centre sat the temple's wind chamber, a sort of tunnel that focused the natural flow of wind. A small structure with a large door lay on the northern side; the stairs down into the royal palace. Around the roof's edge, great stone columns were spaced evenly. Their purpose was unknown to Lashek, as there was no ceiling above them.

The temple was unlike anything else in Pandeia. Regal, ornate, and beautiful.

They gathered at the pedestal. Lashek held his *Kaizuun* in his left hand, leaving his right free to draw the spell's runes. There was a space for each of them to draw at even intervals around the pedestal's outer edge.

Explosions, quiet from the distance, peppered the quiet rush of the wind. Thankfully they were far enough from the fighting that they heard nothing else; no screams or shouting.

"Start casting," Zeera said, "… now."

Each of them launched into motion, gentle scraping sounds filling the air. The runes glowed immediately.

There were layers to the spells. The first were preparation, increasing their magic and tying it to the attack spells they would cast a little later. There was also a spell connecting them to each other.

Lashek risked losing his focus to glance at Aella. She had told the Circle that Sithares was in her head, that she was likely the new chosen Hero of the God of Fire.

She was sweating, a deep and intense frown on her face as she drew the runes. *Sithares must be putting up quite a fight in her head,* he thought, *hopefully she can handle it*. They still didn't know what kind of fight to expect from Sithares when they began their own attack. Would they only need to get the spells right? Or would they have to defend themselves against something? Surely Sithares wouldn't give up so easily…

They finished the first spell quickly; it was by the far simplest of them. An explosion of pure energy instantly rocked his entire being. His heart raced, not just fast but strong, his chest thudding with its force. With the *Kaizuun* in his hand, he felt waves of magic slamming into him from each of the other Heroes. Their auras were stunning; he could barely see from the brightness of their magic.

"Now the linking spell," Zeera said, "We must be perfectly synchronised. It may feel strange."

The spell contained twenty individual runes. They were complex, among the most difficult to remember; for Lashek, at any rate. He drew on the stone, tracing his finger over its rough surface. The lines glowed, layering over each other to create the intricate finished spell.

As soon as they finished, sensations he'd never experienced ripped through his body; a buzzing, intense lightning, searing heat that burned him from the inside, a deep cold that filled his chest, and an almost delirious lightness that made him feel like he was floating. All at once, every sensation flooded his mind and body.

All five magics flowed through him. When the initial feeling subsided, the origin points of each magic emerged; they emanated from each Hero, flowed through those next to them, and then into Lashek.

He was so… powerful. In that moment, he could have destroyed the entire Ermoori army. *Maybe this is how the magicians of old became so powerful*, he thought, *why they were stronger than any magic we have today*. His breathing was steady, and each breath filled him with more strength, more energy. As though his lungs were twice their ordinary size.

The next spell was perhaps the most important; It linked their elemental magic to Deias. Then would come the attack spells. So far, Sithares had made no moves against them.

Just as he thought it, a deafening crack exploded from Aella's hands and she screamed. The spell she had been casting burned up in a harsh orange flame.

Sithares.

It was most likely still attempting to manipulate Aella; even with the extra power gained from their linking spell, her face was tense with effort as she quickly restarted the spell. Zeera glanced at her. A small wave of comfort flowed from the Tarsi woman.

"Stand strong, Aella," she said, "our attack will begin shortly. Focus on the runes."

Aella gave a short, sharp nod. The Fire Magic coming from her was chaotic, like a real fire rushing over dry wood. He wondered distantly if it was always like that, or if the chaos was a result of Sithares fighting with Aella.

The energy he'd gained from the linking spell boosted his mind, too; he was able to recall the runes much easier than he first anticipated. *So far*, he thought, *this is easy. Why were we so worried? We're more powerful, we're linked to each other, and we remember the runes.*

Sithares was all but doomed.

They started on the next spell. Something changed about halfway through; their movements became slower, like they were standing in murky water instead of air. His mind still thought at its usual pace, but he had to force his body to obey.

He glanced around; the others looked like they were struggling with the same obstacle.

Everything moved so slowly. The wind had died down to a crawl that caressed his face like the gentle ripples of the ocean on a quiet day. Even his hair, and that of the others—except Zeera—

swayed slowly sideways as though caught in a full wind. But so, so slowly. Was time something the Gods could manipulate? They seemed to know the future, after all. Or was something else happening?

They were halfway through the spell that channelled their magic into Deias. The runes began glowing different colours, every line sparkling and changing as he watched.

Red, then blue. Purple. Yellow. White, green, then orange. Each line changed colours independently of the others, so that the whole spell was an ever-changing web of pure energy. He had never seen anything like it.

Then, the instant the spell was finished, power flowed from him so fast that he gasped from the rush of its absence. He was suddenly empty, weak.

Above the spells they'd each cast were floating spheres of elemental magic; each of the five types swirled around each other in a condensed ball of pure magic. A loud hum had risen up over the sound of the wind, though everything but the magic still moved too slowly.

The next spell, several spells, were attacks. If there was a time Sithares was likely to fight back, it was now.

Lashek held his breath, recalling the attack spells as well as he could. Now that the incredible magic that had linked them was out of his body, his mind seemed to move as slowly as time itself. They were vulnerable now, far more vulnerable than he thought they could be after the sheer power he'd felt just moments ago.

What would they do if Sithares fought back now? He searched himself for magic; there was almost none. Not enough to create a magic shield against a normal magic attack, let alone an attack from Sithares itself.

I can't say our chances of survival are very high, he thought, *but if we can take Sithares out with us, then I suppose it'll be worth it*. Maybe that was what happened to the original Heroes.

"Aella," Zeera said, "only a moment longer."

The Thearan queen's eyes were screwed shut, beads of sweat all over her face. Her stark white hair waved slowly in the somehow slowed-down wind. Her teeth were gritted, her hands gripping the dais' edge. She didn't react to Zeera's words.

"Cast the first attack spell," Zeera called, "now!"

Just as they began drawing the runes, chaos erupted around them.

Karak

1798

The battle had begun. Karak waited on a rooftop further back in the city, watching dust and smoke rise from the city's entrance to the smoke above. He had been given an Ermoori rifle and some of their armour, pilfered from corpses in Tarsium. There were almost none of them, with how careful the Ermoori were in reclaiming their fallen, but Zeera saw how terrified Karak was, and how wounded he was, and she had given him one of the only sets they had.

To fit into it, he had to shift into a human form; he chose an Omati face and skin tone so he wouldn't be mistaken for the enemy. After that, all he could do was wait.

The sounds were the worst part; at first it was only the booms and rumbles of explosions and gunfire. But gradually, as the Ermoori pushed further into Aethos, he could hear the screams of wounded warriors on both sides. Chaotic shouting as each army attempted to relay orders through the noise and fighting.

Then the fighting was so close he could have thrown a rock and hit an Ermoori soldier.

He heard their ugly language as they shouted battle cries and orders from their superiors. Their weapons boomed as they shot down warriors by the dozen. Occasionally, an Ermoori soldier fell. But for every one of them, close to a hundred Circle warriors died. Even the Austris Arans could not keep up with their impenetrable armour and lethal weapons.

Karak checked the rifle he was given; he knew how they worked, at least in theory. The only problem was, once he started shooting, the Ermoori would know exactly where he was.

I am supposed to watch and alert the guards, he thought, *not make myself a target*. He would be of no use to anyone if he were shot dead now, even if he took one of them out with him. Besides, he didn't even know if their own weapons worked against them.

His decision made, Karak rushed to the south side of the low building and climbed down to the street. The fighting was barely a street over from his position now.

He ran, holding the rifle tightly in case he had to defend himself. The Ermoori were gaining ground fast. It sounded to him like they were running close behind him, though he knew it wasn't true. He glanced behind him all the same.

The neat streets of Aethos looked as pristine as ever. If not for the cacophony, he might have believed all was well. Then, all at once, a home close to Karak exploded. The ground shook from the force of whatever weapon had been used. A group of Circle warriors backed onto the street, facing away from Karak. They kept shuffling backwards as the Ermoori pushed further into the city. They fought ferociously, valiantly, but the Ermoori were too strong. Too powerful.

I have to move fast, he thought, *hopefully I get to the temple before the Ermoori do*.

He was still in an Omati form; he could run faster that way. Magic exploded around him, and blasts from Ermoori rifles slammed into the stone buildings so close to him that chipped shards of stone hit him.

The streets of Aethos were winding and interconnected, forcing Karak through a maze to reach the temple. He ducked behind a wall, trying to get his bearings, the sound of combat coming from seemingly everywhere. The Ermoori moved inexorably further into Aethos.

So much for being out of danger, he thought, *I'm going to be killed just by getting lost.*

He rushed down another street, the booming of Ermoori rifles deafening. The rifle in his own hands was too heavy; hearing the roar they made, seeing deep gashes in foot-thick stone… no weapon should have been so powerful.

No wonder the Ermoori are winning, he thought, *these weapons are horrific.*

The Tarsi were pacifists at heart; even Karak, who had gone against so many of the Circle's tenets, abhorred violence. He had accepted the rifle as a means to defend against the Ermoori, but he wasn't certain he could fire it even if he had to. The damage they did to Omati stone was bad enough; he didn't want to see what they'd do to a person. He was lucky enough to have not seen the fighting up close.

Karak sought the sun's dim glow above the roiling black and orange smoke; he found south, and then the Air Temple's peak just above the rooftops. *There it is.*

He sprinted towards Austris Ara. What more could he do? He had been tasked with watching the battle's progress, and it was progressing quickly. *The Circle can probably see the battle from where they are anyway*, he thought, *why did Zeera need me*?

As he ran, he noticed other Tarsi agents watching the battle. None of them possessed Ermoori armour or rifles. Most were shifted into animals; if the Tarsi couldn't see through their own kind's shapeshifting, he wouldn't have noticed them at all. There were a handful of them, invisibly watching the Ermoori as they pushed further into the city.

It almost would have been better without the armour and rifle, he thought, *then I could have stayed where I was, unnoticed, instead of running for my life and hoping I won't have to use this weapon.*

Footsteps thudded towards him, coming from ahead. Several people; three or four, perhaps five. *No*, he thought, *no, the Ermoori can't be this far in the city already*. He scrambled for the rifle, holding as he'd been shown, forcing himself to be ready. The trigger was steel, cold and buzzing with malice. His entire world shrank to the size of that trigger. It moved under his finger, and he let go instantly. Holding his breath, Karak waited for the group to round the corner onto his street.

Movement caught his eye, and his finger tensed; the rifle's roar swallowed him whole, the cacophony of battle swept away by a keening whistle that rang through his head.

Then he saw them.

Four warriors—Circle warriors—stood ready for combat, facing Karak. There was a *Kaizeluun*, two Thearans, and an Austris Aran. Shock and hatred burned from their eyes.

"No," he said, "no, it was a mistake!"

"Why do you wear their armour?" the Austris Aran said, "and wield *that*?"

"It was given to me," Karak said, "by Zeera. For protection."

“Yet you shot at us,” the *Kaizeluun* said in a thick Shenza accent, “*us*, your supposed allies.”

“I thought you were Ermoori,” Karak said, tripping over the words as sounds of combat grew closer, “they’re breaking further into the city by the moment.”

“That is why we are here,” the Austris Aran said.

Karak nodded, forcing the panic down as an explosion shook the ground. The Kaizeluun glanced towards the sound.

“We need to go,” he said, “you can join us, if you are—”

A crack shot through the street.

One of the Thearan’s heads exploded, their body twitching as it collapsed. The Austris Aran leapt into the sky, a gust of wind buffeting Karak as the other two warriors launched into action.

An Ermoori soldier, alone—presumably not for long—had taken cover behind a corner, his rifle pointed right at Karak. The explosion of the rifle blinded him and he crashed to the floor. By the time he could see again, the Ermoori was grappling with the other warriors.

And Karak wasn’t dead.

How *long will my luck keep going*? he wondered, *surely I can’t keep surviving such close encounters*.

He checked himself over quickly; there were no wounds. Had he been knocked over? He couldn’t remember. The others fought viciously against the lone Ermoori, but even three to one wasn’t quite enough for them to do any real damage. There were almost no gaps in their armour, and they had been trained to fight effectively.

Karak snatched his rifle from the ground and readied it. He aimed at the Ermoori. The fight was intense; every one of them trading blows, the fight spilling over into the street.

The Ermoori slammed the butt of his rifle into the *Kaizeluun*'s face and landed a vicious headbutt to the Thearan. The Austris Aran swooped from above, but in that moment the Ermoori was open. Karak pulled the trigger; the Ermoori's head snapped back, though he couldn't tell if he had broken through the armour.

But it was enough. The Austris Aran rammed into the soldier feet first with enough power to flatten him against the ground. Karak approached, his rifle pointed at the soldier.

"This will not have killed him," the Austris Aran said, "get ready to shoot."

The Austris Aran knelt and dragged off the soldier's helmet. Even for a being as strong as an Austris Aran, it looked difficult. He heard something crunch from within the armour.

When the helmet cleared, a young face emerged. Too young for a soldier. Despite the war, despite the booms of Ermoori rifles growing ever closer, Karak hesitated. This was a child. Tarsi didn't grow hair, but he knew how it grew on human faces; this boy had almost no facial hair, and what he did have was patchy and pale. How many more of these oppressive soldiers were still boys?

"What are you waiting for?" the Austris Aran snapped, "the battle approaches."

"He's—"

The young soldier woke up, his youthful quality twisted by instant rage as he stared up at Karak. He snarled, thrashing under the Austris Aran's ornate silver and blue boot.

"Do it," the Austris Aran said, "now."

A bare instant later, two more Ermoori soldiers rounded a corner, seeing Karak and the others. The trapped soldier went for his rifle. Karak fired.

The ancient stone ground of Aethos was lost in the splattering of dark red blood and viscera as the Ermoori's head exploded. Karak had to fight to stop himself from throwing up. He had no time to think on what he'd just done; the new soldiers spotted them.

Chaos erupted around him as rifles barked and shouts rang out through the street. The three warriors leapt into combat without hesitation; Karak ran for the temple.

He still held the rifle. It was so heavy; he looked forward to the day he could put it down, and never pick it up again.

Mattias

1798

Mattias was close to Riffolk when the Prime Overseer gave the order to attack. Close to the front line. Tanks fired their cannons directly into the city walls beside the gate, and hundreds of soldiers gave war cries as they charged as hundreds more fired at enemy warriors they could see.

Mattias took aim at a Shenza standing on the city wall. At this distance, accuracy wasn't as good, but Mattias had practiced long distance shots a lot in Tarsium. He slowed his breathing, adjusted his aim, and squeezed the trigger.

His rifle roared, and barely an instant later his target toppled, disappearing behind the battlements.

"Sir," one of his men said, "I saw that! Incredible shot, sir."

Mattias smiled.

"Okay lads, there'll be a prize for whoever makes a better shot," Mattias said, "I got him in the chest. Head shots from this distance or further, report to me and I'll come up with something to give you."

A cheer rose up from his squad.

Finally, he thought, *we are back to being a solid team.* The enemy ahead of them, surrounded by their brothers-in-arms.

Above them, the strange blue-skinned beings flew, swooping in every direction as they threw spears into the Ermoori. Their wings were gold, shining brilliantly even in the dim smoke-filled air. If he hadn't believed in magic already… Ermoori soldiers were yanked into the air as though up had become down, and then plummet back down with a sickening crunch.

Prime Overseer Hayne was close to the front of the army. Even so, there were at least a dozen ranks between them and Aethos. Close enough to fire, far enough to avoid most of the damage; Ermoori rifles had a range well beyond even Shenza bows.

Mattias took aim and fired again. He hit his target in the arm; not lethal, but enough to slow him down. The Shenza certainly wouldn't be wielding his bow anymore.

The soldiers around him began to march forward; their tanks were tearing massive holes in the wall, and they would be in the city in no time. Explosions rocked the ground, the booms of Ermoori rifles surrounding him.

From the gaping holes in Aethos' walls, warriors rushed at the Ermoori. Thousands of them, sprinting without hesitation despite the tanks firing right at them. There were just as many Ermoori. But even so, and even with his almost-indestructible armour, Mattias found himself resisting the march forward.

For the first time, the war felt like a real war; nothing but the two armies facing each other. Both out in the open. No hiding, no tricks. Strength against strength.

Thearans, Shenza and the strange blue-skinned beings all rushed at him together. He was certain there were Tarsi among them, but it was impossible to tell. Mattias fired, over and over, growing more desperate the closer they drew. He was only a few ranks back from the front line.

Ahead, the two armies clashed. The clang of steel swords and spears bashing against Ermoori armour was deafening. Up close, the Thearans were far more vicious. Plumes of fire slammed into soldiers around him, as though the One True God Himself was burning the world down. Like the cannon rounds fired by Ermoori tanks, fireballs screamed through the air from the enemy's side, exploding with enough force to throw half a dozen Ermoori soldiers to the ground.

Two Thearans and a Shenza broke through the lines and lunged at Mattias. Their steel wouldn't break through his armour; but that didn't stop fear from viciously gripping his heart as they slashed and stabbed. He fired his rifle one-handed as he tried to fend them off with the other; he missed, but the Shenza flinched.

The Thearans didn't react at all. They shoved in closer, their blades low and pointing up. Mattias just managed to bring his rifle in close, pointed at the closest Thearan, and fired.

Although the warrior was wearing heavy steel armour, the round from Mattias' rifle slammed right through him, a burst of blood exploding over the fighting warriors behind him. The surviving Thearan growled, and fire sprang to life in his hand. Real, burning flame. He rammed his fist into Mattias' chest, and a deafening roared filled his ears as he was launched into the air.

He landed heavily, half-blind and gasping. His rifle lay a metre away, but he had been thrown back into Ermoori ranks, and he didn't have to fight off enemy warriors to get it back. Even so, the soldiers around him were focused on the fight, and he had to shove his way past a couple of them, barely breathing and moving against their push forward, before he retrieved his weapon. By the time he turned back, the Ermoori had advanced closer to Aethos. Soldiers were dying; but nowhere near as many as their opponents.

They moved forward at an almost marching pace. Mattias rushed to get back to his unit. His chest was tight, an ache settling where the Thearan had done… whatever that was. And still, his armour wasn't even dented.

Aethos' walls were close now. They loomed above him, stone thicker than any building in Ermoor, their age evident in the deep pits and dulled colour.

Enemies rushed from the massive hole in hordes. They outnumbered the Ermoori, but Mattias and the others held rank, shooting endlessly into the sea of warriors. Mattias killed so many that he lost count. They stopped being living beings; they were merely targets. All the feelings he might have experienced fled in the wake of so much death. After perhaps an hour of constant fighting, even fear had abandoned him.

Mattias had become a vessel, nothing but the deliverer of death. Every now and then, more warriors broke through to his unit; they fought, working perfectly as a team. Pride dragged its way up from the depths; it was good to feel something. His team were brave and dedicated.

They passed through the great hole in the wall and into the city proper. Despite the fighting, it was much cleaner, newer-looking, than the wall's outer surface looked. The buildings were strange, starkly different from anything in Ermoor. They were made of stone similar to the city walls, but smaller and carved to interesting shapes. Large windows lined the tops of their walls, just under the rooves. There was no glass in any of them.

Streets were narrower, and also made of stone, though countless trees lined every road. Luckily, other than behind doors and around corners, there were few places for their enemies to hide. And since they weren't in Tarsium, he assumed there were no hidden tunnels from which the natives could appear.

The blue-skinned, golden-winged beings soared above them, throwing spears down into the battle. They didn't pierce Ermoori armour, but they hit hard enough that they slammed soldiers to the ground with brutal force. Somehow, random soldiers were yanked up into the air by invisible means and came crashing down to the stone street a few moments later. This, also, didn't kill any soldiers, at least not that Mattias could see; the affected men stood, albeit shakily, and continued fighting.

Fire was everywhere. Even the stone burned. If he hadn't already seen evidence for magic, this final battle showed him that it was real.

Mattias stuck close to his unit, guiding them through Aethos gradually as the fighting grew more intense. Thearans fought with reckless abandon, throwing themselves at the Ermoori with everything they had. Their swords were nowhere near enough to do any damage to his armour, but Mattias still felt every blow.

The Shenza were more difficult to dispatch; their swords were stronger, sharper, and their fighting style was far more precise. Just as he thought it, he heard an Ermoori soldier scream. A Shenza pulled her blade from the soldier's knee, between the armour plates. Mattias shot the enemy down. His unit fought back-to-back in a side street, surrounded by warriors as other soldiers pushed further into the city.

One of the flying creatures landed nearby; Mattias didn't hesitate. He fired, and the booms of several more rifles joined his own as his men saw the enemy. Mattias had become a skilled marksman, but when he fired, nothing happened. The shots of his unit failed to hit the creature too.

He fired again, sighting right down the barrel; nothing. If his rifle hadn't roared, he might have believed he was out of ammo. It was impossible.

"Fire again!" he shouted, "and if we can't hit it with guns, rush it with your knives!"

His unit gave a unified war cry and launched into another attack. The creature growled and moved so quickly towards them that it seemed to be falling forwards. Before he could react, it rammed a fist into Mattias' chest.

He flew through the air, caught roughly on the neck by something an instant later. Another low growl came from behind him, and he was turned around to see the creature.

It brought him close to its face, its teeth bared. Those eyes… they were endless, stark white, with no pupils, and they seemed to glow. What *was* this creature? It certainly wasn't human. A cold, intense wind kicked up around him, and Aethos fell away. The drop in his stomach was sickening, but he managed to hold onto his rifle. The creature's grip on his neck was all that stopped him from falling as they rose into the air.

Mattias gritted his teeth, forcing himself not to gasp for air; he wouldn't give this creature the satisfaction. He stared into its eerie, empty eyes, and carefully brought up the barrel of his rifle.

He didn't know how high they'd come off the ground, but now was his chance.

"You made a mistake," he said, "getting this close."

The rifle bucked in his hand without a shoulder to brace against. At the same time, the creature's face twisted in a scowl of pain. A splash of purple sprayed out behind the blue-skinned being, and it let go of his neck.

He plummeted, dark grey air rushing around him as the sky and ground became a chaotic blur.

Barely a moment passed—though it did feel like longer—before Mattias slammed into the hard stone ground. His vision shrank to a tiny point of grey surrounded by brilliant white. He felt nothing. His lungs had somehow frozen; his entire chest was cold, and he couldn't pull in any air.

A strange kind of buzzing filled his ears. He groaned, but couldn't hear his voice. When he tried to move, the numbness fell away, swiftly replaced by fierce agony.

His hearing slowly returned as he forced himself to his feet.

"Sir!" a young voice called out, "sir, are you okay?"

Mattias tried to respond, but he could barely breathe. A hand came to rest on his shoulder; how he felt it through the pulsing that tore through his body, and his armour, he'd never know. He looked up to see Lewys, one of the young men who'd been added to his unit from the survivors of another.

"Lewys," he managed, "I'm… I'm alright. I just need a moment. Or two."

He couldn't tell where he was. The streets of Aethos all looked the same. Mattias managed to stand upright, just in time to see the rest of his unit rush to his side. Slowly, the buzzing in his ears was replaced by the sound of combat; still nearby, so they couldn't be too far behind the fighting.

"Sir," Petor—the doctor—said, "let me check you over for injuries."

"I'm okay, doctor," Mattias said, "we have fighting to do."

His men nodded, and he could feel their smiles through their helmets. He couldn't afford to let them see him suffer.

"And someone find my rifle," he added.

Danel

1798

Tense fear gripped the entire city. It clawed its way into Danel's chest, ruthless and cold. The darkness, as thick as an ocean, had settled over all of them with suffocating intensity.

Danel spent as much time indoors as possible since arriving in Aethos. He much preferred being outside, but with things as they were, there was no better option. He couldn't breathe properly under the dark, smoky heat.

Lenala agreed with Danel; they sat together now, playing a game of Thrones given to them by a Tarsi agent. Danel was winning, but it was close.

Despite fear and tension filling the already smoke-filled air, the last few months had come with a surprisingly pleasant development; Lenala and Danel were spending most of their time together. They even shared the same quarters now.

"It should be the beginning of winter now," Lenala said, "but it's still so… well…"

"And it won't get better anytime soon," Danel said, "but in the meantime… it's your turn."

Lenala nodded, and moved a soldier piece forward.

"We've been here a little while," she said as Danel answered with a mounted warrior piece, "the Ermoori must be close."

Danel gave a frustrated smile, more of a grimace than anything else. He'd been working hard to forget their situation. The idea of facing the Ermoori again left him feeling sick. He couldn't imagine a scenario in which the Circle could win against them; they had already lost every battle, and nothing much had changed other than the warriors of each country training together as a unified army.

But that would not be enough. Danel knew it, and he had a feeling everyone else in Aethos did too.

"Thanks for the reminder," he said, "I was almost beginning to forget how much danger we're in."

"Sorry," Lenala said, "it's just on my mind."

"It's on all our minds, Lenala. Which is why taking our mind off it is important. When we can."

Lenala nodded.

Their blades were laid to their left, as Shen tradition dictated. Despite sitting down, his waist felt strange without the blade tied in place. Perhaps the looming threat of combat made him yearn for the familiar weight at his side. He had found himself being tempted to wear it while seated, even while sleeping; but it was simply not done. Besides, they were deep within the city. When the Ermoori did arrive, Danel and Lenala would have plenty of notice.

He moved a piece on the board, and Lenala uttered a small laugh as she moved an assassin piece. Danel saw it too late; he'd left an opening for her to attack the king.

"Damn," he said with a laugh of his own, "how did I miss that?"

The rest of the game went quickly; Lenala took two more pieces, and his king was taken. She gave him a lopsided smile, her violet eyes pulling at him. Her face flowed down to an almost pointed chin, lending her an elegance that even other Shenza did not have.

"I win," she said gently, "now it's your turn."

She was beautiful. He couldn't believe he took this long to notice; when he first met her in Tarsium, he'd seen her as just another fellow Shen. Now, everything about her was incredible. Even the slight kink in the bridge of her nose from an Ermoori soldier's vicious attack was beautiful. She took him by the hand to their bed.

A sudden, intoxicating urgency seized them both, and as they gave in to their passion, the war was forgotten.

Barely an hour passed, during which they dressed and played Thrones again, before the news reached them.

They heard the footsteps before the voice called out.

"War!" a man's voice boomed in the silence, "the battle is starting!"

Other voices echoed the call, and their private peace turned instantly to chaos.

They snatched their blades and left their quarters. Just as they stepped out into the dim cold day, Lenala put her hand on Danel's arm. Her purple eyes, normally vibrant, were dark shadows that gripped him with their desperation.

"Danel," she said, "no matter what happens, please promise me... that we'll stick close together."

He nodded, holding her face in his hands.

"We will be side-by-side the whole time," he said.

A distant boom rumbled through the streets.

It was time.

He had spent so long dreading this moment, it was unreal to face it now. His stomach had pulled tight enough that he felt it in his throat. Thousands of people rushed around them through the streets.

Shenza, Thearans and Austris Arans moved together, faces set in grim determination.

Danel and Lenala ran for the battle. It went against every instinct he possessed; he'd seen the Ermoori fight. But this was their last chance.

As they ran, he drew his blade. It was no *Kaizuun*, but it gave him strength nonetheless.

The explosions grew painfully loud as they approached the city's north. Aethos' army crowded around the front gates, so vast that Danel and Lenala couldn't hear the shouts of the warriors at the gates.

Even so, they heard the Ermoori rifles firing well enough. And the cannons on their tanks were deafening; it was these that they'd heard first further into the city.

Either side of the gates, two massive holes had been torn into the thick stone. Danel could see brief flashes of yellow light through them, turning the mass of warriors fighting in the opening into teeming silhouettes.

Above them, Austris Arans soared over the battle, pulling Ermoori soldiers up with Air Magic and letting them drop. Despite their power, and that of all the other warriors combined, Danel watched helplessly as the Ermoori pushed into Aethos. He saw the fighting, the death, the desperation, and almost gave in to the urge to run away.

"They're coming," Lenala said, "they're breaking through our defences!"

“Teaming up is not enough,” Danel said, his stomach twisting, “and it’s too late to make a better plan.”

In that moment, anger was all he knew. It went against the Shenza tenets, but he couldn’t help it. The Circle was supposed to know everything. They were supposed to make plans for the future. Why had they let the war come to them without a real plan with which to fight?

It made no sense to him.

The Circle’s amassed army moved with the shifting line of battle, like the constantly moving leaves of the mighty trees in Shanaken. In several areas, the Ermoori seemed about to break through into the city proper, and areas where the warriors of Aethos were standing fast against them.

But with every moment, the Ermoori drew closer.

Kerberos

1798

Weeks passed in hiding, during which Kerberos and Nomiki read the scrolls he had taken from Austris Ara's temple.

One of them was an extension of the disguise spell he already knew; one that allowed the caster to alter their entire body, not just their head.

Useful, he thought, *most useful*.

They blended into the crowd of Aethos, waiting for the war to finish from an inn room. It was potentially dangerous, but they had heard that the Ermoori spared non-combatants. All they needed to do was lay low, avoid fighting, and let Aethos be taken over.

After that, he could make plans for what to do with Riffolk Hayne. Either that, or at the very least, take Omatus back from the Ermoori.

When the fighting started, Kerberos was out gathering supplies. Luckily, he was in the southern districts, where the biggest markets were. The Ermoori had been outside Aethos' gates a little while, so he knew the fight was coming; but he thought he'd have enough time to stock up on necessities before the battle began.

He heard explosions first. The ground shook, and the streets filled with startled cries and screams. Then, moments later, messengers sprinted down the streets shouting "war!"

The streets became a mess of terror as civilians ran for shelter and warriors ran for the gates.

Kerberos was torn; he wanted to see the fighting, get a sense of how it would play out, but he needed to lay low. He already carried a sack of goods. If he approached now, in the first hours of the battle, it likely wouldn't matter if he appeared to be a civilian; the Ermoori would kill anyone in their way.

Best to return to the inn, then, he thought, *the fighting will reach us anyway. I can watch then.*

The decision made, Kerberos hurried for the inn. He was in disguise as an Omati once again, far shorter than himself. It took focus to complete the picture; outward appearance was only the beginning.

He had to move like a civilian. He cast furtive glances behind him, ran hunched, clutching his bag. Fear was a difficult expression to make on purpose, but as he ran, he performed his best approximation.

It took close to an hour to walk back to the inn. Aethos wasn't as large as Omatus, but it was still a big city. Nomiki sat on the bed, sharpening her sword.

"Did you find enough?" she asked, "at least to last us the next couple days?"

Kerberos nodded.

"The battle has begun," he said, "did you hear it?"

"Some explosions. The combat itself is still too far away."

He set down the bag and cast off his disguise.

"I do not know if they search buildings," Kerberos said, "but we must be ready if they do."

"I'll find a place to hide the weapons," Nomiki said, "other than that, we have nothing to worry about. The disguise spells are quick to cast."

"I want to get a closer look at the fighting," Kerberos said, "when they reach us."

Nomiki put her blade down. She stood, looking intently at Kerberos.

"What will you gain from getting close to the combat?"

"I want to know how I can beat them," Kerberos said, "after they have taken Aethos. I want to know what Hayne will do when they win. And I want to know what happens to the Circle of Shadows."

They had spoken about the Circle many times; Nomiki told him of their offer to Kerberos, and of his infiltration of their headquarters and how he'd read the book of Asheilos.

He knew of their mission to destroy Sithares. With the endless smoke pouring from Sitharkos, Kerberos understood why they would try. But he had to know if it was possible to succeed in such an endeavour; the idea of killing a God was fascinating. Not only would it spare Pandeia from the smoke and heat that choked the air, it would mean the people would be free from Sithares' corrupting influence.

"I looked into their history," Nomiki said, "now that they are here, with an army of thousands, information is easy to come by."

Kerberos waited. He knew he didn't need to ask.

"There was a war of the gods, thousands of years ago. The original Circle was formed to defend Pandeia against Sithares, who decided Pandeia needed to burn down and be created anew from the ashes. At least, that's the legend being told."

"Sithares does not want to create anything," Kerberos said, "it only burns. It wants only chaos. To spread its destruction across everything."

Nomiki nodded, though her brow was creased, her jaw set.

"The people are talking about the Heroes," she said, "a small group of powerful magicians who trapped Sithares in the original war. There are new Heroes now... You met them, I believe, when you attacked Azar."

Kerberos frowned.

"So things are happening now as they did before," he said, "I wonder why the Heroes decided not to trap Sithares again."

"They must have found a way to destroy it that wasn't known before."

"Possibly," Kerberos said, "or perhaps they do not know why Sithares was trapped instead of destroyed. There could be more to the story."

Nomiki glanced back at her sword, on the bed out of its scabbard.

"If they had a reason not to kill it," she mused, "then the Circle attempting it now would be a mistake."

Nodding, Kerberos rifled through the ancient documents they had taken from Austris Ara. Dust still lay on them, though much of it had shaken off when they first read through them.

"The phrasing of this passage," Kerberos said as he looked through the documents, "is interesting. Here. Read this."

Nomiki's eyes darted over the scroll.

"The five Gods of Pandeia are elemental forces controlled by a sentient spiritual mind. They are not mortal, in the same sense that the people of Pandeia are mortal; they will always exist. They may not be killed."

She frowned, reading over it again silently.

"This is... vague. It leaves room for interpretation."

"Exactly," Kerberos said, "and it does not say they cannot be killed. It says they *may* not be killed. An important distinction."

"So it is phrased as a matter of authority, rather than ability... but what does that mean for the Circle?"

"It means there will likely be consequences if Sithares is killed," Kerberos said, "or possibly that it will not end the way they assume. Either way, I want to be there when it happens."

Several hours after their talk, sounds of combat reached them. Nomiki hid their weapons, other than a simple dagger which Kerberos tied to the back of his belt under a travel cloak.

He cast disguise spells again, and ventured out into the dark, smoky chaos.

The fighting was messy, nothing like what Kerberos would have expected. There was almost no organisation on the Circle's side. They tried, and he could see their familiarity with each other in their actions, but whatever training they had done was not enough.

Magic flowed all around him, vibrant and buzzing with lethal energy. There were two massive sources pulling at him from different directions; a single mix of multiple different magic types to the north, which had to be Riffolk Hayne, and a group of incredibly powerful magic types to the south; the Heroes. Both were active, crackling with energy that made the air around him pulse. For the Heroes to be away from the fighting and still using so much magic, their mission must have begun.

They were attempting to destroy Sithares. With a glance towards the fighting, Kerberos turned and ran for Austris Ara.

Karak

1798

The temple loomed above him, even several streets away.

I have to find Zeera, he thought, *report the fighting to her. She must be told how quickly the Ermoori are approaching*.

They were still hours away, but as far as the war went, that was incredibly fast. Zeera would need time to prepare. Though what her reaction would be, he had no idea; she couldn't stop the Ermoori, even with the Heroes fighting for her.

`Still, reporting to her was infinitely better than remaining where he'd been. He just had to plan where to go after speaking with Zeera; there would be almost no safe places to hide in the coming hours and days. The Ermoori were thorough. They had even found Tarsium's hidden tunnels.

There is nowhere to hide, he thought, *I can only hope they see me as a non-combatant and let me live*.

They wouldn't let anyone leave the city after the battle, surely; they cared far too much about asserting control over Pandeia. So there was no hiding, and no escape.

Karak sighed. He was tired of being pessimistic. Tired of the constant fear of death. All he had ever wanted was his own life. To live the way he wanted, free of dangerous responsibility to the Circle. Was it really too much to ask?

Austris Ara was beautiful; the difference between it and Aethos was almost unbelievable. Where Aethos was all ancient stone and old trees, Austris Ara shined as if it had only just been made. The architecture was different, too, though many buildings in Aethos used the same style. It was the royal palace—and the Air Temple on top—that stood out; it could have been a city unto itself, vast both in width and height.

Karak stopped, panting heavily as he looked back the way he had come. Even rushing, the journey had taken long enough to make him worry.

From here, he couldn't see any trace of the Heroes, not even any Circle presence save for a lone Austria Aran guard.

The fastest way to get to Zeera would be shifting into bird form; he could fly up to the roof and start looking from there. It was where the Austris Arans placed their temple, so it stood to reason that Zeera and her Heroes would be there.

Distantly, Karak heard rumbling, punctuated by the tiny cracks of Ermoori rifles from so far away.

Even with the distance, the fighting was uncomfortably close. Karak climbed onto a nearby building; he couldn't leave the rifle and armour on the street. He placed them carefully out of sight of the ground level.

I'll have to remember where they are, he thought, *after all this is done*. They were far too dangerous to risk someone stumbling upon them. But then again, with the likelihood of Ermoor winning the war... They would most likely be found by an Ermoori soldier anyway. And getting back here if they did win was going to be far too dangerous.

He sighed, rubbing his forehead. They were trapped, all of them; cornered by war, smothered by smoke and fire. There was no way out. No good options.

How had it come to this?

An explosion roared from painfully close, and a building nearby collapsed as chunks of stone flew in every direction. An Ermoori tank rolled down the main street, still quite a distance away, a tiny line of smoke curling up from the barrel of its cannon.

Karak ducked low and rushed to the opposite side of the roof. He hid behind the curved dome in the centre of the roof, and then froze as a cold feeling sliced through his chest.

At first, he had no idea where it came from. He looked around the wide street that surrounded the temple, but there was nothing. The battle was still a distance away. There were no people around except one or two Circle agents keeping watch on rooftops.

Except...

Karak's eyes went wide. One of the Circle agents stood facing the wrong way. He stood tall, staring up at the temple.

It took a moment for Karak's eyes to adjust to the disguise spell. But when he saw the person underneath, a dread more vicious than any he had ever known seized him by the heart and squeezed. He couldn't breathe. He couldn't even think.

Kerberos.

Karak was frozen, his heart barely able to beat.

Why him? *Why now*?

He had to escape. *Shift*, he thought, *shift into something and run*. But his mind was stuck. Where could he go? What would he do when he got there? Kerberos couldn't be escaped.

And as he struggled to break out of his paralysing terror, Kerberos' eyes met his own.

Kerberos

1798

It took him a while to reach the temple. He stopped on a rooftop on the other side of the wide circular street that surrounded it, and spared a glance back at Aethos.

Time was running out. The smoke that had been roiling above them was closer, its suffocating heat growing worse each passing moment. At the temple's peak, the smoke spiralled down in a chaotic whirlwind to meet the roof. It looked like Sithares itself reaching down from the Gods' realm and lancing the temple.

An almost constant orange glow shone through from behind the smoke; fire, pure and raging, burning the very sky of Pandeia. Its heat lashed his skin, and memories of his death pulled at his mind.

Unyielding, endless fire, consuming him with vicious hunger. There was nothing but pain in that realm. The worst kind of pain, forever. And even if the Circle somehow succeeded in destroying Sithares—and there were no hidden consequences—Pandeia would belong to the Ermoori.

He remembered a little of what Omatus had looked like under attack by those unstoppable soldiers. And now he was seeing them lay waste to Aethos, one street at a time.

The Circle was attempting to destroy Sithares now. Kerberos turned back to the temple, staring up at its peak, far taller than any other building he had ever seen. The magic rushed from them in waves, powerful enough to distract him from the burning sky above.

Looking at the temple, Kerberos was struck by a strange and sudden gratitude; if he hadn't already gained the ability to fly, getting to the top would have taken far too long.

I must see this fight, he thought, *between Sithares and the Heroes.*

He had to understand how the Heroes were fighting this fight; how they expected to destroy a God. If they could wield that kind of power, then so could he. And he could bring it to bear against Riffolk and his army. That was, if it worked at all.

The far more likely scenario was either Sithares won the fight, or the Heroes destroyed it but at too steep a cost. He only hoped there would be something left of Pandeia after all this was done.

At the point where the fiery smoke met the temple's roof, flashes of yellow lightning arced up into the sky. Brief glimpses of the other magic types slashed through the air, too; blades of pure black, swirls of water, and almost invisible gusts of air swept up into the chaos. Somewhere within the roiling, burning smoke, Kerberos just barely made out a figure.

There was the curve of a calf muscle. Impossibly far above that was the bulge of a muscular shoulder. Somewhere in between those two was a massive hand, curled into a burning fist. And there, at the top, beyond even the line of the clouds; two eyes, shining brighter than the sun.

It was almost the size of the Austria Aran temple. A being so vast, it struck even Kerberos with sickening awe. Nothing alive could possibly be that gargantuan.

Kerberos shook his head.

There is no winning against that, he thought, *an army of Heroes could not destroy that thing.*

For the first time he could remember, real fear gripped Kerberos. He'd seen flashes of Sithares in his memory; a small, deathly-looking figure made of burning logs, dragging itself out of a bonfire. He had made a deal with it. He remembered these things, in fractured moments, flitting images. But he had never seen anything the likes of which stood in the burning air above him now. It could have crushed the Air Temple under its feet.

And yet, its physical body wasn't attacking; it seemed to be locked in a battle of pure magic. *Even at its most powerful*, he thought, *it still can't interact physically with our world*.

Kerberos began preparing a new disguise spell—he couldn't fly above the battle without drawing attention unless he looked like an Austris Aran—when he spotted a lone figure watching him. It was an Omati, a man, atop the roof of a nearby building. Kerberos was still disguised as an Omati himself, but the watching man stared at him with a look of horror. And worse; recognition.

Impossible, Kerberos thought, *no one can see through Deias disguise spells... can they*?

He abandoned the half-formed spell on his palm, letting the runes fade as he brought Fire Magic to the surface.

I do not have time to find out.

Without another moment's hesitation, Kerberos launched himself at the man. Even from across the wide main street, he reached the strange Omati man in an instant.

It was so fast that it shocked even himself; he wasn't quite ready, and the Omati slipped under his arms. He changed before Kerberos' eyes, his body rapidly shrinking, his arms broadening into wings.

Tarsi, Kerberos thought, *of course*.

The man, who had now become a bird, flew over the rooftop's edge, swooping down to build speed before shooting up into the sky. It flew southwest, avoiding the temple and the battle approaching them.

A survivor, and a coward.

Kerberos leapt to the ground, and sprinted through the streets to follow the bird. There was an Austris Aran guard at the temple's main door, and he didn't want her to see what he could do.

With shockingly little effort, Kerberos sent a bolt of lightning at the bird as he ran. He hit its leg, but it was a glancing blow that didn't stop it from flying. It picked up speed, pushing to get out of range of Kerberos' magic.

Out of sight of the main temple doors, he swept himself onto a rooftop with Air Magic. Instead of a lightning bolt, Kerberos willed a shadow blade to materialise in his hand, and imbued it with Air Magic. The blade vibrated with energy, ready to fly. He focused on the bird, attuned his focus to the Air Magic inside him, and let the blade go.

It streaked through the air so fast that it whistled. The bird twirled, banking in every direction; but Kerberos' blade was fixed to his mind, and he watched his target intently.

His blade sliced through the bird's neck. Its head fell instantly, and the body followed.

Satisfied, he turned his attention once again to the temple battle. Despite the cold dread that came over him when he looked at the figure hidden in the firestorm, Kerberos had never felt more powerful. It wasn't just magic; he was used to that feeling, even when he couldn't remember anything. There was something else, deeper than the elemental forces lashing and roiling within him.

A sense of *completeness*. He was more than human now, more even than immortal. He was... God-like. There was a place in his body for all five magics, like there was a place for each of his organs. They all fit together.

He held his hand out, palm up, and summoned a sphere of each magic type. They floated in a perfect circle above his palm, perfectly balanced, completely controlled. In response to his thoughts, they combined to form a single ball that crackled in his hand. It shifted instantly into new shapes as he imagined them, and moved through the air as easily as a breeze.

A vague memory surfaced of the practice he went through to control simple fireballs; now, controlling magic was as easy as moving his hand. It bent to him willingly, as though it was always meant to be his. As though magic itself had been created for Kerberos to wield.

Shouts rang out behind him, and he turned to see a group of Ermoori soldiers break through the ranks of warriors and sprint towards the temple.

The fighting hadn't cooled down; not even with the appearance of Sithares in the sky. He wondered if any of those fighting had even noticed. At a glance, it simply looked like a chaotic storm of sorts; Sithares' form was mostly hidden behind the fire and smoke.

Back the way he'd come, the Ermoori were making good time. The warriors of Aethos' were giving chase, but they were being picked off by the superior weapons of the invaders. They were approaching fast, sprinting down the main street, with nothing in their way.

And at the head of the group of soldiers was Riffolk Hayne.

Riffolk

1798

His suit was everything he'd wanted it to be. It channelled his magic brilliantly. He sent bolt after bolt of searing lightning into the enemy ranks, and blades made of unbreakable, razor-sharp shadow into the flying creatures.

The soldiers around him were shocked by the display; but they fought through it, never breaking rank, never giving in to fear.

As expendable as they were, Riffolk found himself feeling a brief glow of pride. He didn't care if they died, or even if they were wounded. The equipment he'd provided them with was far more important, and it was all working perfectly.

But it still gave him that bit of pride to know his soldiers were fighting with bravery.

His own unit, made up of elite soldiers who had demonstrated the highest loyalty and skill, kept formation around him. They moved as one through the battle, killing everything in their path. Their mission was to get to the temple. Riffolk knew that was where the powerful magicians were; and where he would find Mara.

The rest of his army could be left to their own devices. He knew Aethos was his. At least a third of the soldiers were still outside the walls, waiting for the space to clear up. Even those who were in the city were more than a match for the pitiful forces within.

Riffolk sent waves of magic into the enemy forces. Fireballs shrieked towards him from Thearan warriors.

They fought for hours, moving steadily through the city. His soldiers never let up. More importantly, his technology never failed. The rifles never jammed, a problem that had been present in previous iterations. The armour was almost seamless, impervious to the enemy's swords and arrows.

It was only magic that posed a threat; and even then, most of his soldiers survived direct hits from fireballs. The Shadow Magic imbued within their armour plates was a perfect foil to the Fire's blistering heat.

Riffolk's armour fared even better. The reactive alloy he had designed for his external plates absorbed magic it came into contact with. Any magical attack aimed at him only made him stronger. There was a limit, of course; all technology had its limits. But even the most powerful magicians in this battle couldn't overwhelm his armour.

Another fireball hit him. The impact shuddered through him, but it was more like a rough shove than a lethal attack. The energy from it dissipated through his armour, and the buzz in his weapon told him it was ready to fire.

He aimed at a group of the flying creatures and pulled the trigger. Immediately, a jet of screaming flame lanced through the air and slammed into the creatures. Riffolk barely heard their screaming over the rush and roar of the fire. His soldiers were still too shocked by what Riffolk could do to cheer, but their morale lifted nevertheless, evident in the renewed determination of their attacks.

Rifles barked, and the barely-armoured Thearans, Shenza and Omati fell. Even when the Shenza cast shadow shield spells in time, the magic-imbued ammunition Riffolk had designed was simply too powerful.

He fought his way through the city, killing as many as he could. He had to be seen fighting as much as possible; the enemy would learn that Riffolk Hayne was infallible. They would learn that, as unstoppable as his army was, Riffolk himself was even worse. If he could prove that, send the message as clearly and as forcefully as possible, none would ever dare stand up to the Prime Overseer. His rule would be absolute.

His forces spread around the city's outskirts, surrounding the enemy. The rest pushed up through the centre like a spear, punching through the enemy's main defences. Those at the back of the spear spread through the remaining enemy ranks.

They left nothing in their wake. A dead city made of ancient stone, painted with the blood of those who defied him.

Riffolk's team followed him through the city centre, moving smoothly, taking aim and firing with practiced precision. His own weapon barely needed to be aimed; it was merely a focusing tool for magic. He controlled the magical attacks he cast, so it didn't matter how good of a shot he was.

A large group of warriors approached, led by three of the blue-skinned creatures. They were headed straight for Riffolk.

"Men," he called, "we have a brave group of heroes come to kill the Prime Overseer."

A wave of jeers rose up from the soldiers, even as they continued fighting.

He waved his men to step down.

"Witness what happens," he said, "when people challenge me."

The world fell away from him as a vicious gust of wind swept him up. Around him, the three flying beings followed, moving easily through the air. They didn't even move their wings to fly.

Riffolk fired a wave of fire as he tumbled upward. The creatures disappeared behind a massive wave of flame; but the moment it died off, they were still there. One of them grabbed him, and they came to a stop in mid-air.

Why did their magic not get absorbed by the suit, he wondered, is it too powerful? Or does the alloy not recognise Air Magic?

"Authelium tharal etherethor loretherae," one of the creatures said, "raleuth Austris Ara arae thora."

Its voice was as gentle as the sky, but deep and commanding nonetheless.

Riffolk drew his dagger; it had been built from Shadow Magic blended with regular steel. It created an alloy that was surprisingly strong. He had honed it to the finest edge possible. It couldn't cut through Shenza steel, but it cut through almost everything else.

The creatures took one careless look at his blade and ignored it, preoccupied instead with the firearm he still held.

He drew on the Power Magic within him, willing a bolt of lightning to form in the barrel of the firearm in his hand. One of the creatures grabbed at it, and Riffolk fired. The bolt of magic burst through the forearm of the creature, obliterating it in a flash of yellow light and a spray of purple blood.

All that remained of the creature's hand was a jagged stump halfway up its forearm. Its screech filled Riffolk's helmet, piercing into his head and forcing his eyes shut from the pain.

The wounded creature backed off, nursing its arm as it glared at him. It still flew with no apparent effort; it seemed that flying, to these beings, was as easy as breathing. The other two had drawn in close, one of them snatching Riffolk's wrist instead of the firearm.

They learn reasonably quickly.

One of them—the one not holding him—drew a spear and levelled its ornate head at his neck.

The one that held him in place grinned, a snarling, wicked grin that spoke of pain and vengeance. Riffolk strained against its grip on his wrist, but it was no use; even the enhanced strength he gained from the suit couldn't rival the muscles of these things.

But they had either forgotten, or never realised, that his weapon didn't need to be aimed.

He pictured what he wanted to happen; a bolt of lightning curving from the barrel, slicing through the chest of the creature holding him up. He would fall, but he could survive that in his suit. At least, the likelihood was high.

As the one pointing its spear at him closed the distance between them, Riffolk willed another bolt into his weapon.

Before he could fire, the spear rammed into his chest, forcing the air from his lungs. For a moment he was certain the blade had pierced his chest plate. But the creatures shrieked, and a moment later he saw the ruined spearhead. He launched the lightning bolt, watching with searing satisfaction as it blasted through the spear wielder's face.

It made a cracking sound that rang out through the hot, dim air as it shattered the creature's skull.

The remaining creature pulled Riffolk in close by the throat, glaring at him with its blank white stare. It smashed a fist into Riffolk's head. Then again, and again, until his vision had blurred into a grey storm.

He stabbed at the creature wildly, feeling the blade hit but not knowing if it penetrated flesh. The creature hit him again, but it held with one hand to do so, and Riffolk's weapon was free.

Riffolk used it at first to beat the creature about the head and body, until he could focus enough to create another magical bolt of ammunition. He went to hit the creature in the head again, but it caught his firearm in its free hand. The barrel pointed directly at its face; Riffolk pulled the trigger.

They both plummeted immediately, the creature's head reduced to a mess of meat and bone. Riffolk clicked the firearm into place in its holster and grabbed the corpse with both hands.

As they fell, he angled the dead body underneath himself and gritted his teeth. It was time to see how his armour held up. He had seen many other soldiers be dragged up and dropped; but those had been short falls compared to how high the creatures had taken him.

The ground rushed towards him.

Without thinking, Riffolk shoved the body down, launching himself off it and aiming his firearm straight down. He fired the most powerful blast of magic he could muster.

It hit the stone ground with a deafening boom, and the force of its impact shoved him back up into the sky. He landed roughly on the stone, but his momentum had been reduced enough that he wasn't even winded by the landing.

A cheer rose up from his soldiers; even their fear of magic wasn't enough to stop them this time.

Riffolk stood, checked over his armour and weapons, and then motioned for his soldiers to push forward. His unit rushed to his side.

The remaining warriors that had approached him still stood waiting for him. With their most powerful members dead, Riffolk barely gave them any thought. He formed Shadow bolts in his firearm and fired them just as the warriors rushed at him.

None of them made it more than two steps. The jet-black bolts ripped through each warrior as though they were paper, spraying blood over the stone behind them.

He was running out of magic; the suit could absorb a lot, but it couldn't generate anything on its own.

"Forward!" he called to his unit, "we must reach that building on the far side."

It is time to finish this war.

Mattias

1798

The Prime Overseer led the charge into Aethos. He was terrifying to behold.

Lightning arced from his weapon, killing everything it touched. He barely aimed, and yet he hit dozens of enemies with the precision of a skilled marksman.

Mattias watched in shock as he fired his weapon with almost careless efficiency. He could have sworn the Prime Overseer wasn't even looking where he fired. Enemies died constantly around him, sometimes multiple at a time.

“Captain,” one of his men called through the din, “is he using magic?”

“Of course not,” Mattias said, “his technology is far more powerful. Besides, magic doesn’t exist.”

Mattias didn’t believe it, and he was certain his men knew it; but he had to say it. Especially with the Prime Overseer so close. Loyalty was paramount.

Their first charge had been hours ago. Now, they were most of the way through Aethos. Mattias had forgotten what it was like outside of war. There was a part of him, distant and quiet, that worried murder and death were all he knew now. It was becoming almost impossible to even imagine what a normal life looked like. The shock of seeing Prime Overseer Hayne shoot lightning and black bolts all over the battlefield was the only thing he’d felt in hours. Even that died down quickly.

Then a group of warriors reached the Prime Overseer and attacked. The flying creatures dragged him up into the air, higher than any of their previous victims. A few long moments later, three bodies smashed onto the stone with sickening thuds. After that, a massive explosion rocked the main street. Riffolk Hayne walked out of it, looking as tired as Mattias, but otherwise unharmed.

The Prime Overseer called for them to push forward.

Before Mattias could react, a Thearan warrior forced her way through a rank of soldiers and landed a kick in the centre of Mattias’ chest. He landed roughly on the ground, his breath catching as his rifle skittered over the blood-stained stone.

He struggled to rise; he was sore all over, and exhausted.

The Thearan leapt onto him with a roar, a dagger in each hand. She slammed them down into his chest plate at the same time. The impact jarred him down to his bones. Without waiting to see if she'd caused any damage, the Thearan brought both blades up and swept them down again, stabbing at every part of him.

Mattias brought his hands up, trying to wrestle her weapons from her, but she was unrelenting. The deep, deafening clang of steel blades bashing against his armour was all he could hear.

A thump hit his left shoulder, and pain exploded there an instant later. Mattias screamed, screwing his eyes shut as it flared through his body. A gunshot exploded, incredibly close, and the weight of the Thearan lifted off him.

"Sir, are you okay?" Petor asked.

"No," he said, "the damn thing found a gap between the plates. Who killed it?"

Robert, the youngest of Mattias' men, stepped forward.

"I did, sir," he said, "not a long-distance shot, but I *did* hit it right in the head."

Mattias forced himself to smile through the pain.

"Well done, lad. I'll make sure you get a medal for this."

The young man stood taller, and the others of his unit clapped him on the back and shoulders.

He stood, shaking from the pain. The Thearan's blade only penetrated a few centimetres, but it burned as though the steel had just been pulled from a forge. He moved his arm, stretching it gently to test the injury; he could still move, at least. It would need stitches as soon as they had the time.

But the battle dragged Mattias' attention to the enemy again; more warriors forced themselves through the ranks, heading for Riffolk.

"Protect the Prime Overseer!" Mattias shouted.

His men rushed to intercept the enemy. The fighting was fierce; these savages were throwing everything they had at Ermoor's leader.

Mattias shot a Shenza in the neck, then kicked it to the ground while it clawed at its throat and gurgled its last few breaths. A Thearan swept his sword down onto Mattias' rifle, then punched him in the head. It didn't hurt, but the sound was deafening. The Thearan pulled his hand away, snarling in pain, and Mattias shot him in the gut.

He dropped to a knee, and Mattias kicked him where the bullet had hit. The man howled and crumpled to the ground.

Two more Thearans leapt over their fellow and attacked Mattias at the same time, short swords clanging on his armour. He blocked as much as he could with his rifle; they were made of the same metal as their armour. Their strikes were too wild to hit him in the tiny gaps between armour plates, but the movement jarred his wounded shoulder, and Mattias found himself being overwhelmed. He rushed one of them, shoving the length of his rifle against the warrior's face. A crunch sound came from the man's nose, and it gave Mattias just enough of an opening.

He swivelled and fired point blank into the second warrior's chest. The man went down instantly, without a sound. The other Thearan growled and threw himself at Mattias.

The ache in his shoulder pulsed with a sickening heat, sweat beading all over Mattias' face. He was glad it was his left shoulder, otherwise shooting would have been far too difficult. Even so, it was becoming harder to focus with each passing moment.

Mattias ducked underneath a horizontal swing at his head and rammed the butt of his rifle into the man's knee.

He buckled, collapsing to the ground in a heap. Mattias had no time to aim properly; he fired three shots into the fallen warrior, and managed to reload his rifle just as yet another attack hit him in the head from behind.

Based on the sound in his helmet and force of the attack, it was a sword swung by someone strong. Very strong. Mattias rolled forwards, grunting with the pain of his shoulder, and twirled out of the roll to face behind him, firing before he could even see who had attacked.

It was a Shenza, but one that looked different. Its tunic was sleeveless, and glowing purple runes were carved down the length of its black blade. Even stranger, it was covered in tattoos, which also glowed purple. It wore long, jet black hair, and bright red eyes shone from its pale face. The blade it carried was long, and looked wickedly sharp.

Mattias had hit it in the side, near the ribcage. But it stood at its full height, holding that strange black sword confidently and staring at him with pure loathing on its face.

A memory suddenly flooded his mind; all those years ago, when he'd been fresh in the army, and patrolled the hidden corridors in Tyra. A Shenza had attacked. It was an unstoppable shadow, dealing death with every blindingly fast movement.

He hadn't seen it clearly, but he'd seen enough.

And it looked exactly like the one standing before him now.

It gestured with a free hand, and a shadow faded into existence above its palm, solidifying into a blade of pure black. Mattias' jaw dropped, and distantly, he was glad that his helmet obscured the expression.

He fired, at the same time grunting as his head snapped back and a ringing clang pierced his ears. Then the Shenza was on him. Mattias roared, firing his rifle again, batting the savage creature's hands away and hitting anything he could reach.

His left shoulder screamed at him. Black and white spots filled his vision as another black blade thudded into the faceplate of his helmet.

This may be it, he thought, *I may be about to die*. And still, he felt nothing. He wasn't afraid, or angry, or even saddened. This was merely his life. Fighting, killing, dying, for Ermoor. For the Prime Overseer. There was nothing else.

He was nothing else. A weapon of Hayne's. An extension of his rifle.

The Shenza summoned more weapons from those strange shadows it controlled, and slammed them down onto his helmet. The same spot, every time. He tried blocking, and disarming, and firing his rifle, but nothing seemed to work. Then he heard a *crack*, and a thin line appeared in the faceplate right in front of his eyes.

With a scream, Mattias rammed his left fist into the Shenza's crotch with as much strength as he could manage, then shoved his rifle's barrel into its gut and fired.

Still, the creature attacked. The expression on its face was one of pain and rage, but it showed no other signs of slowing down.

"Robert," he roared, "shoot this thing in the head, will you?"

A moment later—though it felt like much longer to Mattias—a rough hole appeared in the Shenza's cheek, and the back of its head exploded. Its face went slack, its eyes glassy, and it collapsed. Mattias shoved it off him and dragged himself to his feet.

"Thank you, son," he said through deep breaths, "that's two medals."

Robert nodded, but said nothing. He took aim at another enemy and fired. Mattias sighed. Talking was useless now. Mattias had begun to pride himself on his ability to rally his men, but they were beyond that point. There was no time for inspiring speeches, or spirit-lifting jokes.

There was only death.

Danel

1798

It took hours for the battle to reach them. Standing at the back of the amassed army, Danel and Lenala waited for the Ermoori to reach them. He had never been more terrified; even in Tarsium, the fighting was so different that it might as well have been a separate war. In Aethos, there was nothing but the two armies.

There were no hidden tunnels, no forest of massive trees in which to hide.

By Amalus, he thought when he first saw them, *there are so many*! In both Shanaken and Tarsium, he'd only seen a group at a time; half a dozen, perhaps up to a dozen. But there were *thousands* of them.

They pushed further into Aethos with inhuman uniformity, as though all of them were somehow puppets being controlled by one mind. With their helmets on, all facial features were obscured. It was like fighting against an avalanche; a mass of unstoppable destruction moving inexorably towards them.

As they drew close, Danel froze. He grabbed for Lenala, snatching her hand and gripping it tightly.

"What do we do?" she asked him.

They were not warriors, despite going through the training that all Shenza completed. Danel was a fisher, and a cook. Lenala had been a teacher of *Kuulshenza*, the children of Shanaken.

Shenza meant warrior; they were all supposed to be able to fight. But people like Danel simply weren't natural fighters.

His blade felt useless in its scabbard. What would it do against the Ermoori? They had been able to do some damage with surprise attacks in Tarsium, but even that had come at a severe cost. And they were well beyond surprise attacks now. The enemy was bearing down on them, and there was nowhere to hide.

"I... I don't know," he said, "there isn't much we *can* do. Except fight, I suppose."

"Danel, if we fight, we're going to die."

"I know that," he said, "but we can't run. Even if we get out of the city, and even if we're not seen and punished later, there will be nowhere to hide. Pandeia belongs to the Ermoori now."

They stood together, holding hands, watching helplessly as the enemy approached. It looked like the tide coming in; the ocean effortlessly covering the sand more and more with each passing moment. The tides could not be curbed. They could not be stopped. There was no reasoning with the ocean, it simply followed its nature.

And the Ermoori were following theirs. Conquerors. They had been attempting to take Shanaken for lifetimes. It was who they were.

They were so close now. A few streets away. Close enough that he could feel the stomping of their boots in the stone beneath him. The booms of their rifles shook him, even more than their marching footsteps. In the group ahead of them, screams rang out as warriors fell in sprays of blood.

Danel drew his blade, and Lenala drew her own. His heart had never beat so hard, not even when they had been fired on in Tarsium or Shanaken before that. This time, they were standing in the open streets, waiting for death to claim them.

Why were they fighting? Why didn't they surrender, spare their lives to stop the fighting? Surely living under the control of an enemy was better than being wiped out. If they survived, at least they could make some kind of plan; organise a resistance against the Ermoori leader. Shenza and Tarsi would make excellent assassins.

But they had chosen to fight. He wondered how differently things would have turned out if the Shenza had relinquished Shanaken; would the Ermoori still have levelled the forest? Would they have killed as many warriors?

The Ermoori were close enough now that Danel could have spoken to them. If they had any interest in talking, that was. Their rifles flashed and roared, glowing yellow projectiles streaking from them so fast they could barely be seen. Jet black projectiles tore from other rifles; Shadow Magic.

Just before the soldiers reached Danel and Lenala, he saw the man who could only have been the Ermoori leader.

He wore unique armour; the same jet black as the others, but sleeker, and with shining gold trim around each plate. His weapon was strange, too. The others held simple-looking rifles, but the leader wielded an odd one-handed rifle connected to his suit by a cable that glowed with energy. It fired blasts of pure magic instead of projectiles.

The leader made a broad gesture with his weapon and lightning arced from its barrel, snaking from one warrior to the next in a flash until five of them collapsed. He gestured again, and bolts of shadow sprayed from his weapon so rapidly that Danel couldn't tell how many there were.

Again, a slew of warriors died. The Ermoori leader didn't even look at all those he killed; it was so careless, as though the lives of all the people in Pandeia were utterly meaningless.

Then, all at once, the soldiers were upon them. There were still hundreds—if not thousands—of warriors between him and the bulk of Ermoori soldiers, but the fighting was breaking down into skirmishes.

"Danel," Lenala said, "stay with me."

They fought as well as they could, but the Ermoori weren't just well armed and armoured; they were well-trained too.

Danel slashed at one of them, horizontal at the throat, but the soldier blocked with his rifle and shoved him back. Lenala twirled to intercept the soldier before he could level his rifle at Danel. Instead of trying to attack him directly, she swiped her blade at his rifle, knocking it up to fire harmlessly into the sky.

They grappled, and Danel searched the soldier's armour for gaps. There were clear lines between armour plates, but not enough space for Shenza blades to pierce.

It was far beyond what they had faced in Shanaken; back then, the Shenza could target the gaps even with arrows. Now it was almost impossible. How did they have such vastly improved armour in just a few years?

He grasped the soldier's helmet, pulling up with all his strength. It wouldn't budge. Lenala grabbed the helmet's other side. With their combined strength, it began to shift. The soldier fell, Danel and Lenala on him with all their weight.

All three of them grunted with effort; the Ermoori's voice was low, muffled by his helmet, but Danel still heard it. If not for the armour, the man would be dead already.

A flash of yellow and a deafening boom knocked Danel back. The soldier had regained control of his rifle. Something took over Danel, and he rammed the hilt of his blade into the man's face. Despite the helmet, the soldier's head snapped back, cracking into the stone ground, and he lay still.

Danel stood, legs shaking, and checked himself over.

No wound.

"That was close," he said to Lenala.

But her face was pale, her eyes somehow wide and listless at the same time.

"Lenala," he said, "are you..."

A thin line of blood slipped from the corner of her mouth. She blinked, so slow that time itself may as well have been a dream.

Danel rushed to her side. She stared ahead, seemingly unaware of his presence.

"Lenala," he repeated, "can you hear me?"

She made a small strangled sound and blood seeped from her mouth again. Her lips opened and closed, but he heard no breathing. It was then he saw the wound.

Her chest was a ragged mess; deep red blood flowed from it, pulling her life from her too fast. He knew it instantly, sick dread mixing with cold understanding, gripping his mind in a vice from which there was no escape. The battle no longer existed; there was only Lenala, and the life draining from her.

He had no healing potions. His blade lay on the ground, forgotten. He couldn't use Shadow Magic.

"No," he said, "no, no. Lenala. Please."

She took no final breath. Instead, her lips slowed in their opening and closing, slowed until she was utterly still.

Around him, the chaos continued. People fighting for a city they had either never lived in, or barely knew. He stared at Lenala's face. She was so beautiful, even now. How could he go on, when her life had been ripped from her so suddenly?

How could he fight these... monsters? These animals, who destroyed everything they encountered? They were too powerful.

The Circle would never win. But even if they did, what would Danel do? His home was gone. Most of the people he'd known were dead. Lenala had become his whole world. There was nothing left for him now.

For the first time in a long, long time, Danel prayed to Amalus.

Please, Amalus. Let these people face justice for what they've done. Let them suffer.

Mara

1798

Magic screamed around her. There had never been a storm as fierce in all of Pandeia as the one engulfing them now. Sithares' presence loomed above her, so vast her mind stretched to make sense of it.

We really are attempting to kill a god, she thought, *this is insane*.

Fire streaked down at them. One of the spells they had cast was a protection spell; still, Mara winced every time the fire slammed into the protective barrier above them.

"It can't last forever," she said, more to herself than anyone else, "Sithares is too strong."

"Keep to the spells," Zeera called, "we *will* prevail."

From somewhere above them, Mara could have sworn she heard a growl. It was animalistic, vicious in its rage.

Mara traced another spell on the stone dais. They were up to attack spells; each time one of the Heroes completed the runes, a flash of brilliant light shot from them to the book, and then raced upwards to the barely visible, gargantuan form of Sithares.

Each flash exploded on contact, thousands of searing sparks raining down on the Heroes below, adding to the chaotic storm of magic. Mara gritted her teeth. She had never been more terrified, but there was nothing to do but continue fighting. The other members of the Circle didn't look afraid; they wore expressions of grim determination and focus, but no fear.

"How do we know when the fight is over?" Mara shouted over the chaos.

"It'll be over," Lashek said through gritted teeth, "that's how we'll know."

"It doesn't look like anything is changing," Mara said, "how do we know if we're winning?"

"We all know as much as you do, Mara," Aerene said.

"Speak for yourself," Lashek said.

"Heroes," Zeera snapped, "focus. There are no answers to find in wondering. Fight until we win… or until we die."

"Consider me inspired, boss," Lashek called.

How does he make jokes, Mara thought, *at a time like this*?

Just as she thought it, a massive, burning boulder slammed into the magical shield above them. Mara screamed, and the partially cast spell at her fingertips exploded, throwing Mara back. Firm hands caught her; Eliza pushed her gently back to the dais.

A chunk of the dais had hit the floor where Mara's feet were barely a moment before. The break was right where she had been casting her spell.

Her hands burned, tingling and shaking. There was no blood, but they stung as though they had been cut a thousand times.

"It will be okay," Eliza whispered in her ear, "let me give you magic. Start the spell again."

A swell of buzzing energy swept into her from Eliza as her daughter channelled Power Magic into her body.

"Focus," Zeera called, "do not let Sithares distract you from casting the spells! Mara, you must start again."

Mara nodded, drawing the first runes once again. Without knowing how she knew, she could tell the protective spell surrounding them was weaker. They likely wouldn't survive another falling boulder.

I have to catch up, she thought desperately, *now*!

Another growl, deeper than the ocean and inhumanly furious, echoed from above them. It filled the sky, overtaking even the cacophony of magic and the booms of the battle nearby.

There was anger in that voice. But was there something else, hidden underneath? Pain, perhaps? Or even… fear?

She hoped so, but she wasn't certain.

Casting the spells again took most of her focus, but she couldn't stop her own fear from creeping through her mind.

The others were still launching attacks at Sithares. More boulders fell around them, glowing deep red, and Mara realised they weren't really boulders; they were vast coals, pieces of Sithares' body blasted from it with their attacks.

On the pedestal, pages of the book were tearing from it and disintegrating, one by one.

Aella

1798

You will lose. You cannot win. My will is inescapable. Nothing can stop my Fires from ravaging your little world. The time to stop me was decades hence; you are too late, and too weak.

For all the times Aella had heard Sithares' voice in her head, she never once imagined she would see it in the physical world. Its sheer size threatened to overcome her. If it wanted, it could have crushed all six of them with a single finger… so why didn't it?

It stood above them in the sky, barely visible behind roiling orange and black smoke. The presence of it pushed on her mind, like it was taking up as much space in her head as it did above them. Its rage, its determination, shook her to the core. But so did the determination of the Heroes, too; they worked together perfectly, even taking up the slack left by Mara's failed spell.

Their attacks were getting stronger as their confidence grew. Each spell they cast added to the pool of attacks they could launch. Those were launched in waves, first hitting the book, then lancing up to hit Sithares itself.

"Lashek and Aerene," Zeera shouted, "focus on adding to the shield until Mara has caught up."

Your shield is pathetic. I am merely toying with you. You can feel it; you know I do not lie.

They both nodded, Lashek remaining blessedly silent.

Almost immediately, the shield grew. Just in time, too; another massive chunk of burning coal exploded on the shield's curved surface. The stone beneath them shuddered from the impact. But were they wounds, as she suspected, or attacks?

Or… both? Sithares was certainly cunning enough to use a weakness as a strength. To turn its own injuries into weapons.

Other than coals the size of boulders raining down on them, twisting whirls of pure Fire slammed into the magical shield, roaring as the air around them burned. The heat was more intense than any she had ever experienced before; and Aella had been on fire.

She wondered how much worse the heat might be if their shield failed. *We will have to avoid finding out*, she thought.

You will find out, soon enough. You have felt my true power before, when you were killed. Prepare to feel it again.

Magic pulsed around her, the spells of her fellow Heroes flaring with raw power as each was cast. Almost constant attacks arced up from them, slamming into Sithares. Whirlwinds of vicious Fire punched into their magical shield from above, and massive chunks of glowing coal rammed the shield, exploding on impact in a fiery rain of burning detritus and flashing sparks.

Just as Aella readied another attack, the shield exploded. Aerene threw a hand up instantly, just in time to deflect a giant coal with Air Magic. It crashed into the ground next to them; but Aerene's focus had already gone back to the spells, and she didn't catch the chunks of coal that burst outwards from the impact.

Something thumped into her side, so sudden and powerful that she was almost thrown to the ground. Agony ripped through her body; the air fled from her lungs. The dais in front of her faded in a haze of grey. The rush and roar of magic bled into a whisper, a shadow of the chaos she knew was still there.

Consciousness fled from her, too quickly.

Here it is. You are almost mine.

I need only last until you are dead, she thought to Sithares, *then I can let go.*

Except… Kerberos still lived.

He had to pay for everything he'd done.

A swell of rage burned away her pain, and energy erupted within her anew. This would not kill her. She wouldn't let it. There was still too much to do.

She screamed. Gritting her teeth, she summoned all the Fire she could muster, letting it sweep over her body and through her very soul as she changed into Fire Wight form. The pain didn't let up, but she was saved from the worst of the injury; she could still function this way, though it would only last so long.

The strength of her attacks soared tenfold, and she focused everything she had on Sithares.

Bothersome little creatures. You are merely delaying your inevitable fall. Why must you expend so much energy, when you know you cannot win?

Aella growled, sending another attack at Sithares that cracked against the crook of its elbow; an immense explosion shattered the darkness of the bleak cloud cover, and Sithares' entire forearm plummeted to the temple.

Sithares roared, both in the sky above them and in Aella's head. The sound rang so loud that Aella was sure she would go deaf.

"Shield!" Zeera called, "now!"

Aerene dropped the spell she was casting, gesturing away from them; the half-finished spell flew away over the streets beyond the temple and exploded. At the same time, she raised both hands and screamed with effort as the arm twisted slightly in the air.

Aella sent a massive fireball at the arm, focusing on the centre and watching her spell curve to meet it.

Sithares' severed arm was almost on top of them when it exploded into several massive chunks. The explosion threw them clear of the Heroes.

Aella dropped to a knee; her Magic was almost used up. Her body ached, breath coming in short again as her Fire Wight form began fading. Pain radiated from the point in her side where she'd been hit by a chunk of coal. Her lungs began to burn.

As she struggled to stand, gripping the dais with a weakening grip, she heard Sithares laughing in the back of her mind. But behind the laughter, there was something more.

I'm not dead yet, she thought, *save your laughter. I can feel you growing weaker*.

"Heroes," Zeera called, "keep pushing! Attack, with all your strength… we almost have it beaten!"

A couple of them rallied; Mara had caught up and was back to attacking, and Aerene had recast a shield above them.

But Lashek had gone pale. A jagged hole gaped in his stomach. *The coal Aerene diverted*, Aella thought, *hit him too*. He didn't have the luxury of a Fire Wight form. Aella knew that *Kaizeluun* could become living Shadow; perhaps Lashek had forgotten in the chaos.

Or perhaps he simply didn't have enough magic. Her own wight spell went out then, with a rush and a wave of thick smoke, like a fire doused with sand.

Suddenly, she could barely breathe. A sickening grey blur filled her vision, and the pain in her side rose up, threatening to overtake her completely as her mouth grew hot and slick with saliva.

Distantly, she heard Zeera call out her name. She saw nothing, felt nothing but the pain, yet still she focused on pouring her magic into attacks.

If this is how I die, she thought, *at least the legends will say I gave everything I had.*

There will be no legends. Pandeia is done. I will consume this world, and move on to the next. As I have before.

The sounds of roaring flame and raging winds became a curious echo, as though she had only ever imagined them. After that, even the pain faded away, until there was nothing but Aella clinging to the magic she cast, forcing it out of herself with the sheer, furious power of her will.

She heard shouting, like whispers in her mind, but none of it made sense. Merely quiet chaos bubbling away in the depths of her thoughts, background noise as she desperately cast attacks spells with what little magic and strength she had left.

I hope the Circle can continue once I'm spent, she thought, *if not, we really are in trouble*.

Aerene

1798

Aerene grunted with the effort of shoving the falling coal away from them; Air Magic could only do so much at such speed, and against such weight. The coal shattered, pieces flying at them. One hit Aella, and a thump came from Lashek's position too.

Shortly after, vivid orange flame swept over Aella, and she stood straighter, though a grimace of pain was still set on her face. Her attacks grew far more powerful; Aerene was struck by the sheer destructive power of Fire Magic. Though Aerene focused on building layers into the shield that protected them all, she watched in her peripheral vision as Aella sent a blinding bolt of pure magic at Sithares. It tore chunks out of the book in front of them, and ripped off Sithares' entire forearm.

Aerene was halfway through a shield spell. Zeera screamed at them to shield, but she knew there was no protection that could stop the falling mass of red-hot coal.

She threw the spell away, forgetting it as it exploded harmlessly in the air, and put all her magic into shifting the giant God's arm. A tornado of screaming wind formed above them, pulling at the arm as it fell. It shifted slightly in the air, but not enough. Just before it cannoned into them, Aella launched a fireball that blasted it into boulder-sized pieces. They crashed into the temple's roof, its thick stone shuddering but holding.

Aerene bolstered the shield surrounding them as quickly as she could, adding layer after layer while Sithares was distracted with its injury.

In the sky beyond the temple, within Aerene's vision, a thick yellow bolt of lightning streaked by. She knew without thinking that it was one of the Ermoori tanks; and the angle of it placed the enemy close to them.

Very close.

She realised she could hear their cannons booming, and the thin cracks of their rifles, even through the cacophony of their fight with Sithares.

Shaela, she thought, *if the Ermoori get too close before we're done here, she will fight against them alone.*

Aella fell, landing heavily on one knee, the bright orange of her Fire fading fast.

"Heroes," Zeera called, "keep pushing! Attack, with all your strength… we almost have it beaten!"

Aerene gritted her teeth, turning from shield spells to attack. If she could turn the tide now, and defeat Sithares… perhaps she could save Shaela, too.

She sent a spear of bound Air and pure magic into the book, watching with vicious satisfaction as it sliced through several pages, then arced up into Sithares' chest. Its roar rocked her down to her bones.

But she was distracted; she could feel it, pulling at her mind. Shaela could be in danger, right in this moment. If she was killed while Aerene struggled against Sithares, she would never forgive herself. And what if the Ermoori broke through into the temple, before the Heroes were done?

They couldn't defend themselves *and* defeat Sithares. It would mean certain death.

Please, Shaela, Aerene thought, *please survive.*

She tried glancing to the north, from where the Ermoori were approaching. An attack from above slammed into her, fire smashing through the shields, the fury of it forcing a gasp from her.

Sithares is growing desperate, she thought, *perhaps Zeera was right... Perhaps it's almost beaten.*

But even this thought was not enough to stop her distraction. She was accustomed to using Deias, but it still took focus. The fear within her clawed its way through her body, choking her, forcing tears out of her that stung her eyes.

Fire and coal battered the Heroes from above; the spells took their attention, and the sounds of battle grew so close that the thick stone roof vibrated under her feet.

A word, dangerous in its insistent simplicity, arose from somewhere in her mind.

Helpless.

We are outnumbered, overpowered, and exhausted.

But she fought on, against the numbing fear and the cold, certain dread that enveloped her. There *had* to be a chance.

Lashek looked almost dead. Aella's Fire had gone out, her eyes rolled into the back of her head. Mara was uninjured, but her face was a clear picture of absolute terror.

Only Zeera stood strong, a look of total concentration glowing from her large silver eyes.

Behind Mara, Eliza's face was all concern; but not fear. Aerene's heart broke free of the claws of dread gripping it, and soared for a brilliant moment.

She is the best of us, Aerene thought, *not only the most powerful, but also the bravest.*

To have a friend such as her brought a sharp, singing pride to Aerene's heart, despite the desperate situation. She used it to renew her focus, launching another attack, the spell so familiar now that her fingers flew through the runes. Magic swept from her in a giant wave that left her deflated, like having the wind knocked from her lungs. A moment's concentration told her that each of the Heroes were low on magic.

We cannot last much longer, she thought, *Lashek and Aella are almost unconscious, let alone out of magic.*

Then, Aerene heard Aurath's voice; so quiet, like the gentlest breeze, but clear and unmistakeable.

Hold on a little longer. Sithares will be destroyed. Do not worry about Shaela, or the Heroes, or the Ermoori. You have almost won the day.

Along with the voice came a sense of calm so strong that Aerene almost felt like she was in a dream. And with the calm came focus.

She looked closely at the book in front of them for the first time in hours. The fire that bound it had died down, looking more like embers than the hungry, energetic flame that had covered it when they started. It looked weak, a thin black smoke pluming from the barely burning cover.

And there were only a handful of pages left.

Eliza

1798

Eliza was speechless. Sithares had appeared above them when the battle started; she was looking at the form of an actual God. It stood, almost hidden by the thick black smoke choking the sky, vast twisting jets of Fire scorching the air as they shot from its fingers to the temple's roof.

Its eyes were bigger than buildings, gargantuan furnaces of hunger and rage. All around them, the sky itself burned. Eliza had never felt such unstoppable heat.

Even if we win, she thought, *the heat will kill us before long.*

Everywhere she looked was fire. The streets of Austris Ara burned, the white stone stained black where it wasn't glowing deep red. Above them the black smoke flashed and flickered in hues of orange. Even the horizon seemed to glow like a distant bonfire.

The Heroes fought without pause, seemingly without thought of their own deaths. Sithares' attacks pummelled them, battering the shields endlessly.

Eliza watched in awe as the book before them was torn slowly to pieces.

It's working, she thought, *they're killing Sithares*!

And then, before any of them realised it was happening, the tide of battle turned.

Their shields shattered, and a mass of coal as big as a horseless carriage exploded on the roof too close to them; pieces of debris that shot out in every direction hit both Aella and Lashek. Aella managed a brutal counter-attack, but the damage had been done.

They fought on, but Eliza could see them all struggling to maintain the spells they cast.

Sithares only grew more dangerous in its rage and desperation, screaming and growling as it launched a new wave of attacks against them.

"Zeera!" Eliza called, "let me take over! For Lashek, or Aella, or mother… please!"

But the Tarsi woman merely shook her head, her bright silver eyes staring intently at the book.

I could help them, she thought, *I have more magic now than all of them combined, I can feel it*. And, as much as Zeera had initially attempted to discourage her from learning the Circle's secrets, she eventually caved in and allowed her to train with Deias.

Why let me learn, she thought, *if I can't use it to help them*?

All she could do was pour magic into Mara, granting her a massive boost as she cast the spells to attack. She wanted to do so much more—and she could have, if Zeera let her—but she *was* helping.

She pulled Power Magic from the machines nearby, and channelled it directly into Mara along with some of her own magic. Zeera had drained most of the water she had prepared earlier. Aerene would be fine, Eliza knew; Air Magic was everywhere.

Lashek and Aella were the most affected.

Except…

"Aella," Eliza called, "the Fire! It's everywhere!"

But the Thearan woman didn't react; she was too far gone. Her eyes had rolled back, her hand gripping the dais so tightly that her arm shook. And still, Fire Magic poured from her in violent pulses, clashing against Sithares' book in direct attacks, no longer focused into Deias.

She is going to kill herself, Eliza thought, *if Sithares doesn't die soon*.

"Zeera," she shouted again, "let me take over! Now!"

When the Tarsi woman replied, Eliza barely heard her strained, quiet voice.

"Wait," she said, "your time is coming. But we must wait…"

Kerberos

1798

He watched Sithares from near the temple. The God of Fire had become unimaginably powerful. Flame twisted through everything, the entire world a burning ember. Its heat tore through his flesh, his very soul. His breath came out as smoke, hot and dry, his lungs heavy and scorched.

Atop the temple fought the Heroes; Kerberos couldn't see them, but a white spherical glow peeked over the roof. It had to be a magical shield of some type.

Despite its sheer power, Sithares was badly wounded. But the world still burned.

That does not bode well.

His theory that killing Sithares may not mean Pandeia's salvation was becoming more likely accurate with each passing moment.

And what will we do if that is the case? The Heroes were fighting Sithares valiantly; but no one could fight the immense heat, the smothering smoke, the vicious flame consuming everything around them.

An explosion lit up the air close to Kerberos, and the building next to him collapsed.

The Ermoori were on the main street, their tanks firing at the temple, up at Sithares, and randomly into the city. Kerberos leapt behind a taller building, hoping they hadn't seen him. He could kill Ermoori soldiers easily enough, but their tanks were another thing entirely.

Sounds of battle caught up with him, and his heart sank as he saw how few Circle warriors were left. His own warriors were among them; though he couldn't remember much about being King of Omatus, he knew he never would have wanted this much death for anyone. Rage, powerful enough to drive the air from his burnt lungs, threatened to crush him.

They care for nothing but domination, he thought in a cold white blur, *this land means nothing to them. They only want to own it to feel superior*.

Everyone knew of their repeated attempts, over centuries, to take Shanaken. If only the Circle had arisen back then, and taken the fight to Ermoor. They would have been eradicated. Why had they not done so?

Kerberos forced his racing mind to still, breathing as slowly and evenly as he could through the rage, the fire and the smoke. If he kept thinking about the Ermoori, he would be forced to act on his fury. And he had to be careful, now more than ever. His chance would come; assuming, of course, that Pandeia still existed after today.

He would wait until the time was right. When Ermoor had grown fat and complacent, and Riffolk's mind was beginning to slow from age, Kerberos would still be fit and powerful.

Unless our immortality is destroyed along with Sithares, he thought, *then I will run out of time just as quickly as him*.

Whatever happened, Kerberos simply couldn't allow Ermoor to remain in control. All he'd ever wanted was justice and peace. There were snatches of memory, helped along by Nomiki teaching him his own past, of Kerberos growing frustrated with the Omati government, and devoting his life to a mission he'd kept secret for decades as he built a massive Thearan army in the desert.

When he first ventured out, he was not immortal. He had gone into the desert knowing it could mean his death. Knowing it would take decades of his life, and that even then he may not be successful.

I am still that person. I did it then, and I can do it again.

The Ermoori army was close. Ahead of them was a small group of soldiers, rushing past the trundling tanks towards the temple. Kerberos frowned as he watched them, leaning out from behind a rooftop to remain hidden. He gasped, a low grumbling sound as his lungs wheezed from the smoke.

There. That is him.

Despite his broken memory, Kerberos recognised Riffolk Hayne instantly. He was unmistakeably the army's leader. His armour was the same shining black metal as the other soldiers, but the edges were gold, and the armour itself was far sleeker.

Kerberos had never seen armour like it; so closely fit to the wearer that it almost looked organic, and so intricately articulated that it might have been made of fabric.

The weapon he wielded was different, too; as compact as one of the single-handed weapons the Ermoori could shoot, but it seemed to fire blasts of pure magic. As Kerberos watched, Riffolk tore through three Austris Arans with one bolt of Shadow and Power bound together. It swept through the air, ruthlessly efficient, losing no speed as it ripped through the powerful blue-skinned bodies.

He watched Fire Magic explode against the armour, Riffolk barely reacting as he killed the warrior who'd cast it. He seemed to have no weakness, and no limit to the magic he could summon. What would it take to kill such a man?

Even with all five magics, Kerberos thought, *I may not win that fight*.

Riffolk and a small group of soldiers around him reached the temple. They didn't look bothered by the appearance of Sithares above them; but each face was hidden behind a helmet, so Kerberos couldn't read their emotion.

A lone Austris Aran stood guard at the temple's main door. She held a long spear, the metal shining an odd blue-silver, the colour shifting in the volatile darkness.

She moved to greet the Ermoori with confidence, and Kerberos read brilliant skill in her movements even before she engaged them. They exchanged words Kerberos couldn't hear. Then, a bare moment later, one of the Ermoori soldiers suddenly jerked as if struck by lightning, and collapsed in the heap. Blood flowed from the armour's tiny gaps.

Another of the soldiers met the same fate; blood began flooding from his armour before he'd even hit the ground. In the rest of the fighting, Kerberos hadn't seen this kind of attack used by the Austris Arans. He couldn't even tell what she had done.

As Kerberos watched, the Austris Aran warrior killed another soldier, and another, as she narrowly dodged Riffolk's attacks. She killed the last of them and just managed to divert a bolt of lightning from Riffolk's weapon.

But as she gestured towards Riffolk, he finally struck her. A scattershot of blindingly fast Shadow bolts from the Ermoori leader's weapon hit her in the gut, a leg, both arms, and a wing. The limbs that had been hit were decimated; severed completely at the point of impact as dark purple blood sprayed over the stone behind her. She fell back, her screams dulled by the distance.

Riffolk fired one last bolt of Shadow into her head, and her screams were cut short. Then he strolled into the temple, leaving the corpses of his men behind without another glance.

If he fights the Heroes, Kerberos thought, *he may be slightly weakened afterwards. Then I can strike.*

Keeping distance between them, Kerberos flew towards the temple in pursuit.

Riffolk

1798

The war was almost done. All that remained was the group of powerful magicians in the temple.

His forces had taken casualties, but nowhere near his projected losses. An unprecedented success. He had taken Aethos in a matter of hours; barely longer than half a day. Even the combined might of every other army in Pandeia couldn't stand up to his technology.

And still, his suit buzzed with magic. Every attack aimed at him fed its reserves; he barely even used his own magic.

Finally, the temple loomed above them. A single guard stood in his way, deep blue skin mostly hidden behind silver-blue armour. Her golden wings and hair shone even in the darkness.

She approached, her glowing white eyes steady and her lips set in a grim line.

"You are not permitted into the Air Temple," the woman said in perfect Ermoori, "the future of Pandeia is at stake."

"Pandeia is mine," Riffolk said, "and I go where I want. You cannot stop me."

"You know," the woman said, "Air Magic can reach anywhere air itself can. A skilled enough magician can cause irreparable damage to even the most protected opponent."

Her eyes flashed, her brows pulled downwards slightly, and one of Riffolk's soldiers made a choked gasp, convulsed, and fell in a heap. A wet smack came from within the armour when it landed, and blood immediately swept over the stone street.

His soldiers leapt into combat, firing at the blue-skinned woman. She dove to the side, but even so, his rifles should have hit her…

He watched, and noticed that pockmarks appeared all around her in the stone. No matter how many times his men fired, the rounds never hit close enough to wound. She watched them all the time, as she leapt and ducked and swept up into the air.

She is using Air Magic to deflect the projectiles. Her weakness is the limit of her focus.

"Fire at her all at once," he said, "from different angles. You, over there. You, further up."

His soldiers obeyed without hesitation. Riffolk summoned a handful of bolts made of Shadow, holding them ready in his mind as he watched the blue woman deal with the soldiers.

This one is talented.

Just as she killed the last one and turned on Riffolk, he fired. The bolts sliced through her easily, severing most of her limbs, leaving her a bleeding, screaming mess on the stone floor. Riffolk stepped close to her, watching her glowing white eyes shift from pain to rage. He summoned another bolt, aimed at her head, and fired.

Other than the single guard, the temple was abandoned. There had been several of the flying creatures above the temple, but his soldiers took them out with well-placed rifle shots on the approach. Riffolk couldn't believe how easily he strolled through the massive building. He would have gotten lost, if not for the knowledge that he only needed to reach the top.

He searched for every staircase he could find. There were hundreds of them; and thousands of corridors and rooms. It was the largest building Riffolk had ever seen; it could have been a city in its own right. He had to give some credit, albeit begrudgingly, to the blue-skinned people who presumably built it; it was on a scale he never would have dreamed a single building could be.

Moving as quickly as he could, Riffolk still took a long time to find the highest level.

One last, short staircase led to a door. Beyond it, he heard the cacophony of powerful magic being cast repeatedly. Quietly, slowly, Riffolk pushed the door open.

And there she was. Mara. The little waif who had fled him all those years ago. She had caused such trouble. He remembered her being a scared little thing, wide-eyed and pink-cheeked. But now she stood firm, sending blasts of dangerous magic into a book on top of a stone pedestal.

There were six of them, magicians all focusing together on the same task. And only now that he stood on the temple's roof did he see the thing looming above all of them.

It was taller even than the towering mountain in Shanaken's centre. It was burning, glowing red and orange with the intensity of the sun itself.

And it was *alive*.

He stared up at it, watching the movements of its massive body as it growled and threw fire down at the magicians. Though its sheer size was clear, he never got a clear look at it; the smoke and fire filling the air obscured most of its form.

Suddenly, Riffolk caught its eye. They looked directly at each other, a God and a leader of men.

In that moment, despite having smashed through the best Pandeia could throw at him, despite the knowledge of certain victory in the war, Riffolk was a speck of dirt, some small insect facing a full-size human with a foot above Riffolk's head. And briefly—but so vividly—he understood. This world did not belong to humans. He could march over every inch of it, fighting and killing to own the land as he stained it with blood; but he was an insect, infinitesimal, immaterial. Planting a flag in the ground, shooting those in his way... these things did not change the world. It would always be there, regardless of who called it theirs.

And then it was over.

No, he thought, *I refuse to believe that none of it matters. I won Pandeia. It is mine*.

In the back of his mind rose an unsettling sound. A response to his thoughts, coming from the titan above. He didn't know how he knew, but he did.

It was laughing.

Ignoring the laughter, he approached the magicians, slowly and silently.

They were so wrapped up in the ritual they were performing that none of them noticed him. Except the young girl behind Mara. Riffolk drew in a short breath when they locked eyes. There was something about her...

Her face was familiar; she resembled Mara, but some of her features... the high cheekbones, her slim build, and thin eyebrows. Her hair was paler, but he could have sworn she looked like…

Mara fled Ermoori twenty-five years ago. The girl he watched now looked to be about that age. A strange feeling bloomed within him then, something he had never felt. Was it kinship? Did he really feel some kind of familial connection with this girl he'd never met before today?

No. It had to be merely surprise. Surprise that he'd had a daughter all this time. Surprise that Mara managed to keep a secret from him. Whether she was related to him or not, she was on the rebel's side.

But when she saw him, recognition flooded her face, and an expression of pure horror swept over her.

Mara has told her about me, he thought, *pity. It might have been useful to have an heir. No matter; I can make another.*

The girl was still frozen, staring at Riffolk.

With the others busy, now was his time. Mara was finally at his mercy.

At last, he thought, *I can destroy her. At last, I can remove her presence from my mind.*

Before the girl gathered her wits, Riffolk summoned a bolt of Shadow, and bound it with crackling lightning. He would not leave it to chance; she wore no armour, but he would likely only get one shot before the magicians reacted, and he needed to be sure she was dead before focusing on the rest of them.

He took aim at Mara, smiling.

Her eyes snapped to him, and in that moment, her face showed no fear, no outrage. An odd expression shone from her then; acceptance. She knew she was going to die, and she would not fight it.

Finally, he thought, *she is out of my mind.*

He pulled the trigger.

Eliza

1798

The man she knew from her nightmares appeared from behind the temple doors. Her father. Riffolk Hayne, Prime Overseer of Ermoor. He wore a closed helmet, his face obscured; but his presence pushed on her as unmistakeably as if his face had been shown.

He stood watching them, Power Magic crackling within him. Its power reached out to her. There was something dangerous about it; beyond the inherent danger of Power Magic, this was… angry. As though all the rage she'd felt from him over the years had only grown, gathering power, becoming a weapon of its own. A weapon he held now, ready to wield against them.

None of the others had seen him; Sithares took all their focus, the spells they were casting to defeat it took all their energy.

What do I do? Do I warn the Heroes, distract them from their mission? Do I fight him myself?

His armour caught her attention. Even from across the temple's roof, Eliza sensed magic flowing through the suit itself. It was the same sensation she felt from the machines Zeera had positioned around the Heroes for Mara and herself.

A wearable machine, she wondered, *that doubles as armour. He* is *a genius, after all.*

The suit that Mathys had worn as the Spectre contained magic, and even some technology; but nothing like what she saw now. He was terrifying. All five of the Heroes together with Eliza may not have been enough to defeat Riffolk as he was; and that was before they had channelled most of their magic into destroying Sithares. Now, they didn't stand a chance.

Except…

His suit was undeniably intimidating, but once she got past that, she realised something that shocked her even more than his sudden appearance at the temple.

Even with the magic-infused armour, he possessed less magic than Eliza.

If it comes to sheer power against power, she thought, *I might actually be able to kill him.*

But could she do it without distracting the Heroes? What if she lost, or deflected an attack which hit one of them instead? What if she killed him, but the battle itself took too much of a toll on the building? A while ago, her mother had run from Aethos in a panic. She had run into a few travelling merchants, and when they confronted her, her panic had boiled over into a violent magical explosion which collapsed a massive chunk of the cliff where she had stood.

Eliza was more powerful than Mara. And Riffolk was at least as powerful as Mara, if not more so. Particularly with the suit of armour.

She took a look at her mother, and then at the other Heroes. Aella and Lashek were almost dead. Eliza couldn't believe they were still casting magic in their condition. Zeera's face had set into a dense frown, furious concentration sparkling from her eyes.

Zeera forbade me from stepping in for the Heroes, she thought, *fighting Riffolk is the only thing I can do, other than giving mother some energy. Besides, Riffolk is right there. He didn't come here to say hello. We are in grave danger*.

The decision solidified in her mind. As it did, her mother saw Riffolk. Her eyes went wide for the briefest moment. Then, her face settled into a gentle kind of peace.

"No," Eliza whispered.

Just as she spoke, summoning Power Magic to her fingertips, Riffolk fired his weapon at her mother.

The bolt of jagged black and glowing yellow ripped through Mara's body. She gave a short, sharp grunt, and collapsed. Instantly, the magic coming off of her was silenced.

A spray of her mother's blood had splattered the ancient stone. Her body was a mess, a gaping hole in her torso as big as her head, broken chunks of her ribcage jutting from the gore. Her organs had spilled out onto the temple's rough stone roof, some of them torn to shreds. And her face… it was already so pale, her eyes dull and her mouth hanging open, slack and still.

Eliza screamed. She threw a lightning bolt at Riffolk, who simply held up a hand to catch it. The gold trim of his armour glowed.

She summoned more magic, but Zeera shouted.

"Eliza, no!"

"He'll kill us all," Eliza snapped, "look at my mother! You want me to let him do the same to us?"

"I told you your time was coming," Zeera said, "this is the time. We need you to continue the spells."

A sickening cold fog erupted in Eliza's chest as she reeled from Zeera's words.

Did she know? Had she foreseen Mara's death?

"He's right there!" Eliza screamed, "he's going to kill us!"

But Zeera didn't respond.

The Heroes were barely hanging on; Aella and Lashek were swaying, eyes shut, the last dregs of magic draining from them even as Eliza watched.

She had to help them. They were so close, and Sithares was badly injured.

But who would stop Riffolk, if not Eliza?

She stared at him, cold rage blistering her very soul with its intensity. He had to die. This was her chance, right here and now, to kill him. A thump sounded from across the dais, and Lashek tumbled from her view.

Then, somehow, the noise of the magic screaming around her, of the battle raging below, and the rush of fire all around her all fell away. A silence settled over her as gentle as smoke.

With a crackling buzz, an odd voice clawed its way into her mind, clear and loud.

You are the offspring of joined Heroes, and sworn enemies. The daughter of war. This was always your destiny. Destroy Sithares, and end this war.

Taranos, she thought, *it must be*.

She frowned, glancing all around her; Sithares was above them... so where was Taranos?

I am within you. My power is yours, for as long as you wield it against the Fire.

She gritted her teeth, rage still burning her soul.

Why can't you fight your own damned war, she thought, *or better yet, help us win against Ermoor*?

I am *helping. We cannot directly interfere in your world.*

Tell that to Sithares, Eliza thought, *I don't know if you noticed, but it's interfering. It's going to destroy the whole world*!

Taranos said nothing; Eliza's lungs tightened, her jaw aching from gritting her teeth so tightly.

She was on her own. At least, as far as Taranos was concerned.

Fine. I'll *do it*.

She threw one last glance at Riffolk, but what she saw froze her whole body; even her breathing stopped.

A giant of a man appeared behind Riffolk; broad and solid, his bald head shining in the magic glowing around them. He flew, like an Austris Aran, but everything else about him was clearly Thearan. The man wielded no weapons, but still he attacked Riffolk.

Everything that was hopeful within Eliza sang, her spirit erupting in an all-consuming explosion of victory.

Finally, something was going their way.

Riffolk would be distracted by the newcomer, and the Heroes could focus on Sithares. *Eliza* could focus on Sithares.

With a vicious grin on her face, Eliza planted her feet and blasted all the magic she had into the book.

"No!" Zeera screamed, "you have to attack with the spells!"

But it was too late.

Kerberos

1798

Kerberos watched from behind one of the massive columns that lined the temple roof as Riffolk emerged.

Only one of the Heroes noticed him, though the young Ermoori girl wasn't actively casting spells like the others. Perhaps she wasn't a Hero.

Above them all, Sithares roared and growled, bigger than the sky itself; but wounded. Mortally wounded.

They are succeeding, he thought, *they only need a little more time*.

He wondered what Riffolk made of all this. By all accounts, the Ermoori leader was incredibly well informed. But the Circle of Shadows was one of the best-kept secrets in Pandeia.

Whether he knows what they are doing or not, surely he would not interfere with such a powerful display of magic.

Unless...

Perhaps Riffolk believed they were summoning a creature to defeat his army? Or perhaps he was simply intimidated by the chaotic scene before him, and wanted to put a stop to it?

Kerberos watched him notice Sithares. He couldn't see the man's face from here, even if the helmet had been removed, but he could read the body language. Riffolk was awestruck. Kerberos looked up at Sithares too; even mostly obscured by thick black smoke, it was a sight that tore at the belly with hot, gripping fingers.

Before Kerberos turned back down to watch Riffolk, he heard an explosion of magic. Then a piercing scream, and by the time he saw what had happened, the Ermoori woman who had been casting spells was dead on the floor.

A shouted argument rose up between the Tarsi Hero and the young girl. Riffolk watched briefly, head cocked to the side. He seemed to grow bored, and began preparing his strange weapon for another attack. His suit glowed, magic flowing through it, electricity and darkness converging. Kerberos felt it even from where he hid.

Now is the time, he thought, *to strike. The Heroes are busy, and even if they succeed, they look almost dead. They pose no threat to me now.*

He leapt, guiding himself lightly down to the roof with Air Magic. Before Riffolk had time to react, Kerberos slammed a fist into his side, grunting from the unyielding solidity of Riffolk's armour.

Riffolk growled and threw an elbow back at Kerberos; expecting a counter, Kerberos slid beneath it easily.

Riffolk may have been a genius, but he was no warrior. His attacks were slow and poorly executed, easy to deflect or dodge. He never anticipated Kerberos' attacks. If not for the armour, and that viciously powerful weapon, Kerberos would have killed him in one fleeting moment.

But the armour was... perfect. Impenetrable. He had seen Fire Magic explode against it, and if anything, the armour seemed to glow with power in response. No matter what Kerberos did, he couldn't get through it. He ducked underneath a wild punch, grabbed Riffolk around the waist, and hurled him up into the air before slamming him down into the stone temple roof. A deep crack shuddered through the stone. Riffolk's only reaction was a low grunt, then he was up and ready for more.

If only I had my Soul Blade, he thought, *that would have made light work of this.*

As they faced each other, both ready to attack, two massive boulders of coal—pieces of Sithares' broken body—plummeted to the roof where they stood.

Kerberos leapt clear of them, barely avoiding the closest as it crashed into the temple's ancient stone. The roof shattered, a great hole appearing on their side of the temple, near the door that led down into the building. A chunk of coal bigger than Kerberos' head smashed into his shoulder, knocking him back; he almost lost his footing, but managed to stay upright. Light footsteps pattered on the stone, and Kerberos was tackled, both men falling into the hole.

They landed roughly on the smooth stone of a large room. Kerberos grappled with Riffolk, keeping an eye on the weapon. He couldn't afford to die right now, even if he could resurrect later. And it would only take one hit from that weapon.

He brought his knee up sharply into Riffolk's stomach, but all it did was crack against the metal, pain exploding through his leg.

Riffolk rammed a fist into Kerberos' head. An orange-grey blur filled his vision, and he threw Riffolk across the room. He landed roughly, but stood without apparent injury. Kerberos shook his head, blinking hard.

He brought a fireball to life in each fist, and settled into a balanced combat stance.

Riffolk's weapon, a strange one-handed thing that mostly—but not entirely—resembled a smaller, chunkier version of the rifles of his soldiers, hummed as it powered up again.

I need to get rid of that weapon.

He saw the attack coming before Riffolk fired; diving to the side, Kerberos threw a fireball at the floor next to his feet. It exploded, hurling Riffolk off balance. Straight from the dive, Kerberos launched himself at the distracted man, bringing his fire-covered fist into the side of his head.

Riffolk rammed the barrel of his rifle into Kerberos' gut; but there was no attack charged, and Kerberos swept it away. Riffolk looked at him, and then at his rifle.

He heard a muffled laugh, and bolts of lightning cracked into being all around him. They came from above, from Riffolk, and from the air around him, slamming into the floor and ceiling, throwing chunks of ancient stone in every direction.

"Did you think the gun is all I had, Kerberos? Did you forget about our battle in Ermoor all those years ago?"

Of course, Kerberos thought, *he does not need that weapon to wield magic. I should have known. That complicates the fight. Even worse, I cannot use magic directly against him.*

Lightning struck his thigh; it tore through his flesh in a blinding crack of yellow light. The air was ripped from his lungs as brilliant pain threatened to overtake him. He tried to stand, but his thigh flared in vicious defiance.

Riffolk's gun glowed and hummed again. Kerberos couldn't move. Just before Riffolk fired, he finally remembered.

I do not need my legs to move anymore.

He gathered Air Magic around him, and threw himself sideways just as Riffolk fired. The bolt of Power and Shadow hit the wall behind Kerberos, blowing it to pieces. Kerberos glided around Riffolk, trying to keep his leg still.

Another boulder exploded into the stone roof above them. The building shook violently.

Sithares is taking extreme damage, he thought, *it will not be long now before it is dead.*

Air Magic flowed through him, cool and sure. He hadn't the time to train in its use, but already ideas were forming. While behind Riffolk, Kerberos summoned a condensed blade of air next to the man's feet and yanked it into his ankles.

Riffolk was thrown to the ground as effectively as if Kerberos had kicked him.

"Clever," Riffolk said, "but tricks won't save you. You know it's only a matter of time before I get the best of you."

Kerberos threw himself on top of Riffolk, Fire burning in his fists as he pummelled the Ermoori leader about the head and torso as hard as he could.

He heard Riffolk's grunts with each punch, and knew that he was inflicting damage. But even the Fire hitting him was absorbed into his armour. A faint glow flowed through the strange metal plating to the weapon in his hand. It began to hum, and Kerberos growled. The gun was made from the same metal as Riffolk's armour; he couldn't destroy it.

But I can disarm him instead.

Kerberos brought both fists up and roared as he brought them down into Riffolk's helmet as hard as he could. As Riffolk reeled from the attack, Kerberos lunged for the weapon.

It was attached to his armour by two thin but flexible metal tubes. The same metal as everything else. Kerberos had seen armour forged in a similar way before; overlapping plates that could move while maintaining their connection to each other. But to be made into such a fine, thin tube… He hoped it wasn't as unbreakable as the rest of his armour.

There was only one way to find out.

He grabbed the gun, twisting it out of Riffolk's hand. Planting a foot on Riffolk's chest, Kerberos took the gun in both hands and pulled with all his strength.

At first, nothing happened. Then, it shifted, and the tube finally came free with a clink as a link somewhere slipped free of its fellow. Before Riffolk could react, Kerberos threw the weapon hard through the hole in the ceiling, then sent a wave of Air Magic after it. He watched with satisfaction as it disappeared. Riffolk screamed at him, thrashing and hitting like a man insane. He gained footing underneath Kerberos and shoved upwards, sending a wave of lightning bolts at the same time.

Kerberos was hit again, through the left shoulder and the right side just below his ribcage. His teeth chattered from the pain as lightning gripped his entire body.

He landed on the stone floor, his lungs seizing.

I cannot take much more, he thought, *I must kill him. Now.*

Riffolk

1798

Kerberos was fierce. Not only that, he was supremely talented, and shockingly fast for his size. If not for his armour, Riffolk would have died a dozen times by now.

And now he was without his weapon.

The King of Omatus—*the former king*, he reminded himself with a grim smile—lay on the stone roof, open wounds weeping blood as fury turned his face into a terrifying mask.

Somehow, he stood again.

An explosion erupted somewhere above them, brightening the sky in a flash of orange and yellow. The world shook. Coal rained down through the hole in the ceiling, countless tiny pieces that posed no threat, and every now and then a boulder that crashed to the temple roof. Cracks appeared in the room's ceiling

What are those magicians doing up there?

But he would deal with that soon. For now, Kerberos had to die. Though his suit was designed to transfer magic to the gun, he could draw the energy stored within its plates into himself.

He hurled bolt after bolt of pure, thrashing lightning at the wounded man. Despite his injuries, Kerberos moved like a breeze; zipping over the stone, barely touching it as he flew between Riffolk's attacks.

Air Magic, he thought, *he found it. If memory serves, that means Kerberos now wields all five*.

"I expected more," Riffolk said, "from one who possesses all five magics. There were rumours that it would turn one into a God. How disappointing."

Kerberos paused, eyes widening. In the same instant, Riffolk summoned three bolts, streaking from himself to Kerberos. One to either side of him, and one straight in the centre of his chest.

He attempted to dive, but the bolt to his right punched through his chest. Riffolk heard a breathless gasp, and Kerberos landed heavily on the ancient stone roof.

Riffolk smiled.

All too easy.

The magicians on the building's roof were still casting whatever spells they had started. Killing them while they were distracted would be no sport, but it had to be done. Whatever they were doing was about to rip Pandeia apart. He only hoped he wasn't too late in stopping them.

Riffolk sprinted for the nearest staircase, finding his way back to the roof door.

He summoned as much magic as he could, bringing it to his fingertips and targeting the strongest of the magicians. The young Ermoori girl. His… daughter.

A rush of flame through the hole in the roof pulled Riffolk's attention; Kerberos' body was a bonfire, the fire bright and hungry. All around them, the temple's roof was scorched and burning. Black smoke not only sat heavy in the sky, but rose in great drifts from Aethos' streets and buildings. Among the fire and smoke, Kerberos' corpse burned differently; there was energy in that flame.

Then, all at once, Omatus' king rose through the hole, wreathed in flame. Uninjured.

"Tell me," Kerberos said, "are you aware of the limits of that armour? How much magic it can take before it breaks?"

Before Riffolk could reply, he was slammed to the ground on his back, the burning king kneeling on his chest. The heat coming off Kerberos was setting into his skin already.

He threw a bolt of lightning at Kerberos' face, then summoned a blade of Shadow and rammed it into his gut.

Kerberos snarled, but there was no pain in his voice; only annoyance. He brought his fist down on Riffolk's helmet; the metal held, but his head rang from the impact.

As more punches rained down on him, Riffolk gritted his teeth and did his best to deflect them. He couldn't block them directly; Kerberos was far too strong, even before becoming this Fire-coated creature. Now, his strength was mountainous.

Kerberos slammed his fists down into Riffolk's head over and over. Heat flared through the suit, searing his skin. A crunch sounded from the helmet as a web of fine cracks appeared in the faceplate.

No, he thought, *no, no, I cannot lose now*.

His armour was failing. His pistol was gone. Kerberos held him down, pinned and helpless, against the stone floor.

This cannot be how I die. I am supposed to the Prime Overseer of Pandeia!

He brought Shadow Magic up from its pool deep within him, and focused it to both hands; it formed a shield in his left hand, and a punch-blade in his right. Kerberos slammed a fist into the shield, knocking it back into Riffolk's head. Riffolk poured more Shadow Magic into it, building an extension, a base that anchored it to the stone below him. At the same time, he stabbed Kerberos' body over and over. The shield covered most of him. He couldn't see Kerberos anymore; only the pitch-black shield.

The thuds of Kerberos' attacks shuddered through the shield and into the ground. Behind it, Kerberos roared, the ground beneath Riffolk booming as the Thearan man hit harder.

This is no way to fight, he thought, *cowering behind a shield, helpless against the punches of a monster.*

As Riffolk grasped in his mind for ideas, a deep clunk sounded right in his ear, and a crack appeared in the shield he had conjured. He formed a thin plate in the air underneath the crack, and floated it carefully into place, melding it with the shield.

Another clunk sounded, this one louder. But repairing the shield had given him an idea.

If I can cast Shadow Magic, I can manipulate it.

He took hold of the entire shield in his mind, and twisted the anchor around Kerberos' body. Then he launched it straight up, as hard and as far as he could.

It slammed Kerberos up into the ceiling, piercing the stone and lodging itself and the Thearan warrior in place.

With Kerberos temporarily distracted, Riffolk rolled to his feet. He barely regained his balance before Kerberos slammed back down across from him. A moment later, the hunk of Shadow Magic crashed into the burned stone nearby.

"Your time is almost up," Kerberos said in a grating, smoke-filled voice, "I broke that shield. I can break your armour."

His voice echoed through Riffolk's body. Were there more voices? Other people speaking in perfect synchronization? Surely not. But that sound… Kerberos was no longer human.

"With magic?" Riffolk said, "I doubt it."

But both men knew he was lying. His armour was stronger than the shield he'd cast, but not by enough to stop Kerberos. Not for long, anyway.

Kerberos threw a fireball at Riffolk's feet again, but when Riffolk dove to avoid it, another burst in the ground right where he was going to land. The impact sent chunks of stone flying up into him, battering his armour in a hail of thuds and bangs.

He landed badly; the explosion had thrown him off. Rushing to regain his balance, Riffolk spun to face Kerberos.

But he wasn't there.

On instinct, Riffolk leapt into a dive again. Another explosion erupted behind him, and he twisted as he rolled out of the dive to see Kerberos standing in the centre of a small crater.

They threw themselves at each other, magic arcing between them. Kerberos mostly used Fire, but he was talented with all five. Riffolk let his suit absorb any magic Kerberos hit him with, and stuck to Power and Shadow. They made for a deadly combination. But no matter how many times Riffolk hit him, he never seemed wounded.

Riffolk summoned a sheet of Shadow metal, keeping it flexible, and hurled it at Kerberos. He wrapped it around him, and solidified it; sealing him into a metal coffin.

Then he hit the metal with a massive blast of Power Magic. There was a muffled scream from within, but Kerberos was trapped. He wondered, idly, how long it would take the man to die from suffocation.

But the metal shifted; it swept from Kerberos, forming countless sharp blades, and all of them shot straight at Riffolk.

Riffolk caught as many of them as he could in a wave of focus, stopping the blades dead in the air. Some flew past. One hit his shoulder, shoving him back hard but doing no real damage. Kerberos appeared suddenly within an arm's reach of him; when he saw the man's eyes so close, something seized his chest in a cold, tremoring grip.

There was nothing in them but fire. And rage.

Kerberos grabbed Riffolk by the head and screamed, and a flood of Fire rushed over Riffolk. It crackled and roared over every part of him, burning even through the armour. The air inside his helmet scorched his throat as his breathing quickened.

Struggling, growing desperate, Riffolk threw everything he could at Kerberos to break his grip.

"There," Kerberos said, almost to himself, "the armour cannot absorb any more magic. A little more, and you will roast in there."

Through pained gasps, Riffolk forced himself to respond.

"Perhaps," he said, "but how long can you keep this up?"

Just as he finished talking, Riffolk summoned a thick Shadow shield and rammed it into Kerberos' face, forcing it through the air away from him.

It gave him just enough time to take a breath, the metal of his suit cooling only slightly.

Kerberos took control of the Shadow shield again, but he simply let it drop. Then, snarling, he hovered a metre above the temple roof, and flashed his teeth in a smile full of malice.

"I have been going easy on you, boy," Kerberos said, "but I am done with this fight. Say whatever prayers you have. These are your final moments."

In a vibrant rush, the Fire covering Kerberos changed. Instead of Fire alone, all five magics engulfed him in a twisting storm.

Kerberos

1798

F*inally.*

Kerberos unleashed all the magic he possessed, letting it cover his body in a roaring wave.

Even in the armour Riffolk wore, he suddenly looked no more difficult to break than the dead branch of a sickly tree. The world itself changed in front of Kerberos' eyes. Where there had been colours, textures, people and stone, there was now only magic.

The currents of energy that rippled through Air. Within that, particles of Water floated, so small he couldn't have seen them if not for the magic in his body. Fire covered everything; he knew that, of course, but he saw it differently now. It was all simply energy, just the same as Air.

And they all fed into each other; a perfect, circular system. Water was needed to create Air, Air was necessary for Fire, and Fire created Shadow in the spaces it could not reach. In the darkness of storms, Power was given life in the lightning that cracked from the sky, and Water poured from those storms in turn.

But there was something wrong, and in that instant, he knew he'd been right all along.

The world was coming to an end.

Not in danger of ending; the process had already begun. What the Heroes were doing would likely make no difference. Or, worse yet; they might have been the cause.

And yet...

Somehow, he knew it wasn't the end; not really. There would be more. Life—nature, the elements—would find a way to rebuild. Pandeia was so much more than just the people squabbling on its surface.

Riffolk stood in a ready stance, Power Magic crackling at his fingertips. His balance was off, the magic coursing through him sporadic. He was dead already; all that remained was for Kerberos to deliver the killing blow. And he knew he had to, if only to give the Heroes time to finish their task. They had to finish, he knew that now.

Despite the damage they would do, something deep and ineffable told him this was the way of things.

Magic flowed within Kerberos, no longer chaotic as it once had been, but harmonic. Almost musical in its intricate patterns as each type merged with the next. In his youth, Kerberos' parents had taken him to see operas in the Omati amphitheatre. Singers and musicians would each perform their own melody, but together it created a whole far greater than the sum of its parts.

If music had a mind of its own, it would feel the way Kerberos did now. Pieces of a greater work, formed together in perfect balance as the forces of nature had created Pandeia itself.

Riffolk lunged at him, throwing bolts of lightning and Shadow at him. They met his body not as attacks, but as old friends returning home. He watched, felt, as they merged with his body as easily as the air drawn into his lungs.

Nothing could harm him now. It was a strange feeling.

When Riffolk reached him, he let the man strike him; there was no pain, not even the feeling of impact. He merely watched it happen as though it was someone else's body.

Curious, he thought, *I wonder... am I even human, anymore? Or is this what it feels like to become one of them*?

He glanced up at Sithares. It was almost dead, falling to pieces as the remaining Heroes attacked over and over again. The book in between them was a husk; perhaps a few pages were left.

And something was happening; the Fire in Kerberos was growing. Was it coming from Sithares?

"Of course," he whispered to himself, "one does not become *a* God. There are only the five in Pandeia... Never more, never less."

As soon as he said it, the words made perfect sense to him.

There would *always* be Sithares. Fire could never be truly extinguished; without it, there could be no balance.

Riffolk roared, rage evident in the tension of his stance and his erratic attacks. Kerberos wouldn't have thought him to be the kind of man to abandon focus out of anger.

He gestured, barely even thinking about the magic he used, and Riffolk was slammed to the ground on his back, stuck as fast as if one of the coal boulders had landed on him.

"Riffolk," he said, "it is over. You cannot harm me. Accept defeat, and you will walk away."

"Defeat?" Riffolk scoffed, "Pandeia is mine. You are one against the most powerful army this world has ever seen. Your army is destroyed, your city taken. Kill me or don't, it makes no difference; you can't win back the entire world on your own. And my army will follow no one but me. You need me alive."

Kerberos narrowed his eyes, wishing he could see Riffolk's face. He reached out with magic, seeking a way through the armour. It didn't take long; he sensed the air pulling gently into the tiny gaps between the helmet and neck piece. From the feel of it, there was a locking mechanism that kept the helmet firmly in place. Kerberos marvelled at the information he could glean from the way Air Magic flowed around objects. He sensed the Heroes standing behind him around their dais, the thousands of soldiers and warriors fighting below, and the gargantuan form of Sithares above him.

With a little focus, Kerberos twisted the helmet's locking mechanism. Riffolk's helmet came loose, and Kerberos lifted it off with a gesture, throwing it aside. Riffolk's eyes widened for the barest of moments.

Kerberos cast the series of disguise spells he'd memorised, and Riffolk's features flowed over his own as he pulled the spell over his head. The glow of magic that had been emanating from his skin faded underneath the disguise, until he was a perfect copy of Riffolk.

"If I wanted to," he said, "I could take your place. No one would notice the difference until it was too late."

For the first time, Riffolk seemed truly speechless. Then he smiled, though his eyes remained cold and focused.

"That," Riffolk said slowly, "is a very useful trick."

"Useful," Kerberos repeated, "and dangerous to someone like you. I am not the only wielder of this magic, Riffolk. You are not as irreplaceable as you think."

Kerberos pulled the spell off, discarding it as it fell apart. Riffolk seemed to be mulling over his words.

"What do you want?" he asked Riffolk, "with Pandeia? Now that it is yours... what will you do with it?"

Riffolk frowned, as though Kerberos had asked him a question to which everyone should have known the answer.

"Why does it matter?" Riffolk asked, "it's mine either way."

"Your answer will determine your fate, Riffolk. What you say now will make the difference between life and death. And before you scoff at me again, you must know that even if you could not be replaced by a perfect copy, I *can* defeat your entire army, on my own."

Riffolk's frown deepened, his eyes shining in the glow of the Heroes' magic. Finally, he sighed; a short, sharp sound that almost resembled a scoff.

"I will install an organised government," he said, "that answers to me. I will introduce order and civilisation to all of Pandeia. And then, I will create a new age of technology and knowledge so advanced, it will be akin to magic itself."

"Do you swear," Kerberos said quietly, "to protect and serve the people of Pandeia, and act in their best interests at all times?"

Riffolk gave a brisk nod.

"Swear to me, Riffolk Hayne."

His lip pulled up in a grimace of distaste.

"All I ever wanted," he said, "was to work on my designs. To build things no one has ever seen. My loyalty is to science. Taking Pandeia was merely a step on the road to the wealth of resources my inventions require to be built. But if it will pacify you, then fine. I swear it. I will do my best for these people... Provided they live by my laws."

Kerberos stared at him for a long moment. Riffolk's words were hardly comforting; but with the change coming over him, it was the only outcome he could hope for.

As a child, Kerberos had always dreamed of ruling Omatus with justice, integrity, and peace. He had known, even then, that the rulers of his time were ineffective, greedy and corrupt. Riffolk didn't seem to care for politics, which made him a far better candidate than any of the old Omati noble families.

The only question was; would he really keep his word? Could he really act in the best interests of all the people he had conquered? Or would he let the world go to ruin just for the sake of some technological trinkets?

Time would tell. But only if Kerberos made the choice.

"Very well," he said, "Pandeia is yours."

Eliza

1798

We're almost there!" Zeera shouted, "keep pushing, give it everything you've got!"

Even now, Eliza had been holding back; it had always been difficult to let go.

No matter the scenario she found herself in, Mathys' voice emerged in the back of her mind, steady and sure. He had always worked to keep her safe, including the advice to hide her magic. She had lived with the Circle for years now, but still, something within her reeled at showing others what she could do.

But if ever there was time to unleash her magic, it was now. Mathys was dead. Her mother was dead. The Circle knew she was powerful, even if they didn't know the extent of it. And if she didn't unleash her power now…

She glanced at the city, at the horizon. Smoke rose from everywhere, flowing up in thick swathes from the glowing red of the entire world burning. Everything was either smoke, or fire.

All of Pandeia was about to be destroyed.

The book was barely more than a few scraps of paper now, shrouded in flame. She hadn't even looked up at Sithares for what felt like hours.

She knew Zeera was right; they were almost there. The book, and Sithares, were almost dead.

When she first attacked the book, Zeera had screamed for her to stop. But the spells cast by the other Heroes had apparently already done their work; Sithares was too weak now to fight off other attacks. And Eliza was powerful, far more powerful than the other Heroes.

You didn't die in vain, mother, she thought, *I will finish what you started.*

She drew all the Power she possessed to the surface. All of it. Her skin crawled with the pure, chaotic buzz of electricity, her heart racing so fast she couldn't feel individual beats.

Her entire body changed into magic, right down to her bones. She screamed, her soul set alight, her nerves crackling.

A giant chunk of coal smashed into her from above, shattering into countless pieces; she didn't feel it. There was only the Power surging through her being.

She pictured the book dissolving, shredded and inert. Harmless. Useless. Then she reached out to it, and Power Magic leapt from her to the pages. She heard them sizzling. Before her eyes, they crumpled, tearing into flecks of grey ash as the lightning pouring from her decimated them.

It shrank, the air around them blistering as Sithares roared. Despite the speed of its destruction, the world around them decayed even faster.

Sithares isn't attacking us anymore, she realised, *it's trying to tear Pandeia itself apart instead.*

"Eliza!" Zeera shouted, "do it! Bring all your magic to bear!"

She pushed harder, willing all the magic from her body in one massive bolt. The flash of yellow light blinded her, wiping the scene from her eyes as everything disappeared but the magic and Sithares. For the longest moment Eliza had ever experienced, there was no breath in her lungs. Her heart stopped.

Then, in a rush, all the magic left her, and the book exploded. Where there had been an endless pool of brilliant magic within her was a cold, sickening void.

Eliza collapsed, her knees slamming into the rough stone of the temple's roof. Her breath came flooding back, scratching through her dry throat.

It was still so hot. Why was the air still burning?

She glanced at Zeera; the Tarsi woman had collapsed as well, breathing heavily with her eyes shut tight.

Aerene stood like a ghost, her white eyes haunted, her mouth slack. A tear slipped from one of her eyes. Eliza looked up, and saw nothing but fire and smoke. Sithares was gone; but the flame still burned.

Pandeia still burned. Even the stone of ancient buildings, even the great mountains on the horizon, collapsed under the endless searing of the fires.

"What do we do now?" she asked, "how do we stop it?"

Aella grunted, and Eliza had to stifle a gasp.

"I thought you were dead!" she said.

"As did I," Aella said, "it was close."

She raised her hand, and Fire rushed from around them into Aella's body. Her skin flushed immediately. Her wound disappeared, and her eyes took on a renewed shine. She looked around, craning her neck trying to see past the dais.

"Is Lashek okay?" she asked.

"Is Sithares gone?" Zeera asked at the same moment.

"Lashek!" Eliza called.

But she never heard a reply.

A rumbling, deeper and louder than anything Eliza could have imagined, rose up from the ground. The temple shook so savagely that Eliza was thrown sideways.

She glanced to where Riffolk had stood; but Riffolk lay on the ground, and the man she'd seen before hovered above him. But he was something else, now. Magic—every kind—swarmed over his body in writhing patterns. He was a storm made entirely of magic.

Kerberos. It had to be. Eliza never saw him, but she knew enough about him to know that no one else could have obtained all five types of magic.

He floated above Riffolk, who was trapped invisibly against the ground. And they were... talking.

The rumbling picked up, and the roaring of hungry flames rose above even that. It filled the air, consuming everything. Stone, steel, earth and flesh all burned like paper, everything in sight razed to ashes. The flames surrounded her and her skin sizzled, her nerves shrieking as she burned. She reached for her magic to shield herself, but none remained. The world became black, but the sound grew to a deafening boom, drowning out the screams of the Circle's Heroes. And pain ripped at her body, gnawing through her skin, ravenous. Inexorable.

Pandeia tore apart. Deep, unimaginably loud cracks shook the entire world.

Why can't I see?

She was screaming, barely hearing it over the fires that crashed together. She couldn't tell if she heard the screams of everyone else, or if those were imagined; but she could have sworn there were thousands of people screaming around her.

And she realised two things in her last, terrifying moments of life:

The first was that they were never going to win against the Fires of Sithares. They had been doomed from the start.

And the second, which utterly broke her beaten spirit, was the reason she couldn't see.

Before it finished consuming her body, and the world itself, the Fire had melted her eyes.

Sithares

1798

He had known it was coming.

The fall of Pandeia.

He watched, strangely detached, as Fire spread through every particle of his world.

Why was he not devastated? This world, his home, was becoming ash in front of his eyes.

And yet... Kerberos wasn't burning.

No, he was *growing*; his memories rushed back, all at once, and then more... so much more.

Suddenly, everything drew away from him, turning into an endless void of black. He remembered finding the book of Sithares at ten years old. Before the small chamber that contained the book, a narrow passage trapped him in with a powerful Shadow Magic spell. He had experienced terror for the first time then.

But this was different. This was not a trap that stifled his senses. It was an open field, a great pool of pure potential.

The endlessness before him swam with energy. It sang. Though there was nothing visible around him, he felt the immensity of every magic in harmony, the way it had been within him before the void.

Slowly, as if his eyes were adjusting, stars twinkled back into existence. They were so far away, he couldn't feel their presence.

Behind him, the sun shone, brilliant and raging. It emanated energy, nothing but pure magic that flowed into him. There was no end to it; real magic persevered through all time, through all things.

Time had ceased to pass. Kerberos floated in nothingness, a being of magic; a God. It was not pride that whispered to him, but simple truth.

I have become Sithares.

He drifted, the sun behind him, for what could have been a hundred lifetimes, and he was at peace.

Slowly, he began to feel a new presence. Four beings appeared before him. Though he could not see them, they occupied a space in his mind and soul as unique and familiar as the facial features of loved ones.

As they appeared, the four magics beyond Fire slipped from his being. At the same time, a mass of magic and matter formed before him.

Sithares. Welcome—

"—to the fold."

Suddenly, they were there, physically there, floating alongside him. They were vast, gargantuan, dwarfing even the sun. And Kerberos—*no, Sithares*—was too. Each was made of their element, glowing in the void as though they were suns themselves. Sithares looked at his own body; he was pure Fire.

Asheilos had spoken to him; it was a monstrous figure, tentacles spilling from its face, but its presence was cool and deep. Its eyes were swirling pools of rippling water.

Next to Asheilos was Aurath. White, almost transparent Air formed into a great dragon with wings that could have snuffed out the sun itself. From its flowing body came six legs, each ending in vicious claws that shone as though made from sharpness itself.

Then there was Taranos; a jagged beast of flesh and metal, pulsing with furious energy.

Sithares gasped as he saw Amalus' true form; a great snake, feminine in its curves, its eyes as gentle as its fangs were sharp. Instead of the black Shenza steel he expected, Amalus' body was every shade of green, mottled and lush. Its scales were a thousand different shapes, and as he looked closer, he realised they were leaves.

"I do not understand," Sithares said, "are you not God of Shadows?"

"I am God of *Life*, my friend," Amalus said, "the Shadows were merely a tool of defence. My children lost their way over time, forgetting that the protection Shadow afforded them was nothing more than a step towards the balance we all strive for."

Sithares frowned.

"They have been using the wrong magic, all this time?"

"Yes and no."

It was no answer. But what previously might have annoyed him only served to fascinate him now.

"There was still Life," he said, "so your magic endured, even if they were not using it."

Amalus nodded, a gentle smile on its face.

Sithares continued. With each word, he understood more.

"The *real* magic you gave them was different. Life never needed worship, it needed only procreation. And protection. Each generation born was Life Magic enduring."

"That is right."

Sithares smiled, the thought warming him despite the Fire that was his body now.

"What do we do now?" Sithares asked.

"We fulfil our purpose," Amalus said.

He looked at the mass that had formed as the other Gods appeared. His companions did the same. They formed a circle around it, without the need for words between them.

Water, Air, Power, Fire and Life converged into a molten, spinning sphere. He watched it grow and realised what was happening.

They were rebuilding Pandeia.

His heart—if he still possessed one—sang as the Gods worked together to regain what was lost. All he had ever wanted was to create a better world. Now, he could.

"Will it be the same," he asked them, "when it is built? Or do we build anew?"

"We can only tell you what has happened before," Asheilos said, "for this is a cycle, as is everything in the universe."

Sithares waited. All he had was time.

"We have had to build from scratch before," Aurath said, "when Sithares worked against us. Achieving what you desire will require all five of us."

"Then it will be achieved," Sithares said.

"Sithares has said that before," Taranos said, its voice crackling in the heavy silence, "yet always it seeks to destroy."

"Fire need not to be used for destruction," Sithares said, "it is a tool, like the Shadows, like Power. It cooks their food, it warms their homes. Even when it spreads to trees and grass, Life returns to grow from the ashes."

The other four looked at him, as patient as time itself.

"I have no desire to destroy anything," he continued, "I have only ever wanted to build. To create a better world, to give the people of Pandeia a good life."

Amalus smiled, its warmth spreading between the five of them.

"Then from the ashes," it said, "we shall rebuild."

"The same as before?" Sithares asked again, "can we pick up where we left off?"

"Well," Amalus smiled, "not *exactly* the same as before. There was a lot of damage."

"If we work together," Asheilos said, "we can undo what was done, and restore what was lost. But it will cost each of us dearly."

Sithares nodded.

"Any price is worth paying."

As soon as he said it, a connection formed between all five of them, blinding in its intensity. They worked perfectly in tandem, and Sithares poured everything he had into their shared spell.

It was a magic beyond any a human had ever experienced. Even as a God, he was overcome with awe at the blistering scale of the magic they cast.

Layer by layer, they restored what had been. Rock, earth, ocean, atmosphere, plants and creatures; all were spun into being. The complexity in every piece of it humbled him; he only understood as each layer appeared just how magical the entire world had been.

They shared the memory of Pandeia, its land and people alike, exactly as it was before its destruction, and built towards it like a sculptor copying a live model.

And when they were done, he wept; for the world he had fought to create was finally real.

With their work completed, Sithares glanced at his new companions. They were tiny, specks in the distance around the planet that now dwarfed them. And they were fading.

He felt himself fading, too. Though he longed to watch, to see the results of the work he'd done, there was no fear.

There was only peace.

How much time had passed? To the Gods, time was both everything and nothing. Remaking Pandeia had taken them eons, and yet when they were done, it was the moment before the planet had been destroyed.

They had forged a copy, capturing their memory of what had been. Not quite reversing the flow of time; but close enough.

With Pandeia restored, most of the Gods' magic was spent. All they could do was watch and wait for the magic to restore him.

Until then, Sithares was alone. He sensed the other Gods, somewhere out there, but they each existed in their own planes of the spiritual realm. It had only been their sheer power at the peak of the war that they could meet together as they did.

Sithares was on a precipice, standing over a vast ocean of knowledge that would have broken Kerberos' mind. Moments of understanding came to him from the void. But still so much of it remained out of reach that Sithares felt as though he would never learn it all.

There was only the Fire, the magic teeming through Sithares' body, that he knew for sure. That, and what he could see of Pandeia. Glimpses, mostly; snatches of a million conversations, people cooking, fighting, death and eruptions; Fire Magic. It took what could have been countless lifetimes for Sithares to realise that he could only see through the element of fire, and any events that built his magic.

It was no wonder the previous Sithares had been obsessed with burning Pandeia down; all it knew of its planet was chaos and death and burning. But it was not all that Pandeia contained; Sithares knew, and forced himself to remember. Fire was life, warmth, comfort and cleansing. He wouldn't allow himself to forget.

There would never be another war of the Gods again.

Sithares searched for the one who ruled; memory was a difficult thing now, with lifetimes passing for every moment on Pandeia.

What was his name?

Pain. No, Hayne.

The eyes had been blue. The hair black. Those things stood out, even when all else was ethereal.

Now I must try to reach him…

Pandeia had to be protected. Guided into a new era. The man, Hayne, had promised to be the one to guide it; but would he fulfil that promise?

The only way to reach him would be by gaining more power. But Sithares could not do that. Power only came to the God of Fire by chaos, conflict and death. And Sithares refused to tread the same path as his predecessor. Pandeia could not be allowed to burn down again. Never again. Even if it meant Sithares remained weak for the rest of his endless existence.

Ermoor crawled with corruption, even now; but it was gradually changing. Perhaps that was Hayne's influence. Sithares could only hope so. All throughout Pandeia there was still fighting and death. So much suffering, everywhere Sithares looked. He wouldn't be weak for long, influence or not.

Was it Hayne's new world, or was it simply the aftermath of a world war?

I will only know with time.

And to the Gods, time was both everything… and nothing.

Aerene

1798

She came to on her feet. The world faded into view, the sky bright and clean. Austris Ara sparkled in the sunlight. Aerene had to shade her eyes from the dazzling sun.

The Air Temple was half collapsed, scorch marks covering any surface that wasn't smashed to pieces. And yet, there was no sign of danger. No fires or smoke.

Her memories shifted like a cloud, immaterial and elusive. Her body was weak, knees shaking, and a cold emptiness lay within her being. *My magic*, she wondered, *it is... gone. It has never been gone before*. She looked at her pale blue hands, trying to will a sphere of Air Magic to appear.

Nothing happened.

But, thankfully, the emptiness didn't last long. The air around her was clean, clear, eager to flow into her. She breathed it in, its gentle power renewing a mere trickle of her normal strength, but at least she wasn't empty. Whatever had just happened would take time to fully recover from.

She looked about her; the stone dais was cracked through its centre, and the others in her group sat around it, as dazed as herself.

What were we doing?

She remembered the people with her, and the dais, and something on it that they were focused on... but what?

Zeera stood.

"Is everyone okay?" she asked.

Aerene nodded, and then her eyes fell on Lashek. She rushed to his side. Aella, Zeera and Eliza appeared an instant later. They checked him, Aerene looking desperately for any sign of life.

But they were too late.

"Lashek," Zeera whispered, "no."

The crunch of heavy footsteps on stone rose above the gentle breeze. An Ermoori man in sleek black and gold armour approached them from the other side of the temple roof.

Something within her exploded in a cold, vicious panic, and then another memory surfaced.

Riffolk Hayne.

The leader of the Ermoori. They had been fighting against him... hadn't they? His army was taking Pandeia. If he was here, it meant he had succeeded in taking Aethos. And if he was on the temple roof, it meant—

"Shaela!" She screamed.

She gathered what little Air Magic she could around her, ready to fly; but Zeera shouted, her voice clear and strong.

"Aerene! You can't. They are at the doors, in the temple as we speak. If Shaela is dead, there is nothing more you can do. If she's not, she will find us when she can."

Zeera still sat by Lashek's body, holding his head in her hands.

"If she's alive," Aerene said, "I might be able to help her. She could be in grave danger right now!"

"Please, Aerene," Zeera said, "we can do more good for Pandeia from the shadows. We need to surrender, go into hiding. No more fighting. You will only be giving them an excuse to execute us all."

Urgency flooded her body. Every fibre of her being screamed at her to help Shaela, or at least discover her fate.

But Zeera was right. The Ermoori could not be beaten, and if she rushed out to face them now, she would be killed. She prayed silently to Aurath for guidance, for the wind to point her in the right direction; but she heard no answer.

"I promise you," Zeera said, hushing her voice at Riffolk's approach, "we *will* fight back. No matter how long it takes, we will win Pandeia back from them."

Aerene forced herself to slow down. She had been chosen by Aurath, even if it didn't speak to her now; her choice now could change everything. It had to be the right choice.

Shaela, she thought, *please be okay. Please come back to me*.

She sighed, closing her eyes briefly.

"Fine," she said to Zeera, "what do we do, then?"

"We get out of here," Eliza said, and pointed at Riffolk, "before *his* army gets here."

Eliza spat the word out like an insult. Rage emanated from her eyes, her stance, the faint crackling yellow magic at her fingertips.

She is struggling with this choice, too, Aerene thought as the memory of Mara's death came back, *she wants to avenge her mother. If I must sacrifice going to Shaela, at least Eliza and I are together*.

Riffolk stopped near them; carefully out of range of fast attacks, but close enough to talk. He wore an expression of smug victory, his lips curled up in a cruel, sneering smile.

"I want to know what you were doing here," he said, "and why I should spare your lives."

Eliza stepped between him and the Heroes.

"I should be asking you why we should spare *your* life," she snapped, "since you're outnumbered."

"My soldiers will be here within moments," Riffolk replied lightly. "You may be able to kill me, but I doubt you can do it quite that quickly. And even if you can, it will be the last thing you ever do. My soldiers will not hold back if they find you by my corpse."

There was one way out of the temple; for the other Heroes, at any rate. Aerene could have flown away with barely a thought.

"Why do you want to know?" Aerene asked, sidestepping Eliza.

Nearby, Aella shifted on her feet.

"Aerene..." she said.

"I need to know why you almost destroyed Pandeia," Riffolk said, "and if there is a chance you might try again. It's my world, now. I will not tolerate threats of this magnitude."

It was then the memories returned; Sithares, the book on the pedestal, their fight turning desperate towards the end. They had succeeded in destroying the God of Fire, but then... everything had burned anyway. The Fire was most of what she remembered. Even as they fought Sithares, the very air around them had burned.

She gasped from the power of that memory.

They had given everything they had to destroy it; including their lives. And yet they still lived. Something came to their aid, brought them back.

And Riffolk thought the Circle of Shadows were the villains.

Aerene almost laughed.

"You think *we* almost destroyed Pandeia? We are the ones who stopped Sithares. Without us, there would be nothing but ash."

His self-righteous smile never wavered. If he was surprised, he didn't show it.

"If you are lying to me," Riffolk said, stepping close to Eliza as if she were no threat to him at all, "I will find out. If not... well, I thank you for your service to Pandeia." He placed an armoured hand on Eliza's, the sparks of her magic disappearing into the blackness of his suit as she recoiled from his touch.

"You might think yourselves Heroes," he said, "but you are no longer needed."

In that moment, Ermoori soldiers swarmed through the doors.

Epilogue

1805

A seemingly endless desert stretches to the horizon and beyond. Dark grey sand is punctuated by dark stone and occasionally by small, barely living trees. The deserts of Omas resemble a dead, ash-filled wasteland. Even the scarce trees grow in hues of bright red and orange, swaying in the slight breeze, giving the appearance of fires burning. In the dark of night, the effect is even more brutal; deep shadows crowd every tree and boulder and the usually bright trees are dulled to a grey to match the sand. A massive volcano rises from the exact centre of the desert. The top of the volcano is flat, and as wide as a small city.

On the plateau, a bonfire burns in the night. A figure in sleek black armour watches the fire, tending to it until it becomes a massive, roiling inferno.

Nearby is the vehicle that carried him here; a technological marvel of shining black metal, large wings swooping out to either side of its body. It stands ominous in the night, a patient bird of prey waiting to spy its next meal.

The bonfire's light reflects off the black metal, shining brilliant orange ripples over its surface like an ocean made of fire.

The figure removes the gauntlet from his left hand and forearm, and takes a dagger to his wrist, holding a cup underneath to catch the blood. Once the cup is filled, he throws it into the fire and whispers an ancient, forgotten spell.

As his wound bleeds, the fire changes from pale orange to a deep, bright red. A whistling sound emanates from the centre, and a deep rumbling follows soon after. The rumbling grows in volume until the figure flinches in pain, and then it suddenly stops. Burning logs move and shift, and a small, slim, fragile looking creature emerges from the bonfire, crawling out from under the wood. It steps onto the sand gingerly. Its body is made from pieces of still burning wood, its face a jagged stump with two furrowed whorls for eyes, glowing red hot from deep within. Its limbs are spindly, and the fire burning at them makes them look as though they might collapse at any moment.

The creature turns back towards the fire and reaches in, grasping a flickering tongue of flame and pulling, sweeping a cloak of pure orange fire onto its shoulders.

"So, it is true," the armoured figure says, "the Gods can never be truly killed. You are Sithares, renewed. Tell me, how much of Kerberos is still in there? Some, I assume. You Thearans are a stubborn lot. Aella is *still* a thorn in my side."

"*Hush, servant*," replies the fire-cloaked creature in a jagged whisper. "*We haven't much time*."

The armoured man smiles, leaning down to stare directly into the eyes of a Fire God.

"Who is really the servant here? You came to my bidding. I have a deal to make with you."

"*I know. I accept*."

"Because you must," the armoured man says, "I have done my research. Your kind serve he who summons you."

"*You know the price, then*?"

"I do. My soul, such as it is. A mundane price to pay for eternal life. With that, none will pose a threat to me. Aella and the other so-called *heroes*… even the Spectre. There are rumours he is rising again. But it won't matter anymore. I can finish my work, as long as it takes. Pandeia is already changed by my design, but by the time I am done, it will be unrecognisable. My technology will be indistinguishable from magic. And I will control it all." The man smiles, his eyes reflecting the deep red glow of the bonfire. "But I suppose you knew all that already. You knew the deal I came to make, didn't you?"

"*I know all*."

The man smiles again.

"That must be strange, for one to whom Godship is so new."

"*Time is irrelevant, now. The being you once knew is dead. There is only Sithares*."

"I wondered," the man says slowly, carefully, "if you would carry our rivalry with you. I am glad to see you did not."

"*You will maintain peace in Pandeia. Even at the cost of lives, peace is all that matters*."

"You make a better God than you did a king," the armoured man says, "this will be a new era for Pandeia."

"*Then it is done*."

The man nods, and his smile grows wider still, the flames dancing in his eyes.

"For the good of all."

About the Author:

Brendan Wright is an Australian author and musician. He lives in Canberra and spends all of his time writing or watching movies and TV. He loves coffee, Star Wars, and playing piano. Other than the Gods and Heroes series, Brendan is also working on novels in several other genres, such as crime, horror, and science fiction.

Website: brendanwrightauthor.com

Instagram: @brendanwrightauthor
Facebook: /brendanwrightauthor

If you enjoyed this book, please leave a review on Goodreads, Amazon, or Booktopia!

www.ingramcontent.com/pod-product-compliance
Lightning Source LLC
Chambersburg PA
CBHW020718310726
48979CB00004B/972

9781764126410